D0085640

TANCRED.

TANCRED

OR

THE NEW CRUSADE.

BY THE

EARL OF BEACONSFIELD, K.G.

NEW EDITION.

GREENWOOD PRESS, PUBLISHERS
WESTPORT, CONNECTICUT

Originally published in 1877
by Longmans, Green, and Co., London

Reprinted from an original copy in the collections
of the University of Illinois Library

First Greenwood Reprinting 1970

Library of Congress Catalogue Card Number 79-98811

SBN 8371-3072-7

Printed in the United States of America

TANCRED

OR

THE NEW CRUSADE.

BOOK I.

CHAPTER I.

IN that part of the celebrated parish of St. George, which is bounded on one side by Piccadilly and on the other by Curzon Street, is a district of a peculiar character. 'Tis a cluster of small streets of little houses, frequently intersected by mews, which here are numerous, and sometimes gradually, rather than abruptly, terminating in a ramification of those mysterious regions. Sometimes a group of courts develops itself, and you may even chance to find your way into a small market-place. Those, however, who are accustomed to connect these hidden residences of the humble with scenes of misery and characters of violence, need not apprehend in this district any appeal to their sympathies, or any shock to their tastes. All is extremely genteel; and there is almost as much repose as in the golden saloons of the contiguous palaces. At any rate, if there be as much vice, there is as little crime.

No sight or sound can be seen or heard at any hour, which could pain the most precise or the most fastidious. Even if a chance oath may float on the air from the stable-yard to the lodging of a French cook, 'tis of the newest fashion, and, if responded to with less of novel charm, the

repartee is at least conveyed in the language of the most polite
of nations. They bet upon the Derby in these parts a little,
are interested in Goodwood, which they frequent, have
perhaps, in general, a weakness for play, live highly, and
indulge those passions which luxury and refinement encourage; but that is all.

A policeman would as soon think of reconnoitring these
secluded streets as of walking into a house in Park Lane or
Berkeley Square, to which, in fact, this population in a
great measure belongs. For here reside the wives of house-
stewards and of butlers, in tenements furnished by the
honest savings of their husbands, and let in lodgings to
increase their swelling incomes; here dwells the retired
servant, who now devotes his practised energies to the
occasional festival, which, with his accumulations in the
three per cents., or in one of the public-houses of the
quarter, secures him at the same time an easy living, and
the casual enjoyment of that great world which lingers
in his memory. Here may be found his grace's coachman,
and here his lordship's groom, who keeps a book and bleeds
periodically too speculative footmen, by betting odds on his
master's horses. But, above all, it is in this district that
the cooks have ever sought a favourite and elegant abode.
An air of stillness and serenity, of exhausted passions and
suppressed emotion, rather than of sluggishness and of dul-
ness, distinguishes this quarter during the day.

When you turn from the vitality and brightness of Piccadilly, the park, the palace, the terraced mansions, the
sparkling equipages, the cavaliers cantering up the hill,
the swarming multitude, and enter the region of which we
are speaking, the effect is at first almost unearthly. Not a
carriage, not a horseman, scarcely a passenger; there seems
some great and sudden collapse in the metropolitan system,
as if a pest had been announced, or an enemy were expected in alarm by a vanquished capital. The approach
from Curzon Street has not this effect. Hyde Park has
still about it something of Arcadia. There are woods and
waters, and the occasional illusion of an illimitable distance

of sylvan joyance. The spirit is allured to gentle thoughts as we wander in what is still really a lane, and, turning down Stanhope Street, behold that house which the great Lord Chesterfield tells us, in one of his letters, he was 'building among the fields.' The cawing of the rooks in his gardens sustains the tone of mind, and Curzon Street, after a long, straggling, sawney course, ceasing to be a thoroughfare, and losing itself in the gardens of another palace, is quite in keeping with all the accessories.

In the night, however, the quarter of which we are speaking is alive. The manners of the population follow those of their masters. They keep late hours. The banquet and the ball dismiss them to their homes at a time when the trades of ordinary regions move in their last sleep, and dream of opening shutters and decking the windows of their shops. At night, the chariot whirls round the frequent corners of these little streets, and the opening valves of the mews vomit forth their legion of broughams. At night, too, the footman, taking advantage of a ball at Holdernesse, or a concert at Lansdowne House, and knowing that, in either instance, the link-boy will answer when necessary for his summoned name, ventures to look in at his club, reads the paper, talks of his master or his mistress, and perhaps throws a main. The shops of this district, depending almost entirely for their custom on the classes we have indicated, and kept often by their relations, follow the order of the place, and are most busy when other places of business are closed.

A gusty March morning had subsided into a sunshiny afternoon, nearly two years ago, when a young man, slender, above the middle height, with a physiognomy thoughtful yet delicate, his brown hair worn long, slight whiskers, on his chin a tuft, knocked at the door of a house in Carrington Street, May Fair. His mien and his costume denoted a character of the class of artists. He wore a pair of green trousers, braided with a black stripe down their sides, puckered towards the waist, yet fitting with considerable precision to the boot of French leather that enclosed a well-formed foot. His waistcoat was of maroon velvet, displaying a steel watch-chain of refined manufacture, and a black satin cravat, with a coral brooch. His bright blue frockcoat was frogged and braided like his trousers. As the knocker fell from the prim-rose-coloured glove that screened his hand, he uncovered, and passing his fingers rapidly through his hair, resumed his new silk hat, which he placed rather on one side of his head.

' Ah ! Mr. Leander, is it you ? ' exclaimed a pretty girl, who opened the door and blushed.

' And how is the good papa, Eugenie ? Is he at home ? For I want to see him much.'

' I will show you up to him at once, Mr. Leander, for he will be very happy to see you. We have been thinking of hearing of you,' she added, talking as she ushered her guest up the narrow staircase. ' The good papa has a little cold : 'tis not much, I hope ; caught at Sir Wallinger's, a large dinner ; they would have the kitchen windows open, which spoilt all the entrées, and papa got a cold ; but I think, perhaps, it is as much vexation as anything else ; you know if anything goes wrong, especially with the entrées ——'

' He feels as a great artist must,' said Leander, finishing her sentence. ' However, I am not sorry at this moment to find him a prisoner, for I am pressed to see him. It is only this morning that I have returned from Mr. Coningsby's at Hellingsley : the house full, forty covers every day, and some judges. One does not grudge one's labour if we are appreciated,' added Leander ; ' but I have had my troubles. One of my marmitons has disappointed me : I thought I had a genius, but on the third day he lost his head ; and had it not been —— Ah ! good papa,' he ex-claimed, as the door opened, and he came forward and warmly shook the hand of a portly man, advanced in middle life, sitting in an easy chair, with a glass of sugared water by his side, and reading a French newspaper in his cham-ber robe, and with a white cotton nightcap on his head.

'Ah! my child,' said Papa Prevost, 'is it you? You see me a prisoner; Eugenie has told you; a dinner at a merchant's; dressed in a draught; everything spoiled, and I ——' and sighing, Papa Prevost sipped his eau sucrée.

'We have all our troubles,' said Leander, in a consoling tone; 'but we will not speak now of vexations. I have just come from the country; Daubuz has written to me twice; he was at my house last night; I found him on my steps this morning. There is a grand affair on the tapis. The son of the Duke of Bellamont comes of age at Easter; it is to be a business of the thousand and one nights; the whole county to be feasted. Camacho's wedding will do for the peasantry; roasted oxen, and a capon in every platter, with some fountains of ale and good Porto. Our marmitons, too, can easily serve the provincial noblesse; but there is to be a party at the Castle, of double cream; princes of the blood, high relatives and grandees of the Golden Fleece. The duke's cook is not equal to the occasion. 'Tis an hereditary chef who gives dinners of the time of the continental blockade. They have written to Daubuz to send them the first artist of the age,' said Leander; 'and,' added he, with some hesitation, 'Daubuz has written to me.'

'And he did quite right, my child,' said Prevost, 'for there is not a man in Europe that is your equal. What do they say? That Abreu rivals you in flavour, and that Gaillard has not less invention. But who can combine goût with new combinations? 'Tis yourself, Leander; and there is no question, though you have only twenty-five years, that you are the chef of the age.'

'You are always very good to me, sir,' said Leander, bending his head with great respect; 'and I will not deny, that to be famous when you are young is the fortune of the gods. But we must never forget that I had an advantage which Abreu and Gaillard had not, and that I was your pupil.'

'I hope that I have not injured you,' said Papa Prevost, with an air of proud self-content. 'What you learned

from me came at least from a good school. It is something to
have served under Napoleon,' added Prevost, with the grand
air of the Imperial kitchen. ' Had it not been for Waterloo,
I should have had the cross. But the Bourbons and the cooks
of the Empire never could understand each other. They
brought over an emigrant chef, who did not comprehend
the taste of the age. He wished to bring everything back
to the time of the *œil de bœuf.* When Monsieur passed my
soup of Austerlitz untasted, I knew the old family was
doomed. But we gossip. You wished to consult me ? '

' I want not only your advice but your assistance. This
affair of the Duke of Bellamont's requires all our energies.
I hope you will accompany me ; and, indeed, we must
muster all our forces. It is not to be denied that there is
a want, not only of genius, but of men, in our art. The
cooks are like the civil engineers : since the middle class
have taken to giving dinners, the demand exceeds the
supply.'

' There is Andrien,' said Papa Prevost; 'you had some
hopes of him ? '

' He is too young; I took him to Hellingsley, and he lost
his head on the third day. I entrusted the soufflées to him,
and, but for the most desperate personal exertions, all
would have been lost. It was an affair of the bridge of
Arcola.'

' Ah! mon Dieu! those are moments !' exclaimed Prevost. ' Gaillard and Abreu will not serve under you, eh ?
And if they would, they could not be trusted. They would
betray you at the tenth hour.'

' What I want are generals of division, not commanders
in chief. Abreu is sufficiently bon garçon, but he has taken
an engagement with Monsieur de Sidonia, and is not permitted to go out.'

' With Monsieur de Sidonia ! You once thought of that,
my Leander. And what is his salary ? '

' Not too much ; four hundred and some perquisites. It
would not suit me ; besides, I will take no engagement but

with a crowned head. But Abreu likes travelling, and he has his own carriage, which pleases him.'

'There are Philippon and Dumoreau,' said Prevost; 'they are very safe.'

'I was thinking of them,' said Leander, 'they are safe, under you. And there is an Englishman, Smit, he is chef at Sir Stanley's, but his master is away at this moment. He has talent.'

'Yourself, four chefs, with your marmitons; it would do,' said Prevost.

'For the kitchen,' said Leander ; 'but who is to dress the tables?'

'A—h!' exclaimed Papa Prevost, shaking his head.

'Daubuz' head man, Trenton, is the only one I could trust; and he wants fancy, though his style is broad and bold. He made a pyramid of pines relieved with grapes without destroying the outline, very good, this last week. at Hellingsley. But Trenton has been upset on the railroad, and much injured. Even if he recover, his hand will tremble so for the next month that I could have no confidence in him.'

'Perhaps you might find some one at the Duke's?'

'Out of the question!' said Leander; 'I make it always a condition that the head of every department shall be appointed by myself. I take Pellerini with me for the confectionary. How often have I seen the effect of a first-rate dinner spoiled by a vulgar dessert! laid flat on the table, for example, or with ornaments that look as if they had been hired at a pastrycook's: triumphal arches, and Chinese pagodas, and solitary pines springing up out of ice-tubs surrounded with peaches, as if they were in the window of a fruiterer of Covent Garden.'

'Ah! it is incredible what uneducated people will do,' said Prevost. 'The dressing of the tables was a department of itself in the Imperial kitchen.'

'It demands an artist of a high calibre,' said Leander. 'I only know one man who realises my idea, and he is at

St. Petersburgh. You do not know Anastase? There is
a man! But the Emperor has him secure. He can scarcely
complain, however, since he is decorated, and has the rank
of full colonel.'

'Ah!' said Prevost, mournfully, 'there is no recognition
of genius in this country. What think you of Vanesse, my
child? He has had a regular education.'

'In a bad school: as a pis aller one might put up
with him. But his eternal tiers of bon-bons! As if they
were ranged for a supper of the Carnival, and my guests
were going to pelt each other! No, I could not stand
Vanesse, papa.'

The dressing of the table: 'tis a rare talent,' said Prevost, mournfully, 'and always was. In the Imperial
kitchen ——'

'Papa,' said Eugenie, opening the door, and putting in
her head, 'here is Monsieur Vanillette just come from
Brussels. He has brought you a basket of truffles from
Ardennes. I told him you were on business, but to-night,
if you be at home, he could come.'

'Vanillette!' exclaimed Prevost, starting in his chair,
'our little Vanillette! There is your man, Leander. He
was my first pupil, as you were my last, my child. Bring
up our little Vanillette, Eugenie. He is in the household
of King Leopold, and his forte is dressing the table!'

CHAPTER II.

THE Duke of Bellamont was a personage who, from his
rank, his blood, and his wealth, might almost be placed at
the head of the English nobility. Although the grandson
of a mere country gentleman, his fortunate ancestor, in the
decline of the last century, had captivated the heiress of
the Montacutes, Dukes of Bellamont, a celebrated race of
the times of the Plantagenets. The bridegroom, at the
moment of his marriage, had adopted the illustrious name

of his young and beautiful wife. Mr. Montacute was by nature a man of energy and of an enterprising spirit. His vast and early success rapidly developed his native powers. With the castles and domains and boroughs of the Bellamonts, he resolved also to acquire their ancient baronies and their modern coronets. The times were favourable to his projects, though they might require the devotion of a life. He married amid the disasters of the American war. The king and his minister appreciated the independent support afforded them by Mr. Montacute, who represented his county, and who commanded five votes in the House besides his own. He was one of the chief pillars of their cause; but he was not only independent, he was conscientious and had scruples. Saratoga staggered him. The defection of the Montacute votes, at this moment, would have at once terminated the struggle between England and her colonies. A fresh illustration of the advantages of our parliamentary constitution! The independent Mr. Montacute, however, stood by his sovereign; his five votes continued to cheer the noble lord in the blue ribbon, and their master took his seat and the oaths in the House of Lords, as Earl of Bellamont and Viscount Montacute.

This might be considered sufficiently well for one generation; but the silver spoon which some fairy had placed in the cradle of the Earl of Bellamont was of colossal proportions. The French Revolution succeeded the American war, and was occasioned by it. It was but just, therefore, that it also should bring its huge quota to the elevation of the man whom a colonial revolt had made an earl. Amid the panic of Jacobinism, the declamations of the friends of the people, the sovereign having no longer Hanover for a refuge, and the prime minister examined as a witness in favour of the very persons whom he was trying for high treason, the Earl of Bellamont made a calm visit to Downing Street, and requested the revival of all the honours of the ancient Earls and Dukes of Bellamont in his own person. Mr. Pitt, who was far from favourable to the exclusive character which distinguished the English peerage in the last century, was himself not disinclined to accede to the gentle request of his powerful supporter; but the king was less flexible. His Majesty, indeed, was on principle not opposed to the revival of titles in families to whom the domains without the honours of the old nobility had descended ; and he recognised the claim of the present Earls of Bellamont eventually to regain the strawberry leaf which had adorned the coronet of the father of the present countess. But the king was of opinion that this supreme distinction ought only to be conferred on the blood of the old house, and that a generation, therefore, must necessarily elapse before a Duke of Bellamont could again figure in the golden book of the English aristocracy.

But George the Third, with all his firmness, was doomed to frequent discomfiture. His lot was cast in troubled waters, and he had often to deal with individuals as inflexible as himself. Benjamin Franklin was not more calmly contumacious than the individual whom his treason had made an English peer. In that age of violence change and panic, power, directed by a clear brain and an obdurate spirit, could not fail of its aim ; and so it turned out, that, in the very teeth of the royal will, the simple country gentleman, whose very name was forgotten, became, at the commencement of this century, Duke of Bellamont, Marquis of Montacute, Earl of Bellamont, Dacre, and Villeroy, with all the baronies of the Plantagenets in addition. The only revenge of the king was, that he never would give the Duke of Bellamont the garter. It was as well perhaps that there should be something for his son to desire.

The Duke and Duchess of Bellamont were the handsomest couple in England, and devoted to each other, but they had only one child. Fortunately, that child was a son. Precious life ! The Marquis of Montacute was married before he was of age. Not a moment was to be lost to find heirs for all these honours. Perhaps, had his parents been less precipitate, their object might have been more securely obtained. The union was not a happy one. The first duke had, however, the gratification of dying a grandfather. His successor bore no resemblance to him, except in that beauty which became a characteristic of the race. He was born to enjoy, not to create. A man of pleasure, the chosen companion of the Regent in his age of riot, he was cut off in his prime; but he lived long enough to break his wife's heart and his son's spirit; like himself, too, an only child.

The present Duke of Bellamont had inherited something of the clear intelligence of his grandsire, with the gentle disposition of his mother. His fair abilities, and his bene-volent inclinations, had been cultivated. His mother had watched over the child, in whom she found alike the charm and consolation of her life. But, at a certain period of youth, the formation of character requires a masculine im-pulse, and that was wanting. The duke disliked his son; in time he became even jealous of him. The duke had found himself a father at too early a period of life. Himself in his lusty youth, he started with alarm at the form that recalled his earliest and most brilliant hour, and who might prove a rival. The son was of a gentle and affectionate nature, and sighed for the tenderness of his harsh and almost vindictive parent. But he had not that passionate soul which might have appealed, and perhaps not in vain, to the dormant sympathies of the being who had created him. The young Montacute was by nature of an extreme shyness, and the accidents of his life had not tended to dis-sipate his painful want of self-confidence. Physically cou-rageous, his moral timidity was remarkable. He alternately blushed or grew pale in his rare interviews with his father, trembled in silence before the undeserved sarcasm, and often endured the unjust accusation without an attempt to vindicate himself. Alone, and in tears alike of woe and indignation, he cursed the want of resolution or ability which had again missed the opportunity that, both for his mother and himself, might have placed affairs in a happier position. Most persons, under these circumstances, would

have become bitter, but Montacute was too tender for
malice, and so he only turned melancholy.

On the threshold of manhood, Montacute lost his mother,
and this seemed the catastrophe of his unhappy life. His
father neither shared his grief, nor attempted to alleviate it.
On the contrary, he seemed to redouble his efforts to mortify
his son. His great object was to prevent Lord Montacute
from entering society, and he was so complete a master of
the nervous temperament on which he was acting, that
there appeared a fair chance of his succeeding in his bene-
volent intentions. When his son's education was completed, the duke would not furnish him with the means of
moving in the world in a becoming manner, or even sanction his travelling. His grace was resolved to break his
son's spirit by keeping him immured in the country. Other
heirs apparent of a rich seignory would soon have removed
these difficulties. By bill or by bond, by living usury, or
by post-obit liquidation, by all the means that private
friends or public offices could supply, the sinews of war
would have been forthcoming. They would have beaten
their fathers' horses at Newmarket, eclipsed them with
their mistresses, and, sitting for their boroughs, voted
against their party. But Montacute was not one of those
young heroes who rendered so distinguished the earlier part
of this century. He had passed his life so much among
women and clergymen, that he had never emancipated
himself from the old law that enjoined him to honour a
parent. Besides, with all his shyness and timidity, he was
extremely proud. He never forgot that he was a Montacute, though he had forgotten, like the world in general,
that his grandfather once bore a different and humbler
name. All merged in the great fact, that he was the living
representative of those Montacutes of Bellamont, whose
wild and politic achievements, or the sustained splendour of
whose stately life had for seven hundred years formed a
stirring and superb portion of the history and manners of
our country. Death was preferable, in his view, to having

such a name soiled in the haunts of jockeys and courtezans and usurers; and, keen as was the anguish which the conduct of the duke to his mother or himself had often occasioned him, it was sometimes equalled in degree by the sorrow and the shame which he endured when he heard of the name of Bellamont only in connection with some stratagem of the turf or some frantic revel.

Without a friend, almost without an acquaintance, Montacute sought refuge in love. She who shed over his mournful life the divine ray of feminine sympathy was his cousin, the daughter of his mother's brother, an English peer, but resident in the north of Ireland, where he had vast possessions. It was a family otherwise little calculated to dissipate the reserve and gloom of a depressed and melancholy youth; puritanical, severe and formal in their manners, their relaxations a Bible Society, or a meeting for the conversion of the Jews. But Lady Katherine was beautiful, and all were kind to one to whom kindness was strange, and the soft pathos of whose solitary spirit demanded affection.

Montacute requested his father's permission to marry his cousin, and was immediately refused. The duke particularly disliked his wife's family; but the fact is, he had no wish that his son should every marry. He meant to perpetuate his race himself, and was at this moment, in the midst of his orgies, meditating a second alliance, which should compensate him for his boyish blunder. In this state of affairs, Montacute, at length stung to resistance, inspired by the most powerful of passions, and acted upon by a stronger volition than his own, was planning a marriage in spite of his father (love, a cottage by an Irish lake, and seven hundred a-year) when intelligence arrived that his father, whose powerful frame and vigorous health seemed to menace a patriarchal term, was dead.

The new Duke of Bellamont had no experience of the world; but, though long cowed by his father, he had a strong character. Though the circle of his ideas was necessarily contracted, they were all clear and firm. In his moody youth he had imbibed certain impressions and arrived at certain conclusions, and they never quitted him. His mother was his model of feminine perfection, and he had loved his cousin because she bore a remarkable resemblance to her aunt. Again, he was of opinion that the tie between the father and the son ought to be one of intimate confidence and refined tenderness, and he resolved that, if Providence favoured him with offspring, his child should ever find in him absolute devotion of thought and feeling.

A variety of causes and circumstances had impressed him with a conviction that what is called fashionable life was a compound of frivolity and fraud, of folly and vice ; and he resolved never to enter it. To this he was, perhaps, in some degree unconsciously prompted by his reserved disposition, and by his painful sense of inexperience, for he looked forward to this world with almost as much of apprehension as of dislike. To politics, in the vulgar sense of the word, he had an equal repugnance. He had a lofty idea of his duty to his sovereign and his country, and felt within him the energies that would respond to a conjuncture. But he acceded to his title in a period of calmness, when nothing was called in question, and no danger was apprehended ; and as for the fights of factions, the duke altogether held himself aloof from them; he wanted nothing, not even the blue ribbon which he was soon obliged to take. Next to his domestic hearth, all his being was concentrated in his duties as a great proprietor of the soil. On these he had long pondered, and these he attempted to fulfil. That performance, indeed, was as much a source of delight to him as of obligation. He loved the country and a country life. His reserve seemed to melt away the moment he was on his own soil. Courteous he ever was, but then he became gracious and hearty. He liked to assemble ' the county ' around him ; to keep ' the county ' together ; ' the county ' seemed always his first thought ; he was proud of ' the county,' where he reigned supreme, not more from his vast possessions than from the influence of his sweet yet stately character, which made those devoted to him who otherwise were independent of his sway.

From straitened circumstances, and without having had a single fancy of youth gratified, the Duke of Bellamont had been suddenly summoned to the lordship of an estate scarcely inferior in size and revenue to some continental principalities; to dwell in palaces and castles, to be surrounded by a disciplined retinue, and to find every wish and want gratified before they could be expressed or anticipated. Yet he showed no elation, and acceded to his inheritance as serene as if he had never felt a pang or proved a necessity. She whom in the hour of trial he had selected for the future partner of his life, though a remarkable woman, by a singular coincidence of feeling, for it was as much from her original character as from sympathy with her husband, confirmed him in all his moods.

Katherine, Duchess of Bellamont, was beautiful : small and delicate in structure, with a dazzling complexion, and a smile which, though rare, was of the most winning and brilliant character. Her rich brown hair and her deep blue eye might have become a Dryad ; but her brow denoted intellect of a high order, and her mouth spoke inexorable resolution. She was a woman of fixed opinions, and of firm and compact prejudices. Brought up in an austere circle, where on all matters irrevocable judgment had been passed, which enjoyed the advantages of knowing exactly what was true in dogma, what just in conduct, and what correct in manners, she had early acquired the convenient habit of decision, while her studious mind employed its considerable energies in mastering every writer who favoured those opinions which she had previously determined were the right ones. The duchess was deep in the divinity of the seventeenth century. In the controversies between the two churches, she could have perplexed St. Omers or Maynooth. Chillingworth might be found in her boudoir. Not that her grace's reading was confined to divinity ; on the contrary, it was various and extensive. Puritan in religion, she was precisian in morals; but in both she was sincere. She was so in all things. Her nature was frank and simple; if she were inflexible, she at least wished to be just; and though very conscious of the greatness of her position, she was so sensible of its duties, that there was scarcely any exertion which she would evade, or any humility from which she would shrink, if she believed she were doing her duty to her God or to her neighbour.

It will be seen, therefore, that the Duke of Bellamont found no obstacle in his wife, who otherwise much influenced his conduct, to the plans which he had pre-conceived for the conduct of his life after marriage. The duchess shrank, with a feeling of haughty terror from that world of fashion which would have so willingly greeted her. During the greater part of the year, therefore, the Bellamonts resided in their magnificent castle, in their distant county, occupied with all the business and the pleasures of the provinces. While the duke, at the head of the magistracy, in the management of his estates, and in the sports of which he was fond, found ample occupation, his wife gave an impulse to the charity of the county, founded schools, endowed churches, received their neighbours, read her books, and amused herself in the creation of beautiful gardens, for which she had a passion.

After Easter, Parliament requiring their presence, the courtyard of one of the few palaces in London opened, and the world learnt that the Duke and Duchess of Bellamont had arrived at Bellamont House, from Montacute Castle. During their stay in town, which they made as brief as they well could, and which never exceeded three months, they gave a series of great dinners, principally attended by noble relations, and those families of the county who were so fortunate as to have also a residence in London. Regularly every year, also, there was a grand banquet given to some members of the royal family by the Duke and Duchess of Bellamont, and regularly every year the Duke and

Duchess of Bellamont had the honour of dining at the palace. Except at a ball or concert under the royal roof, the duke and duchess were never seen anywhere in the evening. The great ladies indeed, the Lady St. Julians and the Marchionesses of Deloraine, always sent them invitations, though they were ever declined. But the Bellamonts maintained a sort of traditional acquaintance with a few great houses, either by the ties of relationship, which, among the aristocracy, are very ramified, or by occasionally receiving travelling magnificoes at their hospitable castle.

To the great body, however, of what is called 'the World,' the world that lives in St. James' Street and Pall Mall, that looks out of a club window, and surveys mankind as Lucretius from his philosophic tower; the world of the Georges and the Jemmys; of Mr. Cassilis and Mr. Melton; of the Milfords and the Fitzherons, the Berners and the Egertons, the Mr. Ormsbys and the Alfred Mountchesneys, the Duke and Duchess of Bellamont were absolutely unknown. All that the world knew was, that there was a great peer who was called Duke of Bellamont; that there was a great house in London, with a courtyard, which bore his name; that he had a castle in the country, which was one of the boasts of England; and that this great duke had a duchess; but they never met them anywhere, nor did their wives and their sisters, and the ladies whom they admired, or who admired them, either at ball or at breakfast, either at morning dances or at evening déjeuners. It was clear, therefore, that the Bellamonts might be very great people, but they were not in ' society.'

It must have been some organic law, or some fate which uses structure for its fulfilment, but again it seemed that the continuance of the great house of Montacute should depend upon the life of a single being. The duke, like his father and his grandfather, was favoured only with one child, but that child was again a son. From the moment of his birth, the very existence of his parents seemed iden-

tified with his welfare. The duke and his wife mutually
assumed to each other a secondary position, in comparison
with that occupied by their offspring. From the hour of
his birth to the moment when this history opens, and when
he was about to complete his majority, never had such
solicitude been lavished on human being as had been con-
tinuously devoted to the life of the young Lord Montacute.
During his earlier education he scarcely quitted home. He
had, indeed, once been shown to Eton, surrounded by
faithful domestics, and accompanied by a private tutor,
whose vigilance would not have disgraced a superintendent
of police; but the scarlet fever happened to break out
during his first half, and Lord Montacute was instantly
snatched away from the scene of danger, where he was
never again to appear. At eighteen he went to Christchurch. His mother, who had nursed him herself, wrote
to him every day; but this was not found sufficient, and
the duke hired a residence in the neighbourhood of the
university, in order that they might occasionally see their
son during term.

CHAPTER III.

'SAW Eskdale just now,' said Mr. Cassilis, at White's,
'going down to the Duke of Bellamont's. Great doings
there: son comes of age at Easter. Wonder what sort of
fellow he is? Anybody know anything about him?'

'I wonder what his father's rent-roll is?' said Mr.
Ormsby.

'They say it is quite clear,' said Lord Fitzheron.

'Safe for that,' said Lord Milford; 'and plenty of ready
money, too, I should think, for one never heard of the present duke doing anything.'

'He does a good deal in his county,' said Lord Valentine.

'I don't call that anything,' said Lord Milford; 'but I

mean to say he never played, was never seen at Newmarket, or did anything which anybody can remember. In fact, he is a person whose name you never by any chance hear mentioned.'

'He is a sort of cousin of mine,' said Lord Valentine ; 'and we are all going down to the coming of age: that is, we are asked.'

'Then you can tell us what sort of fellow the son is.'

'I never saw him,' said Lord Valentine ; 'but I know the duchess told my mother last year, that Montacute, throughout his life, had never occasioned her a single moment's pain.'

Here there was a general laugh.

'Well, I have no doubt he will make up for lost time,' said Mr. Ormsby, demurely.

'Nothing like mamma's darling for upsetting a coach,' said Lord Milford. 'You ought to bring your cousin here, Valentine ; we would assist the development of his unsophisticated intelligence.'

'If I go down, I will propose it to him.'

'Why if ?' said Mr. Cassilis; ' sort of thing I should like to see once uncommonly : oxen roasted alive, old armour, and the girls of the village all running about as if they were behind the scenes.'

'Is that the way you did it at your majority, George ? ' said Lord Fitzheron.

'Egad, I kept my arrival at years of discretion at Brighton. I believe it was the last fun there ever was at the Pavilion. The poor dear king, God bless him ! proposed my health, and made the devil's own speech ; we all began to pipe. He was Regent then. Your father was there, Valentine ; ask him if he remembers it. That was a scene ! I won't say how it ended ; but the best joke is, I got a letter from my governor a few days after, with an account of what they had all been doing at Brandingham, and rowing me for not coming down, and I found out I had kept my coming of age the wrong day.'

'Did you tell them?'

'Not a word: I was afraid we might have had to go through it over again.'

'I suppose old Bellamont is the devil's own screw,' said Lord Milford. 'Rich governors, who have never been hard up, always are.'

'No: I believe he is a very good sort of fellow,' said Lord Valentine; 'at least my people always say so. I do not know much about him, for they never go anywhere.'

'They have got Leander down at Montacute,' said Mr. Cassilis. 'Had not such a thing as a cook in the whole county. They say Lord Eskdale arranged the cuisine for them; so you will feed well, Valentine.'

'That is something: and one can eat before Easter; but when the balls begin ——'

'Oh! as for that, you will have dancing enough at Montacute; it is expected on these occasions: Sir Roger de Coverley, tenants' daughters, and all that sort of thing. Deuced funny, but I must say, if I am to have a lark, I like Vauxhall.'

'I never met the Bellamonts,' said Lord Milford, musingly. 'Are there any daughters?'

'None.'

'That is a bore. A single daughter, even if there be a son, may be made something of; because, in nine cases out of ten, there is a round sum in the settlements for the younger children, and she takes it all.'

'That is the case of Lady Blanche Bickerstaffe,' said Lord Fitzheron. 'She will have a hundred thousand pounds.'

'You don't mean that!' said Lord Valentine; 'and she is a very nice girl, too.'

'You are quite wrong about the hundred thousand, Fitz,' said Lord Milford; 'for I made it my business to inquire most particularly into the affair: it is only fifty.'

'In these cases, the best rule is only to believe half,' said Mr. Ormsby.

'Then you have only got twenty thousand a-year, Ormsby,' said Lord Milford, laughing, ' because the world gives you forty.'

' Well, we must do the best we can in these hard times,' said Mr. Ormsby, with an air of mock resignation. 'With your Dukes of Bellamont and all these grandees on the stage, we little men shall be scarcely able to hold up our heads.'

' Come, Ormsby,' said Lord Milford, ' tell us the amount of your income tax.'

' They say Sir Robert quite blushed when he saw the figure at which you were sacked, and declared it was down-right spoliation.'

' You young men are always talking about money,' said Mr. Ormsby, shaking his head ; ' you should think of higher things.'

' I wonder what young Montacute will be thinking of this time next year,' said Lord Fitzheron.

' There will be plenty of people thinking of him,' said Mr. Cassilis. ' Egad, you gentlemen must stir yourselves, if you mean to be turned off. You will have rivals.'

' He will be no rival to me,' said Lord Milford ; ' for I am an avowed fortune-hunter, and that you say he does not care for, at least, at present.'

' And I marry only for love,' said Lord Valentine, laughing ; ' and so we shall not clash.'

' Ay, ay ; but if he will not go to the heiresses, the heiresses will go to him,' said Mr. Ormsby. ' I have seen a good deal of these things, and I generally observe the eldest son of a duke takes a fortune out of the market. Why, there is Beaumanoir, he is like Valentine ; I suppose he intends to marry for love, as he is always in that way ; but the heiresses never leave him alone, and in the long run you cannot withstand it ; it is like a bribe ; a man is indignant at the bare thought, refuses the first offer, and pockets the second.'

'It is very immoral, and very unfair,' said Lord Milford, 'that any man should marry for tin, who does not
want it.'

CHAPTER IV.

The Forest of Montacute, in the north of England, is the
name given to an extensive district, which in many parts
offers no evidence of the propriety of its title. The land,
especially during the last century, has been effectively
cleared, and presents, in general, a champaign view; rich
and rural, but far from picturesque. Over a wide expanse,
the eye ranges on cornfields and rich hedgerows, many a
sparkling spire, and many a merry windmill. In the extreme distance, on a clear day, may be discerned the blue
hills of the Border, and towards the north the cultivated
country ceases, and the dark form of the old forest spreads
into the landscape. The traveller, however, who may be
tempted to penetrate these sylvan recesses, will find much
that is beautiful, and little that is savage. He will be
struck by the capital road that winds among the groves of
ancient oak, and the turfy and ferny wilderness which ex-
tends on each side, whence the deer gaze on him with
haughty composure, as if conscious that he was an intruder
into their kingdom of whom they need have no fear. As
he advances, he observes the number of cross routes which
branch off from the main road, and which, though of less
dimensions, are equally remarkable for their masterly structure and compact condition.

Sometimes the land is cleared, and he finds himself by the
homestead of a forest farm, and remarks the buildings, distinguished not only by their neatness, but the propriety of
their rustic architecture. Still advancing, the deer become
rarer, and the road is formed by an avenue of chestnuts;
the forest, on each side, being now transformed into vege-
table gardens. The stir of the population is soon evident.
Persons are moving to and fro on the side path of the road

Horsemen and carts seem returning from market; women with empty baskets, and then the rare vision of a stage coach. The postilion spurs his horses, cracks his whip, and dashes at full gallop into the town of Montacute, the capital of the forest.

It is the prettiest little town in the world, built entirely of hewn stone, the well-paved and well-lighted streets as neat as a Dutch village. There are two churches; one of great antiquity, the other raised by the present duke, but in the best style of Christian architecture. The bridge that spans the little but rapid river Belle, is perhaps a trifle too vast and Roman for its site; but it was built by the first duke of the second dynasty, who was always afraid of underbuilding his position. The town was also indebted to him for their hall, a Palladian palace. Montacute is a corporate town, and, under the old system, returned two members to Parliament. The amount of its population, according to the rule generally observed, might have preserved it from disfranchisement, but, as every house belonged to the duke, and as he was what, in the confused phraseology of the revolutionary war, was called a Tory, the Whigs took care to put Montacute in Schedule A.

The town-hall, the market-place, a literary institution, and the new church, form, with some good houses of recent erection, a handsome square, in which there is a fountain, a gift to the town from the present duchess.

At the extremity of the town, the ground rises, and on a woody steep, which is in fact the termination of a long range of tableland, may be seen the towers of the outer court of Montacute Castle. The principal building, which is vast and of various ages, from the Plantagenets to the Guelphs, rises on a terrace, from which, on the side opposite to the town, you descend into a well-timbered inclosure, called the Home Park. Further on, the forest again appears; the deer again crouch in their fern, or glance along the vistas; nor does this green domain terminate till it touches the vast and purple moors that divide the kingdoms of Great Britain.

It was on an early day of April that the duke was sitting in his private room, a pen in one hand, and looking up with a face of pleasurable emotion at his wife, who stood by his side, her right arm sometimes on the back of his chair and sometimes on his shoulder, while with her other hand, between the intervals of speech, she pressed a handkerchief to her eyes, bedewed with the expression of an affectionate excitement.

'It is too much,' said her grace.

'And done in such a handsome manner!' said the duke.

'I would not tell our dear child of it at this moment,' said the duchess; 'he has so much to go through!'

'You are right, Kate. It will keep till the celebration is over. How delighted he will be!'

'My dear George, I sometimes think we are too happy.'

'You are not half as happy as you deserve to be,' replied her husband, looking up with a smile of affection; and then he finished his reply to the letter of Mr. Hungerford, one of the county members, informing the duke, that now Lord Montacute was of age, he intended at once to withdraw from Parliament, having for a long time fixed on the majority of the heir of the house of Bellamont as the signal for that event. 'I accepted the post,' said Mr. Hungerford, 'much against my will. Your grace behaved to me at the time in the handsomest manner, and, indeed, ever since, with respect to this subject. But a Marquis of Montacute is, in my opinion, and, I believe I may add, in that of the whole county, our proper representative; besides, we want young blood in the House.'

'It certainly is done in the handsomest manner,' said the duke.

'But then you know, George, you behaved to him in the handsomest manner; he says so, as you do indeed to everybody; and this is your reward.'

'I should be very sorry, indeed, if Hungerford did not withdraw with perfect satisfaction to himself, and his family too,' urged the duke; 'they are most respectable people, one of the most respectable families in the county; I should be quite grieved if this step were taken without their entire and hearty concurrence.'

'Of course it is,' said the duchess, 'with the entire and hearty concurrence of every one. Mr. Hungerford says so. And I must say that, though few things could have gratified me more, I quite agree with Mr. Hungerford that a Lord Montacute is the natural member for the county; and I have no doubt that if Mr. Hungerford, or any one else in his position, had not resigned, they never could have met our child without feeling the greatest embarrassment.'

'A man though, and a man of Hungerford's position, an old family in the county, does not like to figure as a warning-pan,' said the duke, thoughtfully. 'I think it has been done in a very handsome manner.'

'And we will show our sense of it,' said the duchess. 'The Hungerfords shall feel, when they come here on Thursday, that they are among our best friends.'

'That is my own Kate! Here is a letter from your brother. They will be here to-morrow. Eskdale cannot come over till Wednesday. He is at home, but detained by a meeting about his new harbour.'

'I am delighted that they will be here to-morrow,' said the duchess. 'I am so anxious that he should see Kate before the castle is full, when he will have a thousand calls upon his time! I feel persuaded that he will love her at first sight. And as for their being cousins, why, we were cousins, and that did not hinder us from loving each other.'

'If she resemble you as much as you resembled your aunt ——' said the duke, looking up.

'She is my perfect image, my very self, Harriet says, in disposition, as well as face and form.'

'Then our son has a good chance of being a very happy man,' said the duke.

'That he should come of age, enter Parliament, and marry in the same year! We ought to be very thankful. What a happy year!'

'But not one of these events has yet occurred,' said the duke, smiling.

'But they all will,' said the duchess, 'under Providence.'

'I would not precipitate marriage.'

'Certainly not; nor should I wish him to think of it before the autumn. I should like him to be married on our wedding-day.'

CHAPTER V.

THE sun shone brightly, there was a triumphal arch at every road; the market-place and the town-hall were caparisoned like steeds for a tournament, every house had its garland; the flags were flying on every tower and steeple. There was such a peal of bells you could scarcely hear your neighbour's voice; then came discharges of artillery, and then bursts of music from various bands, all playing different tunes. The country people came trooping in, some on horseback, some in carts, some in procession. The Temperance band made an immense noise, and the Odd Fellows were loudly cheered. Every now and then one of the duke's yeomanry galloped through the town in his regimentals of green and silver, with his dark flowing plume and clattering sabre, and with an air of business-like desperation, as if he were carrying a message from the commander-in-chief in the thickest of the fight.

Before the eventful day of which this merry morn was the harbinger, the arrivals of guests at the castle had been numerous and important. First came the brother of the duchess, with his countess, and their fair daughter the Lady Katherine, whose fate, unconsciously to herself, had already been sealed by her noble relatives. She was destined to be the third Katherine of Bellamont that her fortunate house had furnished to these illustrious walls. Nor, if unaware of her high lot, did she seem unworthy of it. Her mien was prophetic of the state assigned to her. This was her first visit to Montacute since her early childhood, and she had not encountered her cousin since their nursery days. The day after them, Lord Eskdale came over from his principal seat in the contiguous county, of which he was lord-lieutenant. He was the first-cousin of the duke, his father and the second Duke of Bellamont having married two sisters, and of course intimately related to the duchess and her family. Lord Eskdale exercised a great influence over the house of Montacute, though quite unsought for by him. He was the only man of the world whom they knew, and they never decided upon anything out of the limited circle of their immediate experience without consulting him. Lord Eskdale had been the cause of their son going to Eton ; Lord Eskdale had recommended them to send him to Christchurch. The duke had begged his cousin to be his trustee when he married ; he had made him his executor, and had intended him as the guardian of his son. Although, from the difference of their habits, little thrown together in their earlier youth, Lord Eskdale had shown, even then, kind consideration for his relative ; he had even proposed that they should travel together, but the old duke would not consent to this. After his death, however, being neighbours as well as relatives, Lord Eskdale had become the natural friend and counsellor of his grace.

The duke deservedly reposed in him implicit confidence, and entertained an almost unbounded admiration of his cousin's knowledge of mankind. He was scarcely less a favourite or less an oracle with the duchess, though there were subjects on which she feared Lord Eskdale did not entertain views as serious as her own ; but Lord Eskdale, with an extreme carelessness of manner, and an apparent negligence of the minor arts of pleasing, was a consummate master of the feminine idiosyncrasy, and, from a French actress to an English duchess, was skilled in guiding women without ever letting the curb be felt. Scarcely a week elapsed, when Lord Eskdale was in the country, that a long letter of difficulties was not received by him from Montacute, with an earnest request for his immediate advice. His lordship, singularly averse to letter writing, and especially to long letter writing, used generally in reply to say that, in the course of a day or two, he should be in their part of the world, and would talk the matter over with them.

And, indeed, nothing was more amusing than to see Lord Eskdale, imperturbable, yet not heedless, with his peculiar calmness, something between that of a Turkish pacha and an English jockey, standing up with his back to the fire and his hands in his pockets, and hearing the united statement of a case by the Duke and Duchess of Bellamont; the serious yet quiet and unexaggerated narrative of his grace, the impassioned interruptions, decided opinions, and lively expressions of his wife, when she felt the duke was not doing justice to the circumstances, or her view of them, and the Spartan brevity with which, when both his clients were exhausted, their counsel summed up the whole affair, and said three words which seemed suddenly to remove all doubts, and to solve all difficulties. In all the business of life, Lord Eskdale, though he appreciated their native ability, and respected their considerable acquirements, which he did not share, looked upon his cousins as two children, and managed them as children ; but he was really attached to them, and the sincere attachment of such a character is often worth more than the most passionate devotion. The last great domestic embarrassment at Montacute had been the affair of the cooks. Lord Eskdale had taken this upon his own shoulders, and, writing to Daubuz, had sent down Leander and his friends to open the minds and charm the palates of the north.

Lord Valentine and his noble parents, and their daughter, Lady Florentina, who was a great horsewoman, also arrived. The countess, who had once been a beauty with the reputation of a wit, and now set up for being a wit on the reputation of having been a beauty, was the lady of fashion of the party, and scarcely knew anybody present, though there were many who were her equals and some her superiors in rank. Her way was to be a little fine, always smiling and condescendingly amiable ; when alone with her husband shrugging her shoulders somewhat, and vowing that she was delighted that Lord Eskdale was there, as she had somebody to speak to. It was what she called ' quite a relief.' A relief, perhaps, from Lord and Lady Mountjoy, whom she had been avoiding all her life; unfortunate people, who, with a large fortune, lived in a wrong square, and asked to their house everybody who was nobody ; besides, Lord Mountjoy was vulgar, and laughed too loud, and Lady Mountjoy called you ' my dear,' and showed her teeth. A relief, perhaps, too, from the Hon. and Rev. Montacute Mountjoy, who, with Lady Eleanor, four daughters and two sons, had been invited to celebrate the majority of the future chieftain of their house. The countess had what is called ' a horror of those Mountjoys, and those Montacute Mountjoys,' and what added to her annoyance was, that Lord Valentine was always flirting with the Misses Montacute Mountjoy.

The countess could find no companions in the Duke and Duchess of Clanronald, because, as she told her husband, as they could not speak English and she could not speak Scotch, it was impossible to exchange ideas. The bishop of the diocese was there, toothless and tolerant, and wishing to be on good terms with all sects, provided they pay church-rates, and another bishop far more vigorous and of greater fame. By his administration the heir of Bellamont had entered the Christian church, and by the imposition of his hands had been confirmed in it. His lordship, a great authority with the duchess, was specially invited to be present on the interesting occasion, when the babe that he had held at the font, and the child that he had blessed at the altar, was about thus publicly to adopt and acknowledge the duties and responsibility of a man. But the countess, though she liked bishops, liked them, as she told her husband, ' in their place.' What that exactly was, she did not define ; but probably their palaces or the House of Lords.

It was hardly to be expected that her ladyship would find

any relief in the society of the Marquis and Marchioness of Hampshire; for his lordship passed his life in being the President of scientific and literary societies, and was ready for anything, from the Royal, if his turn ever arrived, to opening a Mechanics' Institute in his neighbouring town. Lady Hampshire was an invalid; but her ailment was one of those mysteries which still remained insoluble, although, in the most liberal manner, she delighted to afford her friends all the information in her power. Never was a votary endowed with a faith at once so lively and so capricious. Each year she believed in some new remedy, and announced herself on the eve of some miraculous cure. But the saint was scarcely canonised, before his claims to beatitude were impugned. One year Lady Hampshire never quitted Leamington; another, she contrived to combine the infinitesimal doses of Hahnemann with the colossal distractions of the metropolis. Now her sole conversation was the water cure. Lady Hampshire was to begin immediately after her visit to Montacute, and she spoke in her sawney voice of factitious enthusiasm, as if she pitied the lot of all those who were not about to sleep in wet sheets.

The members for the county, with their wives and daughters, the Hungerfords and the Ildertons, Sir Russell Malpas, or even Lord Hull, an Irish peer with an English estate, and who represented one of the divisions, were scarcely a relief. Lord Hull was a bachelor, and had twenty thousand a year, and would not have been too old for Florentina, if Lord Hull had only lived in ' society,' learnt how to dress and how to behave, and had avoided that peculiar coarseness of manners and complexion which seem the inevitable results of a provincial life. What are forty-five or even forty-eight years, if a man do not get up too early or go to bed too soon, if he be dressed by the right persons, and, early accustomed to the society of women, he possesses that flexibility of manner and that readiness of gentle repartee which a feminine apprenticeship can alone confer? But Lord Hull was a man with a red face and a grey head, on whom coarse indulgence and the selfish negligence of a country life had already conferred a shapeless form; and who, dressed something like a groom, sate at dinner in stolid silence by Lady Hampshire, who, whatever were her complaints, had certainly the art, if only from her questions, of making her neighbours communicative. The countess examined Lord Hull through her eye-glass with curious pity at so fine a fortune and so good a family being so entirely thrown away. Had he been brought up in a civilised manner, lived six months in May Fair, passed his carnival at Paris, never sported except in Scotland, and occasionally visited a German bath, even Lord Hull might have 'fined down.' His hair need not have been grey if it had been attended to ; his complexion would not have been so glaring ; his hands never could have grown to so huge a shape.

What a party, where the countess was absolutely driven to speculate on the possible destinies of a Lord Hull ! But in this party there was not a single young man, at least not a single young man one had ever heard of, except her son, and he was of no use. The Duke of Bellamont knew no young men; the duke did not even belong to a club ; the Duchess of Bellamont knew no young men ; she never gave and she never attended an evening party. As for the county youth, the young Hungerfords and the young Ildertons, the best of them formed part of the London crowd. Some of them, by complicated manœuvres, might even have made their way into the countess's crowded saloons on a miscellaneous night. She knew the length of their tether. They ranged, as the Price Current says, from eight to three thousand a year. Not the figure that purchases a Lady Florentina !

There were many other guests, and some of them notable, though not of the class and character to interest the fastidious mother of Lord Valentine ; but whoever and whatever they might be, of the sixty or seventy persons who were seated each day in the magnificent banqueting-room of

Montacute Castle, feasting, amid pyramids of gold plate, on the masterpieces of Leander, there was not a single individual who did not possess one of the two great qualifications : they were all of them cousins of the Duke of Bellamont, or proprietors in his county.

But we must not anticipate, the great day of the festival having hardly yet commenced.

CHAPTER VI.

In the Home Park was a colossal pavilion, which held more than two thousand persons, and in which the townsfolk of Montacute were to dine; at equal distances were several smaller tents, each of different colours and patterns, and each bearing on a standard the name of one of the surrounding parishes which belonged to the Duke of Bellamont, and to the convenience and gratification of whose inhabitants these tents were to-day dedicated. There was not a man of Buddleton or Fuddleton; not a yeoman or peasant of Montacute super Mare or Montacute Abbotts, nor of Percy Bellamont nor Friar's Bellamont, nor Winch nor Finch, nor of Mandeville Stokes nor Mandeville Bois; not a goodman true of Carleton and Ingleton and Kirkby and Dent, and Gillamoor and Padmore and Hutton le Hale ; not a stout forester from the glades of Thorp, or the sylvan homes of Hurst Lydgate and Bishopstowe, that knew not where foamed and flowed the duke's ale, that was to quench the longings of his thirsty village. And their wives and daughters were equally welcome. At the entrance of each tent, the duke's servants invited all to enter, supplied them with required refreshments, or indicated their appointed places at the approaching banquet. In general, though there were many miscellaneous parties, each village entered the park in procession, with its flag and its band.

At noon the scene presented the appearance of an immense but well-ordered fair. In the back-ground, men and

boys climbed poles or raced in sacks, while the exploits of
the ginglers, their mischievous manœuvres and subtile
combinations, elicited frequent bursts of laughter. Further
on, two long-menaced cricket matches called forth all the
skill and energy of Fuddleton and Buddleton, and Winch
and Finch. The great throng of the population, however,
was in the precincts of the terrace, where, in the course
of the morning, it was known that the duke and duchess,
with the hero of the day and all their friends, were to
appear, to witness the sports of the people, and especially
the feats of the morrice-dancers, who were at this moment
practising before a very numerous and delighted audience.
In the meantime, bells, drums, and trumpets, an occasional
volley, and the frequent cheers and laughter of the multitude, combined with the brilliancy of the sun and the
brightness of the ale to make a right gladsome scene.

'It's nothing to what it will be at night,' said one of the
duke's footmen to his family, his father and mother, two
sisters and a young brother, listening to him with open
mouths, and staring at his state livery with mingled feelings of awe and affection. They had come over from
Bellamont Friars, and their son had asked the steward to
give him the care of the pavilion of that village, in order
that he might look after his friends. Never was a family
who esteemed themselves so fortunate or felt so happy.
This was having a friend at court, indeed.

'It's nothing to what it will be at night,' said Thomas.
'You will have " Hail, star of Bellamont!" and "God save
the Queen!" a crown, three stars, four flags, and two
coronets, all in coloured lamps, letters six feet high, on the
castle. There will be one hundred beacons lit over the
space of fifty miles the moment a rocket is shot off from
the Round Tower, and as for fireworks, Bob, you'll see
them at last. Bengal lights, and the largest wheels will be
as common as squibs and crackers; and I have heard say,
though it is not to be mentioned ——' And he paused.

'We'll not open our mouths,' said his father, earnestly.

D

'You had better not tell us,' said his mother, in a nervous paroxysm; 'for I am in such a fluster, I am sure I cannot answer for myself, and then Thomas may lose his place for breach of conference.'

'Nonsense, mother,' said his sisters, who snubbed their mother almost as readily as is the gracious habit of their betters. 'Pray tell us, Tom.'

'Ay, ay, Tom,' said his younger brother.

'Well,' said Tom, in a confidential whisper, 'won't there be a transparency! I have heard say the queen never had anything like it. You won't be able to see it for the first quarter of an hour, there will be such a blaze of fire and rockets; but when it does come, they say it's like heaven opening; the young markiss on a cloud, with his hand on his heart, in his new uniform.'

'Dear me!' said the mother. 'I knew him before he was weaned. The duchess suckled him herself, which shows her heart is very true; for they may say what they like, but if another's milk is in your child's veins, he seems, in a sort of way, as much her bairn as your own.'

'Mother's milk makes a true-born Englishman,' said the father; 'and I make no doubt our young markiss will prove the same.'

'How I long to see him!' exclaimed one of the daughters.

'And so do I!' said her sister; 'and in his uniform! How beautiful it must be!'

'Well, I don't know,' said the mother; 'and perhaps you will laugh at me for saying so, but after seeing my Thomas in his state livery, I don't care much for seeing anything else.'

'Mother, how can you say such things! I am afraid the crowd will be very great at the fireworks. We must try to get a good place.'

'I have arranged all that,' said Thomas, with a triumphant look. 'There will be an inner circle for the steward's friends, and you will be let in.'

'Oh!' exclaimed his sisters.

'Well, I hope I shall get through the day,' said his mother; 'but it's rather a trial, after our quiet life.'

'And when will they come on the terrace, Thomas?'

'You see, they are waiting for the corporation, that's the mayor and town council of Montacute; they are coming up with an address. There! Do you hear that? That's the signal gun. They are leaving the town-hall at this same moment. Now, in three-quarters of an hour's time or so, the duke and duchess, and the young markiss, and all of them, will come on the terrace. So you be alive, and draw near, and get a good place. I must look after these people.'

About the same time that the cannon announced that the corporation had quitted the town-hall, some one tapped at the chamber-door of Lord Eskdale, who was sealing a letter in his private room.

'Well, Harris?' said Lord Eskdale, looking up, and recognising his valet.

'His grace has been inquiring for your lordship several times,' replied Mr. Harris, with a perplexed air.

'I shall be with him in good time,' replied his lordship, again looking down.

'If you could manage to come down at once, my lord,' said Mr. Harris.

'Why?'

'Mr. Leander wishes to see your lordship very much.'

'Ah! Leander!' said Lord Eskdale, in a more interested tone. 'What does he want?'

'I have not seen him,' said Mr. Harris; 'but Mr. Prevost tells me that his feelings are hurt.'

'I hope he has not struck,' said Lord Eskdale, with a comical glance.

'Something of that sort,' said Mr. Harris, very seriously.

Lord Eskdale had a great sympathy with artists; he was well acquainted with that irritability which is said to be the characteristic of the creative power; genius always found in him an indulgent arbiter. He was convinced that, if the feelings of a rare spirit like Leander were hurt, they were not to be trifled with. He felt responsible for the presence of one so eminent in a country where, perhaps, he was not properly appreciated; and Lord Eskdale descended to the steward's room with the consciousness of an important, probably a difficult, mission.

The kitchen of Montacute Castle was of the old style, fitted for baronial feasts. It covered a great space, and was very lofty. Now they build them in great houses on a different system; even more distinguished by height, but far more condensed in area, as it is thought that a dish often suffers from the distances which the cook has to move over in collecting its various component parts. The new principle seems sound; the old practice, however, was more picturesque. The kitchen at Montacute was like the preparation for the famous wedding feast of Prince Riquet with the Tuft, when the kind earth opened, and revealed that genial spectacle of white-capped cooks, and endless stoves and stewpans. The steady blaze of two colossal fires was shrouded by vast screens. Everywhere, rich materials and silent artists; business without bustle, and the all-pervading magic of method. Philippon was preparing a sauce; Dumoreau, in another quarter of the spacious chamber, was arranging some truffles; the Englishman, Smit, was fashioning a cutlet. Between these three generals of division aides-de-camp perpetually passed, in the form of active and observant marmitons, more than one of whom, as he looked on the great masters around him, and with the prophetic faculty of genius surveyed the future, exclaimed to himself, like Correggio, 'And I also will be a cook.'

In this animated and interesting scene was only one unoccupied individual, or rather occupied only with his own sad thoughts. This was Papa Prevost, leaning against rather than sitting on a dresser, with his arms folded, his idle knife stuck in his girdle, and the tassel of his cap awry with vexation. His gloomy brow, however, lit up as Mr. Harris, for whom he was waiting with anxious expectation, entered, and summoned him to the presence of Lord Eskdale, who, with a shrewd yet lounging air, which concealed his own foreboding perplexity, said, 'Well, Prevost, what is the matter? The people here been impertinent?'

Prevost shook his head. 'We never were in a house, my lord, where they were more obliging. It is something much worse.'

'Nothing wrong about your fish, I hope? Well, what is it?'

'Leander, my lord, has been dressing dinners for a week: dinners, I will be bound to say, which were never equalled in the Imperial kitchen, and the duke has never made a single observation, or sent him a single message. Yesterday, determined to outdo even himself, he sent up some escalopes de laitances de carpes à la Bellamont. In my time I have seen nothing like it, my lord. Ask Philippon, ask Dumoreau, what they thought of it! Even the Englishman, Smit, who never says anything, opened his mouth and exclaimed; as for the marmitons, they were breathless, and I thought Achille, the youth of whom I spoke to you, my lord, and who appears to me to be born with the true feeling, would have been overcome with emotion. When it was finished, Leander retired to his room; I attended him; and covered his face with his hands. Would you believe it, my lord! Not a word; not even a message. All this morning Leander has waited in the last hope. Nothing, absolutely nothing! How can he compose when he is not appreciated? Had he been appreciated, he would to-day not only have repeated the escalopes à la Bellamont, but perhaps even invented what might have outdone it. It is unheard of, my lord. The late Lord Monmouth would have sent for Leander the very evening, or have written to him a beautiful letter, which would have been preserved in his family; M. de Sidonia would have sent him a tankard from his table. These things in themselves are nothing; but they prove to a man of genius that he is understood. Had Leander been in the Imperial kitchen, or even with the Emperor of Russia, he would have been decorated!'

'Where is he?' said Lord Eskdale.

'He is alone in the cook's room.'

'I will go and say a word to him.'

Alone, in the cook's room, gazing in listless vacancy on the fire, that fire which, under his influence, had often achieved so many master-works, was the great artist who was not appreciated. No longer suffering under mortification, but overwhelmed by that exhaustion which follows acute sensibility and the over-tension of the creative faculty, he looked round as Lord Eskdale entered, and when he perceived who was his visitor, he rose immediately, bowed very low, and then sighed.

'Prevost thinks we are not exactly appreciated here,' said Lord Eskdale.

Leander bowed again, and still sighed.

'Prevost does not understand the affair,' continued Lord Eskdale. 'Why I wished you to come down here, Leander, was not to receive the applause of my cousin and his guests, but to form their taste.'

Here was a great idea; exciting and ennobling. It threw quite a new light upon the position of Leander. He started; his brow seemed to clear. Leander, then, like other eminent men, had duties to perform as well as rights to enjoy; he had a right to fame, but it was also his duty to form and direct public taste. That then was the reason he was brought down to Bellamont Castle; because some of the greatest personages in England, who never had eaten a proper dinner in their lives, would have an opportunity, for the first time, of witnessing art. What could the praise of the Duke of Clanronald, or Lord Hampshire, or Lord Hull, signify to one who had shared the confidence of a Lord Monmouth, and whom Sir Alexander Grant, the first judge in Europe, had declared the only man of genius of the age? Leander erred too in supposing that his achievements had been lost upon the guests at Bellamont. Insensibly his feats had set them a-thinking. They had been like Cossacks in a picture-gallery ; but the Clanronalds, the Hampshires, the Hulls, would return to their homes impressed with a great truth, that there is a difference between eating and dining. Was this nothing for Leander to have effected? Was it nothing, by this development of taste, to assist in supporting that aristocratic influence which he wished to cherish, and which can alone encourage art? If anything can save the aristocracy in this levelling age, it is an appreciation of men of genius. Certainly it would have been very gratifying to Leander if his grace had only sent him a message, or if Lord Montacute had expressed a wish to see him. He had been long musing over some dish à la Montacute, for this very day. The young lord was reputed to have talent; this dish might touch his fancy; the homage of a great artist flatters youth; this offering of genius might colour his destiny. But what, after all, did this signify? Leander had a mission to perform.

'If I were you, I would exert myself, Leander,' said Lord Eskdale.

'Ah! my lord, if all men were like you! If artists were only sure of being appreciated; if we were but understood, a dinner would become a sacrifice to the gods, and a kitchen would be Paradise.'

In the meantime, the mayor and town-councillors of Montacute, in their robes of office, and preceded by their bedels and their mace-bearer, have entered the gates of the castle. They pass into the great hall, the most ancient part of the building, with its open roof of Spanish chestnut, its screen and gallery and dais, its painted windows and marble floor. Ascending the dais, they are ushered into an ante-chamber, the first of that suite of state apartments that opens on the terrace. Leaving on one side the principal dining-room and the library, they proceeded through the green drawing-room, so called from its silken hangings, the red drawing-room, covered with ruby velvet, and both adorned, but not encumbered, with pictures of the choicest art, into the principal or duchesses' drawing-room, thus entitled from its complete collection of portraits of Duchesses of Bellamont. It was a spacious and beautifully proportioned chamber, hung with amber satin, its ceiling by Zucchero, whose rich colours were relieved by the burnished gilding. The corporation trod tremblingly over the gorgeous carpet of Axminster, which displayed, in vivid colours and colossal proportions, the shield and supporters of Bellamont, and threw a hasty glance at the vases of porphyry and malachite, and mosaic tables covered with precious toys, which were grouped about.

Thence they were ushered into the Montacute room, adorned, among many interesting pictures, by perhaps the finest performance of Lawrence, a portrait of the present duke, just after his marriage. Tall and graceful, with a clear dark complexion, regular features, eyes of liquid tenderness, a frank brow, and rich clustering hair, the accomplished artist had seized and conveyed the character of a high-spirited but gentle-hearted cavalier. From the Montacute chamber they entered the ball-room; very spacious, white and gold, a coved ceiling, large Venetian lustres, and the walls of looking-glass, enclosing friezes of festive sculpture. Then followed another antechamber, in the centre of which was one of the master-pieces of Canova. This room, lined with footmen in state liveries, completed the suite that opened on the terrace. The northern side of this chamber consisted of a large door; divided, and decorated in its panels with emblazoned shields of arms.

The valves being thrown open, the mayor and town-council of Montacute were ushered into a gallery one hundred feet long, and which occupied a great portion of the northern side of the castle. The panels of this gallery enclosed a series of pictures in tapestry, which represented the principal achievements of the third crusade. A Montacute had been one of the most distinguished knights in that great adventure, and had saved the life of Cœur de Lion at the siege of Ascalon. In after-ages a Duke of Bellamont, who was our ambassador at Paris, had given orders to the Gobelins factory for the execution of this series of pictures from cartoons by the most celebrated artists of the time. The subjects of the tapestry had obtained for the magnificent chamber, which they adorned and rendered so interesting, the title of ' The Crusaders' Gallery.'

At the end of this gallery, surrounded by their guests, their relatives, and their neighbours ; by high nobility, by reverend prelates, by the members and notables of the county, and by some of the chief tenants of the duke, a portion of whom were never absent from any great carousing or high ceremony that occurred within his walls, the Duke and Duchess of Bellamont and their son, a little in advance of the company, stood to receive the congratulatory addresses of the mayor and corporation of their ancient and faithful town of Montacute ; the town which their fathers had built and adorned, which they had often represented in Parliament in the good old days, and which they took care should then enjoy its fair proportion of the good old things ; a town, every house in which belonged to them, and of which there was not an inhabitant who, in his own person or in that of his ancestry, had not felt the advantages of the noble connection.

The duke bowed to the corporation, with the duchess on his left hand ; and on his right there stood a youth, above the middle height and of a frame completely and gracefully formed. His dark brown hair, in those hyacinthine curls which Grecian poets have celebrated, and which Grecian sculptors have immortalised, clustered over his brow, which, however, they only partially concealed. It was pale, as was his whole countenance, but the liquid richness of the dark brown eye, and the colour of the lip, denoted anything but a languid circulation. The features were regular, and inclined rather to a refinement which might have imparted to the countenance a character of too much delicacy, had it not been for the deep meditation of the brow, and for the lower part of the visage, which intimated indomitable will and an iron resolution.

Placed for the first time in his life in a public position,

and under circumstances which might have occasioned some degree of embarrassment even to those initiated in the world, nothing was more remarkable in the demeanour of Lord Montacute than his self-possession; nor was there in his carriage anything studied, or which had the character of being preconceived. Every movement or gesture was distinguished by what may be called a graceful gravity. With a total absence of that excitement which seemed so natural to his age and situation, there was nothing in his manner which approached to nonchalance or indifference It would appear that he duly estimated the importance of the event they were commemorating, yet was not of a habit of mind that over-estimated anything.

END OF BOOK I.

BOOK II.

CHAPTER I.

THE week of celebration was over: some few guests remained, near relatives, and not very rich, the Montacute Mountjoys, for example. They came from a considerable distance, and the duke insisted that they should remain until the duchess went to London, an event, by the bye, which was to occur very speedily. Lady Eleanor was rather agreeable, and the duchess a little liked her; there were four daughters, to be sure, and not very lively, but they sang in the evening.

It was a bright morning, and the duchess, with a heart prophetic of happiness, wished to disburthen it to her son; she meant to propose to him, therefore, to be her companion in her walk, and she had sent to his rooms in vain, and was inquiring after him, when she was informed that 'Lord Montacute was with his grace.'

A smile of satisfaction flitted over her face, as she recalled the pleasant cause of the conference that was now taking place between the father and the son.

Let us see how it advanced.

The duke is in his private library, consisting chiefly of the statutes at large, Hansard, the Annual Register, Parliamentary Reports, and legal treatises on the powers and duties of justices of the peace. A portrait of his mother is over the mantel-piece: opposite it a huge map of the county. His correspondence on public business with the secretary of state, and the various authorities of the shire, is admirably arranged: for the duke was what is called an excellent man of business, that is to say, methodical, and an adept in all the small arts of routine. These papers were deposited, after having been ticketed with a date and a summary of their contents, and tied with much tape, in a large cabinet, which occupied nearly one side of the room, and on the top of which were busts in marble of Mr. Pitt, George III., and the Duke of Wellington.

The duke was leaning back in his chair, which it seemed, from his air and position, he had pushed back somewhat suddenly from his writing table, and an expression of painful surprise, it cannot be denied, dwelt on his countenance. Lord Montacute was on his legs, leaning with his left arm on the chimney-piece, very serious, and, if possible, paler than usual.

'You take me quite by surprise,' said the duke; 'I thought it was an arrangement that would have deeply gratified you.'

Lord Montacute slightly bowed his head, but said nothing. His father continued.

'Not wish to enter Parliament at present! Why, that is all very well, and if, as was once the case, we could enter Parliament when we liked, and how we liked, the wish might be very reasonable. If I could ring my bell, and return you member for Montacute with as much ease as I could send over to Bellamont to engage a special train to take us to town, you might be justified in indulging a fancy. But how and when, I should like to know, are you to enter Parliament now? This Parliament will last : it will go on to the lees. Lord Eskdale told me so not a week ago. Well then, at any rate, you lose three years : for three years you are an idler. I never thought that was your character. I have always had an impression you would turn your mind to public business, that the county might look up to you. If you have what are called higher views, you should not forget there is a great opening now in public life, which may not offer again. The Duke is resolved to give the preference, in carrying on the business of the country, to the aristocracy. He believes this is our only means of preservation. He told me so himself. If it be so, I fear we are doomed. I hope we may be of some use to our country without being ministers of state. But let that pass. As long as the Duke lives, he is omnipotent, and will have his way. If you come into Parliament now, and show any disposition for office, you may rely upon it you will not long be unemployed. I have no doubt I could arrange that you should move the address of next session. I dare say Lord Eskdale could manage this, and, if he could not, though I abhor asking a minister for anything, I should, under the circumstances, feel perfectly justified in speaking to the Duke on the subject myself, and,' added his grace, in a lowered tone, but with an expression of great earnestness and determination, 'I flatter myself that if the Duke of Bellamont chooses to express a wish, it would not be disregarded.'

Lord Montacute cast his dark, intelligent eyes upon the ground, and seemed plunged in thought.

' Besides,' added the duke, after a moment's pause, and inferring, from the silence of his son, that he was making an impression, ' suppose Hungerford is not in the same humour this time three years which he is in now. Probably he may be; possibly he may not. Men do not like to be balked when they think they are doing a very kind and generous and magnanimous thing. Hungerford is not a warming-pan; we must remember that; he never was originally, and if he had been, he has been member for the county too long to be so considered now. I should be placed in a most painful position, if, this time three years, I had to withdraw my support from Hungerford, in order to secure your return.'

' There would be no necessity, under any circumstances, for that, my dear father,' said Lord Montacute, looking up, and speaking in a voice which, though somewhat low, was of that organ that at once arrests attention; a voice that comes alike from the brain and from the heart, and seems made to convey both profound thought and deep emotion.

There is no index of character so sure as the voice   There are tones, tones brilliant and gushing, which impart a quick and pathetic sensibility: there are others that, deep and yet calm, seem the just interpreters of a serene and exalted intellect. But the rarest and the most precious of all voices is that which combines passion and repose; and whose rich and restrained tones exercise, perhaps, on the human frame a stronger spell than even the fascination of the eye, or that bewitching influence of the hand, which is the privilege of the higher races of Asia.

'There would be no necessity, under any circumstances, for that, my dear father,' said Lord Montacute, 'for, to be frank, I believe I should feel as little disposed to enter Parliament three years hence as now.'

The duke looked still more surprised. 'Mr. Fox was not of age when he took his seat,' said his grace. 'You know how old Mr. Pitt was when he was a minister. Sir Robert, too, was in harness very early. I have always heard the good judges say, Lord Eskdale, for example, that a man might speak in Parliament too soon, but it was impossible to go in too soon.'

'If he wished to succeed in that assembly,' replied Lord Montacute, 'I can easily believe it. In all things an early initiation must be of advantage. But I have not that wish.'

'I don't like to see a man take his seat in the House of Lords who has not been in the House of Commons. He seems to me always, in a manner, unfledged.'

'It will be a long time, I hope, my dear father, before I take my seat in the House of Lords,' said Lord Montacute, 'if, indeed, I ever do.'

'In the course of nature 'tis a certainty.'

'Suppose the Duke's plan for perpetuating an aristocracy do not succeed,' said Lord Montacute, 'and our house ceases to exist?'

His father shrugged his shoulders. 'It is not our business to suppose that. I hope it never will be the business of any one, at least seriously. This is a great country, and it has become great by its aristocracy.'

'You think, then, our sovereigns did nothing for our greatness, Queen Elizabeth, for example, of whose visit to Montacute you are so proud?'

'They performed their part.'

'And have ceased to exist. We may have performed our part, and may meet the same fate.'

'Why, you are talking liberalism!'

'Hardly that, my dear father, for I have not expressed an opinion.'

'I wish I knew what your opinions were, my dear boy, or even your wishes.'

'Well, then, to do my duty.'

'Exactly; you are a pillar of the State; support the State.'

'Ah! if any one would but tell me what the State is,' said Lord Montacute, sighing. 'It seems to me your pillars remain, but they support nothing; in that case, though the shafts may be perpendicular, and the capitals very ornate, they are no longer props, they are a ruin.'

'You would hand us over, then, to the ten-pounders?'

'They do not even pretend to be a State,' said Lord Montacute; 'they do not even profess to support anything; on the contrary, the essence of their philosophy is, that nothing is to be established, and everything is to be left to itself.'

'The common sense of this country and the fifty pound clause will carry us through,' said the duke.

'Through what?' inquired his son.

'This—this state of transition,' replied his father.

'A passage to what?'

'Ah! that is a question the wisest cannot answer.'

'But into which the weakest, among whom I class myself, have surely a right to inquire.'

'Unquestionably; and I know nothing that will tend more to assist you in your researches than acting with practical men.'

'And practising all their blunders,' said Lord Montacute. 'I can conceive an individual who has once been entrapped into their haphazard courses, continuing in the fatal confusion to which he has contributed his quota; but I am at least free, and I wish to continue so.'

'And do nothing?'

'But does it follow that a man is infirm of action because he declines fighting in the dark?'

'And how would you act, then? What are your plans? Have you any?'

'I have.'

'Well, that is satisfactory,' said the duke, with animation. 'Whatever they are, you know you may count upon my doing everything that is possible to forward your wishes. I know they cannot be unworthy ones, for I believe, my child, you are incapable of a thought that is not good or great.'

'I wish I knew what was good and great,' said Lord Montacute; 'I would struggle to accomplish it.'

'But you have formed some views; you have some plans. Speak to me of them, and without reserve; as to a friend, the most affectionate, the most devoted.'

'My father,' said Lord Montacute, and moving, he drew a chair to the table, and seated himself by the duke, 'you possess and have a right to my confidence. I ought not to have said that I doubted about what was good; for I know you.'

'Sons like you make good fathers.'

'It is not always so,' said Lord Montacute; 'you have been to me more than a father, and I bear to you and to my mother a profound and fervent affection; an affection,' he added, in a faltering tone, 'that is rarer, I believe, in this age than it was in old days. I feel it at this moment more deeply,' he continued, in a firmer tone, 'because I am about to propose that we should for a time separate.'

The duke turned pale, and leant forward in his chair, but did not speak.

'You have proposed to me to-day,' continued Lord Montacute, after a momentary pause, 'to enter public life. I do not shrink from its duties. On the contrary, from the position in which I am born, still more from the impulse of my nature, I am desirous to fulfil them. I have meditated on them, I may say, even for years. But I cannot find that it is part of my duty to maintain the order of things, for I will not call it system, which at present prevails in our country. It seems to me that it cannot last, as nothing can endure, or ought to endure, that is not founded upon principle; and its principle I have not discovered. In nothing, whether it be religion, or government, or manners, sacred or political or social life, do I find faith; and if there be no faith, how can there be duty? Is there such a thing as religious truth? Is there such a thing as political right? Is there such a thing as social propriety? Are these facts, or are they mere phrases? And if they be facts, where are they likely to be found in England? Is truth in our Church? Why, then, do you support dissent? Who has the right to govern? The Monarch? You have robbed him of his prerogative. The Aristocracy? You confess to me that we exist by sufferance. The People? They themselves tell you that they are nullities. Every session of that Parliament in which you wish to introduce me, the method by which power is distributed is called in question, altered, patched up, and again impugned. As for our morals, tell me, is charity the supreme virtue, or the greatest of errors? Our social system ought to depend on a clear conception of this point. Our morals differ in different counties, in different towns, in different streets, even in different Acts of Parliament. What is moral in London is immoral in Montacute; what is crime among the multitude is only vice among the few.'

'You are going into first principles,' said the duke, much surprised.

'Give me then second principles,' replied his son; 'give me any.'

B

'We must take a general view of things to form an opinion,' said his father, mildly. 'The general condition of England is superior to that of any other country; it cannot be denied that, on the whole, there is more political freedom, more social happiness, more sound religion, and more material prosperity among us, than in any nation in the world.'

'I might question all that,' said his son; 'but they are considerations that do not affect my views. If other States are worse than we are, and I hope they are not, our condition is not mended, but the contrary, for we then need the salutary stimulus of example.'

'There is no sort of doubt,' said the duke, 'that the state of England at this moment is the most flourishing that has ever existed, certainly in modern times. What with these railroads, even the condition of the poor, which I admit was lately far from satisfactory, is infinitely improved. Every man has work who needs it, and wages are even high.'

'The railroads may have improved, in a certain sense, the condition of the working classes almost as much as that of members of Parliament. They have been a good thing for both of them. And if you think that more labour is all that is wanted by the people of England, we may be easy for a time. I see nothing in this fresh development of material industry, but fresh causes of moral deterioration. You have announced to the millions that their welfare is to be tested by the amount of their wages. Money is to be the cupel of their worth, as it is of all other classes. You propose for their conduct the least ennobling of all impulses. If you have seen an aristocracy invariably become degraded under such influence; if all the vices of a middle class may be traced to such an absorbing motive; why are we to believe that the people should be more pure, or that they should escape the catastrophe of the policy that confounds the happiness with the wealth of nations?'

The duke shook his head, and then said, 'You should not forget we live in an artificial state.'

'So I often hear, sir,' replied his son; 'but where is the art? It seems to me the very quality wanting to our present condition. Art is order, method, harmonious results obtained by fine and powerful principles. I see no art in our condition. The people of this country have ceased to be a nation. They are a crowd, and only kept in some rude provisional discipline by the remains of that old system which they are daily destroying.'

'But what would you do, my dear boy?' said his grace, looking up very distressed. 'Can you remedy the state of things in which we find ourselves?'

'I am not a teacher,' said Lord Montacute, mournfully; 'I only ask you, I supplicate you, my dear father, to save me from contributing to this quick corruption that surrounds us.'

'You shall be master of your own actions. I offer you counsel, I give no commands; and, as for the rest, Providence will guard us.'

'If an angel would but visit our house as he visited the house of Lot!' said Montacute, in a tone almost of anguish.

'Angels have performed their part,' said the duke. 'We have received instruction from one higher than angels. It is enough for all of us.'

'It is not enough for me,' said Lord Montacute, with a glowing cheek, and rising abruptly. 'It was not enough for the Apostles; for though they listened to the sermon on the mount, and partook of the first communion, it was still necessary that He should appear to them again, and promise them a Comforter. I require one,' he added, after a momentary pause, but in an agitated voice. 'I must seek one. Yes! my dear father, it is of this that I would speak to you; it is this which for a long time has oppressed my spirit, and filled me often with intolerable gloom We must separate. I must leave you, I must leave that dear mother, those beloved parents, in whom are concentred all my earthly affections; but I obey an impulse that I believe comes from above. Dearest and best of men, you will not thwart me; you will forgive, you will aid me!' And he advanced and threw himself into the arms of his father.

The duke pressed Lord Montacute to his heart, and endeavoured, though himself agitated and much distressed, to penetrate the mystery of this ebullition. 'He says we must separate,' thought the duke to himself. 'Ah! he has lived too much at home, too much alone; he has read and pondered too much; he has moped. Eskdale was right two years ago. I wish I had sent him to Paris, but his mother was so alarmed; and, indeed, 'tis a precious life! The House of Commons would have been just the thing for him. He would have worked on committees and grown practical. But something must be done for him, dear child! He says we must separate; he wants to travel. And perhaps he ought to travel. But a life on which so much depends! And what will Katherine say? It will kill her. I could screw myself up to it. I would send him well attended. Brace should go with him; he understands the Continent; he was in the Peninsular war; and he should have a skilful physician. I see how it is; I must act with decision, and break it to his mother.'

These ideas passed through the duke's mind during the few seconds that he embraced his son, and endeavoured at the same time to convey consolation by the expression of his affection, and his anxiety at all times to contribute to his child's happiness.

'My dear son,' said the duke, when Lord Montacute had resumed his seat, 'I see how it is; you wish to travel?'

Lord Montacute bent his head, as if in assent.

'It will be a terrible blow to your mother; I say nothing of myself. You know what I feel for you. But neither your mother nor myself have a right to place our feelings in competition with any arrangement for your welfare. It would be in the highest degree selfish and unreasonable; and perhaps it will be well for you to travel awhile; and, as for Parliament, I am to see Hungerford this morning at Bellamont. I will try and arrange with him to postpone his resignation until the autumn, or, if possible, for some little time longer. You will then have accomplished your purpose. It will do you a great deal of good. You will have seen the world, and you can take your seat next year.'

The duke paused. Lord Montacute looked perplexed and distressed; he seemed about to reply, and then, leaning on the table, with his face concealed from his father, he maintained his silence. The duke rose, looked at his watch, said he must be at Bellamont by two o'clock, hoped that Brace would dine at the Castle to-day, thought it not at all impossible Brace might, would send on to Montacute for him, perhaps might meet him at Bellamont. Brace understood the Continent, spoke several languages, Spanish among them, though it was not probable his son would have any need of that, the present state of Spain not being very inviting to the traveller. 'As for France,' continued the duke, 'France is Paris, and I suppose that will be your first step; it generally is. We must see if your cousin, Henry Howard, is there. If so, he will put you in the way of everything. With the embassy and Brace, you would manage very well at Paris. Then, I suppose, you would like to go to Italy; that, I apprehend, is your great point. Your mother will not like your going to Rome. Still, at the same time, a man, they say, should see Rome before he dies. I never did. I have never crossed the sea except to go to Ireland. Your grandfather would never let me travel; I wanted to, but he never would. Not, however, for the same reasons which have kept you at home. Suppose you even winter at Rome, which I believe is the right thing, why, you might very well be back by the spring. However, we must manage your mother a little about remaining over the winter, and, on second thoughts, we will get Bernard to go with you, as well as Brace and a physician, and then she will be much more easy. I think, with Brace, Bernard, and a medical man whom we can really trust, Harry Howard at Paris, and the best letters for every other place, which we will consult Lord Eskdale about, I think the danger will not be extreme.'

'I have no wish to see Paris,' said Lord Montacute
evidently embarrassed, and making a great effort to relieve
his mind of some burthen. 'I have no wish to see Paris.'

'I am very glad to hear that,' said his father, eagerly.

'Nor do I wish either to go to Rome,' continued his son.

'Well, well, you have taken a load off my mind, my
dear boy. I would not confess it, because I wish to save
you pain; but really, I believe the idea of your going to
Rome would have been a serious shock to your mother. It
is not so much the distance, though that is great, nor the
climate, which has its dangers, but, you understand, with
her peculiar views, her very strict——' The duke did not
care to finish his sentence.

'Nor, my dear father,' continued Lord Montacute,
'though I did not like to interrupt you when you were
speaking with so much solicitude and consideration for me,
is it exactly travel, in the common acceptation of the term,
that I feel the need of. I wish, indeed, to leave England;
I wish to make an expedition; a progress to a particular
point; without wandering, without any intervening residence. In a word, it is the Holy Land that occupies my
thought, and I propose to make a pilgrimage to the sepulchre of my Saviour.'

The duke started, and sank again into his chair. 'The
Holy Land! The Holy Sepulchre!' he exclaimed, and repeated to himself, staring at his son.

'Yes, sir, the Holy Sepulchre,' repeated Lord Montacute,
and now speaking with his accustomed repose. 'When I
remember that the Creator, since light sprang out of darkness, has deigned to reveal Himself to His creature only in
one land; that in that land He assumed a manly form, and
met a human death; I feel persuaded that the country
sanctified by such intercourse and such events must be
endowed with marvellous and peculiar qualities, which man
may not in all ages be competent to penetrate, but which,
nevertheless, at all times exercise an irresistible influence
upon his destiny. It is these qualities that many times

drew Europe to Asia during the middle centuries. Our
castle has before this sent forth a De Montacute to Palestine. For three days and three nights he knelt at the
tomb of his Redeemer. Six centuries and more have
elapsed since that great enterprise. It is time to restore
and renovate our communications with the Most High. I,
too, would kneel at that tomb; I, too, surrounded by the
holy hills and sacred groves of Jerusalem, would relieve my
spirit from the bale that bows it down; would lift up my
voice to heaven, and ask, What is DUTY, and what is FAITH?
What ought I to DO, and what ought I to BELIEVE?'

The Duke of Bellamont rose from his seat, and walked
up and down the room for some minutes, in silence and in
deep thought. At length, stopping and leaning against
the cabinet, he said, 'What has occurred to-day between
us, my beloved child, is, you may easily believe, as strange
to me as it is agitating. I will think of all you have said;
I will try to comprehend all you mean and wish. I will
endeavour to do that which is best and wisest; placing
above all things your happiness, and not our own. At this
moment I am not competent to the task: I need quiet, and
to be alone. Your mother, I know, wishes to walk with
you this morning. She may be speaking to you of many
things. Be silent upon this subject, until I have communicated with her. At present I will ride over to Bellamont. I must go; and, besides, it will do me good. I
never can think very well except in the saddle. If Brace
comes, make him dine here. God bless you.'

The duke left the room; his son remained in meditation.
The first step was taken. He had poured into the interview of an hour the results of three years of solitary
thought. A sound roused him; it was his mother. She
had only learnt casually that the duke was gone; she was
surprised he had not come into her room before he went;
it seemed the first time since their marriage that the duke
had gone out without first coming to speak to her. So she
went to seek her son, to congratulate him on being a

member of Parliament, on representing the county of which they were so fond, and of breaking to him a proposition which she doubted not he would find not less interesting and charming. Happy mother, with her only son, on whom she doted and of whom she was so justly proud, about to enter public life in which he was sure to distinguish himself, and to marry a woman who was sure to make him happy! With a bounding heart the duchess opened the library door, where she had been informed she should find Lord Montacute. She had her bonnet on, ready for the walk of confidence, and, her face flushed with delight, she looked even beautiful. 'Ah!' she exclaimed, 'I have been looking for you, TANCRED!'

CHAPTER II.

THE duke returned rather late from Bellamont, and went immediately to his dressing-room. A few minutes before dinner the duchess knocked at his door and entered. She seemed disconcerted, and reminded him, though with great gentleness, that he had gone out to-day without first bidding her adieu; she really believed it was the only time he had done so since their marriage. The duke, who, when she entered, anticipated something about their son, was relieved by her remark, embraced her, and would have affected a gaiety which he did not really feel.

'I am glad to hear that Brace dines here to-day, Kate, for I particularly wanted to see him.'

The duchess did not reply, and seemed absent; the duke, to say something, tying his cravat, kept harping upon Brace.

'Never mind Brace, George,' said the duchess; 'tell me what is this about Tancred? Why is his coming into Parliament put off?'

The duke was perplexed; he wished to know how far at this moment his wife was informed upon the matter; the feminine frankness of the duchess put him out of suspense.

'I have been walking with Tancred,' she continued, 'and intimated, but with great caution, all our plans and hopes. I asked him what he thought of his cousin; he agrees with us she is by far the most charming girl he knows, and one of the most agreeable. I impressed upon him how good she was. I wished to precipitate nothing. I never dreamed of their marrying until late in the autumn. I wished him to become acquainted with his new life, which would not prevent him seeing a great deal of Katherine in London, and then to visit them in Ireland, as you visited us, George; and then, when I was settling everything in the most delightful manner, what he was to do when he was kept up very late at the House, which is the only part I don't like, and begging him to be very strict in making his servant always have coffee ready for him, very hot, and a cold fowl too, or something of the sort, he tells me, to my infinite astonishment, that the vacancy will not immediately occur, that he is not sorry for it, as he thinks it may be as well that he should go abroad. What can all this mean? Pray tell me; for Tancred has told me nothing, and, when I pressed him, waived the subject, and said we would all of us consult together.'

'And so we will, Kate,' said the duke, 'but hardly at this moment, for dinner must be almost served. To be brief,' he added, speaking in a light tone, 'there are reasons which perhaps may make it expedient that Hungerford should not resign at the present moment; and as Tancred has a fancy to travel a little, it may be as well that we should take it into consideration whether he might not profitably occupy the interval in this manner.'

'Profitably!' said the duchess. 'I never can understand how going to Paris and Rome, which young men always mean when they talk of travelling, can be profitable to him; it is the very thing which, all my life, I have been endeavouring to prevent. His body and his soul will be both imperilled; Paris will destroy his constitution, and Rome, perhaps, change his faith.'

' I have more confidence in his physical power and his
religious principle than you, Kate,' said the duke, smiling.
' But make yourself easy on these heads; Tancred told me
this morning that he had no wish to visit either Rome or
Paris.'

' Well!' exclaimed the duchess, somewhat relieved, 'if
he wants to make a little tour in Holland, I think I could
bear it; it is a Protestant country, and there are no vermin.
And then those dear Disbrowes, I am sure, would take care
of him at the Hague.'

' We will talk of all this to-night, my love,' said the duke ;
and offering his arm to his wife, who was more composed, if
not more cheerful, they descended to their guests.

Colonel Brace was there, to the duke's great satisfaction.
The colonel had served as a cornet in a dragoon regiment in
the last campaign of the Peninsular war, and had marched
into Paris. Such an event makes an indelible impression
on the memory of a handsome lad of seventeen, and the
colonel had not yet finished recounting his strange and
fortunate adventures.

He was tall, robust, a little portly, but, well buckled, still
presented a grand military figure. He was what you call a
fine man; florid, with still a good head of hair though
touched with grey, splendid moustaches, large fat hands,
and a courtly demeanour not unmixed with a slight swagger.
The colonel was a Montacute man, and had inherited a
large house in the town and a small estate in the neighbourhood. Having sold out, he had retired to his native place,
where he had become a considerable personage. The duke
had put him in the commission, and he was the active magistrate of the district; he had reorganised the Bellamont
regiment of yeomanry cavalry, which had fallen into sad
decay during the late duke's time, but which now, with
Brace for its lieutenant-colonel, was second to none in the
kingdom. Colonel Brace was one of the best shots in the
county; certainly the boldest rider among the heavy
weights; and bore the palm from all with the rod, and

that, too, in a county famous for its feats in lake and river. The colonel was a man of great energy, of good temper, of ready resource, frank, a little coarse, but hearty and honest. He adored the Duke and Duchess of Bellamont. He was sincere; he was not a parasite; he really believed that they were the best people in the world, and I am not sure that he had not some foundation for his faith. On the whole, he might be esteemed the duke's right-hand man. His grace generally consulted the colonel on county affairs; the command of the yeomanry alone gave him a considerable position; he was the chief also of the militia staff; could give his opinion whether a person was to be made a magistrate or not; and had even been called into council when there was a question of appointing a deputy-lieutenant. The colonel, who was a leading member of the corporation of Montacute, had taken care to be chosen mayor this year; he had been also chairman of the Committee of Management during the celebration of Tancred's majority; had had the entire ordering of the fireworks, and was generally supposed to have given the design, or at least the leading idea, for the transparency.

We should notice also Mr. Bernard, a clergyman, and recently the private tutor of Lord Montacute, a good scholar; in ecclesiastical opinions, what is called high and dry. He was about five-and-thirty; well-looking, bashful. The duke intended to prefer him to a living when one was vacant; in the meantime he remained in the family, and at present discharged the duties of chaplain and librarian at Montacute, and occasionally assisted the duke as private secretary. Of his life, one-third had been passed at a rural home, and the rest might be nearly divided between school and college.

These gentlemen, the distinguished and numerous family of the Montacute Mountjoys, young Hungerford, whom the duke had good-naturedly brought over from Bellamont for the sake of the young ladies, the duke and duchess, and their son, formed the party, which presented rather a

contrast, not only in its numbers, to the series of recent
banquets. They dined in the Montacute chamber. The
party, without intending it, was rather dull and silent.
The duchess was brooding over the disappointment of the
morning ; the duke trembled for the disclosures of the morrow. The Misses Mountjoy sang better than they talked;
their mother, who was more lively, was seated by the duke,
and confined her powers of pleasing to him. The Honourable
and Reverend Montacute himself was an epicure, and disliked conversation during dinner. Lord Montacute spoke
to Mr. Hungerford across the table, but Mr. Hungerford
was whispering despairing nothings in the ear of Arabella
Mountjoy, and replied to his question without originating
any in return, which of course terminates talk.

When the second course had arrived, the duke, who
wanted a little more noise and distraction, fired off in
despair a shot at Colonel Brace, who was on the left hand
of the duchess, and set him on his yeomanry charger.
From this moment affairs improved. The colonel made
continual charges, and carried all before him. Nothing
could be more noisy in a genteel way. His voice sounded
like the bray of a trumpet amid the din of arms ; it seemed
that the moment he began, everybody and everything became animated and inspired by his example. All talked ;
the duke set them the fashion of taking wine with each
other ; Lord Montacute managed to entrap Arminta Mountjoy into a narrative in detail of her morning's ride and
adventures ; and, affecting scepticism as to some of the
incidents, and wonder at some of the feats, produced a
considerable addition to the general hubbub, which he in-
stinctively felt that his father wished to encourage.

'I don't know whether it was the Great Western or the
South Eastern,' continued Colonel Brace ; 'but I know his
leg is broken.'

'God bless me !' said the duke ; 'and only think of my
not hearing of it at Bellamont to-day !'

'I don't suppose they know anything about it,' replied

the colonel. 'The way I know it is this: I was with Roby to-day, when the post came in, and he said to me, " Here is a letter from Lady Malpas ; I hope nothing is the matter with Sir Russell or any of the children." And then it all came out. The train was blown up behind; Sir Russell was in a centre carriage, and was pitched right into a field. They took him into an inn, put him to bed, and sent for some of the top-sawyers from London, Sir Benjamin Brodie, and that sort of thing; and the moment Sir Russell came to himself, he said, " I must have Roby, send for Roby, Roby knows my constitution." And they sent for Roby. And I think he was right. The quantity of young officers I have seen sent rightabout in the Peninsula, because they were attended by a parcel of men who knew nothing of their constitution ! Why, I might have lost my own leg once, if I had not been sharp. I got a scratch in a little affair at Almeidas, charging the enemy a little too briskly ; but we really ought not to speak of these things before the ladies ——'

'My dear colonel,' said Lord Montacute, 'on the contrary, there is nothing more interesting to them. Miss Mountjoy was only saying yesterday, that there was nothing she found so difficult to understand as the account of a battle, and how much she wished to comprehend it.'

'That is because, in general, they are not written by soldiers,' said the colonel; 'but Napier's battles are very clear. I could fight every one of them on this table. That's a great book, that history of Napier; it has faults, but they are rather omissions than mistakes. Now that affair of Almeidas of which I was just speaking, and which nearly cost me my leg, it is very odd, but he has omitted mentioning it altogether.'

'But you saved your leg, colonel,' said the duke.

'Yes, I had the honour of marching into Paris, and that is an event not very easy to be forgotten, let me tell your grace. I saved my leg because I knew my constitution. For the very same reason by which I hope Sir Russell

Malpas will save his leg. Because he will be attended by a person who knows his constitution. He never did a wiser thing than sending for Roby. For my part, if I were in garrison at Gibraltar to-morrow, and laid up, I would do the same ; I would send for Roby. In all these things, depend upon it, knowing the constitution is half the battle.'

All this time, while Colonel Brace was indulging in his garrulous comments, the Duke of Bellamont was drawing his moral. He had a great opinion of Mr. Roby, who was the medical attendant of the castle, and an able man. Mr. Roby was perfectly acquainted with the constitution of his son ; Mr. Roby must go to the Holy Sepulchre. Cost what it might, Mr. Roby must be sent to Jerusalem. The duke was calculating all this time the income that Mr. Roby made. He would not put it down at more than five hundred pounds per annum, and a third of that was certainly afforded by the castle. The duke determined to offer Roby a thousand and his expenses to attend Lord Montacute. He would not be more than a year absent, and his practice could hardly seriously suffer while away, backed as he would be, when he returned, by the castle. And if it did, the duke must guarantee Roby against loss ; it was a necessity, absolute and of the first class, that Tancred should be attended by a medical man who knew his constitution. The duke agreed with Colonel Brace that it was half the battle

---

CHAPTER III.

' MISERABLE mother that I am !' exclaimed the duchess, and she clasped her hands in anguish.

'My dearest Katherine !' said the duke, ' calm yourself.'

' You ought to have prevented this, George ; you ought never to have let things come to this pass.'

' But, my dearest Katherine, the blow was as unlooked-for by me as by yourself. I had not, how could I have, a remote suspicion of what was passing through his mind ?'

' What, then, is the use of your boasted confidence with your child, which you tell me you have always cultivated? Had I been his father, I would have discovered his secret thoughts.'

'Very possibly, my dear Katherine ; but you are at least his mother, tenderly loving him, and tenderly loved by him. The intercourse between you has ever been of an extreme intimacy, and especially on the subjects connected with this fancy of his, and yet, you see, even you are completely taken by surprise.'

' I once had a suspicion he was inclined to the Puseyite heresy, and I spoke to Mr. Bernard on the subject, and afterwards to him, but I was convinced that I was in error. I am sure,' added the duchess, in a mournful tone, ' I have lost no opportunity of instilling into him the principles of religious truth. It was only last year, on his birthday, that I sent him a complete set of the publications of the Parker Society, my own copy of Jewel, full of notes, and my grandfather, the primate's, manuscript commentary on Chillingworth ; a copy made purposely by myself.'

' I well know,' said the duke, ' that you have done everything for his spiritual welfare which ability and affection combined could suggest.'

' And it ends in this ! ' exclaimed the duchess. ' The Holy Land ! Why, if he even reach it, the climate is certain death. The curse of the Almighty, for more than eighteen centuries, has been on that land. Every year it has become more sterile, more savage, more unwholesome, and more unearthly. It is the abomination of desolation. And now my son is to go there ! Oh! he is lost to us for ever !'

' But, my dear Katherine, let us consult a little.'

' Consult! Why should I consult ? You have settled everything, you have agreed to everything. You do not come here to consult me ; I understand all that ; you come here to break a foregone conclusion to a weak and miserable woman.'

' Do not say such things, Katherine!'

'What should I say? What can I say?'

'Anything but that. I hope that nothing will be ever done in this family without your full sanction.'

'Rest assured, then, that I will never sanction the departure of Tancred on this crusade.'

'Then he will never go, at least, with my consent,' said the duke; 'but Katherine, assist me, my dear wife. All shall be, shall ever be, as you wish; but I shrink from being placed, from our being placed, in collision with our child. The mere exercise of parental authority is a last resource; I would appeal first, rather to his reason, to his heart; your arguments, his affection for us, may yet influence him.'

'You tell me you have argued with him,' said the duchess, in a melancholy tone.

'Yes, but you know so much more on these subjects than I do, indeed, upon all subjects; you are so clever, that I do not despair, my dear Katherine, of your producing an impression on him.'

'I would tell him at once,' said the duchess, firmly, 'that the proposition cannot be listened to.'

The duke looked very distressed. After a momentary pause, he said, 'If, indeed, you think that the best; but let us consult before we take that step, because it would seem to terminate all discussion, and discussion may yet do good. Besides, I cannot conceal from myself that Tancred in this affair is acting under the influence of very powerful motives; his feelings are highly strung; you have no idea, you can have no idea from what we have seen of him hitherto, how excited he is. I had no idea of his being capable of such excitement. I always thought him so very calm, and of such a quiet turn. And so, in short, my dear Katherine, were we to be abrupt at this moment, peremptory, you understand, I, I should not be surprised, were Tancred to go without our permission.'

'Impossible!' exclaimed the duchess, starting in her chair, but with as much consternation as confidence in her

countenance. 'Throughout his life he has never dis-
obeyed us.'

'And that is an additional reason,' said the duke, quietly,
but in his sweetest tone, 'why we should not treat as a
light ebullition this first instance of his preferring his own
will to that of his father and mother.'

'He has been so much away from us these last three
years,' said the duchess in a tone of great depression, 'and
they are such important years in the formation of character!
But Mr. Bernard, he ought to have been aware of all this;
he ought to have known what was passing through his
pupil's mind; he ought to have warned us. Let us speak
to him; let us speak to him at once. Ring, my dear George,
and request the attendance of Mr. Bernard.'

That gentleman, who was in the library, kept them waiting but a few minutes. As he entered the room, he perceived, by the countenances of his noble patrons, that
something remarkable, and probably not agreeable, had
occurred. The duke opened the case to Mr. Bernard with
calmness; he gave an outline of the great catastrophe; the
duchess filled up the parts, and invested the whole with a
rich and even terrible colouring.

Nothing could exceed the astonishment of the late private
tutor of Lord Montacute. He was fairly overcome; the
communication itself was startling, the accessories overwhelmed him. The unspoken reproaches that beamed from
the duke's mild eye; the withering glance of maternal
desolation that met him from the duchess; the rapidity of
her anxious and agitated questions; all were too much for
the simple, though correct, mind of one unused to those
passionate developments which are commonly called scenes.
All that Mr. Bernard for some time could do was to sit
with his eyes staring and mouth open, and repeat, with a
bewildered air, 'The Holy Land, the Holy Sepulchre!'
No, most certainly not; most assuredly; never in any way,
by any word or deed, had Lord Montacute ever given him
reason to suppose or imagine that his lordship intended to

make a pilgrimage to the Holy Sepulchre, or that he was influenced by any of those views and opinions which he had so strangely and so uncompromisingly expressed to his father.

'But, Mr. Bernard, you have been his companion, his instructor, for many years,' continued the duchess, 'for the last three years especially, years so important in the formation of character. You have seen much more of Montacute than we have. Surely you must have had some idea of what was passing in his mind; you could not help knowing it; you ought to have known it; you ought to have warned, to have prepared us.'

'Madam,' at length said Mr. Bernard, more collected, and feeling the necessity and excitement of self-vindication, 'Madam, your noble son, under my poor tuition, has taken the highest honours of his university; his moral behaviour during that period has been immaculate; and as for his religious sentiments, even this strange scheme proves that they are, at any rate, of no light and equivocal character.'

'To lose such a son!' exclaimed the duchess, in a tone of anguish, and with streaming eyes.

The duke took her hand, and would have soothed her; and then, turning to Mr. Bernard, he said, in a lowered tone, 'We are very sensible how much we owe you; the duchess equally with myself. All we regret is, that some of us had not obtained a more intimate acquaintance with the character of my son than it appears we have acquired.'

'My lord duke,' said Mr. Bernard, 'had yourself or her grace ever spoken to me on this subject, I would have taken the liberty of expressing what I say now. I have ever found Lord Montacute inscrutable. He has formed himself in solitude, and has ever repelled any advance to intimacy, either from those who were his inferiors or his equals in station. He has never had a companion. As for myself, during the ten years that I have had the honour of being connected with him, I cannot recall a word or a deed on his part which towards me has not been courteous and considerate; but as a child he was shy and silent, and as a man, for I have looked upon him as a man in mind for these four or even five years, he has employed me as his machine to obtain knowledge. It is not very flattering to one's-self to make these confessions, but at Oxford he had the opportunity of communicating with some of the most eminent men of our time, and I have always learnt from them the same result. Lord Montacute never disburthened. His passion for study has been ardent; his power of application is very great; his attention unwearied as long as there is anything to acquire; but he never seeks your opinions, and never offers his own. The interview of yesterday with your grace is the only exception with which I am acquainted, and at length throws some light on the mysteries of his mind.'

The duke looked sad; his wife seemed plunged in profound thought; there was a silence of many moments. At length the duchess looked up, and said, in a calmer tone, and with an air of great seriousness, ' It seems that we have mistaken the character of our son. Thank you very much for coming to us so quickly in our trouble, Mr. Bernard. It was very kind, as you always are.' Mr. Bernard took the hint, rose, bowed, and retired.

The moment that he had quitted the room, the eyes of the Duke and Duchess of Bellamont met. Who was to speak first ? The duke had nothing to say, and therefore he had the advantage; the duchess wished her husband to break the silence, but, having something to say herself, she could not refrain from interrupting it. So she said, with a tearful eye, ' Well, George, what do you think we ought to do ?'

The duke had a great mind to propose his plan of sending Tancred to Jerusalem, with Colonel Brace, Mr. Bernard, and Mr. Roby, to take care of him, but he hardly thought the occasion was ripe enough for that; and so he suggested that the duchess should speak to Tancred herself.

' No,' said her grace, shaking her head, ' I think it better for me to be silent; at least at present. It is necessary, however, that the most energetic means should be adopted to save him, nor is there a moment to be lost. We must shrink from nothing for such an object. I have a plan. We will put the whole matter in the hands of our friend, the bishop. We will get him to speak to Tancred. I entertain not a doubt that the bishop will put his mind all right; clear all his doubts; remove all his scruples. The bishop is the only person, because, you see, it is a case political as well as theological, and the bishop is a great statesman as well as the first theologian of the age. Depend upon it, my dear George, that this is the wisest course, and, with the blessing of Providence, will effect our purpose. It is, perhaps, asking a good deal of the bishop, considering his important and multifarious duties, to undertake this office, but we must not be delicate when everything is at stake; and, considering he christened and confirmed Tancred, and our long friendship, it is quite out of the question that he can refuse. However, there is no time to be lost. We must get to town as soon as possible; to-morrow, if we can. I shall advance affairs by writing to the bishop on the subject, and giving him an outline of the case, so that he may be prepared to see Tancred at once on our arrival. What think you, George, of my plan?'

'I think it quite admirable,' replied his grace, only too happy that there was at least the prospect of a lull of a few days in this great embarrassment.

CHAPTER IV.

ABOUT the time of the marriage of the Duchess of Bellamont, her noble family, and a few of their friends, some of whom also believed in the millennium, were persuaded that the conversion of the Roman Catholic population of Ireland to the true faith, which was their own, was at hand. They had subscribed very liberally for the purpose, and formed an amazing number of sub-committees. As long as their funds lasted, their missionaries found proselytes. It was the last desperate effort of a Church that had from the first betrayed its trust. Twenty years ago, statistics not being so much in vogue, and the people of England being in the full efflorescence of that public ignorance which permitted them to believe themselves the most enlightened nation in the world, the Irish ' difficulty ' was not quite so well understood as at the present day. It was then an established doctrine, that all that was necessary for Ireland was more Protestantism, and it was supposed to be not more difficult to supply the Irish with Protestantism than it had proved, in the instance of a recent famine, 1822, to furnish them with potatoes. What was principally wanted in both cases were, subscriptions.

When the English public, therefore, were assured by their co-religionists on the other side of St. George's Channel, that at last the good work was doing ; that the flame spread, even rapidly ; that not only parishes but provinces were all agog, and that both town and country were quite in a heat of proselytism, they began to believe that at last the scarlet lady was about to be dethroned ; they loosened their purse-strings ; fathers of families contributed their zealous five pounds, followed by every other member of the household, to the babe in arms, who subscribed its fanatical five shillings. The affair looked well. The journals teemed with lists of proselytes and cases of conversion ; and even orderly, orthodox people, who were firm in their own faith, but wished others to be permitted to pursue their errors in peace, began to congratulate each other on the prospect of our at last becoming a united Protestant people.

In the blaze and thick of the affair, Irish Protestants jubilant, Irish Papists denouncing the whole movement as fraud and trumpery, John Bull perplexed, but excited, and still subscribing, a young bishop rose in his place in the House of Lords, and, with a vehemence there unusual, declared that he saw ' the finger of God in this second Reformation,' and, pursuing the prophetic vein and manner, denounced ' woe to those who should presume to lift up their hands and voices in vain and impotent attempts to stem the flood of light that was bursting over Ireland.'

In him, who thus plainly discerned 'the finger of God' in transactions in which her family and feelings were so deeply interested, the young and enthusiastic Duchess of Bellamont instantly recognised the 'man of God;' and, from that moment the right reverend prelate became, in all spiritual affairs, her infallible instructor, although the impending second Reformation did chance to take the untoward form of the emancipation of the Roman Catholics, followed in due season by the destruction of Protestant bishoprics, the sequestration of Protestant tithes, and the endowment of Maynooth.

In speculating on the fate of public institutions and the course of public affairs, it is important that we should not permit our attention to be engrossed by the principles on which they are founded and the circumstances which they present, but that we should also remember how much depends upon the character of the individuals who are in the position to superintend or to direct them.

The Church of England, mainly from its deficiency of oriental knowledge, and from a misconception of the priestly character which has been the consequence of that want, has fallen of late years into great straits; nor has there ever been a season when it has more needed for its guides men possessing the higher qualities both of intellect and disposition. About five-and-twenty years ago, it began to be discerned that the time had gone by, at least in England, for bishoprics to serve as appanages for the younger sons of great families. The Arch-Mediocrity who then governed this country, and the mean tenor of whose prolonged administration we have delineated in another work, was impressed with the necessity of reconstructing the episcopal bench on principles of personal distinction and ability. But his notion of clerical capacity did not soar higher than a private tutor who had suckled a young noble into university honours; and his test of priestly celebrity was the decent editorship of a Greek play. He sought for the successors of the apostles, for the stewards of the mysteries of Sinai and of Calvary, among third-rate hunters after syllables. These men, notwithstanding their elevation, with one exception, subsided into their native insignificance; and during our agitated age, when the principles of all institutions, sacred and secular, have been called in question; when, alike in the senate and the market-place, both the doctrine and the discipline of the Church have been impugned, its power assailed, its authority denied, the amount of its revenues investigated, their disposition criticised, and both attacked; not a voice has been raised by these mitred nullities, either to warn or to vindicate; not a phrase has escaped their lips or their pens, that ever influenced public opinion, touched the heart of nations, or guided the conscience of a perplexed people. If they were ever heard of, it was that they had been pelted in a riot.

The exception which we have mentioned to their sorry careers was that of the too adventurous prophet of the second Reformation; the *ductor dubitantium* appealed to by the Duchess of Bellamont, to convince her son that the principles of religious truth, as well as of political justice, required no further investigation; at least by young marquesses.

The ready audacity with which this right reverend prelate had stood sponsor for the second Reformation is a key to his character. He combined a great talent for action with very limited powers of thought. Bustling, energetic, versatile, gifted with an indomitable perseverance, and stimulated by an ambition that knew no repose, with a capacity for mastering details and an inordinate passion for affairs, he could permit nothing to be done without his interference, and consequently was perpetually involved in transactions which were either failures or blunders. He was one of those leaders who are not guides. Having little

real knowledge, and not endowed with those high qualities
of intellect which permit their possessor to generalise the
details afforded by study and experience, and so deduce
rules of conduct, his lordship, when he received those frequent appeals which were the necessary consequence of his
officious life, became obscure, confused, contradictory, inconsistent, illogical. The oracle was always dark. Placed
in a high post in as age of political analysis, the bustling
intermeddler was unable to supply society with a single
solution. Enunciating second-hand, with characteristic
precipitation, some big principle in vogue, as if he were a
discoverer, he invariably shrank from its subsequent application, the moment that he found it might be unpopular and
inconvenient. All his quandaries terminated in the same
catastrophe; a compromise. Abstract principles with him
ever ended in concrete expediency. The aggregate of circumstances outweighed the isolated cause. The primor-
dial tenet, which had been advocated with uncompromising
arrogance, gently subsided into some second-rate measure
recommended with all the artifice of an impenetrable ambiguity.

Beginning with the second Reformation, which was a
little rash but dashing, the bishop, always ready, had in the
course of his episcopal career placed himself at the head of
every movement in the Church which others had originated,
and had as regularly withdrawn at the right moment, when
the heat was over, or had become, on the contrary, excessive.
Furiously evangelical, soberly high and dry, and fervently
Puseyite, each phasis of his faith concludes with what the
Spaniards term a 'transaction.' The saints are to have
their new churches, but they are also to have their rubrics
and their canons; the universities may supply successors
to the apostles, but they are also presented with a church
commission; even the Puseyites may have candles on their
altars, but they must not be lighted.

It will be seen, therefore, that his lordship was one of
those characters not ill-adapted to an eminent station in an

age like the present, and in a country like our own ; an
age of movement, but of confused ideas ; a country of progress, but too rich to risk much change. Under these
circumstances, the spirit of a period and a people seeks a
safety-valve in bustle. They do something, lest it be said
that they do nothing. At such a time, ministers recommend
their measures as experiments, and parliaments are ever
ready to rescind their votes. Find a man who, totally
destitute of genius, possesses nevertheless considerable
talents ; who has official aptitude, a volubility of routine
rhetoric, great perseverance, a love of affairs ; who, embarrassed neither by the principles of the philosopher nor
by the prejudices of the bigot, can assume, with a cautious
facility, the prevalent tone, and disembarrass himself of it,
with a dexterous ambiguity, the moment it ceases to be pre-
dominant ; recommending himself to the innovator by his
approbation of change 'in the abstract,' and to the conservative by his prudential and practical respect for that
which is established ; such a man, though he be one of an
essentially small mind, though his intellectual qualities
be less than moderate, with feeble powers of thought, no
imagination, contracted sympathies, and a most loose
public morality ; such a man is the individual whom kings
and parliaments would select to govern the State or rule
the Church. Change, 'in the abstract,' is what is wanted
by a people who are at the same time inquiring and
wealthy. Instead of statesmen they desire shufflers ; and
compromise in conduct and ambiguity in speech are, though
nobody will confess it, the public qualities now most in
vogue.

Not exactly, however, those calculated to meet the case
of Tancred. The interview was long, for Tancred listened
with apparent respect and deference to the individual
under whose auspices he had entered the Church of Christ ;
but the replies to his inquiries, though more adroit than
the duke's, were in reality not more satisfactory, and could
not, in any way, meet the inexorable logic of Lord Mont-

acute. The bishop was as little able as the duke to indicate the principle on which the present order of things in England was founded; neither faith nor its consequence, duty, was at all illustrated or invigorated by his handling. He utterly failed in reconciling a belief in ecclesiastical truth with the support of religious dissent. When he tried to define in whom the power of government should repose, he was lost in a maze of phrases, and afforded his pupil not a single fact.

'It cannot be denied,' at length said Tancred, with great calmness, 'that society was once regulated by God, and that now it is regulated by man. For my part, I prefer divine to self-government, and I wish to know how it is to be attained.'

'The Church represents God upon earth,' said the bishop.

'But the Church no longer governs man,' replied Tancred.

'There is a great spirit rising in the Church,' observed the bishop, with thoughtful solemnity; 'a great and excellent spirit. The church of 1845 is not the Church of 1745. We must remember that; we know not what may happen. We shall soon see a bishop at Manchester.'

'But I want to see an angel at Manchester.'

'An angel!'

'Why not? Why should there not be heavenly messengers, when heavenly messages are most wanted?'

'We have received a heavenly message by one greater than the angels,' said the bishop. 'Their visits to man ceased with the mightier advent.'

'Then why did angels appear to Mary and her companions at the holy tomb?' inquired Tancred.

The interview from which so much was anticipated was not satisfactory. The eminent prelate did not realise Tancred's ideal of a bishop, while his lordship did not hesitate to declare that Lord Montacute was a visionary.

CHAPTER V.

WHEN the duchess found that the interview with the bishop
had been fruitless of the anticipated results, she was
staggered, disheartened ; but she was a woman of too high
a spirit to succumb under a first defeat. She was of opinion
that his lordship had misunderstood the case, or had mis-
managed it ; her confidence in him, too, was not so illimitable since he had permitted the Puseyites to have candles
on their altars, although he had forbidden their being
lighted, as when he had declared, twenty years before, that
the finger of God was about to protestantise Ireland. His
lordship had said and had done many things since that
time which had occasioned the duchess many misgivings,
although she had chosen that they should not occur to
her recollection until he failed in convincing her son that
religious truth was to be found in the parish of St. James,
and political justice in the happy haunts of Montacute
Forest.

The bishop had voted for the Church Temporalities' Bill
in 1833, which at one swoop had suppressed ten Irish
episcopates. This was a queer suffrage for the apostle of
the second Reformation. True it is that Whiggism was
then in the ascendant, and two years afterwards, when
Whiggism had received a heavy blow and great discourage-
ment ; when we had been blessed in the interval with a
decided though feeble Conservative administration, and
were blessed at the moment with a strong though undecided
Conservative opposition ; his lordship, with characteristic
activity, had galloped across country into the right line
again, denounced the Appropriation Clause in a spirit
worthy of his earlier days, and, quite forgetting the ten
Irish Bishoprics, that only four-and-twenty months before
he had doomed to destruction, was all for proselytising
Ireland again by the efficacious means of Irish Protestant
bishops.

'The bishop says that Tancred is a visionary,' said the duchess to her husband, with an air of great displeasure. 'Why, it is because he is a visionary that we sent him to the bishop. I want to have his false imaginings removed by one who has the competent powers of learning and argument, and the authority of a high and holy office. A visionary, indeed! Why, so are the Puseyites; they are visionaries, and his lordship has been obliged to deal with them; though, to be sure, if he spoke to Tancred in a similar fashion, I am not surprised that my son has returned unchanged! This is the most vexatious business that ever occurred to us. Something must be done; but what to fix on? What do you think, George? Since speaking to the bishop, of which you so much approved, has failed, what do you recommend?'

While the duchess was speaking, she was seated in her boudoir, looking into the Green Park; the duke's horses were in the courtyard, and he was about to ride down to the House of Lords; he had just looked in, as was his custom, to say farewell till they met again.

'I am sorry that the interview with the bishop has failed,' said the duke, in a hesitating tone, and playing with his riding-stick; and then walking up to the window and looking into the Park, he said, apparently after reflection, 'I always think the best person to deal with a visionary is a man of the world.'

'But what can men of the world know of such questions?' said the duchess, mournfully.

'Very little,' said her husband, 'and therefore they are never betrayed into arguments, which I fancy always make people more obstinate, even if they are confuted. Men of the world have a knack of settling everything without discussion; they do it by tact. It is astonishing how many difficulties I have seen removed; by Eskdale, for example; which it seemed that no power on earth could change, and about which we had been arguing for months. There was the Cheadle churches case, for example; it broke up some

of the oldest friendships in the county; even Hungerford
and Ilderton did not speak. I never had a more anxious
time of it; and, as far as I was personally concerned, I
would have made any sacrifice to keep a good understanding in the county. At last I got the business referred to
Eskdale, and the affair was ultimately arranged to everybody's satisfaction. I don't know how he managed: it was
quite impossible that he could have offered any new arguments, but he did it by tact. Tact does not remove difficulties, but difficulties melt away under tact.'

'Heigho!' sighed the duchess. 'I cannot understand
how tact can tell us what is religious truth, or prevent my
son from going to the Holy Sepulchre.'

'Try,' said the duke.

'Shall you see our cousin to-day, George?'

'He is sure to be at the House,' replied the duke, eagerly.
'I tell you what I propose, Kate: Tancred is gone to the
House of Commons to hear the debate on Maynooth; I will
try and get our cousin to come home and dine with us, and
then we can talk over the whole affair at once. What say
you?'

'Very well.'

'We have failed with a bishop; we will now try a man
of the world; and if we are to have a man of the world, we
had better have a firstrate one, and everybody agrees that
our cousin ——'

'Yes, yes, George,' said the duchess, 'ask him to come;
tell him it is very urgent, that we must consult him immediately; and then, if he be engaged, I dare say he will
manage to come all the same.'

Accordingly, about half-past eight o'clock, the two peers
arrived at Bellamont House together. They were unexpectedly late; they had been detained at the House. The duke
was excited; even Lord Eskdale looked as if something had
happened. Something had happened; there had been a
division in the House of Lords. Rare and startling event!
It seemed as if the peers were about to resume their func-

tions.　Divisions in the House of Lords are now-a-days so thinly scattered, that, when one occurs, the peers cackle as if they had laid an egg.　They are quite proud of the proof of their still procreative powers.　The division to-night had not been on a subject of any public interest or importance; but still it was a division, and, what was more, the Government had been left in a minority.　True, the catastrophe was occasioned by a mistake.　The dictator had been asleep during the debate, woke suddenly from a dyspeptic dream, would make a speech, and spoke on the wrong side. A lively colleague, not yet sufficiently broken in to the frigid discipline of the High Court of Registry, had pulled the great man once by his coat tails, a House of Commons practice, permitted to the Cabinet when their chief is blundering, very necessary sometimes for a lively leader, but of which Sir Robert highly disapproves, as the arrangement of his coat tails, next to beating the red box, forms the most important part of his rhetorical accessories.　The dictator, when he at length comprehended that he had made a mistake, persisted in adhering to it; the division was called, some of the officials escaped, the rest were obliged to vote with their ruthless master; but his other friends, glad of an opportunity of asserting their independence and administering to the dictator a slight check in a quiet inoffensive way, put him in a minority; and the Duke of Bellamont and Lord Eskdale had contributed to this catastrophe.

Dinner was served in the library; the conversation during it was chiefly the event of the morning.　The duchess, who, though not a partisan, was something of a politician, thought it was a pity that the dictator had ever stepped out of his military sphere; her husband, who had never before seen a man's coat tails pulled when he was speaking, dilated much upon the singular circumstance of Lord Spur so disporting himself on the present occasion; while Lord Eskdale, who had sat for a long time in the House of Commons, and who was used to everything, assured his cousin that the custom, though odd, was by no means irregular. 'I remember,' said his lordship, 'seeing Ripon, when he was Robinson, and Huskisson, each pulling one of Canning's coat tails at the same time.'

Throughout dinner not a word about Tancred. Lord Eskdale neither asked where he was nor how he was. At length, to the great relief of the duchess, dinner was finished; the servants had disappeared. The duke pushed away the table; they drew their chairs round the hearth; Lord Eskdale took half a glass of Madeira, then stretched his legs a little, then rose, stirred the fire, and then, standing with his back to it and his hands in his pockets, said, in a careless tone approaching to a drawl, 'And so, duchess, Tancred wants to go to Jerusalem?'

'George has told you, then, all our troubles?'

'Only that; he left the rest to you, and I came to hear it.'

Whereupon the duchess went off, and spoke for a considerable time with great animation and ability, the duke hanging on every word with vigilant interest, Lord Eskdale never interrupting her for an instant; while she stated the case not only with the impassioned feeling of a devoted mother, but occasionally with all the profundity of a theologian. She did not conceal from him the interview between Tancred and the bishop; it was her last effort, and had failed; and so, 'after all our plans,' she ended, 'as far as I can form an opinion, he is absolutely more resolved than ever to go to Jerusalem.'

'Well,' said his lordship, 'it is at least better than going to the Jews, which most men do at his time of life.'

'I cannot agree even to that,' said the duchess; 'for I would rather that he should be ruined than die.'

'Men do not die as they used,' said his lordship. 'Ask the annuity offices; they have all raised their rates.'

'I know nothing about annuity offices, but I know that almost everybody dies who goes to those countries; look at young Fernborough, he was just Tancred's age; the fevers alone must kill him.'

'He must take some quinine in his dressing-case,' said Lord Eskdale.

'You jest, Henry,' said the duchess, disappointed, 'when I am in despair.'

'No,' said Lord Eskdale, looking up to the ceiling, 'I am thinking how you may prevent Tancred from going to Jerusalem, without, at the same time, opposing his wishes.'

'Ay, ay,' said the duke, 'that is it.' And he looked triumphantly to his wife, as much as to say, 'Now you see what it is to be a man of the world.'

'A man cannot go to Jerusalem as he would to Birmingham, by the next train,' continued his lordship; 'he must get something to take him; and if you make the sacrifice of consenting to his departure, you have a right to stipulate as to the manner in which he should depart. Your son ought to travel with a suite; he ought to make the voyage in his own yacht. Yachts are not to be found like hack cabs, though there are several for sale now; but then they are not of the admeasurement of which you approve for such a voyage and such a sea. People talk very lightly of the Mediterranean, but there are such things as white squalls. Anxious parents, and parents so fond of a son as you are, and a son whose life for so many reasons is so precious, have a right to make it a condition of their consent to his departure, that he should embark in a vessel of considerable tonnage. He will find difficulty in buying one second-hand; if he finds one it will not please him. He will get interested in yacht-building, as he is interested now about Jerusalem: both boyish fancies. He will stay another year in England to build a yacht to take him to the Holy Land; the yacht will be finished this time twelvemonths; and, instead of going to Palestine, he will go to Cowes.'

'That is quite my view of the case,' said the duke.

'It never occurred to me,' said the duchess.

Lord Eskdale resumed his seat, and took another half-glass of Madeira.

'Well, I think it is very satisfactory, Katherine,' said the duke, after a short pause.

'And what do you recommend us to do first?' said the duchess to Lord Eskdale.

'Let Tancred go into society : the best way for him to forget Jerusalem is to let him see London.'

'But how can I manage it?' said the duchess. 'I never go anywhere; nobody knows him, and he does not wish to know anybody.'

'I will manage it, with your permission; 'tis not difficult; a young marquess has only to evince an inclination, and in a week's time he will be everywhere. I will tell Lady St. Julians and the great ladies to send him invitations; they will fall like a snow-storm. All that remains is for you to prevail upon him to accept them.'

'And how shall I contrive it?' said the duchess.

'Easily,' said Lord Eskdale. 'Make his going into society, while his yacht is preparing, one of the conditions of the great sacrifice you are making. He cannot refuse you : 'tis but the first step. A youth feels a little repugnance to launching into the great world : 'tis shyness; but after the plunge, the great difficulty is to restrain rather than to incite. Let him but once enter the world, and be tranquil, he will soon find something to engage him.'

'As long as he does not take to play,' said the duke, 'I do not much care what he does.'

'My dear George!' said the duchess, 'how can you say such things! I was in hopes,' she added, in a mournful tone, 'that we might have settled him, without his entering what you call the world, Henry. Dearest child! I fancy him surrounded by pitfalls.'

CHAPTER VI.

AFTER this consultation with Lord Eskdale, the duchess became easier in her mind. She was of a sanguine temper, and with facility believed what she wished. Affairs stood thus : it was agreed by all that Tancred should go to the Holy Land, but he was to go in his own yacht ; which yacht was to be of a firstrate burthen, and to be commanded by an officer in H.M.S. ; and he was to be accompanied by Colonel Brace, Mr. Bernard, and Mr. Roby ; and the servants were to be placed entirely under the control of some trusty foreigner accustomed to the East, and who was to be chosen by Lord Eskdale. In the meantime, Tancred had acceded to the wish of his parents, that until his departure he should mix much in society. The duchess calculated that, under any circumstances, three months must elapse before all the arrangements were concluded ; and she felt persuaded that, during that period, Tancred must become enamoured of his cousin Katherine, and that the only use of the yacht would be to take them all to Ireland. The duke was resolved only on two points : that his son should do exactly as his son liked, and that he himself would never take the advice, on any subject, of any other person than Lord Eskdale.

In the meantime Tancred was launched, almost unconsciously, into the great world. The name of the Marquess of Montacute was foremost in those delicate lists by which an eager and admiring public is apprised who, among their aristocracy, eat, drink, dance, and sometimes pray. From the saloons of Belgrave and Grosvenor Square to the sacred recesses of the Chapel Royal, the movements of Lord Montacute were tracked and registered, and were devoured every morning, oftener with a keener relish than the matin meal of which they formed a regular portion. England is the only country which enjoys the unspeakable advantage of being thus regularly, promptly, and accurately furnished with catalogues of those favoured beings who are deemed qualified to enter the houses of the great. What condescension in those who impart the information! What indubitable evidence of true nobility! What superiority to all petty vanity! And in those who receive it, what freedom from all little feelings! No arrogance on one side; on the other, no envy. It is only countries blessed with a free press that can be thus favoured. Even a free press is not alone sufficient. Besides a free press, you must have a servile public.

After all, let us be just. The uninitiated world is apt to believe that there is sometimes, in the outskirts of fashion, an eagerness, scarcely consistent with self-respect, to enter the mansions of the great. Not at all: few people really want to go to their grand parties. It is not the charms of conversation, the flash of wit or the blaze of beauty, the influential presence of the powerful and celebrated, all the splendour and refinement, which, combined, offer in a polished saloon so much to charm the taste and satisfy the intellect, that the mass of social partisans care anything about. What they want is, not so much to be in her ladyship's house as in her ladyship's list. After the party at Coningsby Castle, our friend, Mrs. Guy Flouncey, at length succeeded in being asked to one of Lady St. Julians' assemblies. It was a great triumph, and Mrs. Guy Flouncey determined to make the most of it. She was worthy of the occasion. But, alas! next morning, though admitted to the rout, Mrs. Guy Flouncey was left out of the list! It was a severe blow! But Mrs. Guy Flouncey is in every list now, and even strikes out names herself. But there never was a woman who advanced with such dexterity.

Lord Montacute was much shocked, when, one morning, taking up a journal, he first saw his name in print. He was alone, and he blushed; felt, indeed, extremely distressed, when he found that the English people were formally made acquainted with the fact, that he had dined on the previous Saturday with the Earl and Countess of St. Julians; 'a grand banquet,' of which he was quite unconscious until he read it; and that he was afterwards ' observed ' at the Opera.

He found that he had become a public character, and he was not by any means conscious of meriting celebrity.   To be pointed at as he walked the streets, were he a hero, or had done, said, or written anything that anybody remembered, though at first painful and embarrassing, for he was shy, he could conceive ultimately becoming endurable, and not without a degree of excitement, for he was ambitious ; but to be looked at because he was a young lord, and that this should be the only reason why the public should be informed where he dined, or where he amused himself, seemed to him not only vexatious but degrading. When he arrived, however, at a bulletin of his devotions, he posted off immediately to the Surrey Canal to look at a yacht there, and resolved not to lose unnecessarily one moment in setting off for Jerusalem.

He had from the first busied himself about the preparations for his voyage with all the ardour of youth ; that is, with all the energy of inexperience, and all the vigour of simplicity.   As everything seemed to depend upon his obtaining a suitable vessel, he trusted to no third person ; had visited Cowes several times ; advertised in every paper ; and had already met with more than one yacht which at least deserved consideration. The duchess was quite frightened at his progress.   ' I am afraid he has found one, she said to Lord Eskdale ; ' he will be off directly.'

Lord Eskdale shook his head.   ' There are always things of this sort in the market.   He will inquire before he purchases, and he will find that he has got hold of a slow coach.'

' A slow coach ! ' said the duchess, looking inquiringly. ' What is that ? '

' A tub that sails like a collier, and which, instead of taking him to Jerusalem, will hardly take him to Newcastle.'

Lord Eskdale was right. Notwithstanding all his ardour, all his inquiries, visits to Cowes and the Surrey Canal, advertisements and answers to advertisements, time flew on, and Tancred was still without a yacht.

In this unsettled state, Tancred found himself one evening at Deloraine House. It was not a ball, it was only a dance, brilliant and select; but, all the same, it seemed to Tancred that the rooms could not be much more crowded. The name of the Marquess of Montacute, as it was sent along by the servants, attracted attention. Tancred had scarcely entered the world, his appearance had made a sensation, everybody talked of him, many had not yet seen him.

'Oh! that is Lord Montacute,' said a great lady, looking through her glass; 'very distinguished!'

'I tell you what,' whispered Mr. Ormsby to Lord Valentine, 'you young men had better look sharp; Lord Montacute will cut you all out!'

'Oh! he is going to Jerusalem,' said Lord Valentine.

'Jerusalem!' said Mr. Ormsby, shrugging his shoulders. 'What can he find to do at Jerusalem?'

'What, indeed,' said Lord Milford. 'My brother was there in '39; he got leave after the bombardment of Acre, and he says there is absolutely no sport of any kind.'

'There used to be partridges in the time of Jeremiah,' said Mr. Ormsby; 'at least they told us so at the Chapel Royal last Sunday, where, by-the-bye, I saw Lord Montacute for the first time; and a deuced good-looking fellow he is,' he added, musingly.

'Well, there is not a bird in the whole country now,' said Lord Milford.

'Montacute does not care for sport,' said Lord Valentine.

'What does he care for?' asked Lord Milford. 'Because, if he wants any horses, I can let him have some.'

'He wants to buy a yacht,' said Lord Valentine; 'and that reminds me that I heard to-day Exmouth wanted to get rid of "The Flower of Yarrow," and I think it would suit my cousin. I'll tell him of it.' And he followed Tancred.

'You and Valentine must rub up your harness, Milford,' said Mr. Ormsby; 'there is a new champion in the field. We are talking of Lord Montacute,' continued Mr. Ormsby, addressing himself to Mr. Melton, who joined them; 'I tell Milford he will cut you all out.'

'Well,' said Mr. Melton, 'for my part I have had so much success, that I have no objection, by way of change, to be for once eclipsed.'

'Well done, Jemmy,' said Lord Milford.

'I see, Melton,' said Mr. Ormsby, 'you are reconciled to your fate like a philosopher.'

'Well, Montacute,' said Lord St. Patrick, a good-tempered, witty Milesian, with a laughing eye, 'when are you going to Jericho?'

'Tell me,' said Tancred, in reply, and rather earnestly, 'who is that?' And he directed the attention of Lord St. Patrick to a young lady, rather tall, a brilliant complexion, classic features, a profusion of light brown hair, a face of intelligence, and a figure rich and yet graceful.

'That is Lady Constance Rawleigh; if you like, I will introduce you to her. She is my cousin, and deuced clever. Come along!'

In the meantime, in the room leading to the sculpture gallery where they are dancing, the throng is even excessive. As the two great divisions, those who would enter the gallery and those who are quitting it, encounter each other, they exchange flying phrases as they pass.

'They told me you had gone to Paris! I have just returned. Dear me, how time flies! Pretty dance, is it not? Very. Do you know whether the Madlethorpes mean to come up this year? I hardly know; their little girl is very ill. Ah! so I hear; what a pity, and such a fortune! Such a pity with such a fortune! How d'ye do? Mr. Coningsby here? No; he's at the House. They say he is a very close attendant. It interests him. Well, Lady Florentina, you never sent me the dances. Pardon, but you will find them when you return. I lent them to Augusta, and she would copy them. Is it true that I am to congratulate you? Why? Lady Blanche? Oh! that is a romance of Easter week. Well, I am really delighted; I think such an excellent match for both; exactly suited to each other. They think so. Well, that is one point. How well Lady Everingham is looking! She is quite herself again. Quite. Tell me, have you seen M. de Talleyrand here? I spoke to him but this moment. Shall you be at Lady Blair's to-morrow? No; I have promised to go to Mrs. Guy Flouncey's. She has taken Craven Cottage, and is to be at home every Saturday. Well, if you are going, I think I shall. I would; everybody will be there.'

Lord Montacute had conversed some time with Lady Constance; then he had danced with her; he had hovered about her during the evening. It was observed, particularly by some of the most experienced mothers. Lady Constance was a distinguished beauty of two seasons; fresh, but adroit. It was understood that she had refused offers of a high calibre; but the rejected still sighed about her, and it was therefore supposed that, though decided, she had the art of not rendering them desperate. One at least of them was of a rank equal to that of Tancred. She had the reputation of being very clever, and of being able, if it pleased her, to breathe scorpions as well as brilliants and roses. It had got about that she admired intellect, and, though she claimed the highest social position, that a booby would not content her, even if his ears were covered with strawberry leaves.

In the cloak-room, Tancred was still at her side, and was presented to her mother, Lady Charmouth.

'I am sorry to separate,' said Tancred.

'And so am I,' said Lady Constance, smiling; 'but one advantage of this life is, we meet our friends every day.'

'I am not going anywhere to-morrow, where I shall meet you,' said Tancred, 'unless you chance to dine at the Archbishop of York's.'

'I am not going to dine with the Archbishop of York,' said Lady Constance, 'but I am going, where everybody else is going, to breakfast with Mrs. Guy Flouncey, at Craven Cottage. Why, will not you be there?'

'I have not the honour of knowing her,' said Tancred.

'That is not of the slightest consequence; she will be very happy to have the honour of knowing you. I saw her in the dancing-room, but it is not worth while waiting to speak to her now. You shall receive an invitation the moment you are awake.'

'But to-morrow I have got an engagement. I have got to look at a yacht.'

'But that you can look at on Monday ; besides, if you wish to know anything about yachts, you had better speak to my brother, Fitzheron, who has built more than any man alive.'

'Perhaps he has got one that he wishes to part with ?' said Tancred.

'I have no doubt of it. You can ask him to-morrow at Mrs. Guy Flouncey's.'

'I will. Lady Charmouth's carriage is called. May I have the honour ?' said Tancred, offering his arm.

CHAPTER VII.

THERE is nothing so remarkable as feminine influence. Although the character of Tancred was not completely formed ; for that result depends, in some degree, upon the effect of circumstances at a certain time of life, as well as on the impulse of a natural bent; still the temper of his being was profound and stedfast. He had arrived, in solitude and by the working of his own thought, at a certain resolution, which had assumed to his strong and fervent imagination a sacred character, and which he was determined to accomplish at all costs. He had brought himself to the point, that he would not conceive an obstacle that should balk him. He had acceded to the conditions which had been made by his parents, for he was by nature dutiful, and wished to fulfil his purpose, if possible, with their sanction.

Yet he had entered society with repugnance, and found nothing in its general tone with which his spirit harmonised. He was alone in the crowd; silent, observing, and not charmed. There seemed to him generally a want of simplicity and repose; too much flutter, not a little affectation. People met in the thronged chambers, and interchanged brief words, as if they were always in a hurry. 'Have you been here long? Where are you going next?' These were the questions which seemed to form the staple of the small talk of a fashionable multitude. Why too was there a smile on every countenance, which often also assumed the character of a grin? No error so common or so grievous as to suppose that a smile is a necessary ingredient of the pleasing. There are few faces that can afford to smile. A smile is sometimes bewitching, in general vapid, often a contortion. But the bewitching smile usually beams from the grave face. It is then irresistible. Tancred, though he was unaware of it, was gifted with this rare spell. He had inherited it from his mother; a woman naturally earnest and serious, and of a singular simplicity, but whose heart when pleased spoke in the dimpling sunshine of her cheek with exquisite beauty. The smiles of the Duchess of Bellamont, however, were like her diamonds, brilliant, but rarely worn.

Tancred had not mounted the staircase of Deloraine House with any anticipation of pleasure. His thoughts were far away amid cities of the desert, and by the palmy banks of ancient rivers. He often took refuge in these exciting and ennobling visions, to maintain himself when he underwent the ceremony of entering a great house. He was so shy in little things, that to hear his name sounded from servant to servant, echoing from landing-place to landing-place, was almost overwhelming. Nothing but his pride, which was just equal to his reserve, prevented him from often turning back on the stairs and precipitately retreating. And yet he had not been ten minutes in Deloraine House, before he had absolutely requested to be introduced to a lady. It was the first time he had ever made such a request.

He returned home, softly musing. A tone lingered in his ear; he recalled the countenance of one absent. In his dressing room he lingered before he retired, with his arm on the mantel-piece, and gazing with abstraction on the fire.

When his servant called him in the morning, the servant brought him a card from Mrs. Guy Flouncey, inviting him on that day to Craven Cottage, at three o'clock : 'déjeûner at four o'clock precisely.' Tancred took the card, looked at it, and the letters seemed to cluster together and form the countenance of Lady Constance. 'It will be a good thing to go,' he said, 'because I want to know Lord Fitzheron; he will be of great use to me about my yacht.' So he ordered his carriage at three o'clock.

The reader must not for a moment suppose that Mrs. Guy Flouncey, though she was quite as well dressed, and almost as pretty, as she was when at Coningsby Castle in 1837, was by any means the same lady who then strove to amuse and struggled to be noticed. By no means. In 1837, Mrs. Guy Flouncey was nobody; in 1845, Mrs. Guy Flouncey was somebody, and somebody of very great importance. Mrs. Guy Flouncey had invaded society, and had conquered it, gradually, but completely, like the English in India. Social invasions are not rare, but they are seldom fortunate, or success, if achieved, is partial, and then only sustained at immense cost, like the French in Algiers.

The Guy Flounceys were not people of great fortune. They had a good fortune ; seven or eight thousand a-year. But then, with an air of great expenditure, even profusion, there was a basis of good management. And a good fortune with good management, and without that equivocal luxury, a great country-house, is almost equal to the great fortune of a peer. But they not only had no country-house, they had no children. And a good fortune, with good management, no country-house, and no children, is Aladdin's lamp.

Mr. Guy Flouncey was a sporting character. His wife had impressed upon him that it was the only way in which he could become fashionable and acquainted with 'the best men.' He knew just enough of the affair not to be ridiculous; and, for the rest, with a great deal of rattle and apparent heedlessness of speech and deed, he was really an extremely selfish and sufficiently shrewd person, who never compromised himself. It is astonishing with what dexterity Guy Flouncey could extricate himself from the jaws of a friend, who, captivated by his thoughtless candour and ostentatiously good heart, might be induced to request Mr. Flouncey to lend him a few hundreds, only for a few months, or, more diplomatically, might beg his friend to become his security for a few thousands, for a few years. Mr. Guy Flouncey never refused these applications, they were exactly those to which it delighted his heart to respond, because nothing pleased him more than serving a friend. But then he always had to write a preliminary letter of preparation to his banker, or his steward, or his confidential solicitor; and, by some contrivance or other, without offending any one, rather with the appearance of conferring an obligation, it ended always by Mr. Guy Flouncey neither advancing the hundreds, nor guaranteeing the thousands. He had, indeed, managed, like many others, to get the reputation of being what is called 'a good fellow;' though it would have puzzled his panegyrists to allege a single act of his that evinced a good heart.

This sort of pseudo reputation, whether for good or for evil, is not uncommon in the world. Man is mimetic; judges of character are rare; we repeat without thought the opinions of some third person, who has adopted them without inquiry; and thus it often happens that a proud generous man obtains in time the reputation of being 'a screw,' because he has refused to lend money to some impudent spendthrift, who from that moment abuses him; and a cold-hearted, civil-spoken personage, profuse in costless services, with a spice of the parasite in him, or perhaps hospitable out of vanity, is invested with all the thoughtless sympathies of society, and passes current as that most popular of characters, ' a good fellow.'

Guy Flouncey's dinners began to be talked of among men; it became a sort of fashion, especially among sporting men, to dine with Mr. Guy Flouncey, and there they met Mrs. Guy Flouncey. Not an opening ever escaped her. If a man had a wife, and that wife was a personage, sooner or later, much as she might toss her head at first, she was sure to visit Mrs. Guy Flouncey, and, when she knew her, she was sure to like her. The Guy Flounceys never lost a moment; the instant the season was over, they were at Cowes, then at a German bath, then at Paris, then at an English country-house, then in London. Seven years, to such people, was half a century of social experience. They had half a dozen seasons in every year. Still it was hard work, and not rapid. At a certain point they stuck, as all do. Most people, then, give it up; but patience, Buffon tells us, is genius, and Mrs. Guy Flouncey was, in her way, a woman of genius. Their dinners were, in a certain sense, established: these in return brought them to a certain degree into the dinner world; but balls, at least balls of a high calibre, were few, and as for giving a ball herself, Mrs. Guy Flouncey could no more presume to think of that, than of attempting to prorogue Parliament. The house, however, got really celebrated for ' the best men.' Mrs. Guy Flouncey invited all the young dancing lords to dinner. Mothers will bring their daughters where there are young lords. Mrs. Guy Flouncey had an opera-box in the best tier, which she took only to lend to her friends; and a box at the French play, which she took only to bribe her foes. They were both at everybody's service, like Mr. Guy Flouncey's yacht, provided the persons who required them were members of that great world in which Mrs. Guy Flouncey had resolved to plant herself.

Mrs. Guy Flouncey was pretty; she was a flirt on principle; thus she had caught the Marquess of Beaumanoir, who, if they chanced to meet, always spoke to her, which gave Mrs. Guy Flouncey fashion. But Mrs. Guy Flouncey was nothing more than a flirt. She never made a mistake; she was born with strong social instincts. She knew that the fine ladies among whom, from the first, she had determined to place herself, were moral martinets with respect to any one not born among themselves. That which is not observed, or, if noticed, playfully alluded to in the conduct of a patrician dame, is visited with scorn and contumely, if committed by some 'shocking woman,' who has deprived perhaps a countess of the affections of a husband who has not spoken to her for 'years. But if the countess is to lose her husband, she ought to lose him to a viscountess, at least. In this way the earl is not lost to 'society.'

A great nobleman met Mrs. Guy Flouncey at a country-house, and was fairly captivated by her. Her pretty looks, her coquettish manner, her vivacity, her charming costume, above all, perhaps, her imperturbable good temper, pierced him to the heart. The great nobleman's wife had the weakness to be annoyed. Mrs. Guy Flouncey saw her opportunity. She threw over the earl, and became the friend of the countess, who could never sufficiently evince her gratitude to the woman who would not make love to her husband. This friendship was the incident for which Mrs. Guy Flouncey had been cruising for years. Men she had vanquished; they had given her a sort of ton which she had prudently managed. She had not destroyed herself by any fatal preference. Still, her fashion among men necessarily made her unfashionable among women, who, if they did not absolutely hate her, which they would have done had she had a noble lover, were determined not to help her up the social ladder. Now she had a great friend, and one of the greatest of ladies. The moment she had pondered over for years had arrived. Mrs. Guy Flouncey determined at once to test her position. Mrs. Guy Flouncey resolved on giving a ball.

But some of our friends in the country will say, ' Is that all ? Surely it required no very great resolution, no very protracted pondering, to determine on giving a ball! Where is the difficulty ? The lady has but to light up her house, hire the fiddlers, line her staircase with American plants, perhaps inclose her balcony, order Mr. Gunter to provide plenty of the best refreshments, and at one o'clock a superb supper, and, with the company of your friends, you have as good a ball as can be desired by the young, or endured by the old.'

Innocent friends in the country ! You might have all these things. Your house might be decorated like a Russian palace, blazing with the most brilliant lights and breathing the richest odours ; you might have Jullien presiding over your orchestra, and a banquet worthy of the Romans. As for your friends, they might dance until daybreak, and agree that there never was an entertainment more tasteful, more sumptuous, and, what would seem of the first importance, more merry. But, having all these things, suppose you have not a list ? You have given a ball, you have not a list. The reason is obvious : you are ashamed of your guests. You are not in ' society.'

But even a list is not sufficient for success. You must also get a day : the most difficult thing in the world. After inquiring among your friends, and studying the columns of the 'Morning Post,' you discover that, five weeks hence, a day is disengaged. You send out your cards ; your house is dismantled ; your lights are arranged ; the American plants have arrived ; the band, perhaps two bands, are engaged. Mr. Gunter has half dressed your supper, and made all your ice, when suddenly, within eight-and-forty hours of the festival which you have been five weeks preparing, the Marchioness of Deloraine sends out cards for a ball in honour of some European sovereign who has just alighted on our isle, and means to stay only a week, and at whose court, twenty years ago, Lord Deloraine was ambassador. Instead of receiving your list, you are obliged to send messengers in all directions to announce that your ball is postponed, although you are perfectly aware that not a single individual would have been present whom you would have cared to welcome.

The ball is postponed; and next day the 'Morning Post' informs us it is postponed to that day week; and the day after you have circulated this interesting intelligence, you *yourself*, perhaps, have the gratification of receiving an invitation, for the same day, to Lady St. Julians: with 'dancing,' neatly engraved in the corner. You yield in despair; and there are some ladies who, with every quali-fication for an excellent ball; guests, Gunter, American plants, pretty daughters; have been watching and waiting for years for an opportunity of giving it; and at last, quite hopeless, at the end of the season, expend their funds in a series of Greenwich banquets, which sometimes fortunately produce the results expected from the more imposing festivity.

You see, therefore, that giving a ball is not that matter-of-course affair you imagined; and that for Mrs. Guy Flouncey to give a ball and succeed, completely, trium-phantly to succeed, was a feat worthy of that fine social general. Yet she did it. The means, like everything that is great, were simple. She induced her noble friend to ask her guests. Her noble friend canvassed for her as if it were a county election of the good old days, when the representation of a shire was the certain avenue to a peerage, instead of being, as it is now, the high road to a poor-law commissionership. Many were very glad to make the acquaintance of Mrs. Guy Flouncey; many only wanted an excuse to make the acquaintance of Mrs. Guy Flouncey; they went to her party because they were asked by their dear friend, Lady Kingcastle. As for the potentates, there is no disguise on these subjects among them. They went to Mrs. Guy Flouncey's ball, because one who was their equal, not only in rank, but in social influence, had re-quested it as a personal favour, she herself, when the

occasion offered, being equally ready to advance their
wishes.   The fact was, that affairs were ripe for the recognition of Mrs. Guy Flouncey as a member of the social
body.   Circumstances had been long maturing.   The Guy
Flounceys, who, in the course of their preparatory career,
had hopped from Park Crescent to Portman Square, had
now perched upon their 'splendid mansion' in Belgrave
Square.   Their dinners were renowned.   Mrs. Guy Flouncey
was seen at all the 'best balls,' and was always surrounded
by the 'best men.'   Though a flirt and a pretty woman,
she was a discreet parvenue, who did not entrap the affections of noble husbands.   Above all, she was the friend of
Lady Kingcastle, who called her and her husband 'those
good Guy Flounceys.'

  The ball was given; you could not pass through Belgrave Square that night.   The list was published; it
formed two columns of the 'Morning Post.'   Lady Kingcastle was honoured by the friendship of a royal duchess.
She put the friendship to the proof, and her royal highness
was seen at Mrs. Guy Flouncey's ball.   Imagine the recep-
tion, the canopy, the scarlet cloth, the 'God save the King'
from the band of the first guards, bivouacked in the hall,
Mrs. Guy Flouncey herself performing her part as if she
had received princesses of the blood all her life; so reverent
and yet so dignified, so very calm and yet with a sort of
winning, sunny innocence.   Her royal highness was quite
charmed with her hostess, praised her much to Lady Kingcastle, told her that she was glad that she had come, and
even stayed half an hour longer than Mrs. Guy Flouncey
had dared to hope.   As for the other guests the peerage
was gutted.   The Dictator himself was there, and, the
moment her royal highness had retired, Mrs. Guy Flouncey
devoted herself to the hero.   All the great ladies, all the
ambassadors, all the beauties, a full chapter of the Garter,
a chorus among the 'best men' that it was without doubt
the 'best ball' of the year, happy Mrs. Guy Flouncey!
She threw a glance at her swing-glass while Mr. Guy

Flouncey, 'who had not had time to get anything the whole evening,' was eating some supper on a tray in her dressing-room at five o'clock in the morning, and said, 'We have done it at last, my love!'

She was right; and from that moment Mrs. Guy Flouncey was asked to all the great houses, and became a lady of the most unexceptionable ton.

But all this time we are forgetting her déjeûner, and that Tancred is winding his way through the garden lanes of Fulham to reach Craven Cottage.

CHAPTER VIII.

THE day was brilliant: music, sunshine, ravishing bonnets, little parasols that looked like large butterflies. The new phaetons glided up, then carriages and four swept by; in general the bachelors were ensconced in their comfortable broughams, with their glasses down and their blinds drawn, to receive the air and to exclude the dust; some less provident were cavaliers, but, notwithstanding the well-watered roads, seemed a little dashed as they cast an anxious glance at the rose which adorned their button-hole, or fancied that they felt a flying black from a London chimney light upon the tip of their nose.

Within, the winding walks dimly echoed whispering words; the lawn was studded with dazzling groups; on the terrace by the river a dainty multitude beheld those celebrated waters which furnish flounders to Richmond and whitebait to Blackwall.

'Mrs. Coningsby shall decide,' said Lord Beaumanoir.

Edith and Lady Theresa Lyle stood by a statue that glittered in the sun surrounded by a group of cavaliers; among them, Lord Beaumanoir, Lord Milford, Lord Eugene de Vere. Her figure was not less lithe and graceful since her marriage, a little more voluptuous; her rich complexion, her radiant and abounding hair, and her long grey eye, now melting with pathos, and now twinkling with mockery, presented one of those faces of witchery which are beyond beauty.

'Mrs. Coningsby shall decide.'

'It is the very thing,' said Edith, 'that Mrs. Coningsby will never do. Decision destroys suspense, and suspense is the charm of existence.'

'But suspense may be agony,' said Lord Eugene de Vere, casting a glance that would read the innermost heart of Edith.

'And decision may be despair,' said Mrs. Coningsby.

'But we agreed the other night that you were to decide everything for us,' said Lord Beaumanoir; 'and you consented.'

'I consented the other night, and I retract my consent to-day; and I am consistent, for that is indecision.'

'You are consistent in being charming,' said Lord Eugene.

'Pleasing and original!' said Edith. 'By-the-bye, when I consented that the melancholy Jaques should be one of my aides-de-camp I expected him to maintain his reputation, not only for gloom but wit. I think you had better go back to the forest, Lord Eugene, and see if you cannot stumble upon a fool who may drill you in repartee. How do you do, Lady Riddlesworth?' and she bowed to two ladies who seemed inclined to stop, but Edith added, 'I heard great applications for you this moment on the terrace.'

'Indeed!' exclaimed the ladies; and they moved on.

'When Lady Riddlesworth joins the conversation it is like a stoppage in the streets. I invented a piece of intelligence to clear the way, as you would call out Fire! or The queen is coming! There used to be things called *vers de société*, which were not poetry; and I do not see why there should not be social illusions which are not fibs.'

'I entirely agree with you,' said Lord Milford; 'and I move that we practise them on a large scale.'

'Like the verses, they might make life more light,' said Lady Theresa.

'We are surrounded by illusions,' said Lord Eugene, in a melancholy tone.

'And shams of all descriptions,' said Edith; 'the greatest, a man who pretends he has a broken heart when all the time he is full of fun.'

'There are a great many men who have broken hearts,' said Lord Beaumanoir, smiling sorrowfully.

'Cracked heads are much commoner,' said Edith, 'you may rely upon it. The only man I really know with a broken heart is Lord Fitzbooby. I do think that paying Mount-Dullard's debts has broken his heart. He takes on so; 'tis piteous. " My dear Mrs. Coningsby," he said to me last night, " only think what that young man might have been; he might have been a lord of the treasury in '35; why, if he had had nothing more in '41, why, there's a loss of between four and five thousand pounds; but with my claims; Sir Robert, having thrown the father over, was bound on his own principle to provide for the son; he might have got something better; and now he comes to me with his debts, and his reason for paying his debts, too, Mrs. Coningsby, because he is going to be married; to be married to a woman who has not a shilling. Why, if he had been in office, and only got 1,500*l.* a-year, and married a woman with only another 1,500*l.*, he would have had 3,000*l.* a-year, Mrs. Coningsby; and now he has nothing of his own except some debts, which he wants me to pay, and settle 3,000*l.* a-year on him besides." '

They all laughed.

'Ah!' said Mrs. Coningsby, with a resemblance which made all start, 'you should have heard it with the Fitzbooby voice.'

The character of a woman rapidly develops after marriage, and sometimes seems to change, when in fact it is only complete. Hitherto we have known Edith only in her girlhood, bred up in a life of great simplicity, and under the influence of a sweet fancy, or an absorbing passion. Coningsby had been a hero to her before they met, the

hero of nursery hours and nursery tales. Experience had
not disturbed those dreams. From the moment they encountered each other at Millbank, he assumed that place in
her heart which he had long occupied in her imagination;
and, after their second meeting at Paris, her existence
was merged in love. All the crosses and vexations of their
early affection only rendered this state of being on her part
more profound and engrossing.

But though Edith was a most happy wife, and blessed
with two children worthy of their parents, love exercises
quite a different influence upon a woman when she has
married, and especially when she has assumed a social
position which deprives life of all its real cares. Under any
circumstances, that suspense, which, with all its occasional
agony, is the great spring of excitement, is over; but,
generally speaking, it will be found, notwithstanding the
proverb, that with persons of a noble nature, the straitened
fortunes which they share together, and manage, and miti-
gate by mutual forbearance, are more conducive to the
sustainment of a high-toned and romantic passion, than a
luxurious and splendid prosperity. The wife of a man of
limited means, who, by contrivance, by the concealed sacrifice of some necessity of her own, supplies him with some
slight enjoyment which he has never asked, but which she
fancies he may have sighed for, experiences, without doubt,
a degree of pleasure far more ravishing than the patrician
dame who stops her barouche at Storr and Mortimer's,
and out of her pin-money buys a trinket for the husband
whom she loves, and which he finds, perhaps, on his dressing table, on the anniversary of their wedding-day. That's
pretty too and touching, and should be encouraged; but
the other thrills, and ends in an embrace that is still poetry.

The Coningsbys shortly after their marriage had been
called to the possession of a great fortune, for which, in
every sense, they were well adapted. But a great fortune
necessarily brings with it a great change of habits. The
claims of society proportionately increase with your income

You live less for yourselves. For a selfish man, merely looking to his luxurious ease, Lord Eskdale's idea of having ten thousand a-year, while the world suppose you have only five, is the right thing. Coningsby, however, looked to a great fortune as one of the means, rightly employed, of obtaining great power. He looked also to his wife to assist him in this enterprise. Edith, from a native impulse, as well as from love for her husband, responded to his wish. When they were in the country, Hellingsley was a perpetual stream and scene of splendid hospitality; there the flower of London society mingled with all the aristocracy of the county. Leander was often retained specially, like a Wilde or a Kelly, to renovate the genius of the habitual chief: not of the circuit, but the kitchen. A noble mansion in Park Lane received them the moment Parliament assembled. Coningsby was then immersed in affairs, and counted entirely on Edith to cherish those social influences which in a public career are not less important than political ones. The whole weight of the management of society rested on her. She had to cultivate his alliances, keep together his friends, arrange his dinner-parties, regulate his engagements. What time for romantic love? They were never an hour alone. Yet they loved not less; but love had taken the character of enjoyment instead of a wild bewitchment; and life had become an airy bustle, instead of a storm, an agony, a hurricane of the heart.

In this change in the disposition, not in the degree, of their affection, for there was the same amount of sweet solicitude, only it was duly apportioned to everything that interested them, instead of being exclusively devoted to each other, the character of Edith, which had been swallowed up by the absorbing passion, rapidly developed itself amid the social circumstances. She was endued with great vivacity, a sanguine and rather saucy spirit, with considerable talents, and a large share of feminine vanity: that divine gift which makes woman charming. Entirely sympathising with her husband, labouring with zeal to advance his views, and living perpetually in the world, all these qualities came to light. During her first season she had been very quiet, not less observant, making herself mistress of the ground. It was prepared for her next campaign. When she evinced a disposition to take a lead, although found faultless the first year, it was suddenly remembered that she was a manufacturer's daughter; and she was once described by a great lady as 'that person whom Mr. Coningsby had married, when Lord Monmouth cut him off with a shilling.'

But Edith had anticipated these difficulties, and was not to be daunted. Proud of her husband, confident in herself, supported by a great establishment, and having many friends, she determined to exchange salutes with these social sharp-shooters, who are scarcely as courageous as they are arrogant. It was discovered that Mrs. Coningsby could be as malicious as her assailants, and far more epigrammatic. She could describe in a sentence and personify in a phrase. The *mot* was circulated, the *nom de nique* repeated. Surrounded by a brilliant band of youth and wit, even her powers of mimickry were revealed to the initiated. More than one social tyrant, whom all disliked, but whom none had ventured to resist, was made ridiculous. Flushed by success and stimulated by admiration, Edith flattered herself that she was assisting her husband while she was gratifying her vanity. Her adversaries soon vanished, but the powers that had vanquished them were too choice to be forgotten or neglected. The tone of raillery she had assumed for the moment, and extended, in self-defence, to persons, was adopted as a habit, and infused itself over affairs in general.

Mrs. Coningsby was the fashion; she was a wit as well as a beauty; a fascinating droll; dazzling and bewitching, the idol of every youth. Eugene de Vere was roused from his premature exhaustion, and at last again found excitement. He threw himself at her feet; she laughed at him. He asked leave to follow her footsteps; she consented. He was only one of a band of slaves. Lord Beaumanoir, still a bachelor, always hovered about her; feeding on her laughing words with a mild melancholy, and sometimes bandying repartee with a kind of tender and stately despair. His sister, Lady Theresa Lyle, was Edith's great friend. Their dispositions had some resemblance. Marriage had developed in both of them a frolic grace. They hunted in couple; and their sport was brilliant. Many things may be said by a strong female alliance, that would assume quite a different character were they even to fall from the lips of an Aspasia to a circle of male votaries; so much depends upon the scene and the characters, the mode and the manner.

The good-natured world would sometimes pause in its amusement, and, after dwelling with statistical accuracy on the number of times Mrs. Coningsby had danced the Polka, on the extraordinary things she said to Lord Eugene de Vere, and the odd things she and Lady Theresa Lyle were perpetually doing, would wonder, with a face and voice of innocence, ' how Mr. Coningsby liked all this ? ' There is no doubt what was the anticipation by the good-natured world of Mr. Coningsby's feelings. But they were quite mistaken. There was nothing that Mr. Coningsby liked more. He wished his wife to become a social power; and he wished his wife to be amused. He saw that, with the surface of a life of levity, she already exercised considerable influence, especially over the young; and independently of such circumstances and considerations, he was delighted to have a wife who was not afraid of going into society by herself; not one whom he was sure to find at home when he returned from the House of Commons, not reproaching him exactly for her social sacrifices, but looking a victim, and thinking that she retained her husband's heart by being a mope. Instead of that, Coningsby wanted to be amused when he came home, and more than that, he wanted to be instructed in the finest learning in the world.

As some men keep up their Greek by reading every day a chapter in the New Testament, so Coningsby kept up his

knowledge of the world, by always, once at least in the four
and twenty hours, having a delightful conversation with
his wife. The processes are equally orthodox. Exempted
from the tax of entering general society, free to follow his
own pursuits, and to live in that political world which alone
interested him, there was not an anecdote, a trait, a good
thing said, or a bad thing done, which did not reach him
by a fine critic and a lively narrator. He was always behind those social scenes which, after all, regulate the political performers, knew the springs of the whole machinery,
the changings and the shiftings, the fiery cars and golden
chariots which men might mount, and the trap-doors down
which men might fall.

But the Marquess of Montacute is making his reverence
to Mrs. Guy Flouncey.

There was not at this moment a human being whom that
lady was more glad to see at her déjeûner; but she did not
show it in the least. Her self-possession, indeed, was the
finest work of art of the day, and ought to be exhibited at
the Adelaide Gallery. Like all mechanical inventions of a
high class, it had been brought to perfection very gradually,
and after many experiments. A variety of combinations,
and an almost infinite number of trials, must have been expended before the too-startling laugh of Coningsby Castle
could have subsided into the haughty suavity of that sunny
glance, which was not familiar enough for a smile, nor
foolish enough for a simper. As for the rattling vein which
distinguished her in the days of our first acquaintance, that
had long ceased. Mrs. Guy Flouncey now seemed to share
the prevalent passion for genuine Saxon, and used only
monosyllables; while Fine-ear himself would have been
sometimes at fault had he attempted to give a name to her
delicate breathings. In short, Mrs. Guy Flouncey never
did or said anything but in 'the best taste.' It may, however, be a question, whether she ever would have captivated
Lord Monmouth, and those who like a little nature and fun,
if she had made her first advances in this style. But that
showed the greatness of the woman. Then she was ready

for anything for promotion. That was the age of forlorn hopes; but now she was a general of division, and had assumed a becoming carriage.

This was the first déjeûner at which Tancred had been present. He rather liked it. The scene, lawns and groves and a glancing river, the air, the music, our beautiful countrywomen, who, with their brilliant complexions and bright bonnets, do not shrink from the daylight, these are circumstances which, combined with youth and health, make a morning festival, say what they like, particularly for the first time, very agreeable, even if one be dreaming of Jerusalem. Strange power of the world, that the moment we enter it, our great conceptions dwarf! In youth it is quick sympathy that degrades them; more advanced, it is the sense of the ridiculous. But perhaps these reveries of solitude may not be really great conceptions; perhaps they are only exaggerations; vague, indefinite, shadowy, formed on no sound principles, founded on no assured basis.

Why should Tancred go to Jerusalem? What does it signify to him whether there be religious truth or political justice? He has youth, beauty, rank, wealth, power, and all in excess. He has a mind that can comprehend their importance and appreciate their advantages. What more does he require? Unreasonable boy! And if he reach Jerusalem, why should he find religious truth and political justice there? He can read of it in the travelling books, written by young gentlemen, with the best letters of introduction to all the consuls. They tell us what it is, a third-rate city in a stony wilderness. Will the Providence of Fashion prevent this great folly about to be perpetrated by one born to be Fashion's most brilliant subject? A folly, too, which may end in a catastrophe? His parents, indeed, have appealed in vain; but the sneer of the world will do more than the supplication of the father. A mother's tear may be disregarded, but the sigh of a mistress has changed the most obdurate. We shall see. At present Lady Constance Rawleigh expresses her pleasure at Tancred's arrival, and his heart beats a little.

CHAPTER IX.

'THEY are talking about it,' said Lord Eskdale to the duchess, as she looked up to him with an expression of the deepest interest.

'He asked St. Patrick to introduce him to her at Deloraine House, danced with her, was with her the whole evening, went to the breakfast on Saturday to meet her, instead of going to Blackwall to see a yacht he was after.'

'If it were only Katherine,' said the duchess, 'I should be quite happy.'

'Don't be uneasy,' said Lord Eskdale; 'there will be plenty of Katherines and Constances, too, before he finishes. This affair is not much, but it shows, as I foretold, that, the moment he found something more amusing, his taste for yachting would pass off.'

'You are right, you always are.'

What really was this affair, which Lord Eskdale held lightly? With a character like Tancred, everything may become important. Profound and yet simple, deep in self-knowledge yet inexperienced, his reserve, which would screen him from a thousand dangers, was just the quality which would insure his thraldom by the individual who could once effectually melt the icy barrier and reach the central heat. At this moment of his life, with all the repose, and sometimes even the high ceremony, on the surface, he was a being formed for high-reaching exploits, ready to dare everything and reckless of all consequences, if he proposed to himself an object which he believed to be just and great. This temper of mind would, in all things, have made him act with that rapidity, which is rashness with the weak, and decision with the strong. The influence of woman on him was novel. It was a disturbing influence, on which he had never counted in those dreams and visions in which there had figured more heroes than heroines. In the imaginary interviews in which he had disciplined his solitary mind, his antagonists had been statesmen, prelates, sages,

and senators, with whom he struggled and whom he vanquished.

He was not unequal in practice to his dreams. His shyness would have vanished in an instant before a great occasion; he could have addressed a public assembly; he was
capable of transacting important affairs. These were all
situations and contingencies which he had foreseen, and
which for him were not strange, for he had become acquainted with them in his reveries. But suddenly he was
arrested by an influence for which he was unprepared; a
precious stone made him stumble who was to have scaled
the Alps. Why should the voice, the glance, of another
agitate his heart? The cherubim of his heroic thoughts
not only deserted him, but he was left without the guardian
angel of his shyness. He melted, and the iceberg might
degenerate into a puddle.

Lord Eskdale drew his conclusions like a clever man of
the world, and in general he would have been right; but a
person like Tancred was in much greater danger of being
captured than a common-place youth entering life with
second-hand experience, and living among those who ruled
his opinions by their sneers and sarcasms. A malicious tale
by a spiteful woman, the chance ribaldry of a club-room
window, have often been the impure agencies which have
saved many a youth from committing a great folly; but
Tancred was beyond all these influences. If they had been
brought to bear on him, they would rather have precipi-
tated the catastrophe. His imagination would have immediately been summoned to the rescue of his offended
pride; he would have invested the object of his regard with
supernatural qualities, and consoled her for the imperti-
nence of society by his devotion.

Lady Constance was clever; she talked like a married
woman, was critical, yet easy; and having guanoed her
mind by reading French novels, had a variety of conclusions
on all social topics, which she threw forth with unfaltering
promptness, and with the well-arranged air of an im-
promptu. These were all new to Tancred, and startling.

He was attracted by the brilliancy, though he often regretted the tone, which he ascribed to the surrounding corruption from which he intended to escape, and almost wished to save her at the same time. Sometimes Tancred looked unusually serious; but at last his rare and brilliant smile beamed upon one who really admired him, was captivated by his intellect, his freshness, his difference from all around, his pensive beauty and his grave innocence. Lady Constance was free from affectation; she was frank and natural; she did not conceal the pleasure she had in his society; she conducted herself with that dignified facility, becoming a young lady who had already refused the hands of two future earls, and of the heir of the Clan-Alpins.

A short time after the déjeûner at Craven Cottage, Lord Montacute called on Lady Charmouth. She was at home, and received him with great cordiality, looking up from her frame of worsted work with a benign maternal expression; while Lady Constance, who was writing an urgent reply to a note that had just arrived, said rapidly some agreeable words of welcome, and continued her task. Tancred seated himself by the mother, made an essay in that small talk in which he was by no means practised, but Lady Charmouth helped him on without seeming to do so. The note was at length dispatched, Tancred of course still remaining at the mother's side, and Lady Constance too distant for his wishes. He had nothing to say to Lady Charmouth; he began to feel that the pleasure of feminine society consisted in talking alone to her daughter.

While he was meditating a retreat, and yet had hardly courage to rise and walk alone down a large long room, a new guest was announced. Tancred rose, and murmured good morning; and yet, somehow or other, instead of quitting the apartment, he went and seated himself by Lady Constance. It really was as much the impulse of shyness, which sought a nook of refuge, as any other feeling that actuated him; but Lady Constance seemed pleased, and said, in a low voice and in a careless tone, ' 'Tis Lady Brancepeth; do you know her? Mamma's great friend;'

which meant, you need give yourself no trouble to talk to any one but myself.

After making herself very agreeable, Lady Constance took up a book which was at hand, and said, 'Do you know this?' And Tancred, opening a volume which he had never seen, and then turning to its titlepage, found it was 'The Revelations of Chaos,' a startling work just published, and of which a rumour had reached him.

'No,' he replied; 'I have not seen it.'

'I will lend it you if you like: it is one of those books one must read. It explains everything, and is written in a very agreeable style.'

'It explains everything!' said Tancred; 'it must, indeed, be a very remarkable book!'

'I think it will just suit you,' said Lady Constance. 'Do you know, I thought so several times while I was reading it.'

'To judge from the title, the subject is rather obscure,' said Tancred.

'No longer so,' said Lady Constance. 'It is treated scientifically; everything is explained by geology and astronomy, and in that way. It shows you exactly how a star is formed; nothing can be so pretty! A cluster of vapour, the cream of the milky way, a sort of celestial cheese, churned into light, you must read it, 'tis charming.'

'Nobody ever saw a star formed,' said Tancred.

'Perhaps not. You must read the "Revelations;" it is all explained. But what is most interesting, is the way in which man has been developed. You know, all is development. The principle is perpetually going on. First, there was nothing, then there was something; then, I forget the next, I think there were shells, then fishes; then we came, let me see, did we come next? Never mind that; we came at last. And the next change there will be something very superior to us, something with wings. Ah! that's it: we were fishes, and I believe we shall be crows. But you must read it.'

'I do not believe I ever was a fish,' said Tancred.

'Oh! but it is all proved; you must not argue on my rapid sketch; read the book. It is impossible to contradict anything in it. You understand, it is all science; it is not like those books in which one says one thing and another the contrary, and both may be wrong. Everything is proved: by geology, you know. You see exactly how everything is made; how many worlds there have been; how long they lasted; what went before, what comes next. We are a link in the chain, as inferior animals were that preceded us: we in turn shall be inferior; all that will remain of us will be some relics in a new red sandstone. This is development. We had fins; we may have wings.'

Tancred grew silent and thoughtful; Lady Brancepeth moved, and he rose at the same time. Lady Charmouth looked as if it were by no means necessary for him to depart, but he bowed very low, and then bade farewell to Lady Constance, who said, 'We shall meet to-night.'

'I was a fish, and I shall be a crow,' said Tancred to himself, when the hall door closed on him. 'What a spiritual mistress! And yesterday, for a moment, I almost dreamed of kneeling with her at the Holy Sepulchre! I must get out of this city as quickly as possible; I cannot cope with its corruption. The acquaintance, however, has been of use to me, for I think I have got a yacht by it. I believe it was providential, and a trial. I will go home and write instantly to Fitzheron, and accept his offer. One hundred and eighty tons: it will do; it must.'

At this moment he met Lord Eskdale, who had observed Tancred from the end of Grosvenor Square, on the steps of Lord Charmouth's door. This circumstance ill prepared Lord Eskdale for Tancred's salutation.

'My dear lord, you are just the person I wanted to meet. You promised to recommend me a servant who had travelled in the East.'

'Well, are you in a hurry?' said Lord Eskdale, gaining time, and pumping.

'1 should like to get off as soon as practicable.'

'Humph!' said Lord Eskdale. 'Have you got a yacht?'

'I have.'

'Oh! So you want a servant?' he added, after a moment's pause.

'I mentioned that, because you were so kind as to say you could help me in that respect.'

'Ah! I did,' said Lord Eskdale, thoughtfully.

'But I want a great many things,' continued Tancred. 'I must make arrangements about money; I suppose I must get some letters; in fact, I want generally your advice.'

'What are you going to do about the colonel and the rest?'

'I have promised my father to take them,' said Tancred, 'though I feel they will only embarrass me. They have engaged to be ready at a week's notice; I shall write to them immediately. If they do not fulfil their engagement, I am absolved from mine.'

'So you have got a yacht, eh?' said Lord Eskdale. 'I suppose you have bought the "Basilisk"?'

'Exactly.'

'She wants a good deal doing to her.'

'Something, but chiefly for show, which I do not care about; but I mean to get away, and refit, if necessary, at Gibraltar. I must go.'

'Well, if you must go,' said his lordship, and then he added, 'and in such a hurry; let me see. You want a firstrate managing man, used to the East, and letters, and money, and advice. Hem! You don't know Sidonia?'

'Not at all.'

'He is the man to get hold of, but that is so difficult now. He never goes anywhere. Let me see, this is Monday; to-morrow is post-day, and I dine with him alone in the City. Well, you shall hear from me on Wednesday morning early, about everything; but I would not write to the colonel and his friends just yet.'

CHAPTER X.

WHAT is most striking in London is its vastness. It is the illimitable feeling that gives it a special character. London is not grand. It possesses only one of the qualifications of a grand city, size; but it wants the equally important one, beauty. It is the union of these two qualities that produced the grand cities, the Romes, the Babylons, the hundred portals of the Pharaohs; multitudes and magnificence; the millions influenced by art. Grand cities are unknown since the beautiful has ceased to be the principle of invention. Paris, of modern capitals, has aspired to this character; but if Paris be a beautiful city, it certainly is not a grand one; its population is too limited, and, from the nature of their dwellings, they cover a comparatively small space. Constantinople is picturesque; nature has furnished a sublime site, but it has little architectural splendour, and you reach the environs with a fatal facility. London overpowers us with its vastness.

Place a Forum or an Acropolis in its centre, and the effect of the metropolitan mass, which now has neither head nor heart, instead of being stupefying, would be ennobling. Nothing more completely represents a nation than a public building. A member of Parliament only represents at the most the united constituencies: but the Palace of the Sovereign, a National Gallery, or a Museum baptized with the name of the country, these are monuments to which all should be able to look up with pride, and which should exercise an elevating influence upon the spirit of the humblest. What is their influence in London? Let us not criticise what all condemn. But how remedy the evil? What is wanted in architecture, as in so many things, is, a man. Shall we find a refuge in a Committee of Taste? Escape from the mediocrity of one to the mediocrity of many? We only multiply our feebleness, and aggravate our deficiencies. But one suggestion might be made. No profession in England has done its duty until it has furnished its victim. The pure administration of justice dates from the deposition of Macclesfield. Even our boasted navy never achieved a great victory until we shot an admiral. Suppose an architect were hanged? Terror has its inspiration as well as competition.

Though London is vast, it is very monotonous. All those new districts that have sprung up within the last half-century, the creatures of our commercial and colonial wealth, it is impossible to conceive anything more tame, more insipid, more uniform. Pancras is like Mary-le-bone, Mary-le-bone is like Paddington; all the streets resemble each other, you must read the names of the squares before you venture to knock at a door. This amount of building capital ought to have produced a great city. What an opportunity for Architecture suddenly summoned to furnish habitations for a population equal to that of the city of Bruxelles, and a population, too, of great wealth. Mary-le-bone alone ought to have produced a revolution in our domestic architecture. It did nothing. It was built by Act of Parliament. Parliament prescribed even a façade. It is Parliament to whom we are indebted for your Glouces-ter Places, and Baker Streets, and Harley Streets, and Wimpole Streets, and all those flat, dull, spiritless streets, resembling each other like a large family of plain children, with Portland Place and Portman Square for their respect-able parents. The influence of our Parliamentary Govern-ment upon the fine arts is a subject worth pursuing. The power that produced Baker Street as a model for street architecture in its celebrated Building Act, is the power that prevented Whitehall from being completed, and which sold to foreigners all the pictures which the King of England had collected to civilise his people.

In our own days we have witnessed the rapid creation of a new metropolitan quarter, built solely for the aristocracy by an aristocrat. The Belgrave district is as monotonous as

I

Mary-le-bone; and is so contrived as to be at the same time insipid and tawdry.

Where London becomes more interesting is Charing Cross. Looking to Northumberland House, and turning your back upon Trafalgar Square, the Strand is perhaps the finest street in Europe, blending the architecture of many periods; and its river ways are a peculiar feature and rich with associations. Fleet Street, with its Temple, is not unworthy of being contiguous to the Strand. The fire of London has deprived us of the delight of a real old quarter of the city; but some bits remain, and everywhere there is a stirring multitude, and a great crush and crash of carts and wains. The Inns of Court, and the quarters in the vicinity of the port, Thames Street, Tower Hill, Billings-gate, Wapping, Rotherhithe, are the best parts of London; they are full of character : the buildings bear a nearer relation to what the people are doing than in the more polished quarters.

The old merchants of the times of the first Georges were a fine race. They knew their position, and built up to it. While the territorial aristocracy, pulling down their family hotels, were raising vulgar streets and squares upon their site, and occupying themselves one of the new tenements, the old merchants filled the straggling lanes, which con-nected the Royal Exchange with the port of London, with mansions which, if not exactly equal to the palaces of stately Venice, might at least vie with many of the hotels of old Paris. Some of these, though the great majority have been broken up into chambers and counting-houses, still remain intact.

In a long, dark, narrow, crooked street, which is still called a lane, and which runs from the south side of the street of the Lombards towards the river, there is one of these old houses of a century past, and which, both in its original design and present condition, is a noble specimen of its order. A pair of massy iron gates, of elaborate workmanship, separate the street from its spacious and airy court-yard, which is formed on either side by a wing of the mansion, itself a building of deep red brick, with a pediment, and pilasters, and copings of stone. A flight of steps leads to the lofty and central doorway; in the middle of the court there is a garden plot, inclosing a fountain, and a fine plane tree.

The stillness, doubly effective after the tumult just quitted, the lulling voice of the water, the soothing aspect of the quivering foliage, the noble building, and the cool and capacious quadrangle, the aspect even of those who enter, and frequently enter, the precinct, and who are generally young men, gliding in and out, earnest and full of thought, all contribute to give to this locality something of the classic repose of a college, instead of a place agitated with the most urgent interests of the current hour; a place that deals with the fortunes of kings and empires, and regulates the most important affairs of nations, for it is the counting-house in the greatest of modern cities of the most celebrated of modern financiers.

It was the visit of Tancred to the City, on the Wednesday morning after he had met Lord Eskdale, that occasions me to touch on some of the characteristics of our capital. It was the first time that Tancred had ever been in the City proper, and it greatly interested him. His visit was prompted by receiving, early on Wednesday morning, the following letter:

'DEAR TANCRED : I saw Sidonia yesterday, and spoke to him of what you want. He is much occupied just now, as his uncle, who attended to affairs here, is dead, and, until he can import another uncle or cousin, he must steer the ship, as times are critical. But he bade me say you might call upon him in the City to-day, at two o'clock. He lives in Sequin Court, near the Bank. You will have no difficulty in finding it. I recommend you to go, as he is the sort of man who will really understand what you mean, which neither your father nor myself do exactly; and, besides, he is a person to know.

'I inclose a line which you will send in, that there may be no mistake. I should tell you, as you are very fresh, that he is of the Hebrew race; so don't go on too much about the Holy Sepulchre.

'Yours faithfully,
'ESKDALE.'

'Spring Gardens, Wednesday morning.'

It is just where the street is most crowded, where it narrows, and losing the name of Cheapside, takes that of the Poultry, that the last of a series of stoppages occurred; a stoppage which, at the end of ten minutes, lost its inert character of mere obstruction, and developed into the livelier qualities of the row. There were oaths, contradictions, menaces: 'No, you sha'n't; Yes, I will; No, I didn't; Yes, you did; No, you hav'n't; Yes, I have;' the lashing of a whip, the interference of a policeman, a crash, a scream. Tancred looked out of the window of his brougham. He saw a chariot in distress, a chariot such as would have become an Ondine by the waters of the Serpentine, and the very last sort of equipage that you could expect to see smashed in the Poultry. It was really breaking a butterfly upon a wheel: to crush its delicate springs, and crack its dark brown panels, soil its dainty hammercloth, and endanger the lives of its young coachman in a flaxen wig, and its two tall footmen in short coats, worthy of Cinderella.

The scream, too, came from a fair owner, who was surrounded by clamorous carmen and city marshals, and who, in an unknown land, was afraid she might be put in a city Compter, because the people in the city had destroyed her beautiful chariot. Tancred let himself out of his brougham, and not without difficulty contrived, through the narrow and crowded passage formed by the two lines, to reach the chariot, which was coming the contrary way to him.

Some ruthless officials were persuading a beautiful woman to leave her carriage, the wheel of which was broken. 'But where am I to go?' she exclaimed. 'I cannot walk. I will not leave my carriage until you bring me some conveyance. You ought to punish these people, who have quite ruined my chariot.'

'They say it was your coachman's fault: we have nothing to do with that; besides, you know who they are. Their employers' name is on the cart, Brown, Bugsby, and Co., Limehouse. You can have your redress against Brown, Bugsby, and Co., Limehouse, if your coachman is not in fault; but you cannot stop up the way, and you had better get out, and let the carriage be removed to the Steel-yard.'

'What am I to do!' exclaimed the lady, with a tearful eye and agitated face.

'I have a carriage at hand,' said Tancred, who at this moment reached her, 'and it is quite at your service.'

The lady cast her beautiful eyes, with an expression of astonishment she could not conceal, at the distinguished youth who thus suddenly appeared in the midst of insolent carmen, brutal policemen, and all the cynical amateurs of a mob. Public opinion in the Poultry was against her; her coachman's wig had excited derision; the footmen had given themselves airs; there was a strong feeling against the shortcoats. As for the lady, though at first awed by her beauty and magnificence, they rebelled against the authority of her manner. Besides, she was not alone. There was a gentleman with her, who wore moustaches, and had taken a part in the proceedings at first, by addressing the carmen in French. This was too much, and the mob declared he was Don Carlos.

'You are too good,' said the lady, with a sweet expression.

Tancred opened the door of the chariot, the policemen pulled down the steps, the servants were told to do the best they could with the wrecked equipage; in a second the lady and her companion were in Tancred's brougham, who, desiring his servants to obey all their orders, disappeared, for the stoppage at this moment began to move, and there was no time for bandying compliments.

He had gained the pavement, and had made his way as far as the Mansion House, when, finding a group of public buildings, he thought it prudent to inquire which was the Bank.

'That is the Bank,' said a good-natured man, in a bustle, but taken by Tancred's unusual appearance. 'What do you want? I am going there.'

'I do not want exactly the Bank,' replied Tancred, 'but a place somewhere near it. Do you happen to know, sir, a place called Sequin Court?'

'I should think I did,' said the man, smiling. 'So you are going to Sidonia's?'

CHAPTER XI.

TANCRED entered Sequin Court; a chariot with a foreign coronet was at the foot of the great steps which he ascended. He was received by a fat hall porter, who would not have disgraced his father's establishment, and who, rising with lazy insolence from his hooded chair, when he observed that Tancred did not advance, asked the new comer what he wanted.

'I want Monsieur de Sidonia.'

'Can't see him now; he is engaged.'

'I have a note for him.'

'Very well, give it me; it will be sent in. You can sit here.' And the porter opened the door of a waiting-room, which Tancred declined to enter. 'I will wait here, thank you,' said Tancred, and he looked round at the old oak hall, on the walls of which were hung several portraits, and from which ascended one of those noble staircases never found in a modern London mansion. At the end of the hall, on a slab of porphyry, was a marble bust, with this inscription on it, ' FUNDATOR.' It was the first Sidonia, by Chantrey.

' I will wait here, thank you,' said Tancred, looking round; and then, with some hesitation, he added, ' I have an appointment here at two o'clock.'

As he spoke, that hour sounded from the belfry of an old city church that was at hand, and then was taken up by the chimes of a large German clock in the hall.

' It may be,' said the porter, ' but I can't disturb master now; the Spanish ambassador is with him, and others are waiting. When he is gone, a clerk will take in your letter with some others that are here.'

At this moment, and while Tancred remained in the hall, various persons entered, and, without noticing the porter, pursued their way across the apartment.

' And where are those persons going?' inquired Tancred.

The porter looked at the enquirer with a blended gaze of curiosity and contempt, and then negligently answered him without looking in Tancred's face, and while he was brushing up the hearth, ' Some are going to the counting-house, and some are going to the Bank, I should think.'

' I wonder if our hall porter is such an infernal bully as Monsieur de Sidonia's ! ' thought Tancred.

There was a stir. ' The ambassador is coming out,' said the hall porter; ' you must not stand in the way.'

The well-trained ear of this guardian of the gate was conversant with every combination of sound which the apartments of Sequin Court could produce. Close as the doors might be shut, you could not rise from your chair without his being aware of it; and in the present instance he was correct. A door at the end of the hall opened, and the Spanish minister came forth.

' Stand aside,' said the hall porter to Tancred; and, summoning the servants without, he ushered his excellency with some reverence to his carriage.

' Now your letter will go in with the others,' he said to Tancred, whom for a few moments he left alone, and then returned, taking no notice of our young friend, but, depositing his bulky form in his hooded chair, he resumed the city article of the ' Times.'

The letter ran thus :

' DEAR SIDONIA : This will be given you by my cousin Montacute, of whom I spoke to you yesterday. He wants to go to Jerusalem, which very much perplexes his family, for he is an only child. I don't suppose the danger is what they imagine. But still there is nothing like experience, and there is no one who knows so much of these things as yourself. I have promised his father and mother, very innocent people, whom, of all my relatives, I most affect, to do what I can for him. If, therefore, you can aid Montacute, you will really serve me. He seems to have character, though I can't well make him out. I fear I indulged in the hock yesterday, for I feel a twinge. Yours faithfully,

' Wednesday morning.'   ' ESKDALE.'

The hall clock had commenced the quarter chimes, when a young man, fair and intelligent, and wearing spectacles, came into the hall, and, opening the door of the waiting room, looked as if he expected to find some one there ; then, turning to the porter, he said, ' Where is Lord Montacute ? '

The porter rose from his hooded chair, and put down the newspaper, but Tancred had advanced when he heard his name, and bowed, and followed the young man in spectacles, who invited Tancred to accompany him.

Tancred was ushered into a spacious and rather long apartment, panelled with old oak up to the white coved ceiling, which was richly ornamented. Four windows looked upon the fountain and the plane tree. A portrait by Lawrence, evidently of the same individual who had furnished the model to Chantrey, was over the high, old-fashioned, but very handsome marble mantel-piece. A Turkey carpet, curtains of crimson damask, some large tables covered with papers, several easy chairs, against the

walls some iron cabinets, these were the furniture of the
room, at one corner of which was a glass door, which led
to a vista of apartments fitted up as counting-houses, filled
with clerks, and which, if expedient, might be covered by
a baize screen, which was now unclosed.

A gentleman writing at a table rose as he came in, and
extending his hand said, as he pointed to a seat, 'I am
afraid I have made you come out at an unusual hour.'

The young man in spectacles in the meanwhile retired;
Tancred had bowed and murmured his compliments: and
his host, drawing his chair a little from the table, continued: 'Lord Eskdale tells me that you have some thoughts
of going to Jerusalem.'

'I have for some time had that intention.'

'It is a pity that you did not set out earlier in the year,
and then you might have been there during the Easter
pilgrimage. It is a fine sight.'

'It is a pity,' said Tancred; 'but to reach Jerusalem is
with me an object of so much moment, that I shall be content to find myself there at any time, and under any circumstances.'

'It is no longer difficult to reach Jerusalem; the real
difficulty is the one experienced by the crusaders, to know
what to do when you have arrived there.'

'It is the land of inspiration,' said Tancred, slightly
blushing; 'and when I am there, I would humbly pray that
my course may be indicated to me.'

'And you think that no prayers, however humble, would
obtain for you that indication before your departure?'

'This is not the land of inspiration,' replied Tancred,
timidly.

'But you have your Church,' said Sidonia.

'Which I hold of divine institution, and which should be
under the immediate influence of the Holy Spirit,' said
Tancred, dropping his eyes, and colouring still more as he
found himself already trespassing on that delicate province
of theology, which always fascinated him, but which it had

been intimated to him by Lord Eskdale that he should avoid.

'Is it wanting to you, then, in this conjuncture?' inquired his companion.

'I find its opinions conflicting, its decrees contradictory, its conduct inconsistent,' replied Tancred. 'I have conferred with one who is esteemed its most eminent prelate, and I have left him with a conviction of what I had for some time suspected, that inspiration is not only a divine but a local quality.'

'You and I have some reason to believe so,' said Sidonia. 'I believe that God spoke to Moses on Mount Horeb, and you believe that he was crucified, in the person of Jesus, on Mount Calvary. Both were, at least carnally, children of Israel: they spoke Hebrew to the Hebrews. The prophets were only Hebrews; the apostles were only Hebrews. The churches of Asia, which have vanished, were founded by a native Hebrew; and the church of Rome, which says it shall last for ever, and which converted this island to the faith of Moses and of Christ, vanquishing the Druids, Jupiter Olympius, and Woden, who had successively invaded it, was also founded by a native Hebrew. Therefore, I say, your suspicion or your conviction is, at least, not a fantastic one.'

Tancred listened to Sidonia as he spoke with great interest, and with an earnest and now quite unembarrassed manner. The height of the argument had immediately surmounted all his social reserve. His intelligence responded to the great theme that had so long occupied his musing hours; and the unexpected character of a conversation which, as he had supposed, would have mainly treated of letters of credit, the more excited him.

'Then,' said Tancred, with animation, 'seeing how things are, that I am born in an age and in a country divided between infidelity on one side and an anarchy of creeds on the other; with none competent to guide me, yet feeling that I must believe, for I hold that duty cannot exist without faith; is it so wild as some would think it, I would say is it unreasonable, that I should wish to do that which, six centuries ago, was done by my ancestor whose name I bear, and that I should cross the seas, and ——?' He hesitated.

'And visit the Holy Sepulchre,' said Sidonia.

'And visit the Holy Sepulchre,' said Tancred, solemnly; ' for that I confess is my sovereign thought.'

'Well, the crusades were of vast advantage to Europe,' said Sidonia, ' and renovated the spiritual hold which Asia has always had upon the North. It seems to wane at present, but it is only the decrease that precedes the new development.'

'It must be so,' said Tancred; ' for who can believe that a country once sanctified by the Divine presence can ever be as other lands? Some celestial quality, distinguishing it from all other climes, must for ever linger about it. I would ask those mountains, that were reached by angels, why they no longer receive heavenly visitants. I would appeal to that Comforter promised to man, on the sacred spot on which the assurance of solace was made. I require a Comforter. I have appealed to the holy influence in vain in England. It has not visited me; I know none here on whom it has descended. I am induced, therefore, to believe that it is part of the divine scheme that its influence should be local; that it should be approached with reverence, not thoughtlessly and hurriedly, but with such difficulties and such an interval of time, as a pilgrimage to a spot sanctified can alone secure.'

Sidonia listened to Tancred with deep attention. Lord Montacute was seated opposite the windows, so that there was a full light upon the play of the countenance, the expression of which Sidonia watched, while his keen and far-reaching vision traced at the same time the formation and development of the head of his visitor. He recognised in this youth not a vain and vague visionary, but a being in whom the faculties of reason and imagination were both of the highest class, and both equally developed. He observed that he was of a nature passionately affectionate, and that he was of a singular audacity. He perceived that though, at this moment, Tancred was as ignorant of the world as a young monk, he possessed all the latent qualities which in future would qualify him to control society. When Tancred had finished speaking, there was a pause of a few seconds, during which Sidonia seemed lost in thought; then, looking up, he said, 'It appears to me, Lord Montacute, that what you want is to penetrate the great Asian mystery.'

'You have touched my inmost thought,' said Tancred, eagerly.

At this moment there entered the room, from the glass door, the same young man who had ushered Tancred into the apartment. He brought a letter to Sidonia. Lord Montacute felt confused; his shyness returned to him; he deplored the unfortunate interruption, but he felt he was in the way. He rose, and began to say good morning, when Sidonia, without taking his eyes off the letter, saw him, and waving his hand, stopped him, saying, 'I settled with Lord Eskdale that you were not to go away if anything occurred which required my momentary attention. So pray sit down, unless you have engagements.' And Tancred again seated himself.

'Write,' continued Sidonia to the clerk, 'that my letters are twelve hours later than the despatches, and that the city continued quite tranquil. Let the extract from the Berlin letter be left at the same time at the Treasury. The last bulletin ?'

'Consols drooping at half-past two; all the foreign funds lower; shares very active.'

They were once more alone.

'When do you propose going ?'

'I hope in a week.'

'Alone ?'

'I fear I shall have many attendants.'

'That is a pity. Well, wnen you arrive at Jerusalem, you will naturally go to the convent of Terra Santa. You will make there the acquaintance of the Spanish prior, Alonzo Lara. He calls me cousin; he is a Nuevo of the fourteenth century. Very orthodox; but the love of the old land and the old language have come out in him, as they will, though his blood is no longer clear, but has been modified by many Gothic intermarriages, which was never our case. We are pure Sephardim. Lara thoroughly comprehends Palestine and all that pertains to it. He has been there a quarter of a century, and might have been Archbishop of Seville. You see, he is master of the old as well as the new learning; this is very important; they often explain each other. Your bishops here know nothing about these things. How can they? A few centuries back they were tattooed savages. This is the advantage which Rome has over you, and which you never can understand. That Church was founded by a Hebrew, and the magnetic influence lingers. But you will go to the fountain head. Theology requires an apprenticeship of some thousand years at least; to say nothing of clime and race. You cannot get on with theology as you do with chemistry and mechanics. Trust me, there is something deeper in it. I shall give you a note to Lara; cultivate him, he is the man you want. You will want others; they will come; but Lara has the first key.'

I am sorry to trouble you about such things,' said Tancred, in a hesitating voice, 'but perhaps I may not have the great pleasure to see you again, and Lord Eskdale said that I was to speak to you about some letters of credit.'

'Oh! we shall meet before you go. But what you say reminds me of something. As for money, there is only one banker in Syria; he is everywhere, at Aleppo, Damascus, Beiroot, Jerusalem. It is Besso. Before the expulsion of the Egyptians, he really ruled Syria, but he is still powerful, though they have endeavoured to crush him at Con-

stantinople. I applied to Metternich about him, and, besides that, he is mine. I shall give you a letter to him, but
not merely for your money affairs. I wish you to know
him. He lives in splendour at Damascus, moderately at
Jerusalem, where there is little to do, but which he loves
as a residence, being a Hebrew. I wish you to know him.
You will, I am sure, agree with me, that he is, without
exception, the most splendid specimen of the animal man
you ever became acquainted with. His name is Adam,
and verily he looks as if he were in the garden of Eden
before the fall. But his soul is as grand and as fine as his
body. You will lean upon this man as you would on a
faithful charger. His divan is charming; you will always
find there the most intelligent people. You must learn to
smoke. There is nothing that Besso cannot do; make him
do everything you want; have no scruples; he will be
gratified. Besides, he is one of those who kiss my signet.
These two letters will open Syria to you, and any other land,
if you care to proceed. Give yourself no trouble about any
other preparations.'

'And how am I to thank you?' said Tancred, rising;
'and how am I to express to you all my gratitude?'

'What are you going to do with yourself to-morrow?'
said Sidonia. 'I never go anywhere; but I have a few
friends who are so kind as to come sometimes to me.
There are two or three persons dining with me to-morrow,
whom you might like to meet. Will you do so?'

'I shall be most proud and pleased.'

'That's well. It is not here; it is in Carlton Gardens;
at sunset.' And Sidonia continued the letter which he
was writing when Tancred entered.

CHAPTER XII.

WHEN Tancred returned home, musing, from his visit to Sidonia, he found the following note:

'Lady Bertie and Bellair returns Lord Montacute his carriage with a thousand compliments and thanks. She fears she greatly incommoded Lord Montacute, but begs to assure him how very sensible she is of his considerate courtesy.

'Upper Brook Street, Wednesday.'

The handwriting was of that form of scripture which attracts; refined yet energetic; full of character. Tancred recognised the titles of Bertie and Bellair as those of two not inconsiderable earldoms, now centred in the same individual. Lady Bertie and Bellair was herself a lady of the high nobility; a daughter of the present Duke of Fitz-Aquitaine; the son of that duke who was the father-in-law of Lord de Mowbray, and whom Lady Firebrace, the present Lady Bardolf, and Tadpole, had dexterously converted to conservatism by persuading him that he was to be Sir Robert's Irish viceroy. Lady Bertie and Bellair, therefore, was first-cousin to Lady Joan Mountchesney, and her sister, who is still Lady Maud Fitz-Warene. Tancred was surprised that he never recollected to have met before one so distinguished and so beautiful. His conversation with Sidonia, however, had driven the little adventure of the morning from his memory, and now that it was thus recalled to him, he did not dwell upon it. His being was absorbed in his paramount purpose. The sympathy of Sidonia, so complete, and as instructive as it was animating, was a sustaining power which we often need when we are meditating great deeds. How often, when all seems dark, and hopeless, and spiritless, and tame, when slight obstacles figure in the cloudy landscape as Alps, and the rushing cataracts of our invention have subsided into drizzle, a single phrase of a great man instantaneously flings sunshine on the intellectual landscape, and the habitual features of power and beauty, over which we have so long mused in secret confidence and love, resume all their energy and lustre.

The haunting thought that occasionally, notwithstanding his strong will, would perplex the soul and agitate the heart of Tancred; the haunting thought that, all this time, he was perhaps the dupe of boyish fantasies, was laid to-day. Sometimes he had felt, Why does no one sympathise with my views; why, though they treat them with conventional respect, is it clear that all I have addressed hold them to be absurd? My parents are pious and instructed; they are predisposed to view everything I say, or do, or think, with an even excessive favour. They think me moonstruck. Lord Eskdale is a perfect man of the world; proverbially shrewd, and celebrated for his judgment; he looks upon me as a raw boy, and believes that, if my father had kept me at Eton and sent me to Paris, I should by this time have exhausted my crudities. The bishop is what the world calls a great scholar; he is a statesman who, aloof from faction, ought to be accustomed to take just and comprehensive views; and a priest who ought to be under the immediate influence of the Holy Spirit. He says I am a visionary. All this might well be disheartening; but now comes one whom no circumstances impel to judge my project with indulgence; who would, at the first glance, appear to have many prejudices arrayed against it, who knows more of the world than Lord Eskdale, and who appears to me to be more learned than the whole bench of bishops, and he welcomes my ideas, approves my conclusions, sympathises with my suggestions; developes, illustrates, enforces them; plainly intimates that I am only on the threshold of initiation, and would aid me to advance to the innermost mysteries.

There was this night a great ball at Lady Bardolf's, in Belgrave Square. One should generally mention localities, because very often they indicate character. Lady Bardolf

lived next door to Mrs. Guy Flouncey. Both had risen in
the world, though it requires some esoteric knowledge to
recognise the patrician parvenue ; and both had finally
settled themselves down in the only quarter which Lady
Bardolf thought worthy of her new coronet, and Mrs. Guy
Flouncey of her new visiting list.

Lady Bardolf had given up the old family mansion of
the Firebraces in Hanover Square, at the same time that she
had resigned their old title. Politics being dead, in consequence of the majority of 1841, who, after a little kicking
for the million, satisfactorily assured the minister that there
was no vice in them, Lady Bardolf had chalked out a new
career, and one of a still more eminent and exciting character than her previous pursuit. Lady Bardolf was one
of those ladies, there are several, who entertain the curious
idea that they need only to be known in certain high
quarters, to be immediately selected as the principal objects
of court favour. Lady Bardolf was always putting herself
in the way of it , she never lost an opportunity ; she never
missed a drawing-room, contrived to be at all the court
balls, plotted to be invited to a costume fête, and expended
the tactics of a campaign to get asked to some grand
château honoured by august presence. Still Her Majesty
had not yet sent for Lady Bardolf. She was still very good
friends with Lord Masque, for he had social influence, and
could assist her ; but as for poor Tadpole, she had sadly
neglected him, his sphere being merely political, and that
being no longer interesting. The honest gentleman still
occasionally buzzed about her, slavering portentous stories
about malcontent country gentlemen, mumbling Maynooth,
and shaking his head at Young England. Tadpole was
wont to say in confidence, that for his part he wished Sir
Robert had left alone religion and commerce, and confined
himself to finance, which was his forte as long as he had a
majority to carry the projects which he found in the pigeon-
holes of the Treasury, and which are always at the service
of every minister.

K

Well, it was at Lady Bardolf's ball, close upon midnight, that Tancred, who had not long entered, and had not very far advanced in the crowded saloons, turning his head, recognised his heroine of the morning, his still more recent correspondent, Lady Bertie and Bellair. She was speaking to Lord Valentine. It was impossible to mistake her; rapid as had been his former observation of her face, it was too remarkable to be forgotten, though the captivating details were only the result of his present more advantageous inspection. A small head and large dark eyes, dark as her rich hair which was quite unadorned, a pale but delicate complexion, small pearly teeth, were charms that crowned a figure rather too much above the middle height, yet undulating and not without grace. Her countenance was calm without being grave; she smiled with her eyes.

She was for a moment alone; she looked round, and recognised Tancred; she bowed to him with a beaming glance. Instantly he was at her side.

'Our second meeting to-day,' she said, in a low, sweet voice.

'How came it that we never met before?' he replied.

'I have just returned from Paris; the first time I have been out; and, had it not been for you,' she added, 'I should not have been here to-night. I think they would have put me in prison.'

'Lady Bardolf ought to be very much obliged to me, and so ought the world.'

'I am,' said Lady Bertie and Bellair.

'That is worth everything else,' said Tancred.

'What a pretty carriage you have! I do not think I shall ever get into mine again. I am almost glad they have destroyed my chariot. I am sure I shall never be able to drive in anything else now except a brougham.'

'Why did you not keep mine?'

'You are magnificent; too gorgeous and oriental for these cold climes. You shower your presents as if you were in the East, which Lord Valentine tells me you are about to visit. When do you leave us?'

' I think of going immediately.'

'Indeed!' said Lady Bertie and Bellair, and her countenance changed. There was a pause, and then she continued playfully, yet as it were half in sadness, ' I almost
wish you had not come to my rescue this morning.'

'And why?'

'Because I do not like to make agreeable acquaintances
only to lose them.'

' I think that I am most to be pitied,' said Tancred.

'You are wearied of the world very soon. Before you
can know us, you leave us.'

' I am not wearied of the world, for indeed, as you say,
I know nothing of it. I am here by accident, as you were
in the stoppage to-day. It will disperse, and then I shall
get on.'

' Lord Valentine tells me that you are going to realise
my dream of dreams, that you are going to Jerusalem.'

'Ah!' said Tancred, kindling, ' you too have felt that
want?'

' But I never can pardon myself for not having satisfied
it,' said Lady Bertie and Bellair in a mournful tone, and
looking in his face with her beautiful dark eyes. ' It is
the mistake of my life, and now can never be remedied.
But I have no energy. I ought, as a girl, when they opposed my purpose, to have taken up my palmer's staff, and
never have rested content till I had gathered my shell on
the strand of Joppa.'

' It is the right feeling,' said Tancred. ' I am persuaded
we ought all to go.'

' But we remain here,' said the lady, in a tone of suppressed and elegant anguish; ' here, where we all complain of our hopeless lives; with not a thought beyond the
passing hour, yet all bewailing its wearisome and insipid
moments.'

' Our lot is cast in a material age,' said Tancred.

' The spiritual can alone satisfy me,' said Lady Bertie
and Bellair.

'Because you have a soul,' continued Tancred, with animation, 'still of a celestial hue. They are rare in the nineteenth century. Nobody now thinks about heaven. They never dream of angels. All their existence is concentrated in steamboats and railways.'

'You are right,' said the lady, earnestly; 'and you fly from it.'

'I go for other purposes; I would say even higher ones,' said Tancred.

'I can understand you; your feelings are my own. Jerusalem has been the dream of my life. I have always been endeavouring to reach it, but somehow or other I never got further than Paris.'

'And yet it is very easy now to get to Jerusalem, said Tancred; 'the great difficulty, as a very remarkable man said to me this morning, is to know what to do when you are there.'

'Who said that to you?' inquired Lady Bertie and Bellair, bending her head.

'It was the person I was going to call upon when I met you; Monsieur de Sidonia.'

'Monsieur de Sidonia!' said the lady, with animation. 'Ah! you know him?'

'Not as much as I could wish. I saw him to-day for the first time. My cousin, Lord Eskdale, gave me a letter of introduction to him, for his advice and assistance about my journey. Sidonia has been a great traveller.'

'There is no person I wish to know so much as M. de Sidonia,' said Lady Bertie and Bellair. 'He is a great friend of Lord Eskdale's, I think? I must get Lord Eskdale,' she added, musingly, 'to give me a little dinner, and ask M. de Sidonia to meet me.'

He never goes anywhere; at least I have heard so,' said Tancred.

'He once used to do, and to give us great fêtes. I remember hearing of them before I was out. We must make him resume them. He is immensely rich.'

'1 dare say he may be,' said Tancred. ' I wonder how a man with his intellect and ideas can think of the accumulation of wealth.'

' 'Tis his destiny,' said Lady Bertie. 'He can no more disembarrass himself of his hereditary millions, than a dynasty of the cares of empire. I wonder if he will get the Great Northern. They talked of nothing else at Paris.'

' Of what ? ' said Tancred.

' Oh! let us talk of Jerusalem!' said Lady Bertie and Bellair. 'Ah, here is Augustus! Let me make you and my husband acquainted.'

Tancred almost expected to see the moustached companion of the morning, but it was not so. Lord Bertie and Bellair was a tall, thin, distinguished, withered-looking young man, who thanked Tancred for his courtesy of the morning with a sort of gracious negligence, and, after some easy talk, asked Tancred to dine with them on the morrow. He was engaged, but he promised to call on Lady Bertie and Bellair immediately, and see some drawings of the Holy Land.

CHAPTER XIII.

PASSING through a marble antechamber, Tancred was ushered into an apartment half saloon and half library; the choicely-bound volumes, which were not too numerous, were ranged on shelves inlaid in the walls, so that they ornamented, without diminishing, the apartment. These walls were painted in encaustic, corresponding with the coved ceiling, which was richly adorned in the same fashion. A curtain of violet velvet covering if necessary the large window, which looked upon a balcony full of flowers, and the umbrageous Park; an Axminster carpet, manufactured to harmonise both in colour and design with the rest of the chamber; a profusion of luxurious seats; a large table of ivory marquetry, bearing a carved silver bell which once belonged to a pope; a Naiad, whose golden urn served as an inkstand; some daggers that acted as paper cutters, and some French books just arrived; a group of beautiful vases recently released from an Egyptian tomb and ranged on a tripod of malachite: the portrait of a statesman, and the bust of an emperor, and a sparkling fire, were all circumstances which made the room both interesting and comfortable in which Sidonia welcomed Tancred and introduced him to a guest who had preceded him, Lord Henry Sidney.

It was a name that touched Tancred, as it has all the youth of England, significant of a career that would rescue public life from that strange union of lax principles and contracted sympathies which now form the special and degrading features of British politics. It was borne by one whose boyhood we have painted amid the fields and schools of Eton, and the springtime of whose earliest youth we traced by the sedgy waters of the Cam. We left him on the threshold of public life; and, in four years, Lord Henry had created that reputation which now made him a source of hope and solace to millions of his countrymen. But they were four years of labour which outweighed the usual exertions of public men in double that space. His regular attendance in the House of Commons alone had given him as much Parliamentary experience as fell to the lot of many of those who had been first returned in 1837, and had been, therefore, twice as long in the House. He was not only a vigilant member of public and private committees, but had succeeded in appointing and conducting several on topics which he esteemed of high importance. Add to this, that he took an habitual part in debate, and was a frequent and effective public writer; and we are furnished with an additional testimony, if that indeed were wanting, that there is no incentive to exertion like the passion for a noble renown. Nor should it be forgotten, that, in all he accomplished, he had but one final purpose, and that the highest. The debate, the committee, the article in the Journal or the Review, the public meeting, the private research, these were all means to advance that which he had proposed as the object of his public life, namely to elevate the condition of the people.

Although there was no public man whose powers had more rapidly ripened, still it was interesting to observe that their maturity had been faithful to the healthy sympathies of his earlier years. The boy, whom we have traced intent upon the revival of the pastimes of the people, had expanded into the statesman, who, in a profound and comprehensive investigation of the elements of public wealth, had shown that a jaded population is not a source of national prosperity. What had been a picturesque emotion had now become a statistical argument. The material system that proposes the supply of constant toil to a people as the perfection of polity, had received a staggering blow from the exertions of a young patrician, who announced his belief that labour had its rights as well as its duties. What was excellent about Lord Henry was, that he was not a mere philanthropist, satisfied to rouse public attention to a great social evil, or instantly to suggest for it some crude remedy.

A scholar and a man of the world, learned in history and not inexperienced in human nature, he was sensible that we must look to the constituent principles of society for the causes and the cures of great national disorders. He therefore went deeply into the question, nor shrank from investigating how far those disorders were produced by the operation or the desuetude of ancient institutions, and how far it might be necessary to call new influences into political existence for their remedy. Richly informed, still studious, fond of labour and indefatigable, of a gentle disposition though of an ardent mind, calm yet energetic, very open to conviction, but possessing an inflexibility amounting even to obstinacy when his course was once taken, a ready and improving speaker, an apt and attrac-

tive writer, affable and sincere, and with the undesigning
faculty of making friends, Lord Henry seemed to possess
all the qualities of a popular leader, if we add to them the
golden ones, high lineage, an engaging appearance, youth,
and a temperament in which the reason had not been developed to the prejudice of the heart.

'And when do you start for the Holy Land?' said Lord
Henry to Tancred, in a tone and with a countenance which
proved his sympathy.

'I have clutched my staff, but the caravan lingers.'

'I envy you!'

'Why do you not go?'

Lord Henry slightly shrugged his shoulders, and said,
'It is too late. I have begun my work and I cannot
leave it.'

'If a Parliamentary career could save this country,' said
Tancred, 'I am sure you would be a public benefactor. I
have observed what you and Mr. Coningsby and some of
your friends have done and said, with great interest. But
Parliament seems to me to be the very place which a man
of action should avoid. A Parliamentary career, that old
superstition of the eighteenth century, was important when
there were no other sources of power and fame. An aristocracy at the head of a people whom they had plundered of
their means of education, required some cultivated tribunal
whose sympathy might stimulate their intelligence and
satisfy their vanity. Parliament was never so great as
when they debated with closed doors. The public opinion,
of which they never dreamed, has superseded the rhetorical
club of our great-grandfathers. They know this well
enough, and try to maintain their unnecessary position by
affecting the character of men of business, but amateur men
of business are very costly conveniences. In this age it
is not Parliament that does the real work. It does not
govern Ireland, for example. If the manufacturers want
to change a tariff, they form a commercial league, and they
effect their purpose. It is the same with the abolition of

slavery, and all our great revolutions. Parliament has become as really insignificant as for two centuries it has kept the monarch. O'Connell has taken a good share of its power; Cobden has taken another; and I am inclined to believe,' said Tancred, 'though I care little about it, that, if our order had any spirit or prescience, they would put themselves at the head of the people, and take the rest.'

'Coningsby dines here to-day,' said Sidonia, who, unobserved, had watched Tancred as he spoke, with a searching glance.

'Notwithstanding what you say,' said Lord Henry, smiling, 'I wish I could induce you to remain and help us. You would be a great ally.'

'I go to a land,' said Tancred, 'that has never been blessed by that fatal drollery called a representative government, though Omniscience once deigned to trace out the polity which should rule it.'

At this moment the servant announced Lord and Lady Marney.

Political sympathy had created a close intimacy between Lord Marney and Coningsby. They were necessary to each other. They were both men entirely devoted to public affairs, and sitting in different Houses, both young, and both masters of fortunes of the first class, they were indicated as individuals who hereafter might take a lead, and, far from clashing, would co-operate with each other. Through Coningsby the Marneys had become acquainted with Sidonia, who liked them both, particularly Sybil. Although received by society with open arms, especially by the high nobility, who affected to look upon Sybil quite as one of themselves, Lady Marney, notwithstanding the homage that everywhere awaited her, had already shown a disposition to retire as much as possible within the precinct of a chosen circle.

This was her second season, and Sybil ventured to think that she had made, in the general gaieties of her first, a sufficient oblation to the genius of fashion, and the immediate requirements of her social position. Her life was faithful to its first impulse. Devoted to the improvement of the condition of the people, she was the moving spring of the charitable development of this great city. Her house, without any pedantic effort, had become the focus of a refined society, who, though obliged to show themselves for the moment in the great carnival, wear their masks, blow their trumpets, and pelt the multitude with sugar-plums, were glad to find a place where they could at all times divest themselves of their mummery, and return to their accustomed garb of propriety and good taste.

Sybil, too, felt alone in the world. Without a relation, without an acquaintance of early and other days, she clung to her husband with a devotion which was peculiar as well as profound. Egremont was to her more than a husband and a lover; he was her only friend; it seemed to Sybil that he could be her only friend. The disposition of Lord Marney was not opposed to the habits of his wife. Men, when they are married, often shrink from the glare and bustle of those social multitudes which are entered by bachelors with the excitement of knights-errant in a fairy wilderness, because they are supposed to be rife with adventures, and, perhaps, fruitful of a heroine. The adventure sometimes turns out to be a catastrophe, and the heroine a copy instead of an original; but let that pass.

Lord Marney liked to be surrounded by those who sympathised with his pursuit; and his pursuit was politics, and politics on a great scale. The common-place career of official distinction was at his command. A great peer, with abilities and ambition, a good speaker, supposed to be a Conservative, he might soon have found his way into the cabinet, and, like the rest, have assisted in registering the decrees of one too powerful individual. But Lord Marney had been taught to think at a period of life when he little dreamed of the responsibility which fortune had in store for him.

The change in his position had not altered the conclusions

at which he had previously arrived. He held that the state of England, notwithstanding the superficies of a material prosperity, was one of impending doom, unless it were timely arrested by those who were in high places. A man of fine mind rather than of brilliant talents, Lord Marney found, in the more vivid and impassioned intelligence of Coningsby, the directing sympathy which he required. Tadpole looked upon his lordship as little short of insane. 'Do you see that man?' he would say, as Lord Marney rode by. 'He might be Privy Seal, and he throws it all away for the nonsense of Young England!'

Mrs. Coningsby entered the room almost on the footsteps of the Marneys.

'I am in despair about Harry,' she said, as she gave a finger to Sidonia, 'but he told me not to wait for him later than eight. I suppose he is kept at the House. Do you know anything of him, Lord Henry?'

'You may make yourself quite easy about him,' said Lord Henry. 'He promised Vava our to support a motion which he has to-day, and perhaps speak on it. I ought to be there too, but Charles Buller told me there would certainly be no division, and so I ventured to pair off with him.'

'He will come with Vavasour,' said Sidonia, 'who makes up our party. They will be here before we have seated ourselves.'

The gentleman had exchanged the usual inquiry, whether there was anything new to-day, without waiting for the answer. Sidonia introduced Tancred and Lord Marney.

'And what have you been doing to-day?' said Edith to Sybil, by whose side she had seated herself. 'Lady Bardolf did nothing last night but *gronder* me, because you never go to her parties. In vain I said that you looked upon her as the most odious of her sex, and her balls the pest of society. She was not in the least satisfied. And how is Gerard?'

'Why, we really have been very uneasy about him,' said

Lady Marney, 'but the last bulletin,' she added, with a
smile, 'announces a tooth.'

'Next year you must give him a pony, and let him ride
with my Harry; I mean my little Harry, Harry of Monmouth I call him; he is so like a portrait Mr. Coningsby
has of his grandfather, the same debauched look.'

'Your dinner is served, sir!'

Sidonia offered his hand to Lady Marney; Edith was
attended by Tancred. A door at the end of the room
opened into a marble corridor, which led to the dining-
room, decorated in the same style as the library. It was a
suite of apartments which Sidonia used for an intimate
circle like the present.

CHAPTER XIV.

THEY seated themselves at a round table, on which everything seemed brilliant and sparkling; nothing heavy,
nothing oppressive. There was scarcely anything that
Sidonia disliked so much as a small table, groaning, as it is
aptly termed, with plate. He shrunk from great masses of
gold and silver; gigantic groups, colossal shields, and mobs
of tankards and flagons; and never used them except on
great occasions, when the banquet assumes an Egyptian
character, and becomes too vast for refinement. At present, the dinner was served on Sevres porcelain of Rose du
Barri, raised on airy golden stands of arabesque workmanship; a mule bore your panniers of salt, or a sea-nymph
proffered it you on a shell just fresh from the ocean, or you
found it in a bird's nest; by every guest a different pattern.
In the centre of the table, mounted on a pedestal, was a
group of pages in Dresden china. Nothing could be more
gay than their bright cloaks and flowing plumes, more
elaborately exquisite than their laced shirts and rosettes, or
more fantastically saucy than their pretty affected faces, as

each, with extended arm, held a light to a guest. The room was otherwise illumined from the sides.

The guests had scarcely seated themselves when the two absent ones arrived.

'Well, you did not divide, Vavasour,' said Lord Henry.

'Did I not?' said Vavasour; 'and nearly beat the Government. You are a pretty fellow!'

'I was paired.'

'With some one who could not stay. Your brother, Mrs. Coningsby, behaved like a man, sacrificed his dinner, and made a capital speech.'

'Oh! Oswald, did he speak? Did you speak, Harry?'

'No; I voted. There was too much speaking as it was; if Vavasour had not replied, I believe we should have won.'

'But then, my dear fellow, think of my points; think how they laid themselves open!'

'A majority is always the best repartee,' said Coningsby.

'I have been talking with Montacute,' whispered Lord Henry to Coningsby, who was seated next to him. 'Wonderful fellow! You can conceive nothing richer! Very wild, but all the right ideas; exaggerated of course. You must get hold of him after dinner.'

'But they say he is going to Jerusalem'

'But he will return.'

'I do not know that; even Napoleon regretted that he had ever re-crossed the Mediterranean. The East is a career.'

Mr. Vavasour was a social favourite; a poet and a real poet, and a troubadour, as well as a member of Parliament; travelled, sweet-tempered, and good-hearted; amusing and clever. With catholic sympathies and an eclectic turn of mind, Mr. Vavasour saw something good in everybody and everything, which is certainly amiable, and perhaps just, but disqualifies a man in some degree for the business of life, which requires for its conduct a certain degree of prejudice. Mr. Vavasour's breakfasts were renowned. Whatever your creed, class, or country, one might almost add your character, you were a welcome guest at his matutinal meal, provided you were celebrated. That qualification, however, was rigidly enforced.

It not rarely happened that never were men more incongruously grouped. Individuals met at his hospitable house who had never met before, but who for years had been cherishing in solitude mutual detestation, with all the irritable exaggeration of the literary character. Vavasour liked to be the Amphitryon of a cluster of personal enemies. He prided himself on figuring as the social medium by which rival reputations became acquainted, and paid each other in his presence the compliments which veiled their ineffable disgust. All this was very well at his rooms in the Albany, and only funny; but when he collected his menageries at his ancestral hall in a distant county, the sport sometimes became tragic.

A real philosopher, alike from his genial disposition and from the influence of his rich and various information, Vavasour moved amid the strife, sympathising with every one; and perhaps, after all, the philanthropy which was his boast was not untinged by a dash of humour, of which rare and charming quality he possessed no inconsiderable portion. Vavasour liked to know everybody who was known, and to see everything which ought to be seen. He also was of opinion that everybody who was known ought to know him; and that the spectacle, however splendid or exciting, was not quite perfect without his presence.

His life was a gyration of energetic curiosity; an insatiable whirl of social celebrity. There was not a congregation of sages and philosophers in any part of Europe which he did not attend as a brother. He was present at the camp of Kalisch in his yeomanry uniform, and assisted at the festivals of Barcelona in an Andalusian jacket. He was everywhere, and at everything; he had gone down in a diving-bell and gone up in a balloon. As for his acquaintances, he was welcomed in every land; his universal sympathies seemed omnipotent. Emperor and king, jacobin and carbonaro, alike cherished him. He was the steward of Polish balls and the vindicator of Russian humanity; he dined with Louis Philippe, and gave dinners to Louis Blanc.

This was a dinner of which the guests came to partake. Though they delighted in each other's society, their meetings were not so rare that they need sacrifice the elegant pleasures of a refined meal for the opportunity of conversation. They let that take its chance, and ate and drank without affectation. Nothing so rare as a female dinner where people eat, and few things more delightful. On the present occasion, some time elapsed, while the admirable performances of Sidonia's cook were discussed, with little interruption; a burst now and then from the ringing voice of Mrs. Coningsby crossing a lance with her habitual opponent, Mr. Vavasour, who, however, generally withdrew from the skirmish when a fresh dish was handed to him.

At length, the second course being served, Mrs. Coningsby said, 'I think you have all eaten enough: I have a piece of information for you. There is going to be a costume ball at the Palace.'

This announcement produced a number of simultaneous remarks and exclamations. 'When was it to be? What was it to be? An age, or a country; or an olio of all ages and all countries?'

'An age is a masquerade,' said Sidonia. 'The more contracted the circle, the more perfect the illusion.'

'Oh, no!' said Vavasour, shaking his head. 'An age is the thing; it is a much higher thing. What can be finer than to represent the spirit of an age?'

'And Mr. Vavasour to perform the principal part,' said Mrs. Coningsby. 'I know exactly what he means. He wants to dance the Polka as Petrarch, and find a Laura in every partner.'

'You have no poetical feeling,' said Mr. Vavasour, waving his hand. 'I have often told you so.'

'You will easily find Lauras, Mr. Vavasour, if you often write such beautiful verses as I have been reading to-day,' said Lady Marney.

'You, on the contrary,' said Mr. Vavasour, bowing, 'have a great deal of poetic feeling, Lady Marney; I have always said so.'

'But give us your news, Edith,' said Coningsby. 'Imagine our suspense, when it is a question, whether we are all to look picturesque or quizzical.'

'Ah, you want to know whether you can go as Cardinal Mazarin, or the Duke of Ripperda, Harry. I know exactly what you all are now thinking of; whether you will draw the prize in the forthcoming lottery, and get exactly the epoch and the character which suit you. Is it not so, Lord Montacute? Would not you like to practise a little with your crusados at the Queen's ball, before you go to the Holy Sepulchre?'

'I would rather hear your description of it,' said Tancred.

'Lord Henry, I see, is half inclined to be your companion as a Redcross Knight,' continued Edith. 'As for Lady Marney, she is the successor of Mrs. Fry, and would wish, I am sure, to go to the ball as her representative.'

'And pray what are you thinking of being?' said Mr. Vavasour. 'We should like very much to be favoured with Mrs. Coningsby's ideal of herself.'

'Mrs. Coningsby leaves the ideal to poets. She is quite satisfied to remain what she is, and it is her intention to do so, though she means to go to Her Majesty's ball.'

'I see that you are in the secret,' said Lord Marney.

'If I could only keep secrets, I might turn out something,' said Mrs. Coningsby. 'I am the depositary of so much that is occult—joys, sorrows, plots, and scrapes; but I always tell Harry, and he always betrays me. Well, you must guess a little. Lady Marney begins.'

'Well, we were at one at Turin,' said Lady Marney, 'and it was oriental, Lalla Rookh. Are you to be a sultana?'

Mrs. Coningsby shook her head.

'Come, Edith,' said her husband ; 'if you know, which I doubt ——'

'Oh ! you doubt ——'

'Valentine told me yesterday,' said Mr. Vavasour, in a mock peremptory tone, ' that there would not be a ball.'

'And Lord Valentine told me yesterday that there would be a ball, and what the ball would be ; and what is more, I have fixed on my dress,' said Mrs. Coningsby.

'Such a rapid decision proves that much antiquarian research is not necessary,' said Sidonia. 'Your period is modern.'

'Ah !' said Edith, looking at Sidonia, 'he always finds me out. Well, Mr. Vavasour, you will not be able to crown yourself with a laurel wreath, for the gentlemen will wear wigs.'

'Louis Quatorze ?' said her husband. 'Peel as Louvois.'

'No, Sir Robert would be content with nothing less than Le Grand Colbert, rue Richelieu, No. 15, grand magasin de nouveautés très-anciennes : prix fixe, avec quelques rabais.'

'A description of Conservatism,' said Coningsby.

The secret was soon revealed : every one had a conjecture and a commentary : gentlemen in wigs, and ladies powdered, patched, and sacked. Vavasour pondered somewhat dolefully on the anti-poetic spirit of the age ; Coningsby hailed him as the author of Leonidas.

'And you, I suppose, will figure as one of the " boys " arrayed against the great Sir Robert ?' said Mr. Vavasour, with a countenance of mock veneration for that eminent personage.

'The " boys " beat him at last,' said Coningsby ; and then, with a rapid precision and a richness of colouring which were peculiar to him, he threw out a sketch which placed the period before them ; and they began to tear it to tatters, select the incidents, and apportion the characters.

Two things which are necessary to a perfect dinner are noiseless attendants, and a precision in serving the various dishes of each course, so that they may all be placed upon

L

the table at the same moment. A deficiency in these respects produces that bustle and delay which distract many an agreeable conversation and spoil many a pleasant dish. These two excellent characteristics were never wanting at the dinners of Sidonia. At no house was there less parade. The appearance of the table changed as if by the waving of a wand, and silently as a dream. And at this moment, the dessert being arranged, fruits and their beautiful companions, flowers, reposed in alabaster baskets raised on silver stands of filagree work.

There was half an hour of merry talk, graceful and gay : a good story, a bon-mot fresh from the mint, some raillery like summer lightning, vivid but not scorching.

' And now,' said Edith, as the ladies rose to return to the library, ' and now we leave you to Maynooth.'

' By-the-bye, what do they say to it in your House, Lord Marney ? ' inquired Henry Sidney, filling his glass.

' It will go down,' said Lord Marney. ' A strong dose for some, but they are used to potent potions.'

' The bishops, they say, have not made up their minds.'

' Fancy bishops not having made up their minds,' exclaimed Tancred : ' the only persons who ought never to doubt.'

' Except when they are offered a bishopric,' said Lord Marney.

' Why I like this Maynooth project,' said Tancred, ' though otherwise it little interests me, is, that all the shopkeepers are against it.'

' Don't tell that to the minister,' said Coningsby, ' or he will give up the measure.'

' Well, that is the very reason,' said Vavasour, ' why, though otherwise inclined to the grant, I hesitate as to my vote. I have the highest opinion of the shopkeepers ; I sympathise even with their prejudices. They are the class of the age ; they represent its order, its decency, its industry.'

' And you represent them,' said Coningsby. ' Vavasour is the quintessence of order, decency, and industry.'

'You may jest,' said Vavasour, shaking his head with a spice of solemn drollery; 'but public opinion must and ought to be respected, right or wrong.'

'What do you mean by public opinion?' said Tancred.

'The opinion of the reflecting majority,' said Vavasour.

'Those who don't read your poems,' said Coningsby.

'Boy, boy!' said Vavasour, who could endure raillery from one he had been at college with, but who was not over-pleased at Coningsby selecting the present occasion to claim his franchise, when a new man was present like Lord Montacute, on whom Vavasour naturally wished to produce an impression. It must be owned that it was not, as they say, very good taste in the husband of Edith, but prosperity had developed in Coningsby a native vein of sauciness which it required all the solemnity of the senate to repress. Indeed, even there, upon the benches, with a grave face, he often indulged in quips and cranks, that convulsed his neighbouring audience, who often, amid the long dreary nights of statistical imposture, sought refuge in his gay sarcasms, his airy personalities, and happy quotations.

'I do not see how there can be opinion without thought,' said Tancred; 'and I do not believe the public ever think. How can they? They have no time. Certainly we live at present under the empire of general ideas, which are extremely powerful. But the public have not invented those ideas. They have adopted them from convenience. No one has confidence in himself; on the contrary, every one has a mean idea of his own strength and has no reliance on his own judgment. Men obey a general impulse, they bow before an external necessity, whether for resistance or action. Individuality is dead; there is a want of inward and personal energy in man; and that is what people feel and mean when they go about complaining there is no faith.'

'You would hold, then,' said Henry Sidney, 'that the progress of public liberty marches with the decay of personal greatness?'

'It would seem so.'

'But the majority will always prefer public liberty to personal greatness,' said Lord Marney.

'But, without personal greatness, you never would have had public liberty,' said Coningsby.

'After all, it is civilisation that you are kicking against,' said Vavasour.

'I do not understand what you mean by civilisation,' said Tancred.

'The progressive development of the faculties of man,' said Vavasour.

'Yes, but what is progressive development?' said Sidonia; 'and what are the faculties of man? If development be progressive, how do you account for the state of Italy? One will tell you it is superstition, indulgences, and the Lady of Loretto; yet three centuries ago, when all these influences were much more powerful, Italy was the soul of Europe. The less prejudiced, a Puseyite for example, like our friend Vavasour, will assure us that the state of Italy has nothing to do with the spirit of its religion, but that it is entirely an affair of commerce; a revolution of commerce has convulsed its destinies. I cannot forget that the world was once conquered by Italians who had no commerce. Has the development of Western Asia been progressive? It is a land of tombs and ruins. Is China progressive, the most ancient and numerous of existing societies? Is Europe itself progressive? Is Spain a tithe as great as she was? Is Germany as great as when she invented printing; as she was under the rule of Charles the Fifth? France herself laments her relative inferiority to the past. But England flourishes. Is it what you call civilisation that makes England flourish? Is it the universal development of the faculties of man that has rendered an island, almost unknown to the ancients, the arbiter of the world? Clearly not. It is her inhabitants that have done this; it is an affair of race. A Saxon race, protected by an insular position, has stamped its diligent and methodic character on the century. And when a superior race, with a superior idea to Work and Order, advances, its state will be progressive, and we shall, perhaps, follow the example of the desolate countries. All is race; there is no other truth.'

'Because it includes all others?' said Lord Henry.

'You have said it.'

'As for Vavasour's definition of civilisation,' said Coningsby, 'civilisation was more advanced in ancient than modern times; then what becomes of the progressive principle? Look at the great centuries of the Roman Empire! You had two hundred millions of human beings governed by a jurisprudence so philosophical that we have been obliged to adopt its laws, and living in perpetual peace. The means of communication, of which we now make such a boast, were far more vast and extensive in those days. What were the Great Western and the London and Birmingham to the Appian and Flaminian roads? After two thousand five hundred years, parts of these are still used. A man under the Antonines might travel from Paris to Antioch with as much ease and security as we go from London to York. As for free trade, there never was a really unshackled commerce except in the days when the whole of the Mediterranean coasts belonged to one power. What a chatter there is now about the towns, and how their development is cited as the peculiarity of the age, and the great security for public improvement. Why, the Roman Empire was the empire of great cities. Man was then essentially municipal.'

'What an empire!' said Sidonia. 'All the superior races in all the superior climes.'

'But how does all this accord with your and Coningsby's favourite theory of the influence of individual character?' said Vavasour to Sidonia; 'which I hold, by-the-bye,' he added rather pompously, 'to be entirely futile.'

'What is individual character but the personification of race,' said Sidonia, 'its perfection and choice exemplar? Instead of being an inconsistency, the belief in the influence

of the individual is a corollary of the original proposition.'

'I look upon a belief in the influence of individual character as a barbarous superstition,' said Vavasour.

'Vavasour believes that there would be no heroes if there
were a police,' said Coningsby; 'but I believe that civilisation is only fatal to minstrels, and that is the reason now
we have no poets.'

'How do you account for the Polish failure in 1831?'
said Lord Marney. 'They had a capital army, they were
backed by the population, but they failed. They had everything but a man.'

'Why were the Whigs smashed in 1834,' said Coningsby,
'but because they had not a man?'

'What is the real explanation of the state of Mexico?' said
Sidonia. 'It has not a man.'

'So much for progress since the days of Charles the Fifth,'
said Henry Sidney. 'The Spaniards then conquered Mexico,
and now they cannot govern it.'

'So much for race,' said Vavasour. 'The race is the
same; why are not the results the same?'

'Because it is worn out,' said Sidonia. 'Why do not
the Ethiopians build another Thebes, or excavate the colossal temples of the cataracts? The decay of a race is an
inevitable necessity, unless it lives in deserts and never
mixes its blood.'

CHAPTER XV.

'I AM sorry, my dear mother, that I cannot accompany you;
but I must go down to my yacht this morning, and on my
return from Greenwich I have an engagement.'

This was said about a week after the dinner at Sidonia's,
by Lord Montacute to the duchess.

'That terrible yacht!' thought the duchess.

Her Grace, a year ago, had she been aware of it, would

have deemed Tancred's engagement as fearful an affair. The idea that her son should have called every day for a week on a married lady, beautiful and attractive, would have filled her with alarm amounting almost to horror. Yet such was the innocent case. It might at the first glance seem difficult to reconcile the rival charms of the Basilisk and Lady Bertie and Bellair, and to understand how Tancred could be so interested in the preparations for a voyage which was to bear him from the individual in whose society he found a daily gratification. But the truth is, that Lady Bertie and Bellair was the only person who sympathised with his adventure.

She listened with the liveliest concern to his account of all his progress; she even made many admirable suggestions, for Lady Bertie and Bellair had been a frequent visitor at Cowes, and was quite initiated in the mysteries of the dilettante service of the Yacht Club. She was a capital sailor; at least she always told Tancred so. But this was not the chief source of sympathy, or the principal bond of union, between them. It was not the voyage, so much as the object of the voyage, that touched all the passion of Lady Bertie and Bellair. Her heart was at Jerusalem. The sacred city was the dream of her life; and, amid the dissipations of May Fair and the distractions of Belgravia, she had in fact all this time only been thinking of Jehoshaphat and Sion. Strange coincidence of sentiment—strange and sweet!

The enamoured Montacute hung over her with pious rapture, as they examined together Mr. Roberts' Syrian drawings, and she alike charmed and astonished him by her familiarity with every locality and each detail. She looked like a beautiful prophetess as she dilated with solemn enthusiasm on the sacred scene. Tancred called on her every day, because when he called the first time, he had announced his immediate departure, and so had been authorised to promise that he would pay his respects to her every day till he went. It was calculated that by these means, that is to say three or four visits, they might perhaps travel through Mr. Roberts' views together before he left England, which would facilitate their correspondence, for Tancred had engaged to write to the only person in the world worthy of receiving his letters. But, though separated, Lady Bertie and Bellair would be with him in spirit; and once she sighed and seemed to murmur, that if his voyage could only be postponed awhile, she might in a manner become his fellowpilgrim, for Lord Bertie, a great sportsman, had a desire to kill antelopes, and, wearied with the monotonous slaughter of English preserves, tired even of the eternal moors, had vague thoughts of seeking new sources of excitement amid the snipes of the Grecian marshes, and the deer and wild boars of the desert and the Syrian hills.

While his captain was repeating his inquiries for instructions on the deck of the Basilisk at Greenwich, moored off the Trafalgar Hotel, Tancred fell into reveries of female pilgrims kneeling at the Holy Sepulchre by his side; then started, gave a hurried reply, and drove back quickly to town, to pass the remainder of the morning in Brook Street.

The two or three days had expanded into two or three weeks, and Tancred continued to call daily on Lady Bertie and Bellair, to say farewell. It was not wonderful: she was the only person in London who understood him; so she delicately intimated, so he profoundly felt. They had the same ideas; they must have the same idiosyncrasy. The lady asked with a sigh why they had not met before; Tancred found some solace in the thought that they had at least become acquainted. There was something about this lady very interesting besides her beauty, her bright intelligence, and her seraphic thoughts. She was evidently the creature of impulse; to a certain degree perhaps the victim of her imagination. She seemed misplaced in life. The tone of the century hardly suited her refined and romantic spirit. Her ethereal nature seemed to shrink from the coarse reality which invades in our days even the boudoirs of May Fair.

There was something in her appearance and the temper of her being which rebuked the material, sordid, calculating genius of our reign of Mammon.

Her presence in this world was a triumphant vindication of the claims of beauty and of sentiment. It was evident that she was not happy; for, though her fair brow always lighted up when she met the glance of Tancred, it was impossible not to observe that she was sometimes strangely depressed, often anxious and excited, frequently absorbed in reverie. Yet her vivid intelligence, the clearness and precision of her thought and fancy, never faltered. In the unknown yet painful contest, the intellectual always triumphed. It was impossible to deny that she was a woman of great ability.

Nor could it for a moment be imagined that these fitful moods were merely the routine intimations that her domestic hearth was not as happy as it deserved to be. On the contrary, Lord and Lady Bertie and Bellair were the very best friends; she always spoke of her husband with interest and kindness; they were much together, and there evidently existed between them mutual confidence. His lordship's heart, indeed, was not at Jerusalem; and perhaps this want of sympathy on a subject of such rare and absorbing interest might account for the occasional musings of his wife, taking refuge in her own solitary and devoutly passionate soul. But this deficiency on the part of his lordship could scarcely be alleged against him as a very heinous fault; it is far from usual to find a British noble who on such a topic entertains the notions and sentiments of Lord Montacute; almost as rare to find a British peeress who could respond to them with the same fervour and facility as the beautiful Lady Bertie and Bellair. The life of a British peer is mainly regulated by Arabian laws and Syrian customs at this moment; but, while he sabbatically abstains from the debate or the rubber, or regulates the quarterly performance of his judicial duties in his province by the advent of the sacred festivals, he thinks little of the land

and the race who, under the immediate superintendence of the Deity, have by their sublime legislation established the principle of periodic rest to man, or by their deeds and their dogmas, commemorated by their holy anniversaries, have elevated the condition and softened the lot of every nation except their own.

'And how does Tancred get on?' asked Lord Eskdale one morning of the Duchess of Bellamont, with a dry smile. 'I understand that, instead of going to Jerusalem, he is going to give us a fish dinner.'

The Duchess of Bellamont had made the acquaintance of Lady Bertie and Bellair, and was delighted with her, although her Grace had been told that Lord Montacute called upon her every day. The proud, intensely proper, and highly prejudiced Duchess of Bellamont took the most charitable view of this sudden and fervent friendship. A female friend, who talked about Jerusalem, but kept her son in London, was in the present estimation of the duchess a real treasure, the most interesting and admirable of her sex. Their intimacy was satisfactorily accounted for by the invaluable information which she imparted to Tancred; what he was to see, do, eat, drink; how he was to avoid being poisoned and assassinated, escape fatal fevers, regularly attend the service of the church of England in countries where there were no churches, and converse in languages of which he had no knowledge. He could not have a better counsellor than Lady Bertie, who had herself travelled, at least to the Faubourg St. Honoré, and, as Horace Walpole says, after Calais nothing astonishes. Certainly Lady Bertie had not been herself to Jerusalem, but she had read about it, and every other place. The duchess was delighted that Tancred had a companion who interested him. With all the impulse of her sanguine temperament, she had already accustomed herself to look upon the long-dreaded yacht as a toy, and rather an amusing one, and was daily more convinced of the prescient shrewdness of her cousin, Lord Eskdale.

Tancred was going to give them a fish dinner! A what? A sort of banquet which might have served for the marriage feast of Neptune and Amphitrite, and be commemorated by a constellation; and which ought to have been administered by the Nereids and the Naiads; terrines of turtle, pools of water souchee, flounders of every hue, and eels in every shape, cutlets of salmon, salmis of carp, ortolans represented by whitebait, and huge roasts carved out of the sturgeon. The appetite is distracted by the variety of objects, and tantalised by the restlessness of perpetual solicitation; not a moment of repose, no pause for enjoyment; eventually, a feeling of satiety without satisfaction, and of repletion without sustenance; till, at night, gradually recovering from the whirl of the anomalous repast, famished yet incapable of flavour, the tortured memory can only recall with an effort, that it has dined off pink champagne and brown bread and butter!

What a ceremony to be presided over by Tancred of Montacute; who, if he deigned to dine at all, ought to have dined at no less a round table than that of King Arthur. What a consummation of a sublime project! What a catastrophe of a spiritual career! A Greenwich party and a tavern bill!

All the world now is philosophical, and therefore they can account for this disaster. Without doubt we are the creatures of circumstances; and, if circumstances take the shape of a charming woman, who insists upon sailing in your yacht, which happens to be at Blackwall or Greenwich, it is not easy to discover how the inevitable consequences can be avoided. It would hardly do, off the Nore, to present your mistress with a sea-pie, or abruptly remind your farewell friends and sorrowing parents of their impending loss, by suddenly serving up soup hermetically sealed, and roasting the embalmed joint, which ought only to have smoked amid the ruins of Thebes or by the cataracts of Nubia.

There are, however, two sides of every picture; a party

may be pleasant, and even a fish dinner not merely a whirl of dishes and a clash of plates. The guests may be not too numerous, and well assorted; the attendance not too devoted, yet regardful; the weather may be charming, which is a great thing, and the giver of the dinner may be charmed, and that is everything.'

The party to see the Basilisk was not only the most agreeable of the season, but the most agreeable ever known. They all said so when they came back. Mr. Vavasour, who was there, went to all his evening parties; to the assembly by the wife of a minister in Carlton Terrace; to a rout by the wife of the leader of Opposition in Whitehall; to a literary soirée in Westminster, and a brace of balls in Portman and Belgrave Squares; and told them all that they were none of them to be compared to the party of the morning, to which, it must be owned, he had greatly contributed by his good humour and merry wit. Mrs. Coningsby declared to every one that, if Lord Montacute would take her, she was quite ready to go to Jerusalem; such a perfect vessel was the Basilisk, and such an admirable sailor was Mrs. Coningsby, which, considering that the river was like a mill-pond, according to Tancred's captain, or like a mirror, according to Lady Bertie and Bellair, was not surprising. The duke protested that he was quite glad that Montacute had taken to yachting, it seemed to agree with him so well: and spoke of his son's future movements as if there were no such place as Palestine in the world. The sanguine duchess dreamed of Cowes regattas, and resolved to agree to any arrangement to meet her son's fancy, provided he would stay at home, which she convinced herself he had now resolved to do.

'Our cousin is so wise,' she said to her husband, as they were returning. 'What could the bishop mean by saying that Tancred was a visionary? I agree with you, George, there is no counsellor like a man of the world.'

'I wish M. de Sidonia had come,' said Lady Bertie and Bellair, gazing from the window of the Trafalgar on the moonlit river with an expression of abstraction, and speaking in a tone almost of melancholy.

'I also wish it, since you do,' said Tancred. 'But they say he goes nowhere. It was almost presumptuous in me to ask him, yet I did so because you wished it.'

'I never shall know him,' said Lady Bertie and Bellair, with some vexation.

'He interests you,' said Tancred, a little piqued.

'I had so many things to say to him,' said her ladyship.

'Indeed!' said Tancred; and then he continued, 'I offered him every inducement to come, for I told him it was to meet you; but perhaps if he had known that you had so many things to say to him, he might have relented.'

'So many things! Oh! yes. You know he has been a great traveller; he has been everywhere; he has been at Jerusalem.'

'Fortunate man!' exclaimed Tancred, half to himself. 'Would I were there!'

'Would we were there, you mean,' said Lady Bertie, in a tone of exquisite melody, and looking at Tancred with her rich charged eyes.

His heart trembled; he was about to give utterance to some wild words, but they died upon his lips. Two great convictions shared his being: the absolute necessity of at once commencing his pilgrimage, and the persuasion that life, without the constant presence of this sympathising companion, must be intolerable. What was to be done? In his long reveries, where he had brooded over so many thoughts, some only of which he had as yet expressed to mortal ear, Tancred had calculated, as he believed, every combination of obstacle which his projects might have to encounter; but one, it now seemed, he had entirely omitted, the influence of woman. Why was he here? Why was he not away? Why had he not departed? The reflection was intolerable; it seemed to him even disgraceful. The being who would be content with nothing less than communing with celestial powers in sacred climes, standing at a tavern window gazing on the moonlit mudbanks of the barbarous Thames, a river which neither angel nor prophet had ever visited ! Before him, softened by the hour, was the Isle of Dogs ! The Isle of Dogs ! It should at least be Cyprus !

The carriages were announced; Lady Bertie and Bellair placed her arm in his.

CHAPTER XVI.

TANCRED passed a night of great disquiet. His mind was agitated, his purposes indefinite; his confidence in himself seemed to falter. Where was that strong will that had always sustained him ? that faculty of instant decision which had given such vigour to his imaginary deeds ? A shadowy haze had suffused his heroic idol, duty, and he could not clearly distinguish either its form or its proportions. Did he wish to go to the Holy Land or not ? What a question ? Had it come to that ? Was it possible that he could whisper such an inquiry, even to his midnight soul ? He did wish to go to the Holy Land; his purpose was not in the least faltering; he most decidedly wished to go to the Holy Land, but he wished also to go thither in the company of Lady Bertie and Bellair.

Tancred could not bring himself to desert the only being perhaps in England, excepting himself, whose heart was at Jerusalem; and that being a woman ! There seemed something about it unknightly, unkind and cowardly, almost base. Lady Bertie was a heroine worthy of ancient Christendom rather than of enlightened Europe. In the old days, truly the good old days, when the magnetic power of Western Asia on the Gothic races had been more puissant, her noble yet delicate spirit might have been found beneath the walls of Ascalon or by the purple waters of Tyre. When Tancred first met her, she was dreaming of Palestine amid her frequent sadness; he could not, utterly void of all self-conceit as he was, be insensible to the fa.. that his sympathy, founded on such a divine congeniality, had often chased the cloud from her brow and lightened the burthen of her drooping spirit. If she were sad before, what would she be now, deprived of the society of the only being to whom she could unfold the spiritual mysteries of her romantic soul ? Was such a character to be left alone in this world of slang and scrip; of coarse motives and coarser words ? Then, too, she was so intelligent and so gentle ; the only person who understood him, and never grated for an instant on his high ideal. Her temper also was the sweetest in the world, eminent as her generous spirit. She spoke of others with so much kindness, and never indulged in that spirit of detraction or that love of personal gossip which Tancred had frankly told her he abhorred. Somehow or other it seemed that their tastes agreed on everything.

The agitated Tancred rose from the bed where the hope of slumber was vain. The fire in his dressing-room was nearly extinguished; wrapped in his chamber robe, he threw himself into a chair, which he drew near the expiring embers, and sighed.

Unhappy youth ! For you commences that great hallucination, which all must prove, but which fortunately can never be repeated, and which, in mockery, we call first love. The physical frame has its infantile disorders ; the cough which it must not escape, the burning skin which it must encounter. The heart has also its childish and cradle malady, which may be fatal, but which, if once surmounted, enables the patient to meet with becoming power all the real convulsions and fevers of passion that are the heir-loom of our after-life. They, too, may bring destruction ; but, in their case, the cause and the effect are more proportioned. The heroine is real, the sympathy is wild but at least genuine, the catastrophe is that of a ship at sea which sinks with a rich cargo in a noble venture.

In our relations with the softer sex it cannot be maintained that ignorance is bliss. On the contrary, experience is the best security for enduring love. Love at first sight is often a genial and genuine sentiment, but first love at first sight is ever eventually branded as spurious. Still more so is that first love which suffuses less rapidly the spirit of the ecstatic votary, when he finds that by degrees his feelings, as the phrase runs, have become engaged. Fondness is so new to him that he has repaid it with exaggerated idolatry, and become intoxicated by the novel gratification of his vanity. Little does he suspect that all this time his seventh heaven is but the crapulence of self-love. In these cases, it is not merely that everything is exaggerated, but everything is factitious. Simultaneously, the imaginary attributes of the idol disappearing, and vanity being satiated, all ends in a crash of iconoclastic surfeit.

The embers became black, the night air had cooled the turbulent blood of Lord Montacute, he shivered, returned to his couch, and found a deep and invigorating repose.

The next morning, about two hours after noon, Tancred called on Lady Bertie. As he drove up to the door, there came forth from it the foreigner who was her companion in the city fray, when Tancred first saw her and went to her rescue. He recognised Lord Montacute, and bowed with much ceremony, though with a certain grace and bearing. He was a man whose wrinkled visage strangely contrasted with his still gallant figure, scrupulously attired; a blue frock coat with a ribboned button-hole, a well-turned boot, hat a little too hidalgoish, but quite new. There was something respectable and substantial about him, notwithstanding his moustaches, and a carriage a degree too debonair for his years. He did not look like a carbonaro or a refugee. Who could he be?

Tancred had asked himself this question before. This was not the first time that he had encountered this distinguished foreigner since their first meeting. Tancred had seen him before this, quitting the door of Lord Bertie and Bellair; had stumbled over him before this, more than once, on the staircase; once, to his surprise, had met him as he entered the personal saloon of Lady Bertie. As it was evident, on that occasion, that his visit had been to the lady, it was thought necessary to say something, and he had been called the Baron, and described, though in a somewhat flurried and excited manner, as a particular friend, a person in whom they had the most entire confidence, who had been most kind to them at Paris, putting them in the way of buying the rarest china for nothing, and who was now over here on some private business of his own, of great importance. The Bertie and Bellairs felt immense interest in his exertions, and wished him every success; Lord Bertie particularly. It was not at all surprising, considering the innumerable kindnesses they had experienced at his hands, was it?

'Nothing more natural,' replied Tancred; and he turned the conversation.

Lady Bertie was much depressed this morning, so much so, that it was impossible for Tancred not to notice her unequal demeanour. Her hand trembled as he touched it; her face, flushed when he entered, became deadly pale.

'You are not well,' he said. 'I fear the open carriage last night has made you already repent our expedition.'

She shook her head. It was not the open carriage, which was delightful, nor the expedition, which was enchanting, that had affected her. Would that life consisted only of such incidents, of barouches and whitebait banquets! Alas! no, it was not these. But she was nervous, her slumbers had been disquieted, she had encountered alarming dreams; she had a profound conviction that something terrible was impending over her. And Tancred took her hand, to prevent, if possible, what appeared to be inevitable hysterics. But Lady Bertie and Bellair was a strong-minded woman, and she commanded herself.

'I can bear anything,' said Tancred, in a trembling voice, 'but to see you unhappy.' And he drew his chair nearer to hers.

M

Her face was hid, her beautiful face in her beautiful hand. There was silence and then a sigh.

'Dear lady,' said Lord Montacute.

'What is it?' murmured Lady Bertie and Bellair.

'Why do you sigh?'

'Because I am miserable.'

'No, no, no, don't use such words,' said the distracted Tancred. 'You must not be miserable; you shall not be.'

'Can I help it? Are we not about to part?'

'We need not part,' he said, in a low voice.

'Then you will remain?' she said, looking up, and her dark brown eyes were fixed with all their fascination on the tortured Tancred.

'Till we all go,' he said, in a soothing voice.

'That can never be,' said Lady Bertie; 'Augustus will never hear of it; he never could be absent more than six weeks from London, he misses his clubs so. If Jerusalem were only a place one could get at, something might be done; if there were a railroad to it for example.'

'A railroad!' exclaimed Tancred, with a look of horror. 'A railroad to Jerusalem!'

'No, I suppose there never can be one,' continued Lady Bertie, in a musing tone. 'There is no traffic. And I am the victim,' she added, in a thrilling voice; 'I am left here among people who do not comprehend me, and among circumstances with which I can have no sympathy. But go, Lord Montacute, go, and be happy, alone. I ought to have been prepared for all this; you have not deceived me. You told me from the first you were a pilgrim, but I indulged in a dream. I believed that I should not only visit Palestine, but even visit it with you.' And she leant back in her chair and covered her face with her hands.

Tancred rose from his seat, and paced the chamber. His heart seemed to burst.

'What is all this?' he thought. 'How came all this to occur? How has arisen this singular combination of unforeseen causes and undreamed-of circumstances, which baffles all my plans and resolutions, and seems, as it were, without my sanction and my agency, to be taking possession of my destiny and life ? I am bewildered, confounded, incapable of thought or deed.'

His tumultuous reverie was broken by the sobs of Lady Bertie.

'By heaven, I cannot endure this!' said Tancred, advancing. 'Death seems to me preferable to her unhappiness. Dearest of women!'

'Do not call me that,' she murmured. 'I can bear anything from your lips but words of fondness. And pardon all this ; I am not myself to-day. I had thought that I had steeled myself to all, to our inevitable separation ; but I have mistaken myself, at least miscalculated my strength. It is weak ; it is very weak and very foolish, but you must pardon it. I am too much interested in your career to wish you to delay your departure a moment for my sake. I can bear our separation, at least I think I can. I shall quit the world, for ever. I should have done so had we not met. I was on the point of doing so when we did meet, when, when my dream was at length realised. Go, go ; do not stay. Bless you, and write to me, if I be alive to receive your letters.'

'I cannot leave her,' thought the harrowed Tancred. 'It never shall be said of me that I could blight a woman's life, or break her heart.' But, just as he was advancing, the door opened, and a servant brought in a note, and, without looking at Tancred, who had turned to the window, disappeared. The desolation and despair which had been impressed on the countenance of Lady Bertie and Bellair vanished in an instant, as she recognised the handwriting of her correspondent. They were succeeded by an expression of singular excitement. She tore open the note ; a stupor seemed to spread over her features, and, giving a faint shriek, she fell into a swoon.

Tancred rushed to her side ; she was quite insensible, and pale as alabaster. The note, which was only two lines, was

open and extended in her hands. It was from no idle
curiosity, but it was impossible for Tancred not to read it.
He had one of those eagle visions that nothing could escape,
and, himself extremely alarmed, it was the first object at
which he unconsciously glanced in his agitation to discover
the cause and the remedy for this crisis. The note ran
thus :

'3 *o'clock.*

' *The Narrow Gauge has won. We are utterly done ; and
Snicks tells me you bought five hundred more yesterday, at ten.
Is it possible ?*

'F.'

' Is it possible ? ' echoed Tancred, as, entrusting Lady
Bertie to her maid, he rapidly descended the staircase of
her mansion. He almost ran to Davies Street, where he
jumped into a cab, not permitting the driver to descend to
let him in.

' Where to ? ' asked the driver.

' The city.'

' What part ? '

' Never mind ; near the Bank.'

Alighting from the cab, Tancred hurried to Sequin Court,
and sent in his card to Sidonia, who in a few moments received him. As he entered the great financier's room,
there came out of it the man called in Brook Street the
Baron.

' Well, how did your dinner go off ? ' said Sidonia, looking
with some surprise at the disturbed countenance of Tancred.

' It seems very ridiculous, very impertinent I fear you
will think it,' said Tancred, in a hesitating confused manner, ' but that person, that person who has just left the
room ; I have a particular reason, I have the greatest
desire, to know who that person is.'

' That is a French capitalist,' replied Sidonia, with a
slight smile, ' an eminent French capitalist, the Baron Villebecque de Chateau Neuf. He wants me to support him in

a great railroad enterprise in his country: a new line to Strasbourg, and looks to a great traffic, I suppose, in pasties. But this cannot much interest you. What do you want really to know about him? I can tell you everything. I have been acquainted with him for years. He was the intendant of Lord Monmouth, who left him thirty thousand pounds, and he set up upon this at Paris as a millionaire. He is in the way of becoming one, has bought lands, is a deputy and a baron. He is rather a favourite of mine,' added Sidonia, 'and I have been able, perhaps, to assist him, for I knew him long before Lord Monmouth did, in a very different position from that which he now fills, though not one for which I have less respect. He was a fine comic actor in the courtly parts, and the most celebrated manager in Europe; always a fearful speculator, but he is an honest fellow, and has a good heart.'

'He is a great friend of Lady Bertie and Bellair,' said Tancred, rather hesitatingly.

'Naturally,' said Sidonia.

'She also,' said Tancred, with a becalmed countenance, but a palpitating heart, 'is, I believe, much interested in railroads?'

'She is the most inveterate female gambler in Europe,' said Sidonia, 'whatever shape her speculations take. Villebecque is a great ally of hers. He always had a weakness for the English aristocracy, and remembers that he owed his fortune to one of them. Lady Bertie was in great tribulation this year at Paris: that was the reason she did not come over before Easter; and Villebecque extricated her from a scrape. He would assist her now if he could. By-the-bye, the day that I had the pleasure of making your acquaintance, she was here with Villebecque, an hour at my door, but I could not see her; she pesters me, too, with her letters. But I do not like feminine finance. I hope the worthy baron will be discreet in his alliance with her, for her affairs, which I know, as I am obliged to know every one's, happen to be at this moment most critical.'

'I am trespassing on you,' said Tancred, after a painful pause, 'but I am about to set sail.'

'When?'

'To-morrow; to-day, if I could; and you were so kind as to promise me ——'

'A letter of introduction and a letter of credit. I have not forgotten, and I will write them for you at once.' And Sidonia took up his pen and wrote

A LETTER OF INTRODUCTION.

To Alonzo Lara, Spanish Prior, at the Convent of Terra Santa at Jerusalem.

'MOST HOLY FATHER: The youth who will deliver to you this is a pilgrim who aspires to penetrate the great Asian mystery. Be to him what you were to me; and may the God of Sinai, in whom we all believe, guard over you, and prosper his enterprise!

'London, May, 1845.'   'SIDONIA.'

'You can read Spanish,' said Sidonia, giving him the letter. 'The other I shall write in Hebrew, which you will soon read.'

A LETTER OF CREDIT.

To Adam Besso at Jerusalem.

'London, May, 1845.

'MY GOOD ADAM: If the youth who bears this require advances, let him have as much gold as would make the right-hand lion on the first step of the throne of Solomon the king; and if he want more, let him have as much as would form the lion that is on the left; and so on, through every stair of the royal seat. For all which will be responsible to you the child of Israel, who among the Gentiles is called   SIDONIA.'

END OF BOOK II.

BOOK III.

CHAPTER I.

THE broad moon lingers on the summit of Mount Olivet, but its beam has long left the garden of Gethsemane and the tomb of Absalom, the waters of Kedron and the dark abyss of Jehoshaphat. Full falls its splendour, however, on the opposite city, vivid and defined in its silver blaze. A lofty wall, with turrets and towers and frequent gates, undulates with the unequal ground which it covers, as it encircles the lost capital of Jehovah. It is a city of hills, far more famous than those of Rome: for all Europe has heard of Sion and of Calvary, while the Arab and the Assyrian, and the tribes and nations beyond, are as ignorant of the Capitolian and Aventine Mounts as they are of the Malvern or the Chiltern Hills.

The broad steep of Sion crowned with the tower of David; nearer still, Mount Moriah, with the gorgeous temple of the God of Abraham, but built, alas! by the child of Hagar, and not by Sarah's chosen one; close to its cedars and its cypresses, its lofty spires and airy arches, the moonlight falls upon Bethesda's pool; further on, entered by the gate of St. Stephen, the eye, though 'tis the noon of night traces with ease the Street of Grief, a long winding ascent to a vast cupolaed pile that now covers Calvary, called the Street of Grief, because there the most illustrious of the human, as well as of the Hebrew, race, the descendant of King David, and the divine Son of the most favoured of women, twice sank under that burden of suffering and shame which is now throughout all Christendom the emblem of triumph and of honour; passing over groups and masses of houses built of stone, with terraced roofs, or surmounted with small domes, we reach the hill of Salem, where Melchisedek built his mystic citadel; and still remains the hill of Scopas, where Titus gazed upon Jerusalem on the eve of his final assault. Titus destroyed the temple. The religion of Judæa has in turn subverted the fanes which were raised to his father and to himself in their imperial capital; and the God of Abraham, of Isaac, and of Jacob is now worshipped before every altar in Rome.

Jerusalem by moonlight! 'Tis a fine spectacle, apart from all its indissoluble associations of awe and beauty. The mitigating hour softens the austerity of a mountain landscape magnificent in outline, however harsh and severe in detail; and, while it retains all its sublimity, removes much of the savage sternness of the strange and unrivalled scene. A fortified city, almost surrounded by ravines, and rising in the centre of chains of far-spreading hills, occasionally offering, through their rocky glens, the gleams of a distant and richer land!

The moon has sunk behind the Mount of Olives, and the stars in the darker sky shine doubly bright over the sacred city. The all-pervading stillness is broken by a breeze that seems to have travelled over the plain of Sharon from the sea. It wails among the tombs, and sighs among the cypress groves. The palm-tree trembles as it passes, as if it were a spirit of woe. Is it the breeze that has travelled over the plain of Sharon from the sea?

Or is it the haunting voice of prophets mourning over the city that they could not save? Their spirits surely would linger on the land where their Creator had deigned to dwell, and over whose impending fate Omnipotence had shed human tears. From this Mount! Who can but believe that, at the midnight hour, from the summit of the Ascension, the great departed of Israel assemble to gaze upon the battlements of their mystic city? There might be counted heroes and sages, who need shrink from no rivalry with the brightest and the wisest of other lands; but the lawgiver of the time of the Pharaohs, whose laws are still obeyed; the monarch, whose reign has ceased for three thousand years, but whose wisdom is a proverb in all nations of the earth ; the teacher, whose doctrines have modelled civilised Europe ; the greatest of legislators, the greatest of administrators, and the greatest of reformers ; what race, extinct or living, can produce three such men as these !

The last light is extinguished in the village of Bethany. The wailing breeze has become a moaning wind ; a white film spreads over the purple sky ; the stars are veiled, the stars are hid ; all becomes as dark as the waters of Kedron and the valley of Jehoshaphat. The tower of David merges into obscurity ; no longer glitter the minarets of the mosque of Omar ; Bethesda's angelic waters, the gate of Stephen, the street of sacred sorrow, the hill of Salem, and the heights of Scopas can no longer be discerned. Alone in the increasing darkness, while the very line of the walls gradually eludes the eye, the church of the Holy Sepulchre is a beacon light.

And why is the church of the Holy Sepulchre a beacon light ? Why, when it is already past the noon of darkness, when every soul slumbers in Jerusalem, and not a sound disturbs the deep repose, except the howl of the wild dog crying to the wilder wind ; why is the cupola of the sanctuary illumined, though the hour has long since been numbered, when pilgrims there kneel and monks pray ?

An armed Turkish guard are bivouacked in the court of the church ; within the church itself, two brethren of the convent of Terra Santa keep holy watch and ward ; while, at the tomb beneath, there kneels a solitary youth, who prostrated himself at sunset, and who will there pass unmoved the whole of the sacred night.

Yet the pilgrim is not in communion with the Latin Church ; neither is he of the Church Armenian, or the Church Greek ; Maronite, Coptic, or Abyssinian ; these also are Christian churches which cannot call him child.

He comes from a distant and a northern isle to bow before the tomb of a descendant of the kings of Israel, because he, in common with all the people of that isle, recognises in that sublime Hebrew incarnation the presence of a Divine Redeemer. Then why does he come alone ? It is not that he has availed himself of the inventions of modern science, to repair first to a spot, which all his countrymen may equally desire to visit, and thus anticipate their hurrying arrival. Before the inventions of modern science, all his countrymen used to flock hither. Then why do they not now ? Is the Holy Land no longer hallowed ? Is it not the land of sacred and mysterious truths ? The land of heavenly messages and earthly miracles ? The land of prophets and apostles ? Is it not the land upon whose mountains the Creator of the Universe parleyed with man, and the flesh of whose anointed race He mystically assumed, when He struck the last blow at the powers of evil ? Is it to be believed, that there are no peculiar and eternal qualities in a land thus visited, which distinguish it from all others ? That Palestine is like Normandy or Yorkshire, or even Attica or Rome.

There may be some who maintain this; there have been some, and those, too, among the wisest and the wittiest of the northern and western races, who, touched by a presumptuous jealousy of the long predominance of that oriental intellect to which they owed their civilisation, would have persuaded themselves and the world that the traditions of Sinai and Calvary were fables. Half a century ago, Europe made a violent and apparently successful effort to disembarrass itself of its Asian faith. The most powerful and the most civilised of its kingdoms, about to conquer the rest, shut up its churches, desecrated its altars, massacred and persecuted their sacred servants, and announced that the Hebrew creeds which Simon Peter brought from Palestine, and which his successors revealed to Clovis, were a mockery and a fiction. What has been the result ? In every city, town, village, and hamlet of that great kingdom, the divine image of the most illustrious of Hebrews has been again raised amid the homage of kneeling millions; while, in the heart of its bright and witty capital, the nation has erected the most gorgeous of modern temples, and consecrated its marble and golden walls to the name, and memory, and celestial efficacy of a Hebrew woman.

The country of which the solitary pilgrim, kneeling at this moment at the Holy Sepulchre, was a native, had not actively shared in that insurrection against the first and second Testament which distinguished the end of the eighteenth century. But, more than six hundred years before, it had sent its king, and the flower of its peers and people, to rescue Jerusalem from those whom they considered infidels! and now, instead of the third crusade, they expend their superfluous energies in the construction of railroads.

The failure of the European kingdom of Jerusalem, on which such vast treasure, such prodigies of valour, and such ardent belief had been wasted, has been one of those circumstances which have tended to disturb the faith of Europe, although it should have carried convictions of a very different character. The Crusaders looked upon the Saracens as infidels, whereas the children of the Desert bore a much nearer affinity to the sacred corpse that had, for a brief space, consecrated the holy sepulchre, than any of the invading host of Europe. The same blood flowed in their veins, and they recognised the divine missions both of Moses and of his greater successor. In an age so deficient in physiological learning as the twelfth century, the mysteries of race were unknown. Jerusalem, it cannot be doubted, will ever remain the appanage either of Israel or of Ishmael; and if, in the course of those great vicissitudes which are no doubt impending for the East, there be any attempt to place upon the throne of David a prince of the House of Coburg or Deuxponts, the same fate will doubtless await him as, with all their brilliant qualities and all the sympathy of Europe, was the final doom of the Godfreys, the Baldwins, and the Lusignans.

Like them, the ancestor of the kneeling pilgrim had come to Jerusalem with his tall lance and his burnished armour ; but his descendant, though not less daring and not less full of faith, could profit by the splendid but fruitless achievements of the first Tancred de Montacute. Our hero came on this new crusade with an humble and contrite spirit, to pour forth his perplexities and sorrows on the tomb of his Redeemer, and to ask counsel of the sacred scenes which the presence of that Redeemer and his great predecessors had consecrated.

CHAPTER II.

NEAR the gate of Sion there is a small, still, hilly street, the houses of which, as is general in the East, present to the passenger, with the exception of an occasional portal, only blank walls, built, as they are at Jerusalem, of stone, and very lofty. These walls commonly enclose a court, and, though their exterior offers always a sombre and often squalid appearance, it by no means follows that within you may not be welcomed with cheerfulness and even luxury.

At this moment a man in the Syrian dress, turban and flowing robe, is passing through one of the gateways of this street, and entering the large quadrangle to which it leads. It is surrounded by arcades ; on one side indications of commerce, piles of chests, cases, and barrels ; the other serving for such simple stables as are sufficient in the East. Crossing this quadrangle, the stranger passed by a corridor into a square garden of orange and lemon trees and fountains. This garden court was surrounded by inhabited chambers, and, at the end of it, passing through a low arch at the side, and then mounting a few steps, he was at once admitted into a spacious and stately chamber. Its lofty ceiling was vaulted and lightly painted in arabesque ; its floor was of white marble, varied with mosaics of fruit and flowers ; it was panelled with cedar, and in six of the principal panels were Arabic inscriptions emblazoned in blue and gold. At the top of this hall, and ranging down its two sides, was a divan or seat raised about one foot from the ground, and covered with silken cushions ; and the marble floor before this divan was spread at intervals with small bright Persian carpets.

In this chamber some half dozen persons were seated in the Eastern fashion, and smoking either the choice tobaccoes of Syria through the cherry-wood or jasmine tube of a Turkish or Egyptian chibouque, or inhaling through rose-water the more artificial flavour of the nargilly, which is the hookah of the Levant. If a guest found his pipe exhausted, he clapped his hands, and immediately a negro page appeared, dressed in scarlet or in white, and. learning his pleasure, returned in a few moments, and bowing presented him with a fresh and illumined chibouque. At intervals, these attendants appeared without a summons, and offered cups of Mocha coffee or vases of sherbet.

The lord of this divan, who was seated at the upper end of the room, reclining on embroidered cushions of various colours, and using a nargilly of fine workmanship, was a man much above the common height, being at least six feet two without his red cap of Fez, though so well proportioned, that you would not at the first glance give him credit for such' a stature. He was extremely handsome, retaining ample remains of one of those countenances of blended regularity and lustre which are found only in the cradle of the human race. Though he was fifty years of age, time had scarcely brought a wrinkle to his still brilliant complexion, while his large, soft, dark eyes, his arched brow, his well-proportioned nose, his small mouth and oval cheek presented altogether one of those faces which, in spite of long centuries of physical suffering and moral degradation, still haunt the cities of Asia Minor, the isles of Greece, and the Syrian coasts. It is the archetype of manly beauty, the tradition of those races who have wandered the least from Paradise ; and who, notwithstanding many vicissitudes and much misery, are still acted upon by the same elemental agencies as influenced the Patriarchs; are warmed by the same sun, freshened by the same air, and nourished by the same earth as cheered and invigorated and sustained the earlier generations. The costume of the East certainly does not exaggerate the fatal progress of time; if a figure becomes too portly, the flowing robe conceals the incumbrance which is aggravated by a western dress; he, too, who wears a turban has little dread of grey hairs; a grizzly beard indeed has few charms, but whether it were the lenity of time or the skill of his barber in those arts in which Asia is as experienced as Europe, the beard of the master of the divan became the rest of his appearance, and flowed to his waist in rich dark curls, lending additional dignity to a countenance of which the expression was at the same time grand and benignant.

Upon the right of the master of the divan was, smoking a jasmine pipe, Scheriff Effendi, an Egyptian merchant, of Arab race, a dark face in a white turban, mild and imperturbable, and seated as erect on his cross legs as if he were administering justice; a remarkable contrast to the individual who was on the left of the host, who might have been mistaken for a mass of brilliant garments huddled together, had not the gurgling sound of the nargilly occasionally assured the spectator that it was animated by human breath. This person was apparently lying on his back, his face hid, his form not to be traced, a wild confusion of shawls and cushions, out of which, like some wily and dangerous reptile, glided the spiral involutions of his pipe. Next to the invisible sat a little wiry man with a red nose, sparkling eyes, and a white beard. His black turban intimated that he was a Hebrew, and indeed he was well known as Barizy of the Tower, a description which he had obtained from his residence near the Tower of David, and which distinguished him from his cousin, who was called Barizy of the Gate. Further on an Armenian from Stambool, in his dark robes and black protuberant head-dress, resembling a colossal truffle, solaced himself with a cherry stick which reminded him of the Bosphorus, and he found a companion in this fashion in the young officer of a French brig of war anchored at Beiroot, and who had obtained leave to visit the Holy Land, as he was anxious to see the women of Bethlehem, of whose beauty he had heard much.

As the new comer entered the hall, he shuffled off his slippers at the threshold, and then advancing, and pressing a hand to his brow his mouth and his heart, a salutation which signifies, that in thought, speech, and feeling he was faithful to his host, and which salutation was immediately returned, he took his seat upon the divan, and the master of the house letting the flexible tube of his nargilly fall on one of the cushions, and clapping his hands, a page immediately brought a pipe to the new guest. This was Signor Pasqualigo, one of those noble Venetian names that every now and then turn up in the Levant, and borne in the present case by a descendant of a family who for centuries had enjoyed a monopoly of some of the smaller consular offices of the Syrian coast. Signor Pasqualigo had installed his son as deputy in the ambiguous agency at Jaffa, which he described as a vice-consulate, and himself principally resided at Jerusalem, of which he was the prime gossip, or second only to his rival, Barizy of the Tower. He had only taken a preliminary puff of his chibouque, to be convinced that there was no fear of its being extinguished, before he said,

'So there was a fine pilgrimage last night; the church of the Holy Sepulchre lighted up from sunset to sunrise, an extra guard in the court, and only the Spanish prior and two brethren permitted to enter. It must be 10,000 piastres at least in the coffers of the Terra Santa. Well, they want something! It is a long time since we have had a Latin pilgrim in El Khuds.'

'And they say, after all, that this was not a Latin pilgrim,' said Barizy of the Tower.

'He could not have been one of my people,' said the Armenian, 'or he never would have gone to the Holy Sepulchre with the Spanish prior,'

'Had he been one of your people,' said Pasqualigo, 'he could not have paid 10,000 piastres for a pilgrimage.'

'I am sure a Greek never would,' said Barizy, 'unless he were a Russian prince.'

'And a Russian does not care much for rosaries unless they are made of diamonds,' said Pasqualigo.

'As far as I can make out this morning,' said Barizy of the Tower, 'it is a brother of the Queen of England.'

'I was thinking it might be that,' said Pasqualigo, nettled at his rival's early information, 'the moment I heard he was an Englishman.'

'The English do not believe in the Holy Sepulchre,' said the Armenian, calmly.

'They do not believe in our blessed Saviour,' said Pasqualigo, ' but they do believe in the Holy Sepulchre.'

Pasqualigo's strong point was theology, and there were few persons in Jerusalem who on this head ventured to maintain an argument with him.

'How do you know that the pilgrim is an Englishman ?' asked their host.

'Because his servants told me so,' said Pasqualigo.

He has got an English general for the principal officer of his household,' said Barizy, 'which looks like blood royal ; a very fine man, who passes the whole day at the English consulate.'

'They have taken a house in the Via Dolorosa,' said Pasqualigo.

'Of Hassan Nejed ?' continued Barizy of the Tower, clutching the words out of his rival's grasp; 'Hassan asked five thousand piastres per month, and they gave it. What think you of that ?'

'He must indeed be an Englishman,' said Scheriff Effendi, taking his pipe slowly from his mouth. There was a dead silence when he spoke ; he was much respected.

'He is very young,' said Barizy of the Tower; 'younger than the queen, which is one reason why he is not on the throne, for in England the eldest always succeeds, except in moveables, and those always go to the youngest.'

Barizy of the Tower, though he gave up to Pasqualigo in theology, partly from delicacy, being a Jew, would yield to no man in Jerusalem in his knowledge of law.

'If he goes on at this rate,' said the Armenian, 'he will soon spend all his money; this place is dearer than Stambool.'

'There is no fear of his spending all his money,' said their host, 'for the young man has brought me such a letter, that if he were to tell me to rebuild the temple, I must do it.'

'And who is this young man, Besso?' exclaimed the Invisible, starting up, and himself exhibiting a youthful countenance; fair, almost effeminate, no beard, a slight moustache, his features too delicate, but his brow finely arched, and his blue eye glittering with fire.

'He is an English lord,' said Besso, 'and one of the greatest; that is all I know.'

'And why does he come here?' inquired the youth. 'The English do not make pilgrimages.'

'Yet you have heard what he has done.'

'And why is this silent Frenchman smoking your Latakia,' he continued in a low voice. 'He comes to Jerusalem at the same time as this Englishman. There is more in this than meets our eye. You do not know the northern nations. They exist only in political combinations. You are not a politician, my Besso. Depend upon it, we shall hear more of this Englishman, and of his doing something else than praying at the Holy Sepulchre.'

'It may be so, most noble Emir, but, as you say, I am no politician.'

'Would that you were, my Besso! It would be well for you and for all of us. See now,' he added in a whisper, 'that apparently inanimate mass, Scheriff Effendi, that

man has a political head, he understands a combination, he
is going to smuggle me five thousand English muskets into
the Desert, he will deliver them to a Bedoueen tribe, who
have engaged to convey them safely to the Mountain.
There, what do you think of that, my Besso! Do you know
now what are politics? Tell the Rose of Sharon of it. She
will say it is beautiful. Ask the Rose what she thinks of
it, my Besso.'

'Well, I shall see her to-morrow.'

'I have done well; have I not?'

'You are satisfied; that is well.'

'Not quite, my Besso; but I can be satisfied if you
please. You see that Scheriff Effendi there, sitting like an
Afrite; he will not give me the muskets unless I pay him
for them; and the Bedoueen chief, he will not carry the
arms unless I give him 10,000 piastres. Now, if you will
pay these people for me, my Besso, and deduct the expenses
from my Lebanon Loan when it is negotiated, that would
be a great service. Now, now, my Besso, shall it be done?'
he continued with the coaxing voice and with the wheed-
ling manner of a girl. 'You shall have any terms you like,
and I will always love you so, my Besso. Let it be done,
let it be done! I will go down on my knees and kiss your
hand before the Frenchman, which will spread your fame
throughout Europe, and make Louis Philippe take you for
the first man in Syria, if you will do it for me. Dear, dear
Besso, you will pay that old camel Scheriff Effendi for me,
will you not? and please the Rose of Sharon as much as
me!'

'My prince,' said Besso, 'have a fresh pipe; I never can
transact business after sunset.'

The reader will remember that Sidonia had given Tancred a letter of credit on Besso. He is the same Besso who
was the friend at Jerusalem of Contarini Fleming, and
this is the same chamber in which Contarini, his host, and
others who were present, inscribed one night, before their
final separation, certain sentences in the panels of the walls.

The original writing remains, but Besso, as we have already seen, has had the sentences emblazoned in a manner more permanent and more striking to the eye. They may, however, be both seen by all those who visit Jerusalem, and who enjoy the flowing hospitality and experience the boundless benevolence of this prince of Hebrew merchants.

CHAPTER III.

THE Christian convents form one of the most remarkable features of modern Jerusalem. There are three principal ones : the Latin Convent of Terra Santa, founded, it is believed, during the last crusade, and richly endowed by the kings of Christendom ; the Armenian and the Greek convents, whose revenues are also considerable, but derived from the numerous pilgrims of their different churches, who annually visit the Holy Sepulchre, and generally during their sojourn reside within the walls of their respective religious houses. To be competent to supply such accommodation, it will easily be apprehended that they are of considerable size. They are in truth monastic establishments of the first class, as large as citadels, and almost as strong. Lofty stone walls enclose an area of acres, in the centre of which rises an irregular mass of buildings and enclosures ; courts of all shapes, galleries of cells, roofs, terraces, gardens, corridors, churches, houses, and even streets. Sometimes as many as five thousand pilgrims have been lodged, fed, and tended during Easter in one of these convents.

Not in that of Terra Santa, of which a Protestant traveller, passing for a pilgrim, is often the only annual guest; as Tancred at present. In a white-washed cell, clean, and sufficiently airy and spacious, Tancred was lying on an iron bedstead, the only permanent furniture of the chamber, with the exception of a crucifix, but well suited to the fervent and procreative clime. He was smoking a Turkish

N 2

pipe which stretched nearly across the apartment, and his
Italian attendant, Baroni, on one knee, was arranging the
bowl.

'I begin rather to like it,' said Tancred.

'I am sure you would, my lord. In this country it is
like mother's milk, nor is it possible to make way without
it. 'Tis the finest tobacco of Latakia, the choicest in the
world, and I have smoked all. I begged it myself from
Signor Besso, whose divan is renowned, the day I called on
him with your lordship's letter.'

Saying this, Baroni quickly rose (a man from thirty-two
to thirty-five); rather under the middle height, slender,
lithe, and pliant; a long black beard, cleared off his chin
when in Europe, and concealed under his cravat, but always
ready for the Orient; whiskers closely shaved but strongly
marked, sallow, an aquiline nose, white teeth, a sparkling
black eye. His costume entirely white, fashion Mamlouk,
that is to say, trowsers of a prodigious width, and a light
jacket; a white shawl wound round his waist, enclosing
his dagger; another forming his spreading turban. Temperament, remarkable vivacity modified by extraordinary
experience.

Availing himself of the previous permission of his master,
Baroni, having arranged the pipe, seated himself cross-
legged on the floor.

'And what are they doing about the house?' inquired
Tancred.

'They will be all stowed to-day,' replied Baroni.

'I shall not quit this place,' said Tancred; 'I wish to be
quite undisturbed.'

'Be not alarmed, my lord; they are amused. The
colonel never quits the consulate; dines there every day,
and tells stories about the Peninsular war and the Bellamont cavalry, just as he did on board. Mr. Bernard is
always with the English bishop, who is delighted to have
an addition to his congregation, which is not too much,
consisting of his own family, the English and Prussian

consuls, and five Jews, whom they have converted at twenty piastres a-week; but I know they are going to strike for wages. As for the doctor, he has not a minute to himself. The governor's wife has already sent for him; he has been admitted to the harem; has felt all their pulses without seeing any of their faces, and his medicine chest is in danger of being exhausted before your lordship requires its aid.'

'Take care that they are comfortable,' said Tancred.

'And what does your lordship wish to do to-day?'

'I must go to Gethsemane.'

''Tis the shot of an arrow; go out by the gate of Sion, pass through the Turkish cemetery, cross the Kedron, which is so dry this weather that you may do so in your slippers, and you will find the remnant of an olive grove at the base of the mount.'

'You talk as if you were giving a direction in London.'

'I wish I knew London as well as I know Jerusalem! This is not a very great place, and I think I have been here twenty times. Why, I made eight visits here in '40 and '41; twice from England, and six times from Egypt.'

'Active work!'

'Ah! those were times! If the Pasha had taken M. de Sidonia's advice, in '41, something would have happened in this city ——' And here Baroni pulled up: 'Your lordship's pipe draws easy?'

'Very well. And when was your first visit here, Baroni?'

'When M. de Sidonia travelled. I came in his suite from Naples, eighteen years ago, the next Annunciation of our blessed Lady,' and he crossed himself.

'You must have been very young then?'

'Young enough; but it was thought, I suppose, that I could light a pipe. We were seven when we left Naples, all picked men; but I was the only one who was in Paraguay with M. de Sidonia, and that was nearly the end of our travels, which lasted five years.'

'And what became of the rest?'

'Got ill or got stupid, no mercy in either case with M. de Sidonia, packed off instantly, wherever you may be; whatever money you like, but go you must. If you were in the middle of the Desert, and the least grumbling, you would be spliced on a camel, and a Bedoueen tribe would be hired to take you to the nearest city, Damascus or Jerusalem, or anywhere, with an order on Signor Besso, or some other signor, to pay them.'

'And you were never invalided?'

'Never; I was young and used to tumble about as long as I can remember day; but it was sharp practice sometimes; five years of such work as few men have been through. It educated me and opened my mind amazingly.'

'It seems to have done so,' said Tancred, quietly.

Shortly after this, Tancred, attended by Baroni, passed the gate of Sion. Not a human being was visible, except the Turkish sentries. It was midsummer, but no words and no experience of other places can convey an idea of the canicular heat of Jerusalem. Bengal, Egypt, even Nubia, are nothing to it; in these countries there are rivers, trees, shade, and breezes; but Jerusalem at midday in midsummer is a city of stone in a land of iron with a sky of brass. The wild glare and savage lustre of the landscape are themselves awful. We have all read of the man who had lost his shadow; this is a shadowless world. Everything is so flaming and so clear, that it would remind one of a Chinese painting, but that the scene is one too bold and wild for the imagination of the Mongol race.

'There,' said Baroni, pointing to a group of most ancient olive trees at the base of the opposite hill, and speaking as if he were showing the way to Kensington, 'there is Gethsemane; the path to the right leads to Bethany.'

'Leave me now,' said Tancred.

There are moments when we must be alone, and Tancred had fixed upon this hour for visiting Gethsemane, because he felt assured that no one would be stirring. Descending Mount Sion, and crossing Kedron, he entered the sacred grove.

CHAPTER IV.

THE sun had been declining for some hours, the glare of the earth had subsided, the fervour of the air was allayed. A caravan came winding round the hills, with many camels and persons in rich, bright Syrian dresses ; a congregation that had assembled at the church of the Ascension on Mount Olivet had broken up, and the side of the hill was studded with brilliant and picturesque groups ; the standard of the Crescent floated on the Tower of David ; there was the clang of Turkish music, and the governor of the city, with a numerous cavalcade, might be discerned on Mount Moriah, caracoling without the walls ; a procession of women bearing classic vases on their heads, who had been fetching the waters of Siloah from the well of Job, came up the valley of Jehoshaphat, to wind their way to the gate of Stephen and enter Jerusalem by the street of Calvary.

Tancred came forth from the garden of Gethsemane, his face was flushed with the rapt stillness of pious ecstasy ; hours had vanished during his passionate reverie, and he stared upon the declining sun.

'The path to the right leads to Bethany.' The force of association brought back the last words that he had heard from a human voice. And can he sleep without seeing Bethany ? He mounts the path. What a landscape surrounds him as he moves! What need for nature to be fair in a scene like this, where not a spot is visible that is not heroic or sacred, consecrated or memorable ; not a rock that is not the cave of prophets; not a valley that is not the valley of heaven-anointed kings; not a mountain that is not the mountain of God !

Before him is a living, a yet breathing and existing city, which Assyrian monarchs came down to besiege, which the chariots of Pharaohs encompassed, which Roman Emperors have personally assailed, for which Saladin and Cœur de Lion, the Desert and Christendom, Asia and Europe, struggled in rival chivalry; a city which Mahomet sighed to rule, and over which the Creator alike of Assyrian kings and Egyptian Pharaohs and Roman Cæsars, the Framer alike of the Desert and of Christendom, poured forth the full effusion of his divinely human sorrow.

What need of cascade and of cataract, the deep green turf, the foliage of the fairest trees, the impenetrable forest, the abounding river, mountains of glaciered crest, the voice of birds, the bounding forms of beauteous animals; all sights and sounds of material loveliness that might become the delicate ruins of some archaic theatre, or the lingering fanes of some forgotten faith! They would not be observed as the eye seized on Sion and Calvary; the gates of Bethlehem and Damascus; the hill of Titus; the Mosque of Mahomet and the tomb of Christ. The view of Jerusalem is the history of the world; it is more, it is the history of earth and of heaven.

The path winding round the southern side of the Mount of Olives at length brought Tancred in sight of a secluded village, situate among the hills on a sunny slope, and shut out from all objects excepting the wide landscape which immediately faced it; the first glimpse of Arabia through the ravines of the Judæan hills; the rapid Jordan quitting its green and happy valley for the bitter waters of Asphaltites, and, in the extreme distance, the blue mountains of Moab.

Ere he turned his reluctant steps towards the city, he was attracted by a garden, which issued, as it were, from a gorge in the hills, so that its limit was not perceptible, and then spread over a considerable space, comparatively with the inclosures in its vicinity, until it reached the village. It was surrounded by high stone walls, which every now and then the dark spiral forms of a cypress or a cedar would overtop, and in the more distant and elevated part rose a tall palm tree, bending its graceful and languid head, on which the sunbeam glittered. It was the first palm that Tancred had ever seen, and his heart throbbed as he beheld that fair and sacred tree.

As he approached the garden, Tancred observed that its portal was open : he stopped before it, and gazed upon its walks of lemon trees with delight and curiosity. Tancred had inherited from his mother a passion for gardens ; and an eastern garden, a garden in the Holy Land, such as Gethsemane might have been in those days of political justice when Jerusalem belonged to the Jews ; the occasion was irresistible ; he could not withstand the temptation of beholding more nearly a palm-tree ; and he entered.

Like a prince in a fairy tale, who has broken the mystic boundary of some enchanted pleasaunce, Tancred traversed the alleys which were formed by the lemon and pomegranate tree, and sometimes by the myrtle and the rose. His ear caught the sound of falling water, bubbling with a gentle noise ; more distinct and more forcible every step that he advanced. The walk in which he now found himself ended in an open space covered with roses; beyond them a gentle acclivity, clothed so thickly with a small bright blue flower that it seemed a bank of turquoise, and on its top was a kiosk of white marble, gilt and painted ; by its side, rising from a group of rich shrubs, was the palm, whose distant crest had charmed Tancred without the gate.

In the centre of the kiosk was the fountain, whose alluring voice had tempted Tancred to proceed further than he had at first dared to project. He must not retire without visiting the waters which had been speaking to him so long. Following the path round the area of roses, he was conducted to the height of the acclivity, and entered the kiosk ; some small beautiful mats were spread upon its floor, and, reposing upon one of them, Tancred watched the bright clear water as it danced and sparkled in its marble basin.

The reader has perhaps experienced the effect of falling water. Its lulling influence is proverbial. In the present instance, we must remember that Tancred had been exposed to the meridian fervour of a Syrian sun, that he had been the whole day under the influence of that excitement which necessarily ends in exhaustion ; and that, in addition to this, he had recently walked some distance ; it will not, therefore, be looked upon as an incident impro- bable or astonishing, that Lord Montacute, after pursuing for some time that train of meditation which was his custom, should have fallen asleep.

His hat had dropped from his head ; his rich curls fell on his outstretched arm that served as a pillow for a counte- nance which in the sweet dignity of its blended beauty and stillness might have become an archangel ; and, lying on one of the mats, in an attitude of unconscious gracefulness, which a painter might have transferred to his portfolio, Tancred sank into a deep and dreamless repose.

He woke refreshed and renovated, but quite insensible of all that had recently occurred. He stretched his limbs ; something seemed to embarrass him ; he found himself covered with a rich robe. He was about to rise, resting on his arm, when turning his head he beheld, the form of a woman.

She was young, even for the East ; her stature rather above the ordinary height, and clothed in the rich dress usual among the Syrian ladies. She wore an amber vest of gold- embroidered silk, fitting closely to her shape, and fastening with buttons of precious stones from the bosom to the waist, there opening like a tunic, so that her limbs were free to range in her huge Mamlouk trowsers, made of that white Cashmere, a shawl of which can be drawn through a ring. These, fastened round her ancles with clasps of rubies, fell again over her small slippered feet. Over her amber vest she had an embroidered pelisse of violet silk, with long hang- ing sleeves, which showed occasionally an arm rarer than the costly jewels which embraced it ; a many-coloured Turk- ish scarf inclosed her waist ; and then, worn loosely over all, was an outer pelisse of amber Cashmere, lined with the fur of the white fox. At the back of her head was a cap, quite unlike the Greek and Turkish caps which we are accustomed to see in England, but somewhat resembling the head-dress of a Mandarin ; round, not flexible, almost flat ; and so

thickly incrusted with pearls, that it was impossible to de-
tect the colour of the velvet which covered it. Beneath
it descended two broad braids of dark brown hair, which
would have swept the ground had they not been turned
half-way up, and there fastened with bunches of precious
stones; these, too, restrained the hair which fell, in rich
braids, on each side of her face.

That face presented the perfection of oriental beauty; such
as it existed in Eden, such as it may yet occasionally be
found among the favoured races in the favoured climes, and
such as it might have been found abundantly and for ever,
had not the folly and malignity of man been equal to the
wisdom and beneficence of Jehovah. The countenance
was oval, yet the head was small. The complexion was
neither fair nor dark, yet it possessed the brilliancy of the
north without its dryness, and the softness peculiar to the
children of the sun without its moisture. A rich subdued
and equable tint overspread this visage, though the skin was
so transparent that you occasionally caught the streaky
splendour of some vein like the dappled shades in the fine
peel of beautiful fruit.

But it was in the eye and its overspreading arch that all
the Orient spake, and you read at once of the starry vaults
of Araby and the splendour of Chaldean skies. Dark,
brilliant, with pupil of great size and prominent from its
socket, its expression and effect, notwithstanding the long
eyelash of the Desert, would have been those of a terrible
fascination, had not the depth of the curve in which it reposed softened the spell and modified irresistible power by
ineffable tenderness. This supreme organisation is always
accompanied, as in the present instance, by a noble forehead, and by an eyebrow of perfect form, spanning its space
with undeviating beauty; very narrow, though its roots are
invisible.

The nose was small, slightly elevated, with long oval nostrils fully developed. The small mouth, the short upper
lip, the teeth like the neighbouring pearls of Ormuz, the

round chin, polished as a statue, were in perfect harmony
with the delicate ears, and the hands with nails shaped like
almonds.

Such was the form that caught the eye of Tancred. She
was on the opposite side of the fountain, and stood gazing
on him with calmness, and with a kind of benignant curiosity. The garden, the kiosk, the falling waters, recalled the
past, which flashed over his mind almost at the moment
when he beheld the beautiful apparition. Half risen, yet
not willing to remain until he was on his legs to apologise
for his presence, Tancred, still leaning on his arm and looking up at his unknown companion, said, 'Lady, I am an
intruder.'

The lady, seating herself on the brink of the fountain,
and motioning at the same time with her hand to Tancred
not to rise, replied, 'We are so near the Desert that you must
not doubt our hospitality.'

'I was tempted by the first sight of a palm-tree to a step
too bold; and then sitting by this fountain, I know not how
it was ——'

'You yielded to our Syrian sun,' said the lady. 'It has
been the doom of many; but you, I trust, will not find it
fatal. Walking in the garden with my maidens, we observed you, and one of us covered your head. If you remain in this land you should wear the turban.'

'This garden seems a paradise,' said Tancred. 'I had
not thought that anything so fair could be found among
these awful mountains. It is a spot that quite becomes
Bethany.'

'You Franks love Bethany?'

'Naturally; a place to us most dear and interesting.'

'Pray, are you of those Franks who worship a Jewess; or
of those other who revile her, break her images, and blas-
pheme her pictures?'

'I venerate, though I do not adore, the mother of God,'
said Tancred, with emotion.

'Ah! the mother of Jesus!' said his companion. 'He is

your God. He lived much in this village. He was a great man, but he was a Jew ; and you worship him.'

'And you do not worship him?' said Tancred, looking up to her with an inquiring glance, and with a reddening cheek.

'It sometimes seems to me that I ought,' said the lady, ' for I am of his race, and you should sympathise with your race.'

'You are, then, a Hebrew?'

'I am of the same blood as Mary whom you venerate, but do not adore.'

'You just now observed,' said Tancred, after a momentary pause, 'that it sometimes almost seems to you, that you ought to acknowledge my Lord and Master. He made many converts at Bethany, and found here some of his gentlest disciples. I wish that you had read the history of his life.'

'I have read it. The English bishop here has given me the book. It is a good one, written, I observe, entirely by Jews. I find in it many things with which I agree ; and if there be some from which I dissent, it may be that I do not comprehend them.'

'You are already half a Christian !' said Tancred, with animation.

'But the Christianity which I draw from your book does not agree with the Christianity which you practise,' said the lady, ' and I fear, therefore, it may be heretical.'

'The Christian Church would be your guide.'

'Which ?' inquired the lady; 'there are so many in Jerusalem. There is the good bishop who presented me with this volume, and who is himself a Hebrew : he is a Church; there is the Latin Church, which was founded by a Hebrew ; there is the Armenian Church, which belongs to an Eastern nation who, like the Hebrews, have lost their country and are scattered in every clime ; there is the Abyssinian Church, who hold us in great honour, and practise many of our rites and ceremonies ; and there are the

Greek, the Maronite, and the Coptic Churches, who do not favour us, but who do not treat us as grossly as they treat each other. In this perplexity it may be wise to remain within the pale of a church older than all of them, the church in which Jesus was born and which he never quitted, for he was born a Jew, lived a Jew, and died a Jew; as became a Prince of the House of David, which you do and must acknowledge him to have been. Your sacred genealogies prove the fact; and if you could not establish it, the whole fabric of your faith falls to the ground.'

' If I had no confidence in any Church,' said Tancred, with agitation, ' I would fall down before God and beseech him to enlighten me; and, in this land,' he added, in a tone of excitement, ' I cannot believe that the appeal to the Mercy-seat would be made in vain.'

' But human wit ought to be exhausted before we presume to invoke divine interposition,' said the lady. ' I observe that Jesus was as fond of asking questions as of performing miracles; an inquiring spirit will solve mysteries. Let me ask you : you think that the present state of my race is penal and miraculous ? '

Tancred gently bowed assent.

' Why do you ? ' asked the lady.

' It is the punishment ordained for their rejection and crucifixion of the Messiah.'

' Where is it ordained ? '

' Upon our heads and upon our children be his blood.'

' The criminals said that, not the judge. Is it a principle of your jurisprudence to permit the guilty to assign their own punishment ? They might deserve a severer one. Why should they transfer any of the infliction to their posterity ? What evidence have you that Omnipotence accepted the offer ? It is not so announced in your histories. Your evidence is the reverse. He, whom you acknowledge as omnipotent, prayed to Jehovah to forgive them on account of their ignorance. But, admit that the offer was accepted, which in my opinion is blasphemy, is

the cry of a rabble at a public execution to bind a nation ?
There was a great party in the country not disinclined to
Jesus at the time, especially in the provinces where he had
laboured for three years, and on the whole with success ;
are they and their children to suffer ? But you will say
they became Christians. Admit it. We were originally
a nation of twelve tribes; ten, long before the advent of
Jesus, had been carried into captivity and scattered over the
East and the Mediterranean world ; they are probably the
source of the greater portion of the existing Hebrews ; for
we know that, even in the time of Jesus, Hebrews came up
to Jerusalem at the Passover from every province of the
Roman Empire. What had they to do with the crucifixion
or the rejection ? '

'The fate of the Ten Tribes is a deeply interesting question,' said Tancred ; 'but involved in, I fear, inexplicable
obscurity. In England there are many who hold them to
be represented by the Affghans, who state that their
ancestors followed the laws of Moses. But perhaps they
ceased to exist and were blended with their conquerors.'

'The Hebrews have never blended with their conquerors,'
said the lady, proudly. 'They were conquered frequently,
like all small states situate amid rival empires. Syria was
the battlefield of the great monarchies. Jerusalem has
not been conquered oftener than Athens, or treated worse ;
but its people, unhappily, fought too bravely and rebelled
too often, so at last they were expatriated. I hold that, to
believe that the Hebrew communities are in a principal
measure the descendants of the Ten Tribes, and of the
other captivities preceding Christ, is a just, and fair, and
sensible inference, which explains circumstances that otherwise could not be explicable. But let that pass. We will
suppose all the Jews in all the cities of the world to be the
lineal descendants of the mob who shouted at the crucifixion.
Yet another question ! My grandfather is a Bedoueen
sheikh, chief of one of the most powerful tribes of the
Desert. My mother was his daughter. He is a Jew ; his

whole tribe are Jews; they read and obey the five books, live in tents, have thousands of camels, ride horses of the Nedjed breed, and care for nothing except Jehovah, Moses, and their mares. Were they at Jerusalem at the crucifixion, and does the shout of the rabble touch them? Yet my mother marries a Hebrew of the cities, and a man, too, fit to sit on the throne of King Solomon; and a little Christian Yahoor with a round hat, who sells figs at Smyrna, will cross the street if he see her, lest he should be contaminated by the blood of one who crucified his Saviour; his Saviour being, by his own statement, one of the princes of our royal house. No; I will never become a Christian, if I am to eat such sand! It is not to be found in your books. They were written by Jews, men far too well acquainted with their subject to indite such tales of the Philistines as these!'

Tancred looked at her with deep interest as her eye flashed fire, and her beautiful cheek was for a moment suffused with the crimson cloud of indignant passion; and then he said, 'You speak of things that deeply interest me, or I should not be in this land. But tell me: it cannot be denied that, whatever the cause, the miracle exists; and that the Hebrews, alone of the ancient races, remain, and are found in every country, a memorial of the mysterious and mighty past.'

'Their state may be miraculous without being penal. But why miraculous? Is it a miracle that Jehovah should guard his people? And can He guard them better than by endowing them with faculties superior to those of the nations among whom they dwell?'

'I cannot believe that merely human agencies could have sustained a career of such duration and such vicissitudes.'

'As for human agencies, we have a proverb: " The will of man is the servant of God." But if you wish to make a race endure, rely upon it you should expatriate them. Conquer them, and they may blend with their conquerors;

exile them, and they will live apart and for ever. To expatriate is purely oriental, quite unknown to the modern world. We were speaking of the Armenians, they are Christians, and good ones, I believe.'

' I have understood very orthodox.'

' Go to Armenia, and you will not find an Armenian. They, too, are an expatriated nation, like the Hebrews. The Persians conquered their land, and drove out the people. The Armenian has a proverb : " In every city of the East I find a home." They are everywhere ; the rivals of my people, for they are one of the great races, and little degenerated : with all our industry, and much of our energy ; I would say, with all our human virtues, though it cannot be expected that they should possess our divine qualities ; they have not produced Gods and prophets, and are proud that they can trace up their faith to one of the obscurest of the Hebrew apostles, and who never knew his great master.'

' But the Armenians are found only in the East,' said Tancred.

' Ah ! ' said the lady, with a sarcastic smile ; ' it is exile to Europe, then, that is the curse : well, I think you have some reason. I do not know much of your quarter of the globe : Europe is to Asia what America is to Europe. But I have felt the winds of the Euxine blowing up the Bosphorus ; and, when the Sultan was once going to cut off our heads for helping the Egyptians, I passed some months at Vienna. Oh ! how I sighed for my beautiful Damascus ! '

' And for your garden at Bethany ? ' said Tancred.

' It did not exist then. This is a recent creation,' said the lady. ' I have built a nest in the chink of the hills, that I might look upon Arabia ; and the palm-tree that invited you to honour my domain was the contribution of my Arab grandfather to the only garden near Jerusalem. But I want to ask you another question. What, on the whole, is the thing most valued in Europe ? '

Tancred pondered; and, after a slight pause, said, 'I think I know what ought to be most valued in Europe; it is something very different from what I fear I must confess is most valued there. My cheek burns while I say it; but I think, in Europe, what is most valued is money.

'On the whole,' said the lady, 'he that has most money there is most honoured?'

'Practically, I apprehend so.'

'Which is the greatest city in Europe?'

'Without doubt, the capital of my country, London.'

'Greater I know it is than Vienna; but is it greater than Paris?'

'Perhaps double the size of Paris.'

'And four times that of Stambool! What a city! Why 'tis Babylon! How rich the most honoured man must be there! Tell me, is he a Christian?'

'I believe he is one of your race and faith.'

'And in Paris; who is the richest man in Paris?'

'The brother, I believe, of the richest man in London.'

'I know all about Vienna,' said the lady, smiling. 'Cæsar makes my countrymen barons of the empire, and rightly, for it would fall to pieces in a week without their support. Well, you must admit that the European part of the curse has not worked very fatally.'

'I do not see,' said Tancred thoughtfully, after a short pause, 'that the penal dispersion of the Hebrew nation is at all essential to the great object of the Christian scheme. If a Jew did not exist, that would equally have been obtained.'

'And what do you hold to be the essential object of the Christian scheme?'

'The Expiation.'

'Ah!' said the lady, in a tone of much solemnity, 'that is a great idea; in harmony with our instincts, with our traditions, our customs. It is deeply impressed upon the convictions of this land. Shaped as you Christians offer the doctrine, it loses none of its sublimity; or its associations, full at the same time of mystery, power, and solace. A sacrificial Mediator with Jehovah, that expiatory intercessor born from the chosen house of the chosen people, yet blending in his inexplicable nature the divine essence with the human elements, appointed before all time, and purifying, by his atoning blood, the myriads that preceded and the myriads that will follow us, without distinction of creed or clime, this is what you believe. I acknowledge the vast conception, dimly as my brain can partially embrace it. I understand thus much : the human race is saved ; and, without the apparent agency of a Hebrew prince, it could not have been saved. Now tell me : suppose the Jews had not prevailed upon the Romans to crucify Jesus, what would have become of the Atonement ?'

' I cannot permit myself to contemplate such contingencies,' said Tancred. ' The subject is too high for me to touch with speculation. I must not even consider an event that had been pre-ordained by the Creator of the world for countless ages.'

'Ah !' said the lady ; ' pre-ordained by the Creator of the world for countless ages ! Where then was the inexpiable crime of those who fulfilled the beneficent intention ? The holy race supplied the victim and the immolators. What other race could have been entrusted with such a consummation ? Was not Abraham prepared to sacrifice even his son ? And with such a doctrine, that embraces all space and time ; nay more, chaos and eternity ; with divine persons for the agents, and the redemption of the whole family of man for the subject ; you can mix up the miserable persecution of a single race ! And this is practical, not doctrinal Christianity. It is not found in your Christian books, which were all written by Jews ; it must have been made by some of those Churches to which you have referred me. Persecute us ! Why, if you believed what you profess, you should kneel to us ! You raise statues to the hero who saves a country. We have saved the human race, and you persecute us for doing it.'

'I am no persecutor,' said Tancred, with emotion; 'and, had I been so, my visit to Bethany would have cleansed my heart of such dark thoughts.'

'We have some conclusions in common,' said his companion, rising. 'We agree that half Christendom worships a Jewess, and the other half a Jew. Now let me ask you one more question. Which do you think should be the superior race, the worshipped or the worshippers?'

Tancred looked up to reply, but the lady had disappeared.

CHAPTER V.

BEFORE Tancred could recover from his surprise, the kiosk was invaded by a crowd of little grinning negro pages, dressed in white tunics, with red caps and slippers. They bore a number of diminutive trays of ebony inlaid with tortoiseshell, and the mother-o'-pearl of Joppa, and covered with a great variety of dishes. It was in vain that he would have signified to them, that he had no wish to partake of the banquet, and that he attempted to rise from his mat. They understood nothing that he said, but always grinning and moving about him with wonderful quickness, they fastened a napkin of the finest linen, fringed with gold, round his neck, covered the mats and the border of the fountain with their dishes and vases of differently-coloured sherbets, and proceeded, notwithstanding all his attempts at refusal, to hand him their dainties in due order. Notwithstanding his present tone of mind, which was ill-adapted to any carnal gratification, Tancred had nevertheless been an unusual number of hours without food. He had made during the period no inconsiderable exertion, and was still some distance from the city. Though he resigned himself perforce to the care of his little attendants, their solicitude therefore was not inappropriate. He partook of some of their dishes, and when he had at length succeeded in conveying to them his resolution to taste no more, they cleared the kiosk with as marvellous a celerity as they had stored it, and then two of them advanced with a nargilly and a chibouque, to offer their choice to their guest. Tancred placed the latter for a moment to his mouth, and then rising, and making signs to the pages that he would now return, they danced before him in the path till he had reached the other side of the area of roses, and then, with a hundred bows, bending, they took their leave of him.

The sun had just sunk as Tancred quitted the garden : a crimson glow, shifting, as he proceeded, into rich tints of purple and of gold, suffused the stern Judæan hills, and lent an almost supernatural lustre to the landscape ; lighting up the wild gorges, gilding the distant glens, and still kindling the superior elevations with its living blaze. The air, yet fervid, was freshened by a slight breeze that came over the wilderness from the Jordan, and the big round stars that were already floating in the skies were the brilliant heralds of the splendour of a Syrian night. The beauteous hour and the sacred scene were alike in unison with the heart of Tancred, softened and serious. He mused in fascinated reverie over the dazzling incident of the day. Who was this lady of Bethany, who seemed not unworthy to have followed Him who had made her abiding place so memorable ? Her beauty might have baffled the most ideal painter of the fair Hebrew saints. Raffaelle himself could not have designed a brow of more delicate supremacy. Her lofty but gracious bearing, the vigour of her clear, frank mind, her earnestness, free from all ecstasy and flimsy enthusiasm, but founded in knowledge and deep thought, and ever sustained by exact expression and ready argument, her sweet witty voice, the great and all-engaging theme on which she was so content to discourse, and which seemed by right to belong to her: all these were circumstances which wonderfully affected the imagination of Tancred.

He was lost in the empyrean of high abstraction, his

gaze apparently fixed on the purple mountains, and the
golden skies, and the glittering orbs of coming night, which
yet in truth he never saw, when a repeated shout at length
roused him.   It bade him stand aside on the narrow path
that winds round the Mount of Olives from Jerusalem to
Bethany, and let a coming horseman pass.   The horseman
was the young Emir who was a guest the night before in
the divan of Besso.   Though habited in the Mamlouk dress,
as if only the attendant of some great man, huge trousers
and jacket of crimson cloth, a white turban, a shawl round
his waist holding his pistols and sabre, the horse he rode
was a Kochlani of the highest breed.   By him was a running footman, holding his nargilly, to which the Emir
frequently applied his mouth as he rode along.   He shot a
keen glance at Tancred as he passed by, and then throwing
his tube to his attendant, he bounded on.

In the meantime, we must not forget the lady of Bethany
after she so suddenly disappeared from the kiosk.   Proceeding up her mountain garden, which narrowed as she
advanced, and attended by two female slaves, who had
been in waiting without the kiosk, she was soon in that
hilly chink in which she had built her nest; a long, low
pavilion, with a shelving roof, and surrounded by a Saracenic arcade; the whole painted in fresco; a golden pattern
of flowing fancy on a white ground.   If there were door or
window, they were entirely concealed by the blinds which
appeared to cover the whole surface of the building.   Stepping into the arcade, the lady entered the pavilion by a side
portal, which opened by a secret spring, and which conducted her into a small corridor, and this again through
two chambers, in both of which were many females, who
mutely saluted her as she passed, without rising from their
employments.   Then she entered a more capacious and
ornate apartment.   Its ceiling, which described the horse-
shoe arch of the Saracens, was encrusted with that honeycomb work which is peculiar to them, and which, in the
present instance, was of rose colour and silver.   Mirrors

were inserted in the cedar panels of the walls; a divan of
rose-coloured silk surrounded the chamber, and on the
thick soft carpet of many colours, which nearly covered
the floor, were several cushions surrounding an antique
marble tripod of wreathed serpents. The lady, disembar-
rassing herself of her slippers, seated herself on the divan
in the fashion of her country; one of her attendants brought
a large silver lamp, which diffused a delicious odour as well
as a brilliant light, and placed it on the tripod; while the
other, clapping her hands, a band of beautiful girls entered
the room, bearing dishes of confectionary, plates of choice
fruits, and vases of delicious sherbets. The lady, partaking
of some of these, directed, after a short time, that they
should be offered to her immediate attendants, who thereupon kissed their hands with a grave face, and pressed
them to their hearts. Then one of the girls, leaving the
apartment for a moment, returned with a nargilly of
crystal, set by the most cunning artists of Damascus, in
a framework of golden filagree crusted with precious stones.
She presented the flexible silver tube, tipped with amber,
to the lady, who, waving her hand that the room should be
cleared, smoked a confection of roses and rare nuts, while
she listened to a volume read by one of her maidens, who
was seated by the silver lamp.

While they were thus employed, an opposite curtain to
that by which they had entered was drawn aside, and a
woman advanced, and whispered some words to the lady,
who seemed to signify her assent. Immediately, a tall
negro of Dongola, richly habited in a flowing crimson vest,
and with a large silver collar round his neck, entered the
hall, and, after the usual salutations of reverence to the
lady, spoke earnestly in a low voice. The lady listened
with great attention, and then, taking out her tablets from
her girdle, she wrote a few words and gave a leaf to the
tall negro, who bowed and retired. Then she waved her
hand, and the maiden who was reading closed her book,
rose, and, pressing her hand to her heart, retired.

It seemed that the young Emir had arrived at the pavilion, and prayed that, without a moment's delay, he might speak with the Lady of Bethany.

The curtain was again withdrawn, a light step was heard, the young man who had recently passed Tancred on the road to Jerusalem bounded into the room.

'How is the Rose of Sharon?' he exclaimed. He threw himself at her feet, and pressed the hem of her garment to his lips with an ecstasy which it would have been difficult for a bystander to decide whether it were mockery or enthusiasm, or genuine feeling, which took a sportive air to veil a devotion which it could not conceal, and which it cared not too gravely to intimate.

'Ah, Fakredeen!' said the lady, 'and when did you leave the Mountain?'

'I arrived at Jerusalem yesterday by sunset; never did I want to see you so much. The foreign consuls have stopped my civil war, which cost me a hundred thousand piastres. We went down to Beiroot and signed articles of peace; I thought it best to attend to escape suspicion. However, there is more stirring than you can conceive : never had I such combinations! First let me shortly tell you what I have done, then what I wish you to do. I have made immense hits, but I am also in a scrape.'

'That I think you always are,' said the lady.

'But you will get me out of it, Rose of Sharon! You always do, brightest and sweetest of friends! What an alliance is ours! My invention, your judgment; my combinations, your criticism. It must carry everything before it.'

'I do not see that it has effected much hitherto,' said the lady. 'However, give me your mountain news. What have you done?'

'In the first place, said Fakredeen, 'until this accursed peace intrigue of the foreign consuls, which will not last as long as the carnival, the Mountain was more troubled than ever, and the Porte, backed up by Sir Canning, is obstinate against any prince of our house exercising the rule.'

'Do you call that good news?'

'It serves. In the first place it keeps my good uncle, the Emir Bescheer and his sons, prisoners at the Seven Towers. Now, I will tell you what I have done. I have sent to my uncle and offered him two hundred thousand piastres a-year for his life and that of his sons, if they will represent to the Porte that none but a prince of the house of Shehaab can possibly pacify and administer Lebanon, and that, to obtain this necessary end, they are ready to resign their rights in favour of any other member of the family.'

'What then?' said the Lady of Bethany, taking her nargilly from her mouth.

'Why then,' said Fakredeen, 'I am by another agent working upon Riza Pacha to this effect, that of all the princes of the great house of Shehaab, there is none so well adapted to support the interests of the Porte as the Emir Fakredeen, and for these three principal reasons: in the first place, because he is a prince of great qualities ——'

'Your proof of them to the vizir would be better than your assertion.'

'Exactly,' said Fakredeen. 'I prove them by my second reason, which is a guarantee to his excellency of the whole revenue of the first year of my princedom, provided I receive the berat.'

'I can tell you something,' said the lady, 'Riza shakes a little. He is too fond of first-fruits. His nomination will not be popular.'

'Yes it will, when the divan takes into consideration the third reason for my appointment,' said the prince. 'Namely, that the Emir Fakredeen is the only prince of the great house of Shehaab who is a good Mussulman.'

'You a good Mussulman! Why, I thought you had sent two months ago Archbishop Murad to Paris, urging King Louis to support you, because, amongst other reasons, being a Christian prince, you would defend the faith and privileges of the Maronites.'

'And devote myself to France,' said Fakredeen. 'It is

very true, and an excellent combination it is, if we could only bring it to bear, which I do not despair of, though affairs, which looked promising at Paris, have taken an unfortunate turn of late.'

'I am sorry for that,' said the lady, 'for really, Fakredeen, of all your innumerable combinations, that did seem to me to be the most practical. I think it might have been worked. The Maronites are powerful; the French nation is interested in them; they are the link between France and Syria; and you, being a Christian prince as well as an emir of the most illustrious house, with your intelligence and such aid as we might give you, I think your prospects were, to say the least, fair.'

'Why, as to being a Christian prince, Eva, you must remember I aspire to a dominion where I have to govern the Maronites who are Christians, the Metoualis who are Mahometans, the Anzareys who are Pagans, and the Druses who are nothing. As for myself, my house, as you well know, is more ancient even than that of Othman. We are literally descended from the standard-bearer of the Prophet, and my own estates, as well as those of the Emir Bescheer, have been in our registered possession for nearly eight hundred years. Our ancestors became Christians to conciliate the Maronites. Now tell me: in Europe, an English or French prince who wants a throne, never hesitates to change his religion, why should I be more nice? I am of that religion which gives me a sceptre; and if a Frank prince adopts a new creed when he quits London or Paris, I cannot understand why mine may not change according to the part of the mountain through which I am passing. What is the use of belonging to an old family unless to have the authority of an ancestor ready for any prejudice, religious or political, which your combinations may require?'

'Ah! Fakredeen,' said the lady, shaking her head, 'you have no self-respect.'

'No Syrian has; it won't do for us. You are an Arabian; it will do for the Desert. Self-respect, too, is a

superstition of past centuries, an affair of the Crusades. It
is not suited to these times; it is much too arrogant, too
self-conceited, too egotistical. No one is important enough
to have self-respect. Don't you see?'

'You boast of being a prince inferior to none in the
antiquity of your lineage, and, as far as the mere fact is
concerned, you are justified in your boast. I cannot comprehend how one who feels this pride should deign to do
anything that is not princely.'

'A prince!' exclaimed Fakredeen. 'Princes go for
nothing now, without a loan. Get me a loan, and then
you turn the prince into a government. That's the thing.'

'You will never get a loan till you are Emir of Lebanon,'
said the lady. 'And you have shown me to-day that the
only chance you have is failing you, for, after all, Paris was
your hope. What has crossed you?'

'In the first place,' said Fakredeen, 'what can the
French do? After having let the Egyptians be driven out,
fortunately for me, for their expulsion ruined my uncle,
the French will never take the initiative in Syria. All
that I wanted of them was, that they should not oppose
Riza Pacha in his nomination of me. But to secure his
success a finer move was necessary. So I instructed Archbishop Murad, whom they received very well at Paris, to
open secret communications over the water with the English. He did so, and offered to cross and explain in detail
to their ministers. I wished to assure them in London that
I was devoted to their interests; and I meant to offer to
let the Protestant missionaries establish themselves in the
mountain, so that Sir Canning should have received instructions to support my nomination by Riza. Then you
see, I should have had the Porte, England, and France.
The game was won. Can you believe it? Lord Aberdeen
enclosed my agent's letter to Guizot. I was crushed.'

'And disgraced. You deserved it. You never will
succeed. Intrigue will be your ruin, Fakredeen.'

'Intrigue!' exclaimed the prince, starting from the

cushion near the tripod, on which he sat, speaking with great animation, and using, as was his custom, a superfluity of expression, both of voice and hands and eyes, 'intrigue! It is life! It is the only thing! How do you think Guizot and Aberdeen got to be ministers without intrigue? Or Rïza Pacha himself? How do you think Mehemet Ali got on? Do you believe Sir Canning never intrigues? He would be recalled in a week if he did not. Why, I have got one of his spies in my castle at this moment, and I make him write home for the English all that I wish them not to believe. Intrigue! Why, England won India by intrigue. Do you think they are not intriguing in the Punjaub at this moment? Intrigue has gained half the thrones of Europe: Greece, France, Belgium, Portugal, Spain, Russia. If you wish to produce a result, you must make combinations; and you call combinations, Eva, in-trigue!'

'And this is the scrape that you are in,' said the lady. 'I do not see how I can help you out of it.'

'Pardon; this is not the scrape: and here comes the point on which I need your aid, daughter of a thousand sheikhs! I can extricate myself from the Paris disaster, even turn it to account. I have made an alliance with the Patriarch of the Lebanon, who manages affairs for the Emir Bescheer. The patriarch hates Murad, whom you see I was to have made patriarch. I am to declare the Arch-bishop an unauthorised agent, an adventurer, and my letter to be a forgery. The patriarch is to go to Stambool, with his long white beard, and put me right with France, through De Bourqueney, with whom he has relations in favour of the Emir Bescheer; my uncle is to be thrown over; all the Maronite chiefs are to sign a declaration supplicating the Porte to institute me; nay, the declaration is signed ——'

'And the Druses? Will not this Maronite manifestation put you wrong with the Druses?'

'I live among the Druses, you see,' said Fakredeen, shak-ing his head, and looking with his glittering eye a thousand meanings. ' The Druses love me. They know that I am one of themselves. They will only think that I have made the Maronites eat sand.'

' And what have you really done for the Maronites to gain all this ? ' asked the lady, quietly.

' There it is,' said Fakredeen, speaking in an affected whisper, ' the greatest stroke of state that ever entered the mind of a king without a kingdom, for I am resolved that the mountain shall be a royalty ! You remember when Ibrahim Pacha laid his plans for disarming the Lebanon, the Maronites, urged by their priests, fell into the snare, while the Druses wisely went with their muskets and scimitars, and lived awhile with the eagle and the antelope. This has been sand to the Maronites ever since. The Druses put their tongues in their cheek whenever they meet, and treat them as so many women. The Porte, of course, will do nothing for the Maronites ; they even take back the muskets which they lent them for the insurrection. Well, as the Porte will not arm them, I have agreed to do it.'

' You ! '

' 'Tis done; at least the caravan is laden; we only want a guide. And this is why I am at Jerusalem. Scheriff Effendi, who met me here yesterday, has got me five thousand English muskets, and I have arranged with the Bedoueen of Zoalia to carry them to the mountain.'

' You have indeed Solomon's signet, my dear Fakredeen.'

' Would that I had ; for then I could pay two hundred thousand piastres to that Egyptian camel, Scheriff Effendi, and he would give me up my muskets, which now, like a true son of Eblis, he obstinately retains.'

' And this is your scrape, Fakredeen. And how much have you towards the sum ? '

' Not a piastre ; nor do I suppose I shall ever see, until I make a great financial stroke, so much of the sultan's gold as is on one of the gilt balls of roses in your nargilly. My crops are sold for next year, my jewels are gone, my studs are to be broken up. There is not a cur in the streets of

Beiroot of whom I have not borrowed money. Riza Pacha is a sponge that would dry the sea of Galilee.'

'It is a great thing to have gained the Patriarch of Lebanon,' said the lady; 'I always felt that, as long as that man was against you, the Maronites never could be depended on. And yet these arms; after all they are of no use, for you would not think of insurrection!'

'No; but they can quarrel with the Druses, and cut each other's throats, and this will make the mountain more unmanageable than ever, and the English will have no customers for their calicoes, don't you see? Lord Palmerston will arraign the minister in the council. I shall pay off Aberdeen for enclosing the Archbishop's letter to Guizot. Combination upon combination! The calico merchants will call out for a prince of the house of Shehaab! Riza will propose me; Bourqueney will not murmur, and Sir Canning, finding he is in a mess, will sign a fine note of words about the peace of Europe and the prosperity of Lebanon, and 'tis finished.'

'And my father, you have seen him?'

'I have seen him,' said the young Emir, and he cast his eyes on the ground.

'He has done so much,' said Eva.

'Ask him to do more, Rose of Sharon,' said Fakredeen, like a child about to cry for a toy, and he threw himself on his knees before Eva, and kept kissing her robe. 'Ask him to do more,' he repeated, in a suppressed tone of heart-rending cajolery; 'he can refuse you nothing. Ask him, ask him, Eva! I have no friend in the world but you; I am so desolate. You have always been my friend, my counsellor, my darling, my ruby, my pearl, my rose of Rocnabad! Ask him, Eva; never mind my faults; you know me by heart; only ask him!'

She shook her head.

'Tell him that you are my sister, that I am his son, that I love you so, that I love him so; tell him anything. Say that he ought to do it because I am a Hebrew.'

'A what?' said Eva.

'A Hebrew; yes, a Hebrew. I am a Hebrew by blood, and we all are by faith.'

'Thou son of a slave!' exclaimed the lady, 'thou masquerade of humanity! Christian or Mussulman, Pagan or Druse, thou mayest figure as; but spare my race, Fakredeen, they are fallen ——'

'But not so base as I am. It may be true, but I love you, Eva, and you love me; and if I had as many virtues as yourself, you could not love me more; perhaps less. Women like to feel their superiority; you are as clever as I am, and have more judgment; you are generous, and I am selfish; honourable, and I am a villain; brave, and I am a coward; rich, and I am poor. Let that satisfy you, and do not trample on the fallen;' and Fakredeen took her hand and bedewed it with his tears.

'Dear Fakredeen,' said Eva, 'I thought you spoke in jest, as I did.'

'How can a man jest, who has to go through what I endure!' said the young Emir, in a desponding tone, and still lying at her feet. 'O, my more than sister, 'tis hell! The object I propose to myself would, with the greatest resources, be difficult; and now I have none.'

'Relinquish it.'

'When I am young and ruined! When I have the two greatest stimulants in the world to action, Youth and Debt! No; such a combination is never to be thrown away. Any young prince ought to win the Lebanon, but a young prince in debt ought to conquer the world!' and the Emir sprang from the floor, and began walking about the apartment.

'I think, Eva,' he said, after a moment's pause, and speaking in his usual tone, 'I think you really might do something with your father; I look upon myself as his son; he saved my life. And I am a Hebrew; I was nourished by your mother's breast, her being flows in my veins; and independent of all that, my ancestor was the standard-bearer of the Prophet, and the Prophet was the descendant of Ishmael, and Ishmael and Israel were brothers. I really think, between my undoubted Arabian origin and being your foster-brother, that I may be looked upon as a Jew, and that your father might do something for me.'

'Whatever my father will do, you and he must decide together,' said Eva; 'after the result of my last interference, I promised my father that I never would speak to him on your affairs again; and you know, therefore, that I cannot. You ought not to urge me, Fakredeen.'

'Ah! you are angry with me,' he exclaimed, and again seated himself at her feet. 'You were saying in your heart he is the most selfish of beings. It is true, I am. But I have glorious aspirations at least. I am not content to live like my fathers in a beautiful palace, amid my woods and mountains, with Kochlani steeds, falcons that would pull down an eagle, and nargillies of rubies and emeralds. I want something more than troops of beautiful slaves, music and dances. I want Europe to talk of me. I am wearied of hearing of nothing but Ibrahim Pacha, Louis Philippe, and Palmerston. I, too, can make combinations; and I am of a better family than all three, for Ibrahim is a child of mud, a Bourbon is not equal to a Shehaab, and Lord Palmerston only sits in the queen's second chamber of council, as I well know from an Englishman who was at Beiroot, and with whom I have formed some political relations, of which perhaps some day you will hear.'

'Well, we have arrived at a stage of your career, Fakredeen, in which no combination presents itself; I am powerless to assist you; my resources, never very great, are quite exhausted.'

'No,' said the Emir, 'the game is yet to be won. Listen, Rose of Sharon, for this is really the point on which I came to hold counsel. A young English lord has arrived at Jerusalem this week or ten days past; he is of the highest dignity, and rich enough to buy the grand bazaar of Damascus; he has letters of credit on your father's house without any limit. No one can discover the object of his mission.

I have some suspicions; there is also a French officer here who never speaks; I watch them both. The Englishman, I learnt this morning, is going to Mount Sinai. It is not a pilgrimage, because the English are really neither Jews nor Christians, but follow a sort of religion of their own, which is made every year by their bishops, one of whom they have sent to Jerusalem, in what they call a parliament, a college of muftis; you understand. Now lend me that ear that is like an almond of Aleppo! I propose that one of the tribes that obey your grandfather shall make this Englishman prisoner as he traverses the Desert. You see? Ah! Rose of Sharon, I am not yet beat; your Fakredeen is not the baffled boy that, a few minutes ago, you looked as if you thought him. I defy Ibrahim, or the King of France, or Palmerston himself, to make a combination superior to this. What a ransom! The English lord will pay Scheriff Effendi for his five thousand muskets, and for their convey- ance to the mountain besides.'

CHAPTER VI.

In one of those civil broils at Damascus which preceded the fall of the Janissaries, an Emir of the house of Shehaab, who lost his life in the fray, had, in the midst of the con- vulsion, placed his infant son in the charge of the merchant Besso, a child most dear to him, not only because the babe was his heir, but because his wife, whom he passionately loved, a beautiful lady of Antioch and of one of the old families of the country, had just sacrificed her life in giving birth to their son.

The wife of Besso placed the orphan infant at her own breast, and the young Fakredeen was brought up in every respect as a child of the house; so that, for some time, he looked upon the little Eva, who was three years younger than himself, as his sister. When Fakredeen had attained an age of sufficient intelligence for the occasion and the cir-

P

cumstances, his real position was explained to him; but he was still too young for the communication to effect any change in his feelings, and the idea that Eva was not his sister only occasioned him sorrow, until his grief was forgotten when he found that the change made no difference in their lives or their love.

Soon after the violent death of the father of Fakredeen, affairs had become more tranquil, and Besso had not neglected the interests of his charge. The infant was heir to a large estate in the Lebanon; a fine castle, an illimitable forest, and cultivated lands, whose produce, chiefly silk, afforded a revenue sufficient to maintain the not inconsiderable state of a mountain prince.

When Fakredeen was about ten years of age, his relative the Emir Bescheer, who then exercised a sovereign and acknowledged sway over all the tribes of the Lebanon, whatever their religion or race, signified his pleasure that his kinsman should be educated at his court, in the company of his sons. So Fakredeen, with many tears, quitted his happy home at Damascus, and proceeded to Beteddeen, the beautiful palace of his uncle, situate among the mountains in the neighbourhood of Beiroot. This was about the time that the Egyptians were effecting the conquest of Syria, and both the Emir Bescheer, the head of the house of Shehaab as well as Prince of the Mountain, and the great commercial confederation of the brothers Besso, had declared in favour of the invader, and were mainly instrumental to the success of Mehemet Ali. Political sympathy, and the feelings of mutual dependence which united the Emir Bescheer and the merchant of Damascus, rendered the communications between the families so frequent that it was not difficult for the family of Besso to cherish those sentiments of affection which were strong and lively in the heart of the young Fakredeen, but which, under any circumstances, depend so much on sustained personal intercourse. Eva saw a great deal of her former brother. and there subsisted between them a romantic friendship. He was their frequent guest at Damascus, and was proud to show her how he excelled in his martial exercises, how skilful he was with his falcon, and what horses of pure race he proudly rode.

In the year '39, Fakredeen being then fifteen years of age, the country entirely tranquil, even if discontented, occupied by a disciplined army of 80,000 men, commanded by captains equal it was supposed to any conjuncture, the Egyptians openly encouraged by the greatest military nation of Europe, the Turks powerless, and only secretly sustained by the countenance of the ambassador of the weakest government that ever tottered in England, a goverrment that had publicly acknowledged that it had forfeited the confidence of the Parliament which yet it did not dissolve; everything being thus in a state of flush and affluent prosperity, and both the house of Shehaab and the house of Besso feeling, each day more strongly, how discreet and how lucky they had been in the course which they had adopted, came the great Syrian crash!

Whatever difference of opinion may exist as to the policy pursued by the foreign minister of England, with respect to the settlement of the Turkish Empire in 1840–41, none can be permitted, by those, at least, competent to decide upon such questions, as to the ability with which that policy was accomplished. When we consider the position of the minister at home, not only deserted by Parliament, but abandoned by his party and even forsaken by his colleagues; the military occupation of Syria by the Egyptians; the rabid demonstration of France; that an accident of time or space, the delay of a month or the gathering of a storm, might alone have baffled all his combinations; it is difficult to fix upon a page in the history of this country which records a superior instance of moral intrepidity. The bold conception and the brilliant performance were worthy of Chatham; but the domestic difficulties with which Lord Palmerston had to struggle place the exploit beyond the happiest achievement of the elder Pitt. Throughout the memorable conjuncture, Lord Palmerston, however, had one great advantage, which was invisible to the millions; he was served by a most vigilant and able diplomacy. The superiority of his information concerning the state of Syria to that furnished to the French minister was the real means by which he baffled the menaced legions of our neighbours. A timid Secretary of State in the position of Lord Palmerston, even with such advantages, might have faltered; but the weapon was placed in the hands of one who did not shrink from its exercise, and the expulsion of the Egyptians from Turkey remains a great historic monument alike of diplomatic skill and administrative energy.

The rout of the Egyptians was fatal to the Emir Bescheer, and it seemed also, for a time, to the Damascus branch of the family of Besso. But in these days a great capitalist has deeper roots than a sovereign prince, unless he is very legitimate. The Prince of the Mountain and his sons were summoned from their luxurious and splendid Beteddeen to Constantinople, where they have ever since remained prisoners. Young Fakredeen, the moment he heard of the fall of Acre, rode out with his falcon, as if for the pastime of a morning, and the moment he was out of sight made for the Desert, and never rested until he reached the tents of the children of Rechab, where he placed himself under the protection of the grandfather of Eva. As for the worthy merchant himself, having ships at his command, he contrived to escape with his wife and his young daughter to Trieste, and he remained in the Austrian dominions between three and four years. At length the influence of Prince Metternich, animated by Sidonia, propitiated the Porte. Adam Besso, after making his submission at Stambool, and satisfactorily explaining his conduct to Riza Pacha, returned to his country, not substantially injured in fortune, though the northern clime had robbed him of his Arabian wife; for his brothers, who, as far as politics were concerned, had ever kept in the shade, had managed affairs in the absence of the more prominent member of their house, and, in truth, the family of Besso were too rich to be long under a cloud. The Pacha of Damascus found his revenue fall very short without their interference; and as for the Divan, the Bessoes could always find a friend there if they chose. The awkwardness of the Syrian catastrophe was, that it was so sudden and so unexpected, that there was then no time for those satisfactory explanations which afterwards took place between Adam Besso and Riza.

Though the situation of Besso remained, therefore, unchanged after the subsidence of the Syrian agitation, the same circumstance could not be predicated of the position of his foster-child. Fakredeen possessed all the qualities of the genuine Syrian character in excess; vain, susceptible, endowed with a brilliant though frothy imagination, and a love of action so unrestrained that restlessness deprived it of energy, with so fine a taste that he was always capricious, and so ingenious that he seemed ever inconsistent. His ambition was as high as his apprehension was quick. He saw everything and understood everybody in a flash; and believed that everything that was said or done ought to be made to contribute to his fortunes. Educated in the sweet order, and amid the decorous virtues of the roof of Besso, Fakredeen, who, from his susceptibility, took the colour of his companions, even when he thought they were his tools, had figured for ten years as a soft-hearted and somewhat timid child, dependent on kind words, and returning kindness with a passionate affection.

His change to the palace of his uncle developed his native qualities, which, under any accidents, could not perhaps have been long restrained, but which the circumstances of the times brought to light, and matured with a celerity peculiar to the East. The character of Fakredeen was formed amid the excitement of the Syrian invasion and its stirring consequences. At ten years of age he was initiated in all the mysteries of political intrigue. His startling vivacity and the keen relish of his infant intelligence for all the passionate interests of men amused and sometimes

delighted his uncle. Everything was spoken before him;
he lived in the centre of intrigues which were to shake
thrones, and perhaps to form them. He became habituated to
the idea that everything could be achieved by dexterity, and
that there was no test of conduct except success. To dissemble and to simulate; to conduct confidential negotiations with contending powers and parties at the same time;
to be ready to adopt any opinion and to possess none; to
fall into the public humour of the moment, and to evade
the impending catastrophe; to look upon every man as a
tool, and never to do anything which had not a definite
though circuitous purpose; these were his political accom-
plishments; and, while he recognised them as the best
means of success, he found in their exercise excitement and
delight. To be the centre of a maze of manœuvres was his
empyrean. He was never without a resource.

Stratagems came to him as naturally as fruit comes to a
tree. He lived in a labyrinth of plans, and he rejoiced to
involve some one in the perplexities which his magic touch
could alone unravel. Fakredeen had no principle of any
kind; he had not a prejudice; a little superstition, perhaps,
like his postponing his journey because a hare crossed his
path. But, as for life and conduct in general, forming his
opinions from the great men of whom he had experience,
princes, pachas, and some others, and from the great transactions with which he was connected, he was convinced
that all was a matter of force or fraud. Fakredeen pre-
ferred the latter, because it was more ingenious, and because
he was of a kind and passionate temperament, loving beauty
and the beautiful, apt to idealise everything, and of too exquisite a taste not to shrink with horror from an unnecessary massacre.

Though it was his profession and his pride to simulate
and to dissemble, he had a native ingenuousness which was
extremely awkward and very surprising, for, the moment he
was intimate with you, he told you everything. Though
he intended to make a person his tool, and often succeeded,

such was his susceptibility, and so strong were his sympathetic qualities, that he was perpetually, without being aware of it, showing his cards. The victim thought himself safe, but the teeming resources of Fakredeen were never wanting, and some fresh and brilliant combination, as he styled it, often secured the prey which so heedlessly he had nearly forfeited. Recklessness with him was a principle of action. He trusted always to his fertile expedients if he failed, and ran the risk in the meanwhile of paramount success, the fortune of those who are entitled to be rash. With all his audacity, which was nearly equal to his craft, he had no moral courage; and, if affairs went wrong, and, from some accident, exhaustion of the nervous system, the weather, or some of those slight causes which occasionally paralyse the creative mind, he felt without a combination, he would begin to cry like a child, and was capable of any action, however base and humiliating, to extricate himself from the impending disaster.

Fakredeen had been too young to have fatally committed himself during the Egyptian occupation. The moment he found that the Emir Bescheer and his sons were prisoners at Constantinople, he returned to Syria, lived quietly at his own castle, affected popularity among the neighbouring chieftains, who were pleased to see a Shehaab among them, and showed himself on every occasion a most loyal subject of the Porte. At seventeen years of age, Fakredeen was at the head of a powerful party, and had opened relations with the Divan. The Porte looked upon him with confidence, and although they intended, if possible, to govern Lebanon in future themselves, a young prince of a great house, and a young prince so perfectly free from all disagreeable antecedents, was not to be treated lightly. All the leaders of all the parties of the mountain frequented the castle of Fakredeen, and each secretly believed that the prince was his pupil and his tool. There was not one of these men, grey though some of them were in years and craft, whom the innocent and ingenuous Fakredeen did not

bend as a nose of wax, and, when Adam Besso returned to
Syria in '43, he found his foster-child by far the most considerable person in the country, and all parties amid their
doubts and distractions looking up to him with hope and
confidence. He was then nineteen years of age, and Eva
was sixteen. Fakredeen came instantly to Damascus to
welcome them, hugged Besso, wept like a child over his
sister, sat up the whole night on the terrace of their house
smoking his nargilly, and telling them all his secrets without the slightest reserve : the most shameful actions of his
career as well as the most brilliant ; and finally proposed
to Besso to raise a loan for the Lebanon, ostensibly to pro-
mote the cultivation of mulberries, really to supply arms to
the discontented population who were to make Fakredeen
and Eva sovereigns of the mountain.

It will have been observed, that to supply the partially
disarmed tribes of the mountain with weapons was still,
though at intervals, the great project of Fakredeen, and to
obtain the result in his present destitution of resources
involved him in endless stratagems. His success would at
the same time bind the tribes, already well affected to him,
with unalterable devotion to a chief capable of such an un-
deniable act of sovereignty, and of course render them proportionately more efficient instruments in accomplishing
his purpose. It was the interest of Fakredeen that the
Lebanon should be powerful and disturbed. Besso, who
had often befriended him, and who had frequently rescued
him from the usurers of Beiroot and Sidon, lent a cold ear
to these suggestions. The great merchant was not inclined
again to embark in a political career, or pass another three
or four years away from his Syrian palaces and gardens.
He had seen the most powerful head that the East had
produced for a century, backed by vast means, and after
having apparently accomplished his purpose, ultimately
recoil before the superstitious fears of Christendom, lest
any change in Syria should precipitate the solution of the
great Eastern problem. He could not believe that it was

reserved for Fakredeen to succeed in that which had baffled
Mehemet Ali.

Eva took the more sanguine view that becomes youth
and woman. She had faith in Fakredeen. Though his
position was not as powerful as that of the great viceroy,
it was, in her opinion, more legitimate. He seemed indicated as the natural ruler of the mountain. She had faith,
too, in his Arabian origin. With Eva, what is called
society assumed the character of a continual struggle
between Asia and the North. She dreaded the idea that,
after having escaped the crusaders, Syria should fall first
under the protection, and then the colonisation of some
European power. A link was wanted in the chain of resistance which connected the ranges of Caucasus with the
Atlas. She idealised her foster-brother into a hero, and
saw his standard on Mount Lebanon, the beacon of the
oriental races, like the spear of Shami, or the pavilion of
Abd el Kader. Eva had often influenced her father for
the advantage of Fakredeen, but at last even Eva felt that
she should sue in vain.

A year before, involved in difficulties which it seemed no
combination could control, and having nearly occasioned
the occupation of Syria by a united French and English
force, Fakredeen burst out a-crying like a little boy, and
came whimpering to Eva, as if somebody had broken his
toy or given him a beating. Then it was that Eva had
obtained for him a final assistance from her father, the
condition being, that this application should be the last.

Eva had given him jewels, had interested other members
of her family in his behalf, and effected for him a thousand
services, which only a kind-hearted and quick-witted
woman could devise. While Fakredeen plundered her
without scruple and used her without remorse, he doted on
her; he held her intellect in absolute reverence; a word
from her guided him; a look of displeasure, and his heart
ached. As long as he was under the influence of her presence, he really had no will, scarcely an idea of his own.

He spoke only to elicit her feelings and opinions. He had a superstition that she was born under a fortunate star, and that it was fatal to go counter to her. But the moment he was away, he would disobey, deceive, and, if necessary, betray her, loving her the same all the time. But what was to be expected from one whose impressions were equally quick and vivid, who felt so much for himself, and so much for others, that his life seemed a perpetual re-action between intense selfishness and morbid sensibility?

Had Fakredeen married Eva, the union might have given him some steadiness of character, or at least its semblance. The young Emir had greatly desired this alliance, not for the moral purpose that we have intimated, not even from love of Eva, for he was totally insensible to domestic joys, but because he wished to connect himself with great capitalists, and hoped to gain the Lebanon loan for a dower. But this alliance was quite out of the question. The hand of Eva was destined, according to the custom of the family, for her cousin, the eldest son of Besso of Aleppo. The engagement had been entered into while she was at Vienna, and it was then agreed that the marriage should take place soon after she had completed her eighteenth year. The ceremony was therefore at hand; it was to occur within a few months.

Accustomed from an early period of life to the contempla-tion of this union, it assumed in the eyes of Eva a character as natural as that of birth or death. It never entered her head to ask herself whether she liked or disliked it. It was one of those inevitable things of which we are always conscious, yet of which we never think, like the years of our life or the colour of our hair. Had her destiny been in her own hands, it is probable that she would not have shared it with Fakredeen, for she had never for an instant entertained the wish that there should be any change in the relations which subsisted between them. According to the custom of the country, it was to Besso that Fakredeen had ex-pressed his wishes and his hopes. The young Emir made liberal offers : his wife and children might follow any religion they pleased ; nay, he was even ready to conform himself to any which they fixed upon. He attempted to dazzle Besso with the prospect of a Hebrew Prince of the Mountains. 'My daughter,' said the merchant, 'would certainly, under any circumstances, marry one of her own faith ; but we need not say another word about it ; she is betrothed, and has been engaged for some years, to her cousin.'

When Fakredeen, during his recent visit to Bethany, found that Eva, notwithstanding her Bedoueen blood, received his proposition for kidnapping a young English nobleman with the utmost alarm and even horror, he immediately relinquished it, diverted her mind from the contemplation of a project, on her disapproval of which, notwithstanding his efforts at distraction, she seemed strangely to dwell, and finally presented her with a new and more innocent scheme in which he required her assistance. According to Fakredeen, his new English acquaintance at Beiroot, whom he had before quoted, was ready to assist him in the fulfilment of his contract, provided he could obtain sufficient time from Scheriff Effendi ; and what he wished Eva to do was personally to request the Egyptian merchant to grant time for this indulgence. This did not seem to Eva an unreasonable favour for her foster-brother to obtain, though she could easily comprehend why his previous irregularities might render him an unsuccessful suitor to his creditor. Glad that it was still in her power in some degree to assist him, and that his present project was at least a harmless one, Eva offered the next day to repair to the city and see Scheriff Effendi on his business. Pressing her hand to his heart, and saluting her with a thousand endearing names, the Emir quitted the Rose of Sharon with the tears in his grateful eyes.

Now the exact position of Fakredeen was this : he had induced the Egyptian merchant to execute the contract for him by an assurance that Besso would be his security for the venture, although the peculiar nature of the transaction rendered it impossible for Besso, in his present delicate position, personally to interfere in it. To keep up appearances, Fakredeen, with his usual audacious craft, had appointed Scheriff Effendi to meet him at Jerusalem, at the house of Besso, for the completion of the contract; and accordingly, on the afternoon of the day preceding his visit to Bethany, Fakredeen had arrived at Jerusalem without money, and without credit, in order to purchase arms for a province.

The greatness of the conjuncture, the delightful climate, his sanguine temperament, combined, however, to sustain him. As he traversed his delicious mountains, with their terraces of mulberries, and olives, and vines, lounged occasionally for a short time at the towns on the coast, and looked in at some of his creditors to chatter charming delusions, or feel his way for a new combination most necessary at this moment, his blood was quick and his brain creative; and although he had ridden nearly two hundred miles when he arrived at the ' Holy City,' he was fresh and full of faith that ' something would turn up.' His Egyptian friend, awfully punctual, was the first figure that welcomed him as he entered the divan of Besso, where the young Emir remained in the position which we have described, smoking interminable nargillies while he revolved his affairs, until the conversation respecting the arrival of Tancred roused him from his brooding meditation.

It was not difficult to avoid Scheriff Effendi for a while. The following morning, Fakredeen passed half a dozen hours at the bath, and then made his visit to Eva with the plot which had occurred to him the night before at the divan, and which had been matured this day while they were shampooing him. The moment that, baffled, he again arrived at Jerusalem, he sought his Egyptian merc ant, and thus addressed him : ' You see, Effendi, that you must not talk on this business to Besso, nor can Besso talk to you about it.'

'Good!' said the Effendi.

'But, if it be managed by another person to your satisfaction, it will be as well.'

'Cne grain is like another.'

'It will be managed by another person to your satisfaction.'

'Good!'

'The Rose of Sharon is the same in this business as her father?'

'He is a ruby and she is a pearl.'

'The Rose of Sharon will see you to-morrow about this business.'

'Good!'

'The Rose of Sharon may ask you for time to settle everything; she has to communicate with other places. You have heard of such a city as Aleppo?'

'If Damascus be an eye, Aleppo is an ear.'

'Don't trouble the Rose of Sharon, Effendi, with any details if she speaks to you; but be content with all she proposes. She will ask, perhaps, for three months; women are nervous; they think robbers may seize the money on its way, or the key of the chest may not be found when it is wanted; you understand? Agree to what she proposes; but, between ourselves, I will meet you at Gaza on the day of the new moon, and it is finished.'

'Good.'

Faithful to her promise, at an early hour of the morrow, Eva, wrapped in a huge and hooded Arab cloak, so that her form could not in the slightest degree be traced, her face covered with a black Arab mask, mounted her horse; her two female attendants, habited in the same manner, followed their mistress; before whom marched her janissary armed to the teeth, while four Arab grooms walked on each side of the cavalcade. In this way, they entered Jerusalem by the gate of Sion, and proceeded to the house of Besso. Fakredeen watched her arrival. He was in due time summoned to her presence, where he learned the success of her mission.

'Scheriff Effendi,' she said, 'has agreed to keep the arms for three months, you paying the usual rate of interest on the money. This is but just. May your new friend at Beiroot be more powerful than I am, and as faithful!'

'Beautiful Rose of Sharon! who can be like you! You inspire me; you always do. I feel persuaded that I shall get the money long before the time has elapsed.' And, so saying, he bade her farewell, to return, as he said, without loss of time to Beiroot.

CHAPTER VII.

THE dawn was about to break in a cloudless sky, when Tancred, accompanied by Baroni and two servants, all well armed and well mounted, and by Hassan, a sheikh of the Jellaheen Bedoueens, tall and grave, with a long spear tufted with ostrich feathers in his hand, his musket slung at his back, and a scimitar at his side, quitted Jerusalem by the gate of Bethlehem.

If it were only to see the sun rise, or to become acquainted with nature at hours excluded from the experience of civilisation, it were worth while to be a traveller. There is something especially in the hour that precedes a Syrian dawn, which invigorates the frame and elevates the spirit. One cannot help fancying that angels may have been resting on the mountain tops during the night, the air is so sweet and the earth so still. Nor, when it wakes, does it wake to the maddening cares of Europe. The beauty of a patriarchal repose still lingers about its existence in spite of its degradation. Notwithstanding all they have suffered during the European development, the manners of the Asiatic races generally are more in harmony with nature than the complicated conventionalisms which harass their fatal rival, and which have increased in exact proportion as the Europeans have seceded from those Arabian and Syrian creeds that redeemed them from their primitive barbarism.

But the light breaks, the rising beam falls on the gazelles still bounding on the hills of Judah, and gladdens the partridge which still calls among the ravines, as it did in the days of the prophets. About half-way between Jerusalem and Bethlehem, Tancred and his companions halted at the tomb of Rachel : here awaited them a chosen band of twenty stout Jellaheens, the subjects of Sheikh Hassan, their escort through the wildernesses of Arabia Petræa. The fringed and ribbed kerchief of the Desert, which must be distinguished from the turban, and is woven by their own women from the hair of the camel, covered the heads of the Bedoueens ; a short white gown, also of home manufacture, and very rude, with a belt of cords, completed, with slippers, their costume.

Each man bore a musket and a dagger.

It was Baroni who had made the arrangement with Sheikh Hassan. Baroni had long known him as a brave and faithful Arab. In general, these contracts with the Bedoueens for convoy through the Desert are made by Franks through their respective consuls, but Tancred was not sorry to be saved from the necessity of such an application, as it would have excited the attention of Colonel Brace, who passed his life at the British Consulate, and who probably would have thought it necessary to put on the uniform of the Bellamont yeomanry calvary, and have attended the heir of Montacute to Mount Sinai. Tancred shuddered at the idea of the presence of such a being at such a place, with his large ruddy face, his swaggering, sweltering figure, his flourishing whiskers, and his fat hands.

It was the fifth morn after the visit of Tancred to Bethany, of which he had said nothing to Baroni, the only person at his command who could afford or obtain any information as to the name and quality of her with whom he had there so singularly become acquainted. He was far

from incurious on the subject; all that he had seen and all
that he had heard at Bethany greatly interested him. But
the reserve which ever controlled him, unless under the
influence of great excitement, a reserve which was the
result of pride and not of caution, would probably have
checked any expression of his wishes on this head, even
had he not been under the influence of those feelings which
now absorbed him. A human being, animated by the hope,
almost by the conviction, that a celestial communication is
impending over his destiny, moves in a supernal sphere,
which no earthly consideration can enter. The long
musings of his voyage had been succeeded on the part of
Tancred, since his arrival in the Holy Land, by one un-
broken and impassioned reverie, heightened, not disturbed,
by frequent and solitary prayer, by habitual fasts, and by
those exciting conferences with Alonzo Lara, in which he
had struggled to penetrate the great Asian mystery, reserved
however, if indeed ever expounded, for a longer initiation
than had yet been proved by the son of the English noble.

After a week of solitary preparation, during which he had
interchanged no word, and maintained an abstinence which
might have rivalled an old eremite of Engedi, Tancred had
kneeled before that empty sepulchre of the divine Prince
of the house of David, for which his ancestor, Tancred de
Montacute, six hundred years before, had struggled with
those followers of Mahound, who, to the consternation and
perplexity of Christendom, continued to retain it. Christendom cares nothing for that tomb now, has indeed forgotten its own name, and calls itself enlightened Europe.
But enlightened Europe is not happy. Its existence is a
fever, which it calls progress. Progress to what?

The youthful votary, during his vigils at the sacred tomb,
had received solace but not inspiration. No voice from
heaven had yet sounded, but his spirit was filled with the
sanctity of the place, and he returned to his cell to prepare
for fresh pilgrimages.

One day, in conference with Lara, the Spanish Prior had

let drop these words : ' Sinai led to Calvary ; it may be wise to trace your steps from Calvary to Sinai.'

At this moment, Tancred and his escort are in sight of Bethlehem, with the population of a village but the walls of a town, situate on an eminence overlooking a valley, which seems fertile after passing the stony plain of Rephaim. The first beams of the sun, too, were rising from the mountains of Arabia and resting on the noble convent of the Nativity.

From Bethlehem to Hebron, Canaan is still a land of milk and honey, though not so rich and picturesque as in the great expanse of Palestine to the north of the Holy City. The beauty and the abundance of the promised land may still be found in Samaria and Galilee ; in the magnificent plains of Esdraelon, Zabulon, and Gennesareth ; and ever by the gushing waters of the bowery Jordan.

About an hour after leaving Bethlehem, in a secluded valley, is one of the few remaining public works of the great Hebrew Kings. It is in every respect worthy of them. I speak of those colossal reservoirs cut out of the native rock and fed by a single spring, discharging their waters into an aqueduct of perforated stone, which, until a comparatively recent period, still conveyed them to Jerusalem. They are three in number, of varying lengths from five to six hundred feet, and almost as broad ; their depth still undiscovered. They communicate with each other, so that the water of the uppermost reservoir, flowing through the intermediate one, reached the third, which fed the aqueduct. They are lined with a hard cement like that which coats the pyramids, and which remains uninjured ; and it appears that hanging gardens once surrounded them. The Arabs still call these reservoirs the pools of Solomon, nor is there any reason to doubt the tradition. Tradition, perhaps often more faithful than written documents, is a sure and almost infallible guide in the minds of the people where there has been no complicated variety of historic incidents to confuse and break the chain of memory ; where their

Q

rare revolutions have consisted of an eruption once in a thousand years into the cultivated world; where society has never been broken up, but their domestic manners have remained the same; where, too, they revere truth, and are rigid in its oral delivery, since that is their only means of disseminating knowledge.

There is no reason to doubt that these reservoirs were the works of Solomon. This secluded valley, then, was once the scene of his imaginative and delicious life. Here were his pleasure gardens; these slopes were covered with his fantastic terraces, and the high places glittered with his pavilions. The fountain that supplied these treasured waters was perhaps the 'sealed fountain,' to which he compared his bride; and here was the garden palace where the charming Queen of Sheba vainly expected to pose the wisdom of Israel, as she held at a distance before the most dexterous of men the two garlands of flowers, alike in form and colour, and asked the great king, before his trembling court, to decide which of the wreaths was the real one.

They are gone, they are vanished, these deeds of beauty and these words of wit! The bright and glorious gardens of the tiaraed poet and the royal sage, that once echoed with his lyric voice, or with the startling truths of his pregnant aphorisms, end in this wild and solitary valley, in which with folded arms and musing eye of long abstraction, Tancred halts in his ardent pilgrimage, nor can refrain from asking himself, ' Can it then be true that all is Vanity? '

Why, what, is this desolation? Why are there no more kings, whose words are the treasured wisdom of countless ages, and the mention of whose name to this moment thrills the heart of the Oriental, from the waves of the midland ocean to the broad rivers of the farthest Ind? Why are there no longer bright-witted queens to step out of their Arabian palaces and pay visits to the gorgeous ' house of the forest of Lebanon,' or to where Baalbec, or Tadmor in the wilderness, rose on those plains now strewn with the superb relics of their inimitable magnificence?

And yet some flat-nosed Frank, full of bustle and puffed

up with self-conceit (a race spawned perhaps in the morasses of some Northern forest hardly yet cleared), talks of Progress! Progress to what, and from whence? Amid empires shrivelled into deserts, amid the wrecks of great cities, a single column or obelisk of which nations import for the prime ornament of their mud-built capitals, amid arts forgotten, commerce annihilated, fragmentary literatures and populations destroyed, the European talks of progress, because, by an ingenious application of some scientific acquirements, he has established a society which has mistaken comfort for civilisation.

The soft beam of the declining sun fell upon a serene landscape; gentle undulations covered with rich shrubs or highly cultivated; corn-fields and olive groves; sometimes numerous flocks; and then vineyards fortified with walls and with watch-towers, as in the time of David, whose city Tancred was approaching. Hebron, too, was the home of the great Sheikh Abraham; and the Arabs here possess his tomb, which no Christian is permitted to visit. It is strange and touching, that the children of Ishmael should have treated the name and memory of the Sheikh Abraham with so much reverence and affection. But the circumstance that he was the friend of Allah appears with them entirely to have outweighed the recollection of his harsh treatment of their great progenitor. Hebron has even lost with them its ancient Judæan name, and they always call it, in honour of the tomb of the Sheikh, the 'City of the Friend.'

About an hour after Hebron, in a fair pasture, and near an olive grove, Tancred pitched his tent, prepared on the morrow to quit the land of promise, and approach that 'great and terrible wilderness where there was no water.'

'The children of Israel,' as they were called according to the custom then and now universally prevalent among the Arabian tribes (as, for example, the Beni Kahtan, Beni Kelb, Beni Salem, Beni Sobh, Beni Ghamed, Beni Seydan, Beni Ali, Beni Hateym, all adopting for their description the name of their founder) the 'children of Israel' were

originally a tribe of Arabia Petræa. Under the guidance
of sheikhs of great ability, they emerged from their stony
wilderness and settled on the Syrian border.

But they could not maintain themselves against the disciplined nations of Palestine, and they fell back to their
desert, which they found intolerable. Like some of the
Bedoueen tribes of modern times in the rocky wastes contiguous to the Red Sea, they were unable to resist the temp-
tations of the Egyptian cities ; they left their free but
distressful wilderness, and became Fellaheen. The Pharaohs,
however, made them pay for their ready means of sustenance, as Mehemet Ali has made the Arabs of our days
who have quitted the Desert to eat the harvests of the Nile.
They enslaved them, and worked them as beasts of burden.
But this was not to be long borne by a race whose chiefs in
the early ages had been favoured by Jehovah ; the Patriarch
Emirs, who, issuing from the Caucasian cradle of the great
races, spread over the plains of Mesopotamia, and disseminated their illustrious seed throughout the Arabian wilderness. Their fiery imaginations brooded over the great
traditions of their tribe, and at length there arose among
them one of those men whose existence is an epoch in the
history of human nature : a great creative spirit and organ-
ising mind, in whom the faculties of conception and of
action are equally balanced and possessed in the highest
degree ; in every respect a man of the complete Caucasian
model, and almost as perfect as Adam when he was just
finished and placed in Eden.

But Jehovah recognised in Moses a human instrument too
rare merely to be entrusted with the redemption of an Arabian tribe from a state of Fellaheen to Bedoueen existence.
And, therefore, he was summoned to be the organ of an
eternal revelation of the Divine will, and his tribe were
appointed to be the hereditary ministers of that mighty and
mysterious dispensation.

It is to be noted, although the Omnipotent Creator might
have found, had it pleased him, in the humblest of his crea-

tions, an efficient agent for his purpose, however difficult and sublime, that Divine Majesty has never thought fit to communicate except with human beings of the very highest powers. They are always men who have manifested an extraordinary aptitude for great affairs, and the possession of a fervent and commanding genius. They are great legislators, or great warriors, or great poets, or orators of the most vehement and impassioned spirit. Such were Moses, Joshua, the heroic youth of Hebron, and his magnificent son; such, too, was Isaiah, a man, humanly speaking, not inferior to Demosthenes, and struggling for a similar and as beautiful a cause, the independence of a small state, eminent for its intellectual power, against the barbarian grandeur of a military empire. All the great things have been done by the little nations. It is the Jordan and the Ilyssus that have civilised the modern races. An Arabian tribe, a clan of the Ægean, have been the promulgators of all our knowledge; and we should never have heard of the Pharaohs, of Babylon the great and Nineveh the superb, of Cyrus and of Xerxes, had not it been for Athens and Jerusalem.

Tancred rose with the sun from his encampment at Hebron, to traverse, probably, the same route pursued by the spies when they entered the Land of Promise. The transition from Canaan to the stony Arabia is not abrupt. A range of hills separates Palestine from a high but level country similar to the Syrian Desert, sandy in some places, but covered in all with grass and shrubs; a vast expanse of downs. Gradually the herbage disappears, and the shrubs are only found tufting the ridgy tops of low undulating sandhills. Soon the sand becomes stony, and no trace of vegetation is ever visible excepting occasionally some thorny plant. Then comes a land which alternates between plains of sand and dull ranges of monotonous hills covered with loose flints; sometimes the pilgrim winds his way through their dull ravines, sometimes he mounts the heights and beholds a prospect of interminable desolation.

For three nights had Tancred encamped in this wilder-

ness, halting at some spot where they could find some
Desert shrubs that might serve as food for the camels and
fuel for themselves. His tent was soon pitched, the night
fires soon crackling, and himself seated at one with the
Sheikh and Baroni, he beheld with interest and amusement the picturesque and flashing groups around him.
Their fare was scant and simple: bread baked upon the
spot, the dried tongue of a gazelle, the coffee of the neighbouring Mocha, and the pipe that ever consoles, if indeed
the traveller, whatever his hardships, could need any sustenance but his own high thoughts in such a scene, canopied,
too, by the most beautiful sky and the most delicious climate
in the world.

They were in the vicinity of Mount Seir; on the morrow
they were to commence the passage of the lofty range which
stretches on to Sinai. The Sheikh, who had a feud with a
neighbouring tribe, and had been anxious and vigilant while
they crossed the open country, riding on with an advanced
guard before his charge, reconnoitring from sandhill to
sandhill, often creeping up and lying on his breast, so as not
to be visible to the enemy, congratulated Tancred that all
imminent danger was past.

'Not that I am afraid of them,' said Hassan, proudly;
'but we must kill them or they will kill us.' Hassan,
though Sheikh of his own immediate family and followers,
was dependent on the great Sheikh of the Jellaheen tribe,
and was bound to obey his commands in case the complete
clan were summoned to congregate in any particular part of
the Desert.

On the morrow they commenced their passage of the
mountains, and, after clearing several ranges, found themselves two hours after noon in a defile so strangely beautiful, that to behold it would alone have repaid all the
exertions and perils of the expedition. It was formed by
precipitous rocks of a picturesque shape and of great
height, and of colours so brilliant and so blended that to
imagine them you must fancy the richest sunset you have

ever witnessed, and that would be inferior, from the inevitable defect of its fleeting character. Here the tints, sometimes vivid, sometimes shadowed down, were always equally fair : light blue heights, streaked, perhaps, with scarlet and shaded off to lilac or purple ; a cleft of bright orange ; a broad peach-coloured expanse, veined in delicate circles and wavy lines of exquisite grace ; sometimes yellow and purple stripes ; sometimes an isolated steep of every hue flaming in the sun, and then, like a young queen on a gorgeous throne, from a vast rock of crimson and gold rose a milk-white summit. The frequent fissures of this defile were filled with rich woods of oleander and shrubs of every shade of green, from which rose acacia, and other trees unknown to Tancred. Over all this was a deep and cloudless sky, and through it a path winding amid a natural shrubbery, which princes would have built colossal conservatories to preserve.

' 'Tis a scene of enchantment that has risen to mock us in the middle of the Desert,' exclaimed the enraptured pilgrim; ' surely it must vanish even as we gaze!'

About half-way up the defile, when they had traversed it for about a quarter of an hour, Sheikh Hassan suddenly galloped forward and hurled his spear with great force at an isolated crag, the base of which was covered with oleanders, and then looking back he shouted to his companions. Tancred and the foremost hurried up to him.

' Here are tracks of horses and camels that have entered the valley thus far and not passed through it. They are fresh ; let all be prepared.'

' We are twenty-five men well armed,' said Baroni. ' It is not the Tyahas that will attack such a band.'

' Nor are they the Gherashi or the Mezeines,' said the Sheikh, ' for we know what they are after, and we are brothers.'

' They must be Alouins,' said an Arab.

At this moment the little caravan was apparently landlocked, the defile again winding, but presently it became quite straight, and its termination was visible, though at a considerable distance.

'I see horsemen,' said the Sheikh; 'several of them advance; they are not Alouins.'

He rode forward to meet them, accompanied by Tancred and Baroni.

'Salaam,' said the Sheikh, 'how is it?' and then he added, aside to Baroni, 'They are strangers; why are they here?'

'Aleikoum! We know where you come from,' was the reply of one of the horsemen. 'Is that the brother of the Queen of the English? Let him ride with us, and you may go on in peace.'

'He is my brother,' said Sheikh Hassan, 'and the brother of all here. There is no feud between us. Who are you?'

'We are children of Jethro, and the great Sheikh has sent us a long way to give you salaam. Your desert here is not fit for the camel that your Prophet cursed. Come, let us finish our business, for we wish to see a place where there are palm-trees.'

'Are these children of Eblis?' said Sheikh Hassan to Baroni.

'It is the day of judgment,' said Baroni, looking pale; 'such a thing has not happened in my time. I am lost.'

'What do these people say?' inquired Tancred.

'There is but one God,' said Sheikh Hassan, whose men had now reached him, 'and Mahomet is his Prophet. Stand aside, sons of Eblis, or you shall bite the earth which curses you!'

A wild shout from every height of the defile was the answer. They looked up, they looked round; the crest of every steep was covered with armed Arabs, each man with his musket levelled.

'My lord,' said Baroni, 'there is something hidden in all this. This is not an ordinary Desert foray. You are known, and this tribe comes from a distance to plunder you;' and then he rapidly detailed what had already passed.

' What is your force, sons of Eblis ? ' said the Sheikh to the horsemen.

' Count your men, and your muskets, and your swords, and your horses, and your camels ; and if they were all double, they would not be our force. Our great Sheikh would have come in person with ten thousand men, were not your wilderness here fit only for Giaours.'

' Tell the young chief,' said the Sheikh to Baroni, ' that I am his brother, and will shed the last drop of my blood in his service, as I am bound to do, as much as he is bound to give me ten thousand piastres for the journey, and ask him what he wishes ? '

' Demand to know distinctly what these men want,' said Tancred to Baroni, who then conferred with them.

' They want your lordship,' said Baroni, ' whom they call the brother of the Queen of the English ; their business is clearly to carry you to their great Sheikh, who will release you for a large ransom.'

' And they have no feud with the Jellaheens? '

' None ; they are strangers ; they come from a distance for this purpose ; nor can it be doubted that this plan has been concocted at Jerusalem.'

' Our position, I fear, is fatal in this defile,' said Tancred; ' it is bitter to be the cause of exposing so many brave men to almost inevitable slaughter. Tell them, Baroni, that I am not the brother of the Queen of the English ; that they are ridiculously misled, and that their aim is hopeless, for all that will be ransomed will be my corpse.'

Sheikh Hassan sat on his horse like a statue, with his spear in his hand and his eye on his enemy ; Baroni, advancing to the strange horsemen, who were in position about ten yards from Tancred and his guardian, was soon engaged in animated conversation. He did all that an able diplomatist could effect ; told lies with admirable grace, and made a hundred propositions that did not commit his principal. He assured them very heartily that Tancred was not the brother of the Queen of the English ; that he was only a young Sheikh, whose father was alive, and in possession of all the flocks and herds, camels and horses; that he had quarrelled with his father; that his father, perhaps, would not be sorry if he were got rid of, and would not give a hundred piastres to save his life. Then he offered, if he would let Tancred pass, himself to go with them as prisoner to their great Sheikh, and even proposed Hassan and half his men for additional hostages, whilst some just and equitable arrangement could be effected. All, however, was in vain. The enemy had no discretion; dead or alive, the young Englishman must be carried to their chief.

'I can do nothing,' said Baroni, returning; 'there is something in all this which I do not understand. It has never happened in my time.'

'There is, then, but one course to be taken,' said Tancred; 'we must charge through the defile. At any rate we shall have the satisfaction of dying like men. Let us each fix on our opponent. That audacious-looking Arab in a red kefia shall be my victim, or my destroyer. Speak to the Sheikh, and tell him to prepare his men. Freeman and Trueman,' said Tancred, looking round to his English servants, 'we are in extreme peril; I took you from your homes; if we outlive this day, and return to Montacute, you shall live on your own land.'

'Never mind us, my lord: if it worn't for those rocks we would beat these niggers.'

'Are you all ready?' said Tancred to Baroni.

'We are all ready.'

'Then I commend my soul to Jesus Christ, and to the God of Sinai, in whose cause I perish.' So saying, Tancred shot the Arab in the red kefia through the head, and with his remaining pistol disabled another of the enemy. This he did, while he and his band were charging, so suddenly and so boldly, that those immediately opposed to them were scattered. There was a continuous volley, however, from every part of the defile, and the scene was so involved in smoke that it was impossible for Tancred to see a yard around him; still he galloped on and felt conscious that he had companions, though the shouting was so great that it was impossible to communicate. The smoke suddenly drifting, Tancred caught a glimpse of his position; he was at the mouth of the defile, followed by several of his men, whom he had not time to distinguish, and awaited by innumerable foes.

'Let us sell our lives dearly!' was all that he could exclaim. His sword fell from his wounded arm; his horse, stabbed underneath, sank with him to the ground. He was overpowered and bound. 'Every drop of his blood,' exclaimed the leader of the strange Arabs, 'is worth ten thousand piastres.'

END OF BOOK III.

BOOK IV.

CHAPTER I.

' Where is Besso? ' said Barizy of the Tower, as the Consul Pasqualigo entered the divan of the merchant, about ten days after the departure of Tancred from Jerusalem for Mount Sinai.

'Where is Besso? I have already smoked two chibouques, and no one has entered except yourself. I suppose you have heard the news? '

' Who has not? It is in every one's mouth.'

'What have you heard?' asked Barizy of the Tower, with an air of malicious curiosity.

' Some things that everybody knows,' replied Pasqualigo, ' and some things that nobody knows.'

'Hah, hah!' said Barizy of the Tower, pricking up his ears, and preparing for one of those diplomatic encounters of mutual pumping, in which he and his rival were practised. ' I suppose you have seen somebody, eh? '

' Somebody has been seen,' replied Pasqualigo, and then he busied himself with his pipe just arrived.

' But nobody has seen somebody who was on the spot? ' said Barizy.

' It depends upon what you mean by the spot,' replied Pasqualigo.

' Your information is second-hand,' observed Barizy.

'But you acknowledge it is correct? ' said Pasqualigo, more eagerly.

' It depends upon whether your friend was present——' and here Barizy hesitated.

' It does,' said Pasqualigo·

'Then he was present?' said Barizy.

'He was.'

'Then he knows,' said Barizy, eagerly, 'whether the young English prince was murdered intentionally or by hazard.'

'A—h,' said Pasqualigo, whom not the slighest rumour of the affair had yet reached, 'that is a great question.'

'But everything depends upon it,' said Barizy. 'If he was killed accidentally, there will be negotiations, but the business will be compromised; the English want Cyprus, and they will take it as compensation. If it is an affair of malice prepense, there will be war, for the laws of England require war if blood royal be spilt.'

The Consul Pasqualigo looked very grave; then, withdrawing his lips for a moment from his amber mouthpiece, he observed, 'It is a crisis.'

'It will be a crisis,' said Barizy of the Tower, excited by finding his rival a listener, 'but not for a long time. The crisis has not commenced. The first question is : to whom does the Desert belong; to the Porte, or to the Viceroy?'

'It depends upon what part of the Desert is in question,' said Pasqualigo.

'Of course the part where it took place. I say the Arabian Desert belongs to the Viceroy; my cousin, Barizy of the Gate, says "No, it belongs to the Porte." Raphael Tafna says it belongs to neither. The Bedoueens are independent.'

'But they are not recognised,' said the Consul Pasqualigo. 'Without a diplomatic existence, they are nullities. England will hold all the recognised powers in the vicinity responsible. You will see! The murder of an English prince, under such circumstances too, will not pass unavenged. The whole of the Turkish garrison of the city will march out directly into the Desert.'

'The Arabs care shroff for your Turkish garrison of the city,' said Barizy, with great derision.

''They are eight hundred strong,' said Pasqualigo.

'Eight hundred weak, you mean. No, as Raphael Tafna was saying, when Mehemet Ali was master, the tribes were quiet enough. But the Turks could never manage the Arabs, even in their best days. If the Pacha of Damascus were to go himself, the Bedoueens would unveil his harem while he was smoking his nargilly.'

'Then England will call upon the Egyptians,' said the Consul.

'Hah!' said Barizy of the Tower, 'have I got you at last? Now comes your crisis, I grant you. The English will send a ship of war with a protocol, and one of their lords who is a sailor: that is the way. They will call upon the pacha to exterminate the tribe who have murdered the brother of their queen; the pacha will reply, that when he was in Syria the brothers of queens were never murdered, and put the protocol in his turban. This will never satisfy Palmerston; he will order ——'

'Palmerston has nothing to do with it,' screamed out Pasqualigo; 'he is no longer Reis Effendi; he is in exile; he is governor of the Isle of Wight.'

'Do you think I do not know that?' said Barizy of the Tower; 'but he will be recalled for this purpose. The English will not go to war in Syria without Palmerston. Palmerston will have the command of the fleet as well as of the army, that no one shall say "No" when he says "Yes." The English will not do the business of the Turks again for nothing. They will take this city; they will keep it. They want a new market for their cottons. Mark me: England will never be satisfied till the people of Jerusalem wear calico turbans.'

Let us inquire also with Barizy of the Tower, where was Besso? Alone in his private chamber, agitated and troubled, awaiting the return of his daughter from the bath; and even now, the arrival may be heard of herself and her attendants in the inner court.

'You want me, my father?' said Eva, as she entered. 'Ah! you are disturbed. What has happened?'

'The tenth plague of Pharaoh, my child,' replied Besso, in a tone of great vexation. ' Since the expulsion of Ibrahim, there has been nothing which has crossed me so much.'

' Fakredeen ? '

' No, no ; 'tis nothing to do with him, poor boy ; but of one as young, and whose interests, though I know him not, scarcely less concern me.'

' You know him not ; 'tis not then my cousin. You perplex me, my father. Tell me at once.'

' It is the most vexatious of all conceivable occurrences,' replied Besso, ' and yet it is about a person of whom you never heard, and whom I never saw ; and yet there are circumstances connected with him. Alas ! alas ! you must know, my Eva, there is a young Englishman here, and a young English lord, of one of their princely families ——'

' Yes ! ' said Eva, in a subdued but earnest tone.

' He brought me a letter from the best and greatest of men,' said Besso, with much emotion, ' to whom I, to whom we, owe everything : our fortunes, our presence here, perhaps our lives. There was nothing which I was not bound to do for him, which I was not ready and prepared to do. I ought to have guarded over him ; to have forced my services on his acceptance ; I blame myself now when it is too late. But he sent me his letter by the Intendant of his household, whom I knew. I was fearful to obtrude myself. I learnt he was fanatically Christian, and thought perhaps he might shrink from my acquaintance.'

' And what has happened ? ' inquired Eva, with an agitation which proved her sympathy with her father's sorrow.

' He left the city some days ago to visit Sinai ; well armed and properly escorted. He has been waylaid in the wilderness and captured after a bloody struggle.'

' A bloody struggle ? '

' Yes ; they of course would gladly not have fought, but, though entrapped into an ambush, the young Englishman would not yield, but fought with desperation. His assailants have suffered considerably; his own party comparatively little, for they were so placed; surrounded, you understand, in a mountain defile, that they might have been all massacred, but the fear of destroying their prize restrained at first the marksmen on the heights; and, by a daring and violent charge, the young Englishman and his followers forced the pass, but they were overpowered by numbers.'

'And he wounded?'

'I hope not severely. But you have heard nothing. They have sent his Intendant to Jerusalem with a guard of Arabs to bring back his ransom. What do you think they want?'

Eva signified her inability to conjecture.

'Two millions of piastres!'

'Two millions of piastres! Did you say two? 'Tis a great sum; but we might negotiate. They would accept less, perhaps much less, than two millions of piastres.'

'If it were four millions of piastres, I must pay it,' said Besso. ''Tis not the sum alone that so crosses me. The father of this young noble is a great prince, and could doubtless pay, without serious injury to himself, two millions of piastres for the ransom of his son; but that's not it. He comes here; he is sent to me. I was to care for him, think for him, guard over him: I have never even seen him; and he is wounded, plundered, and a prisoner!'

'But if he avoided you, my father?' murmured Eva, with her eyes fixed upon the ground.

'Avoided me!' said Besso; 'he never thought of me but as of a Jew banker, to whom he would send his servant for money when he needed it. Was I to stand on punctilios with a great Christian noble? I ought to have waited at his gate every day when he came forth, and bowed to the earth, until it pleased him to notice me; I ought ——'

'No, no, no, my father! you are bitter. This youth is not such as you think; at least, in all probability is not,' said Eva. 'You hear he is fanatically Christian; he may be but deeply religious, and his thoughts at this moment may rest on other things than the business of the world.

He who makes a pilgrimage to Sinai can scarcely think us so vile as you would intimate.'

'What will he think of those whom he is among? Here is the wound, Eva! Guess, then, child, who has shot this arrow. 'Tis my father!'

'O traitor! traitor!' said Eva, quickly covering her face with her hands. 'My terror was prophetic! There is none so base!'

'Nay, nay,' said Besso; 'these, indeed, are women's words. The great Sheikh in this has touched me nearly, but I see no baseness in it. He could not know the intimate relation that should subsist between me and this young Englishman. He has captured him in the Desert, according to the custom of his tribe. Much as Amalek may injure me, I must acquit him of treason and of baseness.'

'Yes, yes,' said Eva, with an abstracted air. 'You misconceive me. I was thinking of others; and what do you purpose, my father?'

'First, to clear myself of the deep stain that I now feel upon my life,' said Besso. 'This Englishman comes to Jerusalem with an unbounded credit on my house: he visits the wilderness, and is made prisoner by my father-in-law, who is in ambush in a part of the Desert which his tribe never frequents, and who sends to me for a princely ransom for his captive. These are the apparent circumstances. These are the facts. There is but one inference from them. I dare say 'tis drawn already by all the gossips of the city: they are hard at it, I doubt not, at this moment, in my own divan, winking their eyes and shrugging their shoulders, while they are smoking my choice tobaccos, and drinking my sherbet of pomegranate. And can I blame them?'

'A pure conscience may defy city gossips.'

'A pure conscience must pay the ransom out of my own coffers. I am not over fond of paying two millions of piastres, or even half, for one whose shadow never fell upon my threshold. And yet I must do it: do it for my father-in-law, the Sheikh of the Rechabites, whose peace I made with

E

Mehemet Ali, for whom I gained the guardianship of the Mecca caravan through the Syrian Desert for five years, who has twelve thousand camels which he made by that office. Oh, were it not for you, my daughter, I would curse the hour that I ever mixed my blood with the children of Jethro. After all, if the truth were known, they are sons of Ishmael.'

'No, no, dear father, say not such things. You will send to the great Sheikh; he will listen ——'

'I send to the great Sheikh! You know not your grandfather, and you know not me. The truth is, the Sheikh and myself mutually despise each other, and we have never met without parting in bitterness. No, no; I would rather pay the ransom myself than ask a favour of the great Sheikh. But how can I pay the ransom, even if I chose? This young Englishman is a fiery youth: he will not yield even to an ambush and countless odds. Do you think a man who charges through a defile crowned with matchlocks, and shoots men through the head, as I am told he did, in the name of Christ, will owe his freedom to my Jewish charity? He will burn the Temple first. This young man has the sword of Gideon. You know little of the world, Eva, and nothing of young Englishmen. There is not a race so proud, so wilful, so rash, and so obstinate. They live in a misty clime, on raw meats, and wines of fire. They laugh at their fathers, and never say a prayer. They pass their days in the chase, gaming, and all violent courses. They have all the power of the State, and all its wealth; and when they can wring no more from their peasants, they plunder the kings of India.'

'But this young Englishman, you say, is pious?' said Eva.

'Ah! this young Englishman; why did he come here? What is Jerusalem to him, or he to Jerusalem? His Intendant, himself a prisoner, waits here. I must see him; he is one of the people of my patron, which proves our great friend's interest in this youth. O day thrice cursed! day of a thousand evil eyes! day of a new captivity ——'

'My father, my dear father, these bursts of grief do

not become your fame for wisdom. We must inquire, we must hold counsel. Let me see the Intendant of this English youth, and hear more than I have yet learnt. I cannot think that affairs are so hopeless as you paint them: I will believe that there is a spring near.'

CHAPTER II.

IN an almost circular valley, surrounded by mountains, Amalek, great Sheikh of the Rechabite Bedoueen, after having crossed the peninsula of Petræa from the great Syrian Desert, pitched his camp amid the magnificent ruins of an ancient Idumæan city. The pavilion of the chief, facing the sunset, was raised in the arena of an amphitheatre cut out of the solid rock, and almost the whole of the seats of which were entire. The sides of the mountains were covered with excavated tombs and temples, and, perhaps, dwelling-places; at any rate, many of them were now occupied by human beings. Fragments of columns were lying about, and masses of unknown walls. From a defile in the mountains issued a stream, which wound about in the plain, its waters almost hid, but its course beautifully indicated by the undulating shrubbery of oleanders, fig-trees, and willows. On one side of these, between the water and the amphitheatre, was a crescent of black tents, groups of horses, and crouching camels. Over the whole scene the sunset threw a violet hue, while the moon, broad and white, floated over the opposite hills.

The carpet of the great Sheikh was placed before his pavilion, and, seated on it alone, and smoking a chibouque of date wood, the patriarch ruminated. He had no appearance of age, except from a snowy beard, which was very long: a wiry man, with an unwrinkled face; dark, regular, and noble features, beautiful teeth. Over his head, a crimson kefia, ribbed and fringed with gold; his robe was of the same colour, and his boots were of red leather; the chief of one of the great tribes, and said, when they were united, to be able to bring ten thousand horsemen into the field.

One at full gallop, with a long spear, at this moment darted from the ravine, and, without stopping to answer several who addressed him, hurried across the plain, and did not halt until he reached the Sheikh.

'Salaam, Sheikh of Sheikhs, it is done; the brother of the Queen of the English is your slave.'

'Good!' said Sheikh Amalek, very gravely, and taking his pipe from his mouth. 'May your mother eat the hump of a young camel! When will they be here?'

'They will be the first shadows of the moon.'

'Good! is the brother of the Queen with Sheikh Salem?'

'There is only one God: Sheikh Salem will never drink leban again, unless he drink it in Paradise.'

'Certainly, there is only one God. What! has he fallen asleep into the well of Nummula?'

'No; but we have seen many evil eyes. Four hares crossed our path this morning. Our salaam to the English prince was not a salaam of peace. The brother of the Queen of the English is no less than an Antar. He will fight, yea or nay; and he has shot Sheikh Salem through the head.'

'There is but one God, and his will be done. I have lost the apple of mine eye. The Prince of the English is alive?'

'He is alive.'

'Good! camels shall be given to the widow of Sheikh Salem, and she shall be married to a new husband. Are there other deeds of Gin?'

'One grape will not make a bunch, even though it be a great one.'

'Let truth always be spoken. Let your words flow as the rock of Moses.'

'There is only one God: if you call to Ibrahim-ben-Hassan, to Molgrabi Teuba, and Teuba-ben-Amin, they will not be roused from their sleep: there are also wounds.'

'Tell all the people there is only one God: is it the Sheikh of the Jellaheens that has done these deeds of Gin?'

'Let truth always be spoken; my words shall flow as the rock of Moses. The Sheikh of the Jellaheens counselled the young man not to fight, but the young man is a very Zatanai. Certainly there are many devils, but there is no devil like a Frank in a round hat.'

The evening advanced; the white moon, that had only gleamed, now glittered; the necks of the camels looked tall and silvery in its beam. The night-fires began to blaze, the lamps to twinkle in the crescent of dark tents. There was a shout, a general stir, the heads of spears were seen glistening in the ravine. They came; a winding line of warriors. Some, as they emerged into the plain, galloped forward and threw their spears into the air; but the main body preserved an appearance of discipline, and proceeded at a slow pace to the pavilion of the Sheikh. A body of horsemen came first; then warriors on dromedaries; Sheikh Hassan next, grave and erect as if nothing had happened, though he was wounded, and followed by his men, disarmed, though their chief retained his spear. Baroni followed. He was unhurt, and rode between two Bedoueens, with whom he continually conversed. After them, the bodies of Sheikh Salem and his comrades, covered with cloaks and stowed on camels. And then came the great prize, Tancred, mounted on a dromedary, his right arm bound up in a sling which Baroni had hastily made, and surrounded and followed by a large troop of horsemen, who treated him with the highest consideration, not only because he was a great prince, whose ransom could bring many camels to their tribe, but because he had shown those feats of valour which the wild Desert honours.

Notwithstanding his wound, which, though slight, began to be painful, and the extreme vexation of the whole affair, Tancred could not be insensible to the strange beauty of the scene which welcomed him. He had read of these deserted cities, carved out of the rocks of the wilderness, and once the capitals of flourishing and abounding kingdoms.

They stopped before the pavilion of the great Sheikh:

the arena of the amphitheatre became filled with camels, horses, groups of warriors; many mounted on the seats, that they might overlook the scene, their arms and shawled heads glistening in the silver blaze of the moon or the ruddy flames of the watch-fires. They assisted Tancred to descend, they ushered him with courtesy to their chief, who made room for Tancred on his own carpet, and motioned that he should be seated by his side. A small carpet was placed for Sheikh Hassan, and another for Baroni.

'Salaam, brother of many queens, all that you see is yours; Salaam Sheikh Hassan, we are brothers. Salaam,' added Amalek, looking at Baroni, 'they tell me that you can speak our language, which is beautiful as the moon and many palm-trees; tell the prince, brother of many queens, that he mistook the message that I sent him this morning, which was an invitation to a feast, not to a war. Tell him we are brothers.'

'Tell the Sheikh,' said Tancred, 'that I have no appetite for feasting, and desire to be informed why he has made me a prisoner.'

'Tell the prince, brother of many queens, that he is not a prisoner, but a guest.'

'Ask the Sheikh, then, whether we can depart at once.'

'Tell the prince, brother of many queens, that it would be rude in me to let him depart to-night.'

'Ask the Sheikh whether I may depart in the morning.'

'Tell the prince that, when the morning comes, he will find I am his brother.' So saying, the great Sheikh took his pipe from his mouth and gave it to Tancred: the greatest of distinctions. In a few moments, pipes were also brought to Sheikh Hassan and Baroni.

'No harm can come to you, my lord, after smoking that pipe,' said Baroni. 'We must make the best of affairs. I have been in worse straits with M. de Sidonia. What think you of Malay pirates? These are all gentlemen.'

While Baroni was speaking, a young man slowly and with dignity passed through the by-standers, advanced, and, looking very earnestly at Tancred, seated himself on the same carpet as the grand Sheikh. This action alone would have betokened the quality of the new comer, had not his kefia, similar to that of Sheikh Amalek, and his whole bearing, clearly denoted his princely character. He was very young; and Tancred, while he was struck by his earnest gaze, was attracted by his physiognomy, which, indeed, from its refined beauty and cast of impassioned intelligence, was highly interesting.

Preparations all this time had been making for the feast. Half a dozen sheep had been given to the returning band; everywhere resounded the grinding of coffee; men passed, carrying pitchers of leban and panniers of bread cakes hot from their simple oven. The great Sheikh, who had asked many questions after the oriental fashion: which was the most powerful nation, England or France; what was the name of a third European nation of which he had heard, white men with flat noses in green coats; whether the nation of white men with flat noses in green coats could have taken Acre as the English had, the taking of Acre being the test of military prowess; how many horses the Queen of the English had, and how many slaves; whether English pistols are good; whether the English drink wine; whether the English are Christian giaours or Pagan giaours? and so on, now invited Tancred, Sheikh Hassan, and two or three others, to enter his pavilion and partake of the banquet.

'The Sheikh must excuse me,' said Tancred to Baroni; 'I am wearied and wounded. Ask if I can retire and have a tent.'

'Are you wounded?' said the young Sheikh, who was sitting on the carpet of Amalek, and speaking, not only in a tone of touching sympathy, but in the language of Franguestan.

'Not severely,' said Tancred, less abruptly than he had yet spoken, for the manner and the appearance of the youth touched him; 'but this is my first fight, and perhaps

I make too much of it. However, my arm is painful and
stiff, and indeed, you may conceive after all this, I could
wish for a little repose.'

'The great Sheikh has allotted you a compartment of his
pavilion,' said the youth; ' but it will prove a noisy resting-
place, I fear, for a wounded man. I have a tent here, an
humbler one, but which is at least tranquil. Let me be
your host!'

'You are most gracious, and I should be much inclined
to be your guest, but I am a prisoner,' he said, haughtily,
'and cannot presume to follow my own will.'

'I will arrange all,' said the youth, and he conversed
with Sheikh Amalek for some moments. Then they all
rose, the young man advancing to Tancred, and saying in
a sweet coaxing voice, 'You are under my care. I will
not be a cruel gaoler; I could not be to you.' So saying,
making their reverence to the great Sheikh, the two young
men retired together from the arena. Baroni would have
followed them, when the youth stopped him, saying, with
decision, 'The great Sheikh expects your presence; you
must on no account be absent. I will tend your chief:
you will permit me?' he inquired in a tone of sympathy,
and then, offering to support the arm of Tancred, he murmured, ' It kills me to think that you are wounded.'

Tancred was attracted to the young stranger: his pre-
possessing appearance, his soft manners, the contrast which
they afforded to all around, and to the scenes and circumstances which Tancred had recently experienced, were
winning. Tancred, therefore, gladly accompanied him to
his pavilion, which was pitched outside the amphitheatre,
and stood apart. Notwithstanding the modest description
of his tent by the young Sheikh, it was by no means inconsiderable in size, for it possessed several compartments, and
was of a different colour and fashion from those of the rest
of the tribe. Several steeds were picketed in Arab fashion
near its entrance, and a group of attendants, smoking and
conversing with great animation, were sitting in a circle

close at hand. They pressed their hands to their hearts as
Tancred and his host passed them, but did not rise. Within
the pavilion, Tancred found a luxurious medley of cushions
and soft carpets, forming a delightful divan; pipes and
arms, and, to his great surprise, several numbers of a
French newspaper published at Smyrna.

'Ah !' exclaimed Tancred, throwing himself on the divan,
'after all I have gone through to-day, this is indeed a great
and an unexpected relief.'

''Tis your own divan,' said the young Arab, clapping
his hands; 'and when I have given some orders for your
comfort, I shall only be your guest, though not a distant
one.' He spoke some words in Arabic to an attendant who
entered, and who returned very shortly with a silver lamp
fed with palm oil, which he placed on the ground.

'I have two poor Englishmen here,' said Tancred, 'my
servants; they must be in sad straits; unable to speak a
word ——'

'I will give orders that they shall attend you. In the
meantime you must refresh yourself, however lightly,
before you repose.' At this moment there entered the tent
several attendants with a variety of dishes, which Tancred
would have declined, but the young Sheikh, selecting one
of them, said, 'This, at least, I must urge you to taste, for
it is a favourite refreshment with us after great fatigue, and
has some properties of great virtue.' So saying, he handed
to Tancred a dish of bread, dates, and prepared cream,
which Tancred, notwithstanding his previous want of
relish, cheerfully admitted to be excellent. After this, as
Tancred would partake of no other dish, pipes were brought
to the two young men, who, reclining on the divan, smoked
and conversed.

'Of all the strange things that have happened to me
to-day,' said Tancred, 'not the least surprising, and certainly the most agreeable, has been making your acquaintance. Your courtesy has much compensated me for the
rude treatment of your tribe; but, I confess, such refinement

is what, under any circumstances, I should not have expected to find among the tents of the Desert, any more than
this French journal.'

'I am not an Arab,' said the young man, speaking slowly
and with an air of some embarrassment.

'Ah!' exclaimed Tancred.

'I am a Christian prince.'

'Yes!'

'A prince of the Lebanon, devoted to the English, and
one who has suffered much in their cause.'

'You are not a prisoner here, like myself?'

'No, I am here, seeking some assistance for those suf-
ferers who should be my subjects, were I not deprived of
my sceptre, and they of a prince whose family has reigned
over and protected them for more than seven centuries.
The powerful tribe of which Sheikh Amalek is the head
often pitch their tents in the great Syrian Desert, in the
neighbourhood of Damascus, and there are affairs in which
they can aid my unhappy people.'

'It is a great position, yours,' said Tancred, in an animated tone, 'at the same time a Syrian and a Christian
prince!'

'Yes,' said the young Emir, eagerly, 'if the English
would only understand their own interests, with my co-
operation Syria might be theirs.'

'The English!' said Tancred, 'why should the English
take Syria?'

'France will take it if they do not.'

'I hope not,' said Tancred.

'But something must be done,' said the Emir. 'The
Porte never could govern it. Do you think anybody in
Lebanon really cares for the Pacha of Damascus? If the
Egyptians had not disarmed the mountain, the Turks would
be driven out of Syria in a week.'

'A Syrian and a Christian prince!' said Tancred, musingly, 'There are elements in that position stronger than
the Porte, stronger than England, stronger than united

Europe. Syria was a great country when France and England were forests. The tricolour has crossed the Alps and the Rhine, and the flag of England has beaten even the tricolour; but if I were a Syrian prince, I would raise the cross of Christ and ask for the aid of no foreign banner.'

' If I could only raise a loan,' said the Emir, ' I could do without France and England.'

' A loan!' exclaimed Tancred; 'I see the poison of modern liberalism has penetrated even the Desert. Believe me, national redemption is not an affair of usury.'

At this moment there was some little disturbance without the tent, which it seems was occasioned by the arrival of Tancred's servants, Freeman and Trueman. These excellent young men persisted in addressing the Arabs in their native English, and, though we cannot for a moment believe that they fancied themselves understood, still, from a mixture of pride and perverseness peculiarly British, they continued their valuable discourse as if every word told, or, if not apprehended, was a striking proof of the sheer stupidity of their new companions. The noise became louder and louder, and at length Freeman and Trueman entered.

' Well,' said Tancred, ' and how have you been getting on?'

' Well, my lord, I don't know,' said Freeman, with a sort of jolly sneer; ' we have been dining with the savages.'

' They are not savages, Freeman.'

' Well, my lord, they have not much more clothes, anyhow; and as for knives and forks, there is not such a thing known.'

' As for that, there was not such a thing known as a fork in England little more than two hundred years ago, and we were not savages then; for the best part of Montacute Castle was built long before that time.'

' I wish we were there, my lord!'

' I dare say you do: however, we must make the best of present circumstances. I wanted to know, in the first place,

whether you had food ; as for lodging, Mr. Baroni, I dare
say, will manage something for you; and if not, you had
better quarter yourselves by the side of this tent. With
your own cloaks and mine, you will manage very well.'

'Thank you, my lord. We have brought your lordship's
things with us. I don't know what I shall do to-morrow
about your lordship's boots. The savages have got hold of
the bottle of blacking and have been drinking it like anything.'

'Never mind my boots,' said Tancred; 'we have got
other things to think of now.'

'I told them what it was,' said Freeman, ' but they went
on just the same.'

'Obstinate dogs ! ' said Tancred.

'I think they took it for wine, my lord,' said Trueman.
'I never see such ignorant creatures.'

'You find now the advantage of a good education, Trueman.'

'Yes, my lord, we do, and feel very grateful to your lordship's honoured mother for the same. When we came down
out of the mountains and see those blazing fires, if I didn't
think they were going to burn us alive, unless we changed
our religion! I said the catechism as hard as I could the
whole way, and felt as much like a blessed martyr as
could be.'

'Well, well,' said Tancred, 'I dare say they will spare
our lives. I cannot much assist you here ; but if there be
anything you particularly want, I will try and see what can
be done.'

Freeman and Trueman looked at each other, and their
speaking faces held common consultation. At length, the
former, with some slight hesitation, said, ' We don't like to
be troublesome, my lord, but if your lordship would ask
for some sugar for us ; we cannot drink their coffee without
sugar.'

CHAPTER III.

' I WOULD not mention it to your lordship last night,' said Baroni; ' I thought enough had happened for one day.'

' But now you think I am sufficiently fresh for new troubles.'

' He spoke it in Hebrew, that myself and Sheikh Hassan should not understand him, but I know something of that dialect.'

' In Hebrew ! And why in Hebrew ? '

' They follow the laws of Moses, this tribe.'

' Do you mean that they are Jews ? '

' The Arabs are only Jews upon horseback,' said Baroni. ' This tribe, I find, call themselves Rechabites.'

' Ah ! ' exclaimed Tancred, and he began to muse. ' I have heard of that name before. Is it possible,' thought he, ' that my visit to Bethany should have led to this captivity ? '

' This affair must have been planned at Jerusalem,' said Baroni ; ' I saw from the first it was not a common foray. These people know everything. They will send immediately to Besso ; they know he is your banker, and that if you want to build the Temple, he must pay for it, and unless a most immoderate ransom is given, they will carry us all into the interior of the Desert.'

' And what do you counsel ? '

' In this, as in all things, to gain time ; and principally because I am without resource, but with time expedients develope themselves. Naturally, what is wanted will come ; expediency is a law of nature. The camel is a wonderful animal, but the Desert made the camel. I have already impressed upon the great Sheikh that you are not a prince of the blood ; that your father is ruined, that there has been a murrain for three years among his herds and flocks ; and that, though you appear to be travelling for amusement, you are, in fact, a political exile. All these are grounds for

a reduced ransom. At present he believes nothing that I
say, because his mind has been previously impressed with
contrary and more cogent representations, but what I say
will begin to work when he has experienced some disappointment, and the period of re-action arrives. Re-action
is the law of society; it is inevitable. All success depends
upon seizing it.'

'It appears to me that you are a great philosopher, Baroni,' said Tancred.

'I travelled five years with M. de Sidonia,' said Baroni.
'We were in perpetual scrapes, often worse than this, and
my master moralised upon every one of them. I shared his
adventures, and I imbibed some of his wisdom; and the
consequence is, that I always ought to know what to say,
and generally what to do.'

'Well, here at least is some theatre for your practice;
though, as far as I can form an opinion, our course is
simple, though ignominious. We must redeem ourselves
from captivity. If it were only the end of my crusade, one
might submit to it, like Cœur de Lion, after due suffering;
but occurring at the commencement, the catastrophe is
mortifying, and I doubt whether I shall have heart enough
to pursue my way. Were I alone, I certainly would not
submit to ransom. I would look upon captivity as one of
those trials that await me, and I would endeavour to extricate myself from it by courage and address, relying ever
on Divine aid; but I am not alone. I have involved you in
this mischance, and these poor Englishmen, and, it would
seem, the brave Hassan and his tribe. I can hardly ask you
to make the sacrifice which I would cheerfully endure; and
therefore it seems to me that we have only one course, to
march under the forks.'

'With submission,' said Baroni, 'I cannot agree with any
of your lordship's propositions. You take an extreme view
of our case. Extreme views are never just; something
always turns up which disturbs the calculations formed
upon their decided data. This something is Circumstance.

Circumstance has decided every crisis which I have experienced, and not the primitive facts on which we have consulted. Rest assured that Circumstance will clear us now.'

'I see no room, in our situation, for the accidents on which you rely,' said Tancred. 'Circumstance, as you call it, is the creature of cities, where the action of a multitude, influenced by different motives, produces innumerable and ever-changing combinations; but we are in the Desert. The great Sheikh will never change his mind any more than his habits of life, which are the same as his ancestors pursued thousands of years ago; and, for an identical reason, he is isolated and superior to all influences.'

'Something always turns up,' said Baroni.

'It seems to me that we are in a *cul-de-sac*,' said Tancred.

'There is always an outlet; one can escape from a *cul-de-sac* by a window.'

'Do you think it would be advisable to consult the master of this tent?' said Tancred, in a lower tone. 'He is very friendly.'

'The Emir Fakredeen,' said Baroni.

'Is that his name?'

'So I learnt last night. He is a prince of the house of Shehaab; a great house, but fallen.'

'He is a Christian,' said Tancred, earnestly.

'Is he?' said Baroni carelessly; 'I have known a good many Shehaabs, and if you will tell me their company, I will tell you their creed.'

'He might give us some advice.'

'No doubt of it, my lord; if advice could break our chains, we should soon be free; but in these countries my only confidant is my camel. Assuming that this affair is to end in a ransom, what we want now is to change the impressions of the great Sheikh respecting your wealth. This can only be done from the same spot where the original ideas emanated. I must induce him to permit me to accompany his messenger to Besso. This mission will take time,

and he who gains time gains everything, as M. de Sidonia
said to me when the savages were going to burn us alive,
and there came on a thunder-storm which extinguished
their fagots.'

'You must really tell me your history some day, Baroni,'
said Tancred.

'When my mission has failed. It will perhaps relieve
your imprisonment; at present, I repeat, we must work for
a moderate ransom, instead of the millions of which they
talk, and during the negotiation take the chance of some
incident which will more agreeably free us.'

'Ah! I despair of that.'

'I do not, for it is presumptuous to believe that man can
foresee the future, which will be your lordship's case, if you
owe your freedom only to your piastres.'

'But they say that everything is Calculation, Baroni.'

'No,' said Baroni, with energy, 'everything is Adventure.'

In the meantime the Emir Fakredeen was the prey of
contending emotions. Tancred had from the first, and in
an instant, exercised over his susceptible temperament that
magnetic influence to which he was so strangely subject.
In the heart of the wilderness and in the person of his
victim, the young Emir suddenly recognised the heroic
character which he had himself so vaguely and, as it now
seemed to him, so vainly attempted to realise. The appearance and the courage of Tancred, the thoughtful repose of his manner, his high bearing amid the distressful
circumstances in which he was involved, and the large
views which the few words that had escaped from him on
the preceding evening would intimate that he took of public
transactions, completely captivated Fakredeen, who seemed
at length to have found the friend for whom he had often
sighed; the steadfast and commanding spirit, whose control,
he felt conscious, was often required by his quick but whimsical temperament. And in what relation did he stand to
this being whom he longed to press to his heart, and then

go forth with him and conquer the world? It would not bear contemplation. The arming of the Maronites became quite a secondary object in comparison with obtaining the friendship of Tancred. Would that he had not involved himself in this conspiracy! and yet, but for this conspiracy, Tancred and himself might never have met. It was impossible to grapple with the question; circumstances must be watched, and some new combination formed to extricate both of them from their present perplexed position.

Fakredeen sent one of his attendants in the morning to offer Tancred horses, should his guest, as is the custom of Englishmen, care to explore the neighbouring ruins which were celebrated; but Tancred's wound kept him confined to his tent. Then the Emir begged permission to pay him a visit, which was to have lasted only a quarter of an hour; but when Fakredeen had once established himself in the divan with his nargilly, he never quitted it. It would have been difficult for Tancred to have found a more interesting companion; impossible to have made an acquaintance more singularly unreserved. His frankness was startling. Tancred had no experience of such self-revelations; such a jumble of sublime aspirations and equivocal conduct; such a total disregard of means, such complicated plots, such a fertility of perplexed and tenebrous intrigue! The animated manner and the picturesque phrase, too, in which all this was communicated, heightened the interest and effect. Fakredeen sketched a character in a sentence, and you knew instantly the individual whom he described without any personal knowledge. Unlike the Orientals in general, his gestures were as vivid as his words. He acted the interviews, he achieved the adventures before you. His voice could take every tone and his countenance every form. In the midst of all this, bursts of plaintive melancholy; sometimes the anguish of a sensibility too exquisite, alternating with a devilish mockery and a fatal absence of all self-respect.

'It appears to me,' said Tancred, when the young Emir

S

had declared his star accursed, since, after the ceaseless exertions of years, he was still as distant as ever from the accomplishment of his purpose, 'it appears to me that your system is essentially erroneous. I do not believe that anything great is ever effected by management. All this intrigue, in which you seem such an adept, might be of some service in a court or in an exclusive senate; but to free a nation you require something more vigorous and more simple. This system of intrigue in Europe is quite oldfashioned. It is one of the superstitions left us by the wretched eighteenth century, a period when aristocracy was rampant throughout Christendom; and what were the consequences? All faith in God or man, all grandeur of purpose, all nobility of thought, and all beauty of sentiment, withered and shrivelled up. Then the dexterous management of a few individuals, base or dull, was the only means of success. But we live in a different age: there are popular sympathies, however imperfect, to appeal to; we must recur to the high primeval practice, and address nations now as the heroes, and prophets, and legislators of antiquity. If you wish to free your country, and make the Syrians a nation, it is not to be done by sending secret envoys to Paris or London, cities themselves which are perhaps both doomed to fall; you must act like Moses and Mahomet.'

'But you forget the religions,' said Fakredeen. 'I have so many religions to deal with. If my fellows were all Christians, or all Moslemin, or all Jews, or all Pagans, I grant you, something might be effected: the cross, the crescent, the ark, or an old stone, anything would do: I would plant it on the highest range in the centre of the country, and I would carry Damascus and Aleppo both in one campaign; but I am debarred from this immense support; I could only preach nationality, and, as they all hate each other worse almost than they do the Turks, that would not be very inviting; nationality, without race as a plea, is like the smoke of this nargilly, a fragrant puff.

Well, then, there remains only personal influence: ancient family, vast possessions, and traditionary power; mere personal influence can only be maintained by management, by what you stigmatise as intrigue; and the most dexterous member of the Shehaab family will be, in the long run, Prince of Lebanon.'

'And if you wish only to be Prince of the Lebanon, I dare say you may succeed,' said Tancred, 'and perhaps with much less pains than you at present give yourself. But what becomes of all your great plans of an hour ago, when you were to conquer the East, and establish the independence of the Oriental races?'

'Ah!' exclaimed Fakredeen with a sigh, 'these are the only ideas for which it is worth while to live.'

'The world was never conquered by intrigue: it was conquered by faith. Now, I do not see that you have faith in anything.'

'Faith,' said Fakredeen, musingly, as if his ear had caught the word for the first time, 'faith! that is a grand idea. If one could only have faith in something and conquer the world!'

'See now,' said Tancred, with unusual animation, 'I find no charm in conquering the world to establish a dynasty: a dynasty, like everything else, wears out; indeed, it does not last as long as most things; it has a precipitate tendency to decay. There are reasons; we will not now dwell on them. One should conquer the world not to enthrone a man, but an idea, for ideas exist for ever. But what idea? There is the touchstone of all philosophy! Amid the wreck of creeds, the crash of empires, French revolutions, English reforms, Catholicism in agony, and Protestantism in convulsions, discordant Europe demands the key-note, which none can sound. If Asia be in decay, Europe is in confusion. Your repose may be death, but our life is anarchy.'

'I am thinking,' said Fakredeen, thoughtfully, 'how we in Syria could possibly manage to have faith in anything;

I had faith in Mehemet Ali, but he is a Turk, and that upset him. If, instead of being merely a rebellious Pacha, he had placed himself at the head of the Arabs, and revived the Caliphate, you would have seen something. Head the Desert and you may do anything. But it is so difficult. If you can once get the tribes out of it, they will go anywhere. See what they did when they last came forth. It is a simoom, a kamsin, fatal, irresistible. They are as fresh, too, as ever. The Arabs are always young; it is the only race that never withers. I am an Arab myself; from my ancestor who was the standard-bearer of the Prophet, the consciousness of race is the only circumstance that sometimes keeps up my spirit.'

'I am an Arab only in religion,' said Tancred, 'but the consciousness of creed sustains me. I know well, though born in a distant and northern isle, that the Creator of the world speaks with man only in this land; and that is why I am here.'

The young Emir threw an earnest glance at his companion, whose countenance, though grave, was calm. 'Then you have faith?' said Fakredeen, inquiringly.

'I have passive faith,' said Tancred. 'I know that there is a Deity who has revealed his will at intervals during different ages; but of his present purpose I feel ignorant, and therefore I have not active faith; I know not what to do, and should be reduced to a mere spiritual slothfulness, had I not resolved to struggle with this fearful necessity, and so embarked in this great pilgrimage which has so strangely brought us together.'

'But you have your sacred books to consult?' said Fakredeen.

'There were sacred books when Jehovah conferred with Solomon; there was a still greater number of sacred books when Jehovah inspired the prophets; the sacred writings were yet more voluminous when the Creator ordained that there should be for human edification a completely new series of inspired literature. Nearly two thousand years have passed since the last of those works appeared. It is a greater interval than elapsed between the writings of Malachi and the writings of Matthew.'

'The prior of the Maronite convent, at Mar Hanna, has often urged on me, as conclusive evidence of the falseness of Mahomet's mission, that our Lord Jesus declared that after him "many false prophets should arise," and warned his followers.'

'There spoke the Prince of Israel,' said Tancred, 'not the universal Redeemer. He warned his tribe against the advent of false Messiahs, no more. Far from terminating by his coming the direct communication between God and man, his appearance was only the herald of a relation between the Creator and his creatures more fine, more permanent, and more express. The inspiring and consoling influence of the Paraclete only commenced with the ascension of the Divine Son. In this fact, perhaps, may be found a sufficient reason why no written expression of the celestial will has subsequently appeared. But, instead of foreclosing my desire for express communication, it would, on the contrary, be a circumstance to authorise it.'

'Then how do you know that Mahomet was not inspired?' said Fakredeen.

'Far be it from me to impugn the divine commission of any of the seed of Abraham,' replied Tancred. 'There are doctors of our church who recognise the sacred office of Mahomet, though they hold it to be, what divine commissions, with the great exception, have ever been, limited and local.'

'God has never spoken to a European?' said Fakredeen, inquiringly.

'Never.'

'But you are a European?'

'And your inference is just,' said Tancred, in an agitated voice, and with a changing countenance. 'It is one that has for some time haunted my soul. In England, when I prayed in vain for enlightenment, I at last induced myself

to believe that the Supreme Being would not deign to reveal his will unless in the land which his presence had
rendered holy; but since I have been a dweller within its
borders, and poured forth my passionate prayers at all its
holy places, and received no sign, the desolating thought
has sometimes come over my spirit, that there is a qualification of blood as well as of locality necessary for this
communion, and that the favoured votary must not only
kneel in the Holy Land but be of the holy race.'

'I am an Arab,' said Fakredeen. 'It is something.'

'If I were an Arab in race as well as in religion,' said
Tancred, 'I would not pass my life in schemes to govern
some mountain tribes.'

'I'll tell you,' said the Emir, springing from his divan,
and flinging the tube of his nargilly to the other end of the
tent: 'the game is in our hands, if we have energy. There
is a combination which would entirely change the whole
face of the world, and bring back empire to the East.
Though you are not the brother of the Queen of the English, you are nevertheless a great English prince, and the
Queen will listen to what you say; especially if you talk to
her as you talk to me, and say such fine things in such a
beautiful voice. Nobody ever opened my mind like you.
You will magnetise the Queen as you have magnetised me.
Go back to England and arrange this. You see, gloze it
over as they may, one thing is clear, it is finished with
England. There are three things which alone must destroy it. Primo, O'Connell appropriating to himself the
revenues of half of Her Majesty's dominions. Secondo, the
cottons; the world begins to get a little disgusted with
those cottons; naturally everybody prefers silk; I am sure
that the Lebanon in time could supply the whole world
with silk, if it were properly administered. Thirdly, steam;
with this steam your great ships have become a respectable
Noah's ark. The game is up; Louis Philippe can take
Windsor Castle whenever he pleases, as you took Acre,
with the wind in his teeth. It is all over, then. Now, see

a *coup d'état* that saves all. You must perform the Portuguese scheme on a great scale; quit a petty and exhausted position for a vast and prolific empire. Let the Queen of the English collect a great fleet, let her stow away all her treasure, bullion, gold plate, and precious arms; be accompanied by all her court and chief people, and transfer the seat of her empire from London to Delhi. There she will find an immense empire ready made, a firstrate army, and a large revenue. In the meantime I will arrange with Mehemet Ali. He shall have Bagdad and Mesopotamia, and pour the Bedoueen cavalry into Persia. I will take care of Syria and Asia Minor. The only way to manage the Affghans is by Persia and by the Arabs. We will acknowledge the Empress of India as our suzerain, and secure for her the Levantine coast. If she like, she shall have Alexandria as she now has Malta: it could be arranged. Your queen is young; she has an *avenir.* Aberdeen and Sir Peel will never give her this advice; their habits are formed. They are too old, too *rusés.* But, you see! the greatest empire that ever existed; besides which she gets rid of the embarrassment of her Chambers! And quite practicable; for the only difficult part, the conquest of India, which baffled Alexander, is all done!'

CHAPTER IV.

It was not so much a conviction as a suspicion that Tancred had conveyed to the young Emir, when the pilgrim had confessed that the depressing thought sometimes came over him, that he was deficient in that qualification of race which was necessary for the high communion to which he aspired. Four-and-twenty hours before he was not thus dejected. Almost within sight of Sinai, he was still full of faith. But his vexatious captivity, and the enfeebling consequences of his wound, dulled his spirit. Alone, among strangers and foes, in pain and in peril, and without that energy which finds excitement in difficulty, and can mock at danger, which requires no counsellor but our own quick brain, and no champion but our own right arm, the high spirit of Tancred for the first time flagged. As the twilight descended over the rocky city, its sculptured tombs and excavated temples, and its strewn remains of palaces and theatres, his heart recurred with tenderness to the halls and towers of Montacute and Bellamont, and the beautiful affections beneath those stately roofs, that, urged on, as he had once thought, by a divine influence, now, as he was half tempted to credit, by a fantastic impulse, he had dared to desert. Brooding in dejection, his eyes were suffused with tears.

It was one of those moments of amiable weakness which make us all akin, when sublime ambition, the mystical predispositions of genius, the solemn sense of duty, all the heaped-up lore of ages, and the dogmas of a high philosophy alike desert us, or sink into nothingness. The voice of his mother sounded in his ear, and he was haunted by his father's anxious glance. Why was he there? Why was he, the child of a northern isle, in the heart of the Stony Arabia, far from the scene of his birth and of his duties? A disheartening, an awful question, which, if it could not be satisfactorily answered by Tancred of Montacute, it seemed to him that his future, wherever or however passed, must be one of intolerable bale.

Was he, then, a stranger there? uncalled, unexpected, intrusive, unwelcome? Was it a morbid curiosity, or the proverbial restlessness of a satiated aristocrat, that had drawn him to these wilds? What wilds? Had he no connection with them? Had he not from his infancy repeated, in the congregation of his people, the laws which, from the awful summit of these surrounding mountains, the Father of all had himself delivered for the government of mankind? These Arabian laws regulated his life. And the wanderings of an Arabian tribe in this 'great and terrible wilderness,' under the immediate direction of the Creator, sanctified by his miracles, governed by his counsels, illumined by his presence, had been the first and guiding history that had been entrusted to his young intelligence, from which it had drawn its first pregnant examples of human conduct and divine inter-position, and formed its first dim conceptions of the rela-tions between man and God. Why, then, he had a right to be here! He had a connection with these regions; they had a hold upon him. He was not here like an Indian Brahmin, who visits Europe from a principle of curiosity, however rational or however refined. The land which the Hindoo visits is not his land, nor his father's land; the laws which regulate it are not his laws, and the faith which fills its temples is not the revelation that floats upon his sacred Ganges. But for this English youth, words had been uttered and things done, more than thirty centuries ago, in this stony wilderness, which influenced his opinions and regulated his conduct every day of his life, in that distant and seagirt home, which, at the time of their occur-rence, was not as advanced in civilisation as the Polynesian groups or the islands of New Zealand. The life and pro-perty of England are protected by the laws of Sinai. The hard-working people of England are secured in every seven days a day of rest by the laws of Sinai. And yet they persecute the Jews, and hold up to odium the race to whom they are indebted for the sublime legislation which alleviates the inevitable lot of the labouring multitude!

And when that labouring multitude cease for a while from a toil which equals almost Egyptian bondage, and demands that exponent of the mysteries of the heart, that soother of the troubled spirit, which poetry can alone afford, to whose harp do the people of England fly for sympathy and solace? Who is the most popular poet in this country? Is he to be found among the Mr. Words-worths and the Lord Byrons, amid sauntering reveries or monologues of sublime satiety? Shall we seek him among the wits of Queen Anne? Even to the myriad-minded

Shakspeare can we award the palm? No; the most popular poet in England is the sweet singer of Israel. Since the days of the heritage, when every man dwelt safely under his vine and under his fig-tree, there never was a race who sang so often the odes of David as the people of Great Britain.

Vast as the obligations of the whole human family are to the Hebrew race, there is no portion of the modern populations so much indebted to them as the British people. It was 'the sword of the Lord and of Gideon' that won the boasted liberties of England; chanting the same canticles that cheered the heart of Judah amid their glens, the Scotch, upon their hill-sides, achieved their religious freedom.

Then why do these Saxon and Celtic societies persecute an Arabian race, from whom they have adopted laws of sublime benevolence, and in the pages of whose literature they have found perpetual delight, instruction, and consolation? That is a great question, which, in an enlightened age, may be fairly asked, but to which even the self-complacent nineteenth century would find some difficulty in contributing a reply. Does it stand thus? Independently of their admirable laws which have elevated our condition, and of their exquisite poetry which has charmed it; independently of their heroic history which has animated us to the pursuit of public liberty, we are indebted to the Hebrew people for our knowledge of the true God and for the redemption from our sins.

'Then I have a right to be here,' said Tancred of Montacute, as his eyes were fixed in abstraction on the stars of Arabia; 'I am not a travelling dilettante, mourning over a ruin, or in ecstasies at a deciphered inscription. I come to the land whose laws I obey, whose religion I profess, and I seek, upon its sacred soil, those sanctions which for ages were abundantly accorded. The angels who visited the Patriarchs, and announced the advent of the Judges, who guided the pens of Prophets and bore tidings to the Apostles, spoke also to the Shepherds in the field. I look upon the host of heaven; do they no longer stand before the Lord? Where are the Cherubim, where the Seraphs? Where is Michael the Destroyer? Gabriel of a thousand missions?'

At this moment, the sound of horsemen recalled Tancred from his reverie, and, looking up, he observed a group of Arabs approaching him, three of whom were mounted. Soon he recognised the great Sheikh Amalek, and Hassan, the late commander of his escort. The young Syrian Emir was their companion. This was a visit of hospitable ceremony from the great Sheikh to his distinguished prisoner. Amalek, pressing his hand to his heart, gave Tancred the salute of peace, and then, followed by Hassan, who had lost nothing of his calm self-respect, but who conducted himself as if he were still free, the great Sheikh seated himself on the carpet that was spread before the tent, and took the pipe, which was immediately offered him by Freeman and Trueman, following the instructions of an attendant of the Emir Fakredeen.

After the usual compliments and some customary observations about horses and pistols, Fakredeen, who had seated himself close to Tancred, with a kind of shrinking cajolery, as if he were seeking the protection of some superior being, addressing Amalek in a tone of easy assurance, which remarkably contrasted with the sentimental deference he displayed towards his prisoner, said:

'Sheikh of Sheikhs, there is but one God: now is it Allah, or Jehovah?'

'The palm-tree is sometimes called a date-tree,' replied Amalek, 'but there is only one tree.'

'Good,' said Fakredeen, 'but you do not pray to Allah?'

'I pray as my fathers prayed,' said Amalek.

'And you pray to Jehovah?'

'It is said.'

'Sheikh Hassan,' said the Emir, 'there is but one God, and his name is Jehovah. Why do you not pray to Jehovah?'

'Truly there is but one God,' said Sheikh Hassan, 'and

Mahomet is his Prophet. He told my fathers to pray to Allah, and to Allah I pray.'

'Is Mahomet the prophet of God, Sheikh of Sheikhs?'

'It may be,' replied Amalek, with a nod of assent.

'Then why do you not pray as Sheikh Hassan?'

'Because Moses, without doubt the prophet of God, for all believe in him, Sheikh Hassan, and Emir Fakredeen, and you too, Prince, brother of queens, married into our family and taught us to pray to Jehovah. There may be other prophets, but the children of Jethro would indeed ride on asses were they not content with Moses.'

'And you have his five books?' inquired Tancred.

'We had them from the beginning, and we shall keep them to the end.'

'And you learnt in them that Moses married the daughter of Jethro?'

'Did I learn in them that I have wells and camels? We want no books to tell us who married our daughters.'

'And yet it is not yesterday that Moses fled from Egypt into Midian?'

'It is not yesterday for those who live in cities, where they say at one gate that it is morning, and at another it is night. Where men tell lies, the deed of the dawn is the secret of sunset. But in the Desert nothing changes; neither the acts of a man's life, nor the words of a man's lips. We drink at the same well where Moses helped Zipporah, we tend the same flocks, we live under the same tents; our words have changed as little as our waters, our habits, or our dwellings. What my father learnt from those before him, he delivered to me, and I have told it to my son. What is time and what is truth, that I should forget that a prophet of Jehovah married into my house?'

'Where little is done, little is said,' observed Sheikh Hassan, 'and Silence is the mother of Truth. Since the Hegira, nothing has happened in Arabia, and before that was Moses, and before him the giants.'

'Let truth always be spoken,' said Amalek; 'your words

are a flowing stream, and the children of Rechab and the tribes of the Senites never joined him of Mecca, for they had the five books, and they said, " Is not that enough ? " They withdrew to the Syrian wilderness, and they multiplied. But the sons of Koreidha, who also had the five books, but who were not children of Rechab, but who came into the Desert near Medina after Nebuchadnezzar had destroyed El Khuds, they first joined him of Mecca, and then they made war on him, and he broke their bows and led them into captivity; and they are to be found in the cities of Yemen to this day; the children of Israel who live in the cities of Yemen are the tribe of Koreidha.'

'Unhappy sons of Koreidha, who made war upon the Prophet, and who live in cities!' said Sheikh Hassan, taking a fresh pipe.

'And perhaps,' said the young Emir, 'if you had not been children of Jethro, you might have acknowledged him of Mecca, Sheikh of Sheikhs.'

'There is but one God,' said Amalek ; 'but there may be many prophets. It becomes not a son of Jethro to seek other than Moses. But I will not say that the Koran comes not from God, since it was written by one who was of the tribe of Koreish, and the tribe of Koreish are the lineal descendants of Ibrahim.'

'And you believe that the Word of God could come only to the seed of Abraham ?' asked Tancred, eagerly.

'I and my fathers have watered our flocks in the wilderness since time was,' replied Amalek; 'we have seen the Pharaohs, and Nebuchadnezzar, and Iskander, and the Romans, and the Sultan of the French : they conquered everything except us; and where are they ? They are sand. Let men doubt of unicorns : but of one thing there can be no doubt, that God never spoke except to an Arab.'

Tancred covered his face with his hands. Then, after a few moments' pause, looking up, he said, 'Sheikh of Sheikhs, I am your prisoner; and was, when you captured me, a pilgrim to Mount Sinai, a spot which, in your belief, is not less sacred than in mine. We are, as I have learned, only two days' journey from that holy place. Grant me this boon, that I may at once proceed thither, guarded as you will. I pledge you the word of a Christian noble, that I will not attempt to escape. Long before you have received a reply from Jerusalem, I shall have returned; and, whatever may be the result of the visit of Baroni, I shall, at least, have fulfilled my pilgrimage.'

'Prince, brother of queens,' replied Amalek, with that politeness which is the characteristic of the Arabian chieftains; 'under my tents you have only to command; go where you like, return when you please. My children shall attend you as your guardians, not as your guards.' And the great Sheikh rose and retired.

Tancred re-entered his tent, and, reclining, fell into a reverie of distracting thoughts. The history of his life and mind seemed with a whirling power to pass before him; his birth, in a clime unknown to the Patriarchs; his education, unconsciously to himself, in an Arabian literature; his imbibing, from his tender infancy, oriental ideas and oriental creeds; the contrast that the occidental society in which he had been reared presented to them; his dissatisfaction with that social system; his conviction of the growing melancholy of enlightened Europe, veiled, as it may be, with sometimes a conceited bustle, sometimes a desperate shipwreck gaiety, sometimes with all the exciting empiricism of science; his perplexity that, between the Asian revelation and the European practice, there should be so little conformity, and why the relations between them should be so limited and imperfect; above all, his passionate desire to penetrate the mystery of the elder world, and share its celestial privileges and divine prerogative. Tancred sighed.

He looked round; some one had gently drawn his hand. It was the young Emir kneeling, his beautiful blue eyes bedewed with tears.

'You are unhappy,' said Fakredeen, in a tone of plaintiveness.

'It is the doom of man,' replied Tancred; 'and in my position sadness should not seem strange.'

'The curse of ten thousand mothers on those who made you a prisoner; the curse of twenty thousand mothers on him who inflicted on you a wound!'

''Tis the fortune of life,' said Tancred, more cheerfully; 'and in truth I was perhaps thinking of other things.'

'Do you know why I trouble you when your heart is dark?' said the young Emir. 'See now, if you will it, you are free. The great Sheikh has consented that you should go to Sinai. I have two dromedaries here, fleeter than the Kamsin. At the well of Mokatteb, where we encamp for the night, I will serve raki to the Bedoueens; I have some with me, strong enough to melt the snow of Lebanon; if it will not do, they shall smoke some timbak, that will make them sleep like pachas. I know this Desert as a man knows his father's house; we shall be at Hebron before they untie their eyelids. Tell me, is it good?'

'Were I alone,' said Tancred, 'without a single guard, I must return.'

'Why?'

'Because I have pledged the word of a Christian noble.'

'To a man who does not believe in Christ. Faugh! Is it not itself a sin to keep faith with heretics?'

'But is he one?' said Tancred. 'He believes in Moses; he disbelieves in none of the seed of Abraham. He is of that seed himself! Would I were such a heretic as Sheikh Amalek!'

'If you will only pay me a visit in the Lebanon, I would introduce you to our patriarch, and he would talk as much theology with you as you like. For my own part it is not a kind of knowledge that I have much cultivated; you know I am peculiarly situated, we have so many religions on the mountain; but time presses; tell me, my prince, shall Hebron be our point?'

'If Amalek believed in Baal, I must return,' said Tancred; 'even if it were to certain death. Besides, I could not desert my men; and Baroni, what would become of him?'

'We could easily make some plan that would extricate them. Dismiss them from your mind, and trust yourself to me. I know nothing that would delight me more than to balk these robbers of their prey.'

'I should not talk of such things,' said Tancred; 'I must remain here, or I must return.'

'What can you want to do on Mount Sinai?' murmured the prince rather pettishly. 'Now if it were Mount Lebanon, and you had a wish to employ yourself, there is an immense field! We might improve the condition of the people; we might establish manufactures, stimulate agriculture, extend commerce, get an appalto of the silk, buy it all up at sixty piastres per oke, and sell it at Marseilles at two hundred, and at the same time advance the interests of true religion as much as you please.'

CHAPTER V.

TEN days had elapsed since the capture of Tancred; Amalek and his Arabs were still encamped in the rocky city; the beams of the early sun were just rising over the crest of the amphitheatre, when four horsemen, who were recognised as the children of Rechab, issued from the ravine. They galloped over the plain, shouted, and threw their lances in the air. From the crescent of black tents came forth the warriors, some mounted their horses and met their returning brethren, others prepared their welcome. The horses neighed, the camels stirred their long necks. All living things seemed conscious that an event had occurred.

The four horsemen were surrounded by their brethren; but one of them, giving and returning blessings, darted forward to the pavilion of the great Sheikh.

'Have you brought camels, Shedad, son of Amroo?' inquired one of the welcomers to the welcomed.

'We have been to El Khuds,' was the reply. 'What we have brought back is a seal of Solomon.'

'From Mount Seir to the City of the Friend, what have you seen in the joyful land?'

'We found the sons of Hamar by the well-side of Jumda we found the marks of many camels in the pass of Gharendel, and the marks in the pass of Gharendel were not the marks of the camels of the Beni-Hamar.'

'I had a dream, and the children of Tora said to me, "Who art thou in the lands of our father's flocks? Are none but the sons of Rechab to drink the sweet waters of Edom?" Methinks the marks in the pass of Gharendel were the marks of the camels of the children of Tora.'

'There is feud between the Beni-Tora and the Beni-Hamar,' replied the other Arab, shaking his head. 'The Beni-Tora are in the wilderness of Akiba, and the Beni-Hamar have burnt their tents and captured their camels and their women. This is why the sons of Hamar are watering their flocks by the well of Jumda.'

In the meantime, the caravan, of which the four horsemen were the advanced guard, issued from the pass into the plain.

'Shedad, son of Amroo,' exclaimed one of the Bedoueens, 'what! have you captured an hareem?' For he beheld dromedaries and veiled women.

The great Sheikh came forth from his pavilion and sniffed the morning air; a dignified smile played over his benignant features, and once he smoothed his venerable beard.

'My son-in-law is a true son of Israel,' he murmured complacently to himself. 'He will trust his gold only to his own blood.'

The caravan wound about the plain, then crossed the stream at the accustomed ford, and approached the amphitheatre.

The horsemen halted, some dismounted, the dromedaries knelt down, Baroni assisted one of the riders from her seat; the great Sheikh advanced and said, 'Welcome in the name of God! welcome with a thousand blessings!'

T

'I come in the name of God; I come with a thousand blessings,' replied the lady.

'And with a thousand something else,' thought Amalek to himself; but the Arabs are so polished, that they never make unnecessary allusions to business.

'Had I thought the Queen of Sheba was going to pay me a visit,' said the great Sheikh, ' I would have brought the pavilion of Miriam.   How is the Rose of Sharon?' he continued, as he ushered Eva into his tent.   'How is the son of my heart; how is Besso, more generous than a thousand kings?'

'Speak not of the son of thy heart,' said Eva, seating herself on the divan.   'Speak not of Besso, the generous and the good, for his head is strewn with ashes, and his mouth is full of sand.'

'What is this?' thought Amalek.   'Besso is not ill, or his daughter would not be here.   This arrow flies not straight.   Does he want to scrape my piastres?   These sons of Israel that dwell in cities will mix their pens with our spears.   I will be obstinate as an Azafeer camel.'

Slaves now entered, bringing coffee and bread, the Sheikh asking questions as they ate, as to the time Eva quitted Jerusalem, her halting-places in the Desert, whether she had met with any tribes; then he offered to his granddaughter his own chibouque, which she took with ceremony, and instantly returned, while they brought her aromatic nargilly.

Eva scanned the imperturbable countenance of her grandfather : calm, polite, benignant, she knew the great Sheikh too well to suppose for a moment that its superficial expression was any indication of his innermost purpose.   Suddenly she said, in a somewhat careless tone, ' And why is the Lord of the Syrian pastures in this wilderness, that has been so long accursed?'

The great Sheikh took his pipe from his mouth, and then slowly sent forth its smoke through his nostrils, a feat of which he was proud.   Then he placidly replied : ' For the same reason that the man named Baroni made a visit to El Khuds.'

'The man named Baroni came to demand succour for his lord, who is your prisoner.'

'And also to obtain two millions of piastres,' added Amalek.

'Two millions of piastres! Why not at once ask for the throne of Solomon?'

'Which would be given, if required,' rejoined Amalek. 'Was it not said in the divan of Besso, that if this Prince of Franguestan wished to rebuild the Temple, the treasure would not be wanting?'

'Said by some city gossip,' said Eva, scornfully.

'Said by your father, daughter of Besso, who, though he lives in cities, is not a man who will say that almonds are pearls.'

Eva controlled her countenance, though it was difficult to conceal her mortification as she perceived how well informed her grandfather was of all that passed under their roof, and of the resources of his prisoner. It was necessary, after the last remark of the great Sheikh, to take new ground, and, instead of dwelling, as she was about to do, on the exaggeration of public report, and attempting to ridicule the vast expectations of her host, she said, in a soft tone, 'You did not ask me why Besso was in such affliction, father of my mother?'

'There are many sorrows: has he lost ships? If a man is in sound health, all the rest are dreams. And Besso needs no hakeem, or you would not be here, my Rose of Sharon.'

'The light may have become darkness in our eyes, though we may still eat and drink,' said Eva. 'And that has happened to Besso which might have turned a child's hair grey in its cradle.'

'Who has poisoned his well? Has he quarrelled with the Porte?' said the Sheikh, without looking at her.

'It is not his enemies who have pierced him in the back.'

'Humph,' said the great Sheikh.

'And that makes his heart more heavy,' said Eva.

'He dwells too much in walls,' said the great Sheikh. 'He should have rode into the Desert, instead of you, my child. He should have brought the ransom himself;' and the great Sheikh sent two curling streams out of his nostrils.

'Whoever be the bearer, he is the payer,' said Eva. 'It is he who is the prisoner, not this son of Franguestan, who, you think, is your captive.'

'Your father wishes to scrape my piastres,' said the great Sheikh, in a stern voice, and looking his grand-daughter full in the face.

'If he wanted to scrape piastres from the Desert,' said Eva, in a sweet but mournful voice, 'would Besso have given you the convoy of the Hadj without condition or abatement?'

The great Sheikh drew a long breath from his chibouque. After a momentary pause, he said, 'In a family there should ever be unity and concord; above all things, words should not be dark. How much will the Queen of the English give for her brother?'

'He is not the brother of the Queen of the English,' said Eva.

'Not when he is my spoil, in my tent,' said Amalek, with a cunning smile; 'but put him on a round hat in a walled city, and then he is the brother of the Queen of the English.'

'Whatever his rank, he is the charge of Besso, my father and your son,' said Eva; 'and Besso has pledged his heart, his life, and his honour, that this young prince shall not be hurt. For him he feels, for him he speaks, for him he thinks. Is it to be told in the bazaars of Franguestan that his first office of devotion was to send this youth into the Desert to be spoiled by the father of his wife?'

'Why did my daughters marry men who live in cities?' exclaimed the old Sheikh.

'Why did they marry men who made your peace with

the Egyptian, when not even the Desert could screen you? Why did they marry men who gained you the convoy of the Hadj, and gave you the milk of ten thousand camels?'

'Truly, there is but one God in the Desert and in the city,' said Amalek. 'Now, tell me, Rose of Sharon, how many piastres nave you brought me?'

'If you be in trouble, Besso will aid you as he has done; if you wish to buy camels, Besso will assist you as before; but, if you expect ransom for his charge, whom you ought to have placed on your best mare of Nedgid, then I have not brought a para.'

'It is clearly the end of the world,' said Amalek, with a savage sigh.

'Why I am here,' said Eva, 'I am only the child of your child, a woman without spears; why do you not seize me and send to Besso? He must ransom me, for I am the only offspring of his loins. Ask for four millions of piastres! He can raise them. Let him send round to all the cities of Syria, and tell his brethren that a Bedoueen Sheikh has made his daughter and her maidens captive, and, trust me, the treasure will be forthcoming. He need not say it is one on whom he has lavished a thousand favours, whose visage was darker than the simoom when he made the great Pacha smile on him; who, however he may talk of living in cities now, could come cringing to El Sham to ask for the contract of the Hadj, by which he had gained ten thousand camels; he need say nothing of all this, and, least of all, need he say that the spoiler is his father!'

'What is this Prince of Franguestan to thee and thine?' said Amalek. 'He comes to our land like his brethren, to see the sun and seek for treasure in our ruins, and he bears, like all of them, some written words to your father, saying, Give to this man what he asks, and we will give to your people what they ask. I understand all this: they all come to your father because he deals in money, and is the only man in Syria who has money. What he pays, he is again paid. Is it not so, Eva? Daughter of my blood, let there not be strife between us ; give me a million piastres, and a hundred camels to the widow of Sheikh Salem, and take the brother of the queen.'

'Camels shall be given to the widow of Sheikh Salem,' said Eva, in a conciliatory voice; 'but for this ransom of which you speak, my father, it is not a question as to the number of piastres. If you want a million of piastres, shall it be said that Besso would not lend, perhaps give, them to the great Sheikh he loves? But, you see, my father of fathers, piastres and this Frank stranger are not of the same leaven. Name them not together, I pray you; mix not their waters. It concerns the honour, and welfare, and safety, and glory of Besso that you should cover this youth with a robe of power, and place him upon your best dromedary, and send him back to El Khuds.'

The great Sheikh groaned.

'Have I opened a gate that I am unable to close?' he at length said. 'What is begun shall be finished. Have the children of Rechab been brought from the sweet wells of Costal to this wilderness ever accursed to fill their purses with stones? Will they not return and say that my beard is too white? Yet do I wish that this day was finished. Name then at once, my daughter, the piastres that you will give ; for the prince, the brother of queens, may to-morrow be dust.'

'How so?' eagerly inquired Eva.

'He is a Mejnoun,' replied Amalek. 'After the man named Baroni departed for El Khuds, the Prince of Franguestan would not rest until he visited Gibel Mousa, and I said "Yes" to all his wishes. Whether it were his wound inflamed by his journey, or grief at his captivity, for these Franks are the slaves of useless sorrow, he returned as wild as Kais, and now lies in his tent, fancying he is still on Mount Sinai. 'Tis the fifth day of the fever, and Shedad, the son of Amroo, tells me that the sixth will be fatal unless we can give him the gall of a phœnix, and such a bird is not to be found in this part of Arabia. Now,

you are a great hakeem, my child of children; go then to
the young prince, and see what can be done : for if he die,
we can scarcely ransom him, and I shall lose the piastres,
and your father the backsheesh which I meant to have
given him on the transaction.'

'This is very woful,' murmured Eva to herself, and not
listening to the latter observations of her grandfather.

At this moment the curtain of the pavilion was withdrawn, and there stood before them Fakredeen. The moment his eyes met those of Eva, he covered his face with
both his hands.

'How is the Prince of Franguestan?' inquired Amalek.

The young Emir advanced, and threw himself at the feet
of Eva. 'We must entreat the Rose of Sharon to visit
him,' he said, 'for there is no hakeem in Arabia equal to
her. Yes, I came to welcome you, and to entreat you to
do this kind office for the most gifted and the most interesting of beings;' and he looked up in her face with a
supplicating glance.

'And you too, are you fearful,' said Eva, in a tone of
tender reproach, 'that by his death you may lose your
portion of the spoil?'

The Emir gave a deprecating glance of anguish, and
then, bending his head, pressed his lips to the Bedoueen
robes which she wore. ' 'Tis the most unfortunate of coin-
cidences, but believe me, dearest of friends, 'tis only a
coincidence. I am here merely by accident; I was hunting, I was ——'

'You will make me doubt your intelligence as well as
your good faith,' said Eva, 'if you persist in such assurances.'

'Ah! if you but knew him,' exclaimed Fakredeen, 'you
would believe me when I tell you that I am ready to
sacrifice even my life for his. Far from sharing the spoil,'
he added, in a rapid and earnest whisper, 'I had already
proposed, and could have insured, his escape; when he
went to Sinai, to that unfortunate Sinai. I had two
dromedaries here, thorough bred, we might have reached
Hebron before ——'

' You went with him to Sinai ?'

' He would not suffer it; he desired, he said, to be silent
and to be alone. One of the Bedoueens, who accompanied
him, told me that they halted in the valley, and that he
went up alone into the mountain, where he remained a day
and night. When he returned hither, I perceived a great
change in him. His words were quick, his eye glittered
like fire ; he told me that he had seen an angel, and in the
morning he was as he is now. I have wept, I have prayed
for him in the prayers of every religion, I have bathed his
temples with liban, and hung his tent with charms. O
Rose of Sharon! Eva, beloved, darling Eva, I have faith in
no one but in you. See him, I beseech you, see him! If
you but knew him, if you had but listened to his voice, and
felt the greatness of his thoughts and spirit, it would not
need that I should make this entreaty. But, alas ! you
know him not; you have never listened to him ; you have
never seen him; or neither he, nor I, nor any of us, would
have been here, and have been thus.'

CHAPTER VI.

NOTWITHSTANDING all the prescient care of the Duke and
Duchess of Bellamont, it was destined that the stout arm of
Colonel Brace should not wave by the side of their son
when he was first attacked by the enemy, and now that he
was afflicted by a most severe, if not fatal illness, the practised skill of the Doctor Roby was also absent. Fresh
exemplification of what all of us so frequently experience,
that the most sagacious and matured arrangements are of
little avail; that no one is present when he is wanted, and
that nothing occurs as it was foreseen. Nor should we
forget that the principal cause of all these mischances might
perhaps be recognised in the inefficiency of the third person
whom the parents of Tancred had, with so much solicitude
and at so great an expense, secured to him as a companion

and counsellor in his travels. It cannot be denied, that if the theological attainments of the Rev. Mr. Bernard had been of a more profound and comprehensive character, it is possible that Lord Montacute might not have deemed it necessary to embark upon this new crusade, and ultimately to find himself in the deserts of Mount Sinai. However this may be, one thing was certain, that Tancred had been wounded without a single sabre of the Bellamont yeomanry being brandished in his defence; was now lying dangerously ill in an Arabian tent, without the slightest medical assistance; and perhaps was destined to quit this world, not only without the consolation of a priest of his holy church, but surrounded by heretics and infidels.

'We have never let any of the savages come near my lord,' said Freeman to Baroni, on his return.

'Except the fair young gentleman,' added Trueman, 'and he is a Christian, or as good.'

'He is a prince,' said Freeman, reproachfully. 'Have I not told you so twenty times? He is what they call in this country a Hameer, and lives in a castle, where he wanted my lord to visit him. I only wish he had gone with my lord to Mount Siny; I think it would have come to more good.'

'He has been very attentive to my lord all the time,' said Trueman; 'indeed, he has never quitted my lord night or day; and only left his side when we heard the caravan had returned.'

'I have seen him,' said Baroni; 'and now let us enter the tent.'

Upon the divan, his head supported by many cushions, clad in a Syrian robe of the young Emir, and partly covered with a Bedoueen cloak, lay Tancred, deadly pale, his eyes open and fixed, and apparently unconscious of their presence. He was lying on his back, gazing on the roof of the tent, and was motionless. Fakredeen had raised his wounded arm, which had fallen from the couch, and had supported it with a pile made of cloaks and pillows. The countenance of Tancred was much changed since Baroni last beheld him; it was greatly attenuated, but the eyes glittered with an unearthly fire.

'We don't think he has ever slept,' said Freeman, in a whisper.

'He did nothing but talk to himself the first two days,' said Trueman; 'but yesterday he has been more quiet.'

Baroni advanced to the divan behind the head of Tancred, so that he might not be observed, and then, letting himself fall noiselessly on the carpet, he touched with a light finger the pulse of Lord Montacute.

'There is not too much blood here,' he said, shaking his head.

'You don't think it is hopeless?' said Freeman, beginning to blubber.

'And all the great doings of my lord's coming of age to end in this!' said Trueman. 'They sat down only two less than a hundred at the steward's table for more than a week!'

Baroni made a sign to them to leave the tent. 'God of my fathers!' he said, still seated on the ground, his arms folded, and watching Tancred earnestly with his bright black eyes; 'this is a bad business. This is death or madness, perhaps both. What will M. de Sidonia say? He loves not men who fail. All will be visited on me. I shall be shelved. In Europe they would bleed him, and they would kill him; here they will not bleed him, and he may die. Such is medicine, and such is life! Now, if I only had as much opium as would fill the pipe of a mandarin, that would be something. God of my fathers! this is a bad business.'

He rose softly; he approached nearer to Tancred, and examined his countenance more closely; there was a slight foam upon the lip, which he gently wiped away.

'The brain has worked too much,' said Baroni to himself. 'Often have I watched him pacing the deck during our voyage; never have I witnessed an abstraction so prolonged and so profound. He thinks as much as M. de Sidonia, and feels more. There is his weakness. The strength of my master is his superiority to all sentiment. No affections and a great brain; these are the men to command the world. No affections and a little brain; such is the stuff of which they make petty villains. And a great brain and a great heart, what do they make? Ah! I do not know. The last, perhaps, wears off with time; and yet I wish I could save this youth, for he ever attracts me to him.'

Thus he remained for some time seated on the carpet by the side of the divan, revolving in his mind every possible expedient that might benefit Tancred, and finally being convinced that none was in his power. What roused him from his watchful reverie was a voice that called his name very softly, and, looking round, he beheld the Emir Fakredeen on tiptoe, with his finger on his mouth. Baroni rose, and, Fakredeen inviting him with a gesture to leave the tent, he found without the lady of the caravan.

' I want the Rose of Sharon to see your lord,' said the young Emir, very anxiously, ' for she is a great hakeem among our people.'

' Perhaps in the Desert, where there is none to be useful, I might not be useless,' said Eva, with some reluctance and reserve.

' Hope has only one arrow left,' said Baroni, mournfully.

' Is it indeed so bad ? '

' Oh! save him, Eva, save him ! ' exclaimed Fakredeen, distractedly.

She placed her finger on her lip.

' Or I shall die,' continued Fakredeen; ' nor indeed have I any wish to live, if he depart from us.'

Eva conversed apart for a few minutes with Baroni, in a low voice, and then drawing aside the curtain of the tent, they entered.

There was no change in the appearance of Tancred, but as they approached him he spoke. Baroni dropped into his former position, Fakredeen fell upon his knees, Eva alone was visible when the eyes of Tancred met hers. His vision was not unconscious of her presence; he stared at her with intentness. The change in her dress, however, would, in all probability, have prevented his recognising her even under indifferent circumstances. She was habited as a Bedoueen girl; a leathern girdle encircled her blue robe, a few gold coins were braided in her hair, and her head was covered with a fringed kefia.

Whatever was the impression made upon Tancred by this unusual apparition, it appeared to be only transient. His glance withdrawn, his voice again broke into incoherent but violent exclamations. Suddenly he said, with more moderation, but with firmness and distinctness, ' I am guarded by angels.'

Fakredeen shot a glance at Eva and Baroni, as if to remind them of the tenor of the discourse for which he had prepared them.

After a pause, he became somewhat violent, and seemed as if he would have waved his wounded arm; but Baroni, whose eye, though himself unobserved, never quitted his charge, laid his finger upon the arm, and Tancred did not struggle. Again he spoke of angels, but in a milder and mournful tone.

' Methinks you look like one,' thought Eva, as she beheld his spiritual countenance lit up by a superhuman fire.

After a few minutes, she glanced at Baroni, to signify her wish to leave the tent, and he rose and accompanied her. Fakredeen also rose, with streaming eyes, and making the sign of the cross.

' Forgive me,' he said to Eva, ' but I cannot help it. Whenever I am in affliction I cannot help remembering that I am a Christian.'

' I wish you would remember it at all times,' said Eva, ' and then, perhaps, none of us need have been here;' and then not waiting for his reply, she addressed herself to Baroni. ' I agree with you,' she said. ' If we cannot give him sleep, he will soon sleep for ever.'

'Oh, give him sleep, Eva,' said Fakredeen, wringing his hands ; 'you can do anything.'

'I suppose,' said Baroni, 'it is hopeless to think of finding any opium here.'

'Utterly,' said Eva ; 'its practice is quite unknown among them.'

'Send for some from El Khuds,' said Fakredeen.

'Idle !' said Baroni ; 'this is an affair of hours, not of days.'

'Oh, but I will go,' exclaimed Fakredeen ; 'you do not know what I can do on one of my dromedaries ! I will——'

Eva placed her hand on his arm without looking at him, and then continued to address Baroni. 'Through the pass I several times observed a small white and yellow flower in patches. I lost it as we advanced, and yet I should think it must have followed the stream. If it be, as I think, but I did not observe it with much attention, the flower of the mountain Arnica, I know a preparation from that shrub which has a marvellous action on the nervous system.'

'I am sure it is the mountain Arnica, and I am sure it will cure him,' said Fakredeen.

'Time presses,' said Eva to Baroni. 'Call my maidens to our aid ; and first of all let us examine the borders of the stream.'

While his friends departed to exert themselves, Fakredeen remained behind, and passed his time partly in watching Tancred, partly in weeping, and partly in calculating the amount of his debts. This latter was a frequent, and to him inexhaustible, source of interest and excitement. His creative brain was soon lost in reverie. He conjured up Tancred restored to health, a devoted friendship between them, immense plans, not inferior achievements, and inexhaustible resources. Then, when he remembered that he was himself the cause of the peril of that precious life on which all his future happiness and success were to depend, he cursed himself. Involved as were the circumstances in which he habitually found himself entangled, the present complication was certainly not inferior to any of the perplexities which he had hitherto experienced.

He was to become the bosom friend of a being whom he had successfully plotted to make a prisoner and plunder, and whose life was consequently endangered; he had to prevail on Amalek to relinquish the ransom which had induced the great Sheikh to quit his Syrian pastures, and had cost the lives of some of his most valuable followers; while, on the other hand, the new moon was rapidly approaching, when the young Emir had appointed to meet Scheriff Effendi at Gaza, to receive the arms and munitions which were to raise him to empire, and for which he had purposed to pay by a portion of his share in the great plunder which he had himself projected. His baffled brain whirled with wild and impracticable combinations, till, at length, frightened and exhausted, he called for his nargilly, and sought, as was his custom, serenity from its magic tube. In this wise more than three hours had elapsed, the young Emir was himself again, and was calculating the average of the various rates of interest in every town in Syria, from Gaza to Aleppo, when Baroni returned, bearing in his hand an Egyptian vase.

'You have found the magic flowers?' asked Fakredeen, eagerly.

'The flowers of Arnica, noble Emir, of which the lady Eva spoke. I wish the potion had been made in the new moon; however, it has been blessed. Two things alone now are wanting, that my lord should drink it, and that it should cure him.'

It was not yet noon when Tancred quaffed the potion. He took it without difficulty, though apparently unconscious of the act. As the sun reached its meridian height, Tancred sank into a profound slumber. Fakredeen rushed away to tell Eva, who had now retired into the innermost apartments of the pavilion of Amalek; Baroni never quitted the tent of his lord.

The sun set; the same beautiful rosy tint suffused the

tombs and temples of the city as on the evening of their first forced arrival : still Tancred slept. The camels returned from the river, the lights began to sparkle in the circle of black tents : still Tancred slept. He slept during the day, and he slept during the twilight, and, when the night came, still Tancred slept. The silver lamp, fed by the oil of the palm tree, threw its delicate white light over the couch on which he rested. Mute, but ever vigilant, Fakredeen and Baroni gazed on their friend and master: still Tancred slept.

It seemed a night that would never end, and, when the first beam of the morning came, the Emir and his companion mutually recognised on their respective countenances an expression of distrust, even of terror. Still Tancred slept; in the same posture and with the same expression, unmoved and pale. Was it, indeed, sleep? Baroni touched his wrist, but could find no pulse ; Fakredeen held his bright dagger over the mouth, yet its brilliancy was not for a moment clouded. But he was not cold.

The brow of Baroni was knit with deep thought, and his searching eye fixed upon the recumbent form ; Fakredeen, frightened, ran away to Eva.

'I am frightened, because you are frightened,' said Fakredeen, 'whom nothing ever alarms. O Rose of Sharon! why are you so pale ?'

'It is a stain upon our tents if this youth be lost,' said Eva in a low voice, yet attempting to speak with calmness.

'But what is it on me!' exclaimed Fakredeen, distractedly. 'A stain! I shall be branded like Cain. No, I will never enter Damascus again, or any of the cities of the coast. I will give up all my castles to my cousin Francis El Kazin, on condition that he does not pay my creditors. I will retire to Mar Hanna. I will look upon man no more.'

'Be calm, my Fakredeen ; there is yet hope ; my responsibility at this moment is surely not lighter than yours.'

'Ah! you did not know him, Eva !' exclaimed Fakredeen, passionately; 'you never listened to him ! He cannot be to you what he is to me. I loved him !'

She pressed her finger to her lips, for they had arrived at the tent of Tancred. The young Emir, drying his streaming eyes, entered first, and then came back and ushered in Eva. They stood together by the couch of Tancred. The expression of distress, of suffering, of extreme tension, which had not marred, but which, at least, had mingled with the spiritual character of his countenance the previous day, had disappeared. If it were death, it was at least beautiful. Softness and repose suffused his features, and his brow looked as if it had been the temple of an immortal spirit.

Eva gazed upon the form with a fond, deep melancholy ; Fakredeen and Baroni exchanged glances. Suddenly Tancred moved, heaved a deep sigh, and opened his dark eyes. The unnatural fire which had yesterday lit them up had fled. Calmly and thoughtfully he surveyed those around him, and then he said, ' The Lady of Bethany !'

CHAPTER VII.

BETWEEN the Egyptian and the Arabian Deserts, formed by two gulfs of the Erythræan Sea, is a peninsula of granite mountains. It seems as if an ocean of lava, when its waves were literally running mountains high, had been suddenly commanded to stand still. These successive summits, with their peaks and pinnacles, enclose a series of valleys, in general stern and savage, yet some of which are not devoid of pastoral beauty. There may be found brooks of silver brightness, and occasionally groves of palms and gardens of dates, while the neighbouring heights command sublime landscapes, the opposing mountains of Asia and of Afric, and the blue bosom of two seas. On one of these elevations, more than five thousand feet above the ocean, is a convent ; again, nearly three thousand feet above this convent, is a towering peak, and this is Mount Sinai.

On the top of Mount Sinai are two ruins, a Christian church and a Mahometan mosque. In this, the sublimest scene of Arabian glory, Israel and Ishmael alike raised their altars to the great God of Abraham. Why are they in ruins? Is it that human structures are not to be endured amid the awful temples of nature and revelation; and that the column and the cupola crumble into nothingness in sight of the hallowed Horeb and on the soil of the eternal Sinai?

Ascending the mountain, about half way between the convent and the utmost height of the towering peak, is a small plain surrounded by rocks. In its centre are a cypress tree and a fountain. This is the traditional scene of the greatest event of time.

'Tis night; a solitary pilgrim, long kneeling on the sacred soil, slowly raises his agitated glance to the starry vault of Araby, and, clasping his hands in the anguish of devotion, thus prays :—

' O Lord God of Israel, Creator of the Universe, ineffable Jehovah! a child of Christendom, I come to thine ancient Arabian altars to pour forth the heart of tortured Europe. Why art thou silent? Why no longer do the messages of thy renovating will descend on earth? Faith fades and duty dies. A profound melancholy has fallen on the spirit of man. The priest doubts, the monarch cannot rule, the multitude moans and toils, and calls in its frenzy upon unknown gods. If this transfigured mount may not again behold Thee; if not again, upon thy sacred Syrian plains, Divinity may teach and solace men ; if prophets may not rise again to herald hope ; at least, of all the starry messengers that guard thy throne, let one appear, to save thy creatures from a terrible despair !'

A dimness suffused the stars of Arabia; the surrounding heights, that had risen sharp and black in the clear purple air, blended in shadowy and fleeting masses, the huge branches of the cypress tree seemed to stir, and the kneeling pilgrim sank upon the earth senseless and in a trance.

And there appeared to him a form; a shape that should be human, but vast as the surrounding hills. Yet such was the symmetry of the vision that the visionary felt his little-ness rather than the colossal proportions of the apparition. It was the semblance of one who, though not young, was still untouched by time; a countenance like an oriental night, dark yet lustrous, mystical yet clear. Thought, rather than melancholy, spoke from the pensive passion of his eyes, while on his lofty forehead glittered a star that threw a solemn radiance on the repose of his majestic features.

' Child of Christendom,' said the mighty form, as he seemed slowly to wave a sceptre fashioned like a palm tree, ' I am the angel of Arabia, the guardian spirit of that land which governs the world ; for power is neither the sword nor the shield, for these pass away, but ideas, which are divine. The thoughts of all lands come from a higher source than man, but the intellect of Arabia comes from the Most High. Therefore it is that from this spot issue the principles which regulate the human destiny.

' That Christendom which thou hast quitted, and over whose expiring attributes thou art a mourner, was a savage forest while the cedars of Lebanon, for countless ages, had built the palaces of mighty kings. Yet in that forest brooded infinite races that were to spread over the globe, and give a new impulse to its ancient life. It was decreed that, when they burst from their wild woods, the Arabian principles should meet them on the threshold of the old world to guide and to civilise them. All had been prepared. The Cæsars had conquered the world to place the Laws of Sinai on the throne of the Capitol, and a Galilean Arab advanced and traced on the front of the rude conquerors of the Cæsars the subduing symbol of the last development of Arabian principles.

' Yet again, and Europe is in the throes of a great birth. The multitudes again are brooding ; but they are not now in the forest ; they are in the cities and in the fertile plains. Since the first sun of this century rose, the intellectual colony of Arabia, once called Christendom, has been in a

state of partial and blind revolt. Discontented, they attri-
buted their suffering to the principles to which they owed
all their happiness, and in receding from which they had
become proportionably miserable. They have hankered after
other gods than the God of Sinai and of Calvary, and they
have achieved only desolation. Now they despair. But
the eternal principles that controlled barbarian vigour can
alone cope with morbid civilisation. The equality of man
can only be accomplished by the sovereignty of God. The
longing for fraternity can never be satisfied but under the
sway of a common father. The relations between Jehovah
and his creatures can be neither too numerous nor too near.
In the increased distance between God and man have grown
up all those developments that have made life mournful.
Cease, then, to seek in a vain philosophy the solution of the
social problem that perplexes you. Announce the sublime
and solacing doctrine of theocratic equality. Fear not,
faint not, falter not. Obey the impulse of thine own spirit,
and find a ready instrument in every human being.'

A sound, as of thunder, roused Tancred from his trance.
He looked around and above. There rose the mountains
sharp and black in the clear purple air; there shone, with
undimmed lustre, the Arabian stars; but the voice of the
angel still lingered in his ear. He descended the mountain:
at its base, near the convent, were his slumbering guards,
some steeds, and crouching camels.

CHAPTER VIII.

THE beautiful daughter of Besso, pensive and abstracted,
played with her beads in the pavilion of her grandfather.
Two of her maidens, who had attended her, in a corner of
this inner compartment, accompanied the wild murmur of
their voices on a stringed instrument, which might in the
old days have been a psaltery. They sang the loves of

Antar and of Ibla, of Leila and of Mejnoun; the romance
of the Desert, tales of passion and of plunder, of the rescue
of women and the capture of camels, of heroes with a lion
heart, and heroines brighter and softer than the moon.

The beautiful daughter of Besso, pensive and abstracted,
played with her beads in the pavilion of her grandfather.
Why is the beautiful daughter of Besso pensive and abstracted? What thoughts are flitting over her mind,
silent and soft, like the shadows of birds over the sunshiny earth?

Something that was neither silent nor soft disturbed the
lady from her reverie; the voice of the great Sheikh, in a
tone of altitude and harshness, with him most unusual. He
was in an adjacent apartment, vowing that he would sooner
eat the mother of some third person, who was attempting
to influence him, than adopt the suggestion offered. Then
there were softer and more persuasive tones from his companion, but evidently ineffectual. Then the voices of both
rose together in emulous clamour—one roaring like a bull,
the other shrieking like some wild bird; one full of menace,
and the other taunting and impertinent. All this was followed by a dead silence, which continuing, Eva assumed
that the Sheikh and his companion had quitted his tent.
While her mind was recurring to those thoughts which
occupied them previously to this outbreak, the voice of
Fakredeen was heard outside her tent, saying, 'Rose of
Sharon, let me come into the hareem;' and, scarcely
waiting for permission, the young Emir, flushed and excited, entered, and almost breathless threw himself on the
divan.

'Who says I am a coward?' he exclaimed, with a glance
of devilish mockery. 'I may run away sometimes, but what
of that? I have got moral courage, the only thing worth
having, since the invention of gunpowder. The beast is not
killed, but I have looked into the den; 'tis something.
Courage, my fragrant Rose, have faith in me at last. I may
make an imbroglio sometimes, but, for getting out of a

scrape, I would back myself against any picaroon in the
Levant; and that is saying a good deal.'

'Another imbroglio?'

'Oh, no! the same; part of the great blunder. You must
have heard us raging like a thousand Afrites. I never knew
the great Sheikh so wild.'

'And why?'

'He should take a lesson from Mehemet Ali,' continued
the Emir. 'Giving up Syria, after the conquest, was a much
greater sacrifice than giving up plunder which he has not
yet touched. And the great Pacha did it as quietly as if he
were marching into Stambool instead, which he might have
done if he had been an Arab instead of a Turk. Everything comes from Arabia, my dear Eva, at least everything
that is worth anything. We two ought to thank our stars
every day that we were born Arabs.'

'And the great Sheikh still harps upon this ransom?'
inquired Eva.

'He does, and most unreasonably. For, after all, what
do we ask him to give up? a bagatelle.'

'Hardly that,' said Eva; 'two millions of piastres can
scarcely be called a bagatelle.'

'It is not two millions of piastres,' said Fakredeen; 'there
is your fallacy, 'tis the same as your grandfather's. In the
first place, he would have taken one million; then half belonged to me, which reduces his share to five hundred
thousand; then I meant to have borrowed his share of him.'

'Borrowed his share!' said Eva.

'Of course I should have allowed him interest, good interest. What could the great Sheikh want five hundred
thousand piastres for? He has camels enough; he has so
many horses, that he wants to change some with me for
arms at this moment. Is he to dig a hole in the sand by
a well-side to put his treasure in, like the treasure of
Solomon; or to sew up his bills of exchange in his turban?
The thing is ridiculous. I never contemplated, for a
moment, that the great Sheikh should take any hard

piastres out of circulation, to lock them up in the wilderness. It might disturb the currency of all Syria, upset the
exchanges, and very much injure your family, Eva, of
whose interests I am never unmindful. I meant the great
Sheikh to invest his capital; he might have made a good
thing of it. I could have afforded to pay him thirty per
cent. for his share, and made as much by the transaction
myself; for you see, as I am paying sixty per cent. at
Beiroot, Tripoli, Latakia, and every accursed town of the
coast at this moment, the thing is clear; and I wish you
would only get your father to view it in the same light, and
we might do immense things! Think of this, my Rose of
Sharon, dear, dear Eva, think of this: your father might
make his fortune and mine too, if he would only lend me
money at thirty per cent.'

'You frighten me always, Fakredeen, by these allusions
to your affairs. Can it be possible that they are so very
bad!'

'Good, Eva, you mean good. I should be incapable of
anything, if it were not for my debts. I am naturally so
indolent, that if I did not remember in the morning that I
was ruined, I should never be able to distinguish myself.'

'You never will distinguish yourself,' said Eva; 'you
never can, with these dreadful embarrassments.'

'Shall I not?' said Fakredeen, triumphantly. 'What
are my debts to my resources? That is the point. You
cannot judge of a man by only knowing what his debts are;
you must be acquainted with his resources.'

'But your estates are mortgaged, your crops sold, at
least you tell me so,' said Eva, mournfully.

'Estates! crops! A man may have an idea worth
twenty estates, a principle of action that will bring him in
a greater harvest than all Lebanon.'

'A principle of action is indeed precious,' said Eva; 'but
although you certainly have ideas, and very ingenious ones,
a principle of action is exactly the thing which I have
always thought you wanted.'

'Well, I have got it at last,' said Fakredeen; 'everything comes if a man will only wait.'

'And what is your principle of action?'

'Faith.'

'In yourself? Surely in that respect you have not hitherto been sceptical?'

'No; in Mount Sinai.'

'In Mount Sinai!'

'You may well be astonished; but so it is. The English prince has been to Mount Sinai, and he has seen an angel. What passed between them I do not yet know; but one thing is certain, he is quite changed by the interview. He is all for action: so far as I can form an opinion in the present crude state of affairs, it is not at all impossible that he may put himself at the head of the Asian movement. If you have faith, there is nothing you may not do. One thing is quite settled, that he will not at present return to Jerusalem, but, for change of air and other reasons, make a visit with me to Canobia.'

'He seems to have great purpose in him,' said Eva, with an air of some constraint.

'By-the-bye,' said Fakredeen, 'how came you, Eva, never to tell me that you were acquainted with him?'

'Acquainted with him?' said Eva.

'Yes; he recognised you immediately when he recovered himself, and he has admitted to me since that he has seen you before, though I could not get much out of him about it. He will talk for ever about Arabia, faith, war, and angels; but, if you touch on anything personal, I observe he is always very shy. He has not my fatal frankness. Did you know him at Jerusalem?'

'I met him by hazard for a moment at Bethany. I neither asked then, nor did he impart to me, his name. How then could I tell you we were acquainted? or be aware that the stranger of my casual interview was this young Englishman whom you have made a captive?'

'Hush!' said Fakredeen, with an air of real or affected

alarm. 'He is going to be my guest at my principal castle. What do you mean by captive? You mean whom I have saved from captivity, or am about to save?'

'Well, that would appear to be the real question to which you ought to address yourself at this moment,' said Eva. 'Were I you, I should postpone the great Asian movement until you had disembarrassed yourself from your present position, rather an equivocal one both for a patriot and a friend.'

'Oh! I'll manage the great Sheikh,' said Fakredeen, carelessly. 'There is too much plunder in the future for Amalek to quarrel with me. When he scents the possibility of the Bedoueen cavalry being poured into Syria and Asia Minor, we shall find him more manageable. The only thing now is to heal the present disappointment by extenuating circumstances. If I could screw up a few thousand piastres for backsheesh,' and he looked Eva in the face, 'or could put anything in his way! What do you think, Eva?'

Eva shook her head.

'What an obstinate Jew dog he is!' said Fakredeen. 'His rapacity is revolting!'

'An obstinate Jew dog!' exclaimed Eva, rising, her eyes flashing, her nostrils dilating with contemptuous rage. The manner of Fakredeen had not pleased her this morning. His temper was very uncertain, and, when crossed, he was deficient in delicacy. Indeed, he was too selfish, with all his sensibility and refined breeding, to be ever sufficiently considerate of the feelings of others. He was piqued also that he had not been informed of the previous acquaintance of Eva and Tancred. Her reason for not apprising him of their interview at Bethany, though not easily impugnable, was not as satisfactory to his understanding as to his ear. Again, his mind and heart were so absorbed at this moment by the image of Tancred, and he was so entirely under the influence of his own idealised conceptions of his new and latest friend, that, according to his custom, no other being

could interest him. Although he was himself the sole
cause of all the difficult and annoying circumstances in
which he found himself involved, the moment that his
passions and his interests alike required that Tancred
should be free and uninjured, he acted, and indeed felt, as
if Amalek alone were responsible for the capture and the
detention of Lord Montacute.

The young Emir indeed was, at this moment, in one of
those moods, which had often marred his popularity, but
in which he had never indulged towards Eva before. She
had, throughout his life, been the commanding influence of
his being. He adored and feared her, and knew that she
loved, and rather despised him. But Eva had ceased to be
the commanding influence over Fakredeen. At this moment Fakredeen would have sacrificed the whole family
of Besso to secure the devotion of Tancred ; and the coarse
and rude exclamation to which he had given vent, indicated the current of his feelings and the general tenor of
his mind.

Eva knew him by heart. Her clear sagacious intellect
acting upon an individual, whom sympathy and circumstances had combined to make her comprehend, analysed
with marvellous facility his complicated motives, and in
general successfully penetrated his sovereign design.

'An obstinate Jew dog!' she exclaimed ; 'and who art
thou, thou jackal of this lion! who should dare to speak
thus ? Is it not enough that you have involved us all in
unspeakable difficulty and possible disgrace, that we are to
receive words of contumely from lips like yours ? One
would think you were the English Consul arrived here to
make a representation in favour of his countryman, instead
of being the individual who planned his plunder, occasioned
his captivity, and endangered his life! It is a pity that
this young noble is not acquainted with your claims to his
confidence.'

The possibility that in a moment of irritation Eva might
reveal his secret, some rising remorse at what he had said,

and the superstitious reverence with which he still clung to
her, all acting upon Fakredeen at the same time, he felt
that he had gone too far, and thereupon he sprang from
the divan, on which he had been insolently lolling, and
threw himself at the feet of his foster-sister, whimpering
and kissing her slippers, and calling her, between his sobs,
a thousand fond names.

'I am a villain,' he said, 'but you know it; you have
always known it. For God's sake stand by me now; 'tis
my only chance. You are the only being I love in the
world, except your family. You know how I respect them.
Is not Besso my father? And the great Sheikh, I honour
the great Sheikh. He is one of my allies. Even this accursed business proves it. Besides, what do you mean, by
words of contumely from my lips? Am I not a Jew myself, or as good? Why should I insult them? I only wish
we were in the Land of Promise, instead of this infernal
wilderness.'

'Well, well, let us consult together,' said Eva, 'reproaches
are barren.'

'Ah! Eva,' said Fakredeen, 'I am not reproaching you;
but if, the evening I was at Bethany, you had only told me
that you had just parted with this Englishman, all this
would not have occurred.'

'How do you know that I had then just parted with this
Englishman?' said Eva, colouring and confused.

'Because I marked him on the road. I little thought
then that he had been in your retreat. I took him for
some Frank, looking after the tomb of Lazarus.'

'I found him in my garden,' said Eva, not entirely at
her ease, 'and sent my attendants to him.'

Fakredeen was walking up and down the tent, and
seemed lost in thought. Suddenly he stopped and said,
'I see it all; I have a combination that will put all right.'

'Put all right?'

'See, the day after to-morrow I have appointed to meet
a friend of mine at Gaza, who has a caravan that wants

convoy through the Desert to the mountain. The Sheikh of Sheikhs shall have it. It will be as good as ten thousand piastres. That will be honey in his mouth. He will forget the past, and our English friend can return with you and me to El Khuds.'

' I shall not return to El Khuds,' said Eva. ' The great Sheikh will convoy me to Damascus, where I shall remain till I go to Aleppo.'

' May you never reach Aleppo ! ' said Fakredeen, with a clouded countenance, for Eva in fact alluded to her approaching marriage with her cousin.

' But after all,' resumed Eva, wishing to change the current of his thoughts, ' all these arrangements, so far as I am interested, depend upon the success of my mission to the great Sheikh. If he will not release my father's charge, the spears of his people will never guard me again. And I see little prospect of my success; nor do I think ten thousand piastres, however honestly gained, will be more tempting than the inclination to oblige our house.'

' Ten thousand piastres is not much,' said Fakredeen. ' I give it every three months for interest to a little Copt at Beiroot, whose property I will confiscate the moment I have the government of the country in my hands. But then I only add my ten thousand piastres to the amount of my debt. Ten thousand piastres in coin are a very different affair. They will jingle in the great Sheikh's purse. His people will think he has got the treasure of Solomon. It will do; he will give them all a gold kaireen apiece, and they will braid them in their girls' hair.'

' It will scarcely buy camels for Sheikh Salem's widow,' said Eva.

' I will manage that,' said Fakredeen. ' The great Sheikh has camels enough, and I will give him arms in exchange.'

' Arms at Canobia will not reach the Stony wilderness.'

' No; but I have got arms nearer at hand ; that is, my friend, my friend whom I am going to meet at Gaza, has some ; enough, and to spare. By the Holy Sepulchre, I see it !' said Fakredeen. 'I tell you how I will manage the whole business. The great Sheikh wants arms; well, I will give him five hundred muskets for the ransom, and he shall have the convoy besides. He'll take it. I know him. He thinks now all is lost, and, when he finds that he is to have a jingling purse and English muskets enough to conquer Tadmor, he will close.'

'But how are we to get these arms?' said Eva.

'Why, Scheriff Effendi, to be sure. You know I am to meet him at Gaza the day after to-morrow, and receive his five thousand muskets. Well, five hundred for the great Sheikh will make them four thousand five hundred; no great difference.'

'Scheriff Effendi!' said Eva, with some surprise. 'I thought I had obtained three months' indulgence for you with Scheriff Effendi.'

'Ah! yes, no,' said Fakredeen, blushing. 'The fact is, Eva, darling, beloved Eva, it is no use telling any more lies. I only asked you to speak to Scheriff Effendi to obtain time for me about payment, to throw you off the scent, as you so strongly disapproved of my buccaneering project. But Scheriff Effendi is a camel. I was obliged to agree to meet him at Gaza on the new moon, pay him his two hundred thousand piastres, and receive the cargo. Well, I turn circumstances to account. The great Sheikh will convey the muskets to the mountains.'

'But who is to pay for them?' inquired Eva.

'Why, if men want to head the Asian movement, they must have muskets,' said Fakredeen; 'and, after all, as we are going to save the English prince two millions of piastres, I do not think he can object to paying Scheriff Effendi for his goods; particularly as he will have the muskets for his money.'

CHAPTER IX.

TANCRED rapidly recovered. On the second day after his recognition of Eva, he had held that conversation with Fakredeon, which had determined the young Emir not to lose a moment in making the effort to induce Amalek to forego his ransom, the result of which he had communicated to Eva on their subsequent interview. On the third day, Tancred rose from his couch, and would even have quitted the tent, had not Baroni dissuaded him. He was the more induced to do so, for on this day he missed his amusing companion, the Emir. It appeared from the account of Baroni, that his highness had departed at dawn, on his dromedary and without an attendant. According to Baroni, nothing was yet settled either as to the ransom or the release of Tancred. It seemed that the great Sheikh had been impatient to return to his chief encampment, and nothing but the illness of Tancred would probably have induced him to remain in the Stony Arabia as long as he had done. The lady Eva had not, since her arrival at the ruined city, encouraged Baroni in any communication on the subject, which heretofore during their journey had entirely occupied her consideration, from which he inferred that she had nothing very satisfactory to relate; yet he was not without hope, as he felt assured that Eva would not have remained a day were she convinced that there was no chance of effecting her original purpose. The comparative contentment of the great Sheikh at this moment, her silence, and the sudden departure of Fakredeen, induced Baroni to believe that there was yet something on the cards, and, being of a sanguine disposition, he sincerely encouraged his master, who, however, did not appear to be very desponding.

' The Emir told me yesterday that he was certain to arrange everything,' said Tancred, ' without in any way compromising us. We cannot expect such an adventure to end like a day of hunting. Some camels must be given, and,

perhaps, something else. I am sure the Emir will manage
it all, especially with the aid and counsel of that beauteous
Lady of Bethany, in whose wisdom and goodness I have
implicit faith.'

'I have more faith in her than in the Emir,' said Baroni.
'I never know what these Shehaabs are after. Now he has
not gone to El Khuds this morning; of that I am sure.'

'I am under the greatest obligations to the Emir Fakredeen,' said Tancred, 'and, independently of such circumstances, I very much like him.'

'I know nothing against the noble Emir,' said Baroni,
'and I am sure he has been extremely polite and attentive
to your lordship; but still those Shehaabs, they are such a
set, always after something!'

'He is ardent and ambitious,' said Tancred, 'and he is
young. Are these faults? Besides, he has not had the
advantage of our stricter training. He has been without
guides; and is somewhat undisciplined, and self-formed.
But he has a great and interesting position, and is brilliant
and energetic. Providence may have appointed him to fulfil great ends.'

'A Shehaab will look after the main chance,' said Baroni.

'But his main chance may be the salvation of his country,' said Tancred.

'Nothing can save his country,' said Baroni. 'The
Syrians were ever slaves.'

'I do not call them slaves now,' said Tancred; 'why,
they are armed and are warlike! All that they want is a
cause.'

'And that they never will have,' said Baroni.

'Why?'

'The East is used up.'

'It is not more used up than when Mahomet arose,' said
Tancred. 'Weak and withering as may be the government
of the Turks, it is not more feeble and enervated than that
of the Greek empire and the Chosroes.'

'I don't know anything about them,' replied Baroni;
but I know there is nothing to be done with the people

here. I have seen something of them,' said Baroni. ' M. de Sidonia tried to do something in '39, and, if there had been a spark of spirit or of sense in Syria, that was the time, but ——' and here Baroni shrugged his shoulders.

' But what was your principle of action in '39 ?' inquired Tancred, evidently interested.

' The only principle of action in this world,' said Baroni ; ' we had plenty of money ; we might have had three millions.'

' And if you had had six, or sixteen, your efforts would have been equally fruitless. I do not believe in national regeneration in the shape of a foreign loan. Look at Greece ! And yet a man might climb Mount Carmel, and utter three words which would bring the Arabs again to Grenada, and perhaps further.'

' They have no artillery,' said Baroni.

' And the Turks have artillery and cannot use it,' said Lord Montacute. 'Why, the most favoured part of the globe at this moment is entirely defenceless ; there is not a soldier worth firing at in Asia except the Sepoys. The Persian, Assyrian, and Babylonian monarchies might be gained in a morning with faith and the flourish of a sabre.'

' You would have the Great Powers interfering,' said Baroni.

' What should I care for the Great Powers, if the Lord of Hosts were on my side ! '

' Why, to be sure they could not do much at Bagdad or Ispahan.'

' Work out a great religious truth on the Persian and Mesopotamian plains, the most exuberant soils in the world with the scantiest population, it would revivify Asia. It must spread. The peninsula of Arabia, when in action, must always command the peninsula of the Lesser Asia. Asia revivified would act upon Europe. The European comfort, which they call civilisation, is, after all, confined to a very small space : the island of Great Britain, France, and the course of a single river, the Rhine. The greater part of Europe is as dead as Asia, without the consolation of climate and the influence of immortal traditions.'

' I just found time, my lord, when I was at Jerusalem, to
call in at the Consulate, and see the Colonel,' said Baroni;
'I thought it as well to explain the affair a little to him. I
found that even the rumour of our mischance had not
reached him; so I said enough to prevent any alarm when
it arrived; he will believe that we furnished him with the
priority of intelligence, and he expects your daily return.'

' You did well to call; we know not what may happen.
I doubt, however, whether I shall return to Jerusalem. If
affairs are pleasantly arranged here, I think of visiting the
Emir, at his castle of Canobia. A change of air must be
the best thing for me, and Lebanon, by his account, is delicious at this season. Indeed, I want air, and I must go out
now, Baroni; I cannot stay in this close tent any longer;
the sun has set, and there is no longer any fear of those
fatal heats of which you are in such dread for me.'

It was the first night of the new moon, and the white
beams of the young crescent were just beginning to steal
over the lately flushed and empurpled scene. The air was
still glowing, and the evening breeze, which sometimes
wandered through the ravines from the gulf of Akabah, had
not yet arrived. Tancred, shrouded in his Bedoueen cloak,
and accompanied by Baroni, visited the circle of black tents,
which they found almost empty, the whole band, with the
exception of the scouts, who are always on duty in an Arab
encampment, being assembled in the ruins of the amphitheatre, in whose arena, opposite to the pavilion of the great
Sheikh, a celebrated poet was reciting the visit of Antar to
the temple of the fire-worshippers, and the adventures
of that greatest of Arabian heroes among the effeminate
and astonished courtiers of the generous and magnificent
Nushirvan.

The audience was not a scanty one, for this chosen detachment of the children of Rechab had been two hundred
strong, and the great majority of them were now assembled; some seated, as the ancient Idumæans, on the still
entire seats of the amphitheatre; most squatted in groups

upon the ground, though at a respectful distance from the poet; others standing amid the crumbling pile and leaning against the tall dark fragments just beginning to be silvered by the moon-beam; but in all their countenances, their quivering features, their flashing eyes, the mouth open with absorbing suspense, were expressed a wild and vivid excitement, the heat of sympathy, and a ravishing delight.

When Antar, in the tournament, overthrew the famous Greek knight, who had travelled from Constantinople to beard the court of Persia; when he caught in his hand the assassin spear of the Persian satrap, envious of his Arabian chivalry, and returned it to his adversary's heart; when he shouted from his saddle that he was the lover of Ibla and the horseman of the age; the audience exclaimed with rapturous earnestness, 'It is true, it is true!' although they were guaranteeing the assertions of a hero who lived, and loved, and fought more than fourteen hundred years before. Antar is the Iliad of the Desert; the hero is the passion of the Bedoueens. They will listen for ever to his forays, when he raised the triumphant cry of his tribe, 'Oh! by Abs; oh! by Adnan,' to the narratives of the camels he captured, the men he slew, and the maidens to whose charms he was indifferent, for he was 'ever the lover of Ibla.' What makes this great Arabian invention still more interesting is, that it was composed at a period antecedent to the Prophet; it describes the Desert before the Koran; and it teaches us how little the dwellers in it were changed by the introduction and adoption of Islamism.

As Tancred and his companion reached the amphitheatre, a ringing laugh resounded.

'Antar is dining with the King of Persia after his victory,' said Baroni; 'this is a favourite scene with the Arabs. Antar asks the courtiers the name of every dish, and whether the king dines so every day. He bares his arms, and chucks the food into his mouth without ever moving his jaws. They have heard this all their lives, but always

laugh at it with the same heartiness. Why, Shedad, son
of Amroo,' continued Baroni to an Arab near him, ' you
have listened to this ever since you first tasted liban, and it
still pleases you ! '

' I am never wearied with listening to fine language,' said
the Bedoueen ; ' perfumes are always sweet, though you may
have smelt them a thousand times.'

Except when there was some expression of feeling elicited
by the performance, a shout or a laugh, the silence was absolute. Not a whisper could be heard ; and it was in a
muffled tone that Baroni intimated to Tancred that the
great Sheikh was present, and that, as this was his first
appearance since his illness, he must pay his respects to
Amalek. So saying, and preceding Tancred, in order that
he might announce his arrival, Baroni approached the pavilion. The great Sheikh welcomed Tancred with a benignant
smile, motioned to him to sit upon his carpet ; rejoiced that
he was recovered ; hoped that he should live a thousand
years ; gave him his pipe, and then, turning again to the
poet, was instantly lost in the interest of his narrative.
Baroni, standing as near Tancred as the carpet would permit him, occasionally leant over and gave his lord an intimation of what was occurring.

After a little while, the poet ceased. Then there was a
general hum and great praise, and many men said to each
other, ' All this is true, for my father told it to me before.'
The great Sheikh, who was highly pleased, ordered his
slaves to give the poet a cup of coffee, and, taking from his
own vest an immense purse, more than a foot in length, he
extracted from it, after a vast deal of research, one of the
smallest of conceivable coins, which the poet pressed to his
lips, and, notwithstanding the exiguity of the donation,
declared that God was great.

' O Sheikh of Sheikhs,' said the poet, ' what I have recited, though it is by the gift of God, is in fact written, and
has been ever since the days of the giants ; but I have also
dipped my pen into my own brain, and now I would recite

a poem which I hope some day may be suspended in the temple of Mecca. It is in honour of one who, were she to rise to our sight, would be as the full moon when it rises over the Desert. Yes, I sing of Eva, the daughter of Amalek (the Bedoueens always omitted Besso in her genealogy), Eva, the daughter of a thousand chiefs. May she never quit the tents of her race! May she always ride upon Nejid steeds and dromedaries, with harness of silver! May she live among us for ever! May she show herself to the people like a free Arabian maiden!'

'They are the thoughts of truth,' said the delighted Bedoueens to one another; 'every word is a pearl.'

And the great Sheikh sent a slave to express his wish that Eva and her maidens should appear. So she came to listen to the ode which the poet had composed in her honour. He had seen palm trees, but they were not as tall and graceful as Eva; he had beheld the eyes of doves and antelopes, but they were not as bright and soft as hers; he had tasted the fresh springs in the wilderness, but they were not more welcome than she; and the soft splendour of the Desert moon was not equal to her brow. She was the daughter of Amalek, the daughter of a thousand chiefs. Might she live for ever in their tents; ever ride on Nejid steeds and on dromedaries with silver harness; ever show herself to the people like a free Arabian maiden!

The poet, after many variations on this theme, ceased amid great plaudits.

'He is a true poet,' said an Arab, who was, like most of his brethren, a critic; 'he is in truth a second Antar.'

'If he had recited these verses before the King of Persia, he would have given him a thousand camels,' replied his neighbour, gravely.

'They ought to be suspended in the temple of Mecca,' said a third.

'What I most admire is his image of the full moon; that cannot be too often introduced,' said a fourth.

'Truly the moon should ever shine,' said a fifth. 'Also

in all truly fine verses there should be palm trees and fresh springs.'

Tancred, to whom Baroni had conveyed the meaning of the verses, was also pleased: having observed that, on a previous occasion, the great Sheikh had rewarded the bard, Tancred ventured to take a chain, which he fortunately chanced to wear, from his neck, and sent it to the poet of Eva. This made a great sensation, and highly delighted the Arabs.

'Truly this is the brother of queens,' they whispered to each other.

Now the audience was breaking up and dispersing, and Tancred, rising, begged permission of his host to approach Eva, who was seated at the entrance of the pavilion, somewhat withdrawn from them.

'If I were a poet,' said Tancred, bending before her, 'I would attempt to express my gratitude to the Lady of Bethany. I hope,' he added, after a moment's pause, 'that Baroni laid my message at your feet. When I begged your permission to thank you in person to-morrow, I had not imagined that I should have been so wilful as to quit the tent to-night.'

'It will not harm you,' said Eva; 'our Arabian nights bear balm.'

'I feel it,' said Tancred; 'this evening will complete the cure you so benignantly commenced.'

'Mine were slender knowledge and simple means,' said Eva; 'but I rejoice that they were of use, more especially as I learn that we are all interested in your pilgrimage.'

'The Emir Fakredeen has spoken to you?' said Tancred, inquiringly, and with a countenance a little agitated.

'He has spoken to me of some things, for which our previous conversation had not entirely unprepared me.'

'Ah!' said Tancred, musingly, 'our previous conversation. It is not very long ago since I slumbered by the side of your fountain, and yet it seems to me an age, an age of thought and events.'

'Yet even then your heart was turned towards our unhappy Asia,' said the Lady of Bethany.

'Unhappy Asia! Do you call it unhappy Asia! This land of divine deeds and divine thoughts! Its slumber is more vital than the waking life of the rest of the globe, as the dream of genius is more precious than the vigils of ordinary men. Unhappy Asia, do you call it? It is the unhappiness of Europe over which I mourn.'

'Europe, that has conquered Hindostan, protects Persia and Asia Minor, affects to have saved Syria,' said Eva, with some bitterness. 'Oh! what can we do against Europe?'

'Save it,' said Tancred.

'We cannot save ourselves; what means have we to save others?'

'The same you have ever exercised, Divine Truth. Send forth a great thought, as you have done before, from Mount Sinai, from the villages of Galilee, from the deserts of Arabia, and you may again remodel all their institutions, change their principles of action, and breathe a new spirit into the whole scope of their existence.'

'I have sometimes dreamed such dreams,' murmured Eva, looking down. 'No, no,' she exclaimed, raising her head, after a moment's pause, 'it is impossible. Europe is too proud, with its new command over nature, to listen even to prophets. Levelling mountains, riding without horses, sailing without winds, how can these men believe that there is any power, human or divine, superior to themselves?'

'As for their command over nature,' said Tancred, 'let us see how it will operate in a second deluge. Command over nature! Why the humblest root that serves for the food of man has mysteriously withered throughout Europe, and they are already pale at the possible consequences. This slight eccentricity of that nature, which they boast they can command, has already shaken empires, and may decide the fate of nations. No, gentle lady, Europe is not happy. Amid its false excitement, its bustling invention, and its endless toil, a profound melancholy broods over its spirit and gnaws at its heart. In vain they baptize their tumult by the name of progress; the whisper of a demon is ever asking them, "Progress, from whence and to what?" Excepting those who still cling to your Arabian creeds, Europe, that quarter of the globe to which God has never spoken, Europe is without consolation.'

CHAPTER X.

THREE or four days had elapsed since the departure of Fakredeen, and during each of them Tancred saw Eva; indeed, his hours were much passed in the pavilion of the great Sheikh, and, though he was never alone with the daughter of Besso, the language which they spoke, unknown to those about them, permitted them to confer without restraint on those subjects in which they were interested. Tancred opened his mind without reserve to Eva, for he liked to test the soundness of his conclusions by her clear intelligence. Her lofty spirit harmonised with his own high-toned soul. He found both sympathy and inspiration in her heroic purposes. Her passionate love of her race, her deep faith in the destiny and genius of her Asian land, greatly interested him. To his present position she referred occasionally, but with reluctance; it seemed as if she thought it unkind entirely to pass it over, yet that to be reminded of it was not satisfactory. Of Fakredeen she spoke much and frequently. She expressed with frankness, even with warmth, her natural and deep regard for him, the interest she took in his career, and the high opinion she entertained of his powers; but she lamented his inventive restlessness, which often arrested action, and intimated how much he might profit by the counsels of a friend more distinguished for consistency and sternness of purpose.

In the midst of all this, Fakredeen returned. He came in the early morning, and immediately repaired to the

pavilion of the great Sheikh, with whom he was long
closeted. Baroni first brought the news to Tancred, and
subsequently told him that the quantity of nargillies
smoked by the young Emir indicated not only a prolonged,
but a difficult, controversy. Some time after this, Tancred,
lounging in front of his tent, and watching the shadows as
they stole over the mountain tombs, observed Fakredeen
issue from the pavilion of Amalek. His flushed and radiant
countenance would seem to indicate good news. As he recognised Tancred, he saluted him in the Eastern fashion,
hastily touching his heart, his lip, and his brow. When he
had reached Tancred, Fakredeen threw himself in his arms,
and, embracing him, whispered in an agitated voice on the
breast of Lord Montacute, 'Friend of my heart, you are free!'

In the meantime, Amalek announced to his tribe that
at sunset the encampment would break up, and they would
commence their return to the Syrian wilderness, through
the regions eastward of the Dead Sea. The lady Eva
would accompany them, and the children of Rechab were
to have the honour of escorting her and her attendants to
the gates of Damascus. A detachment of five-and-twenty
Beni-Rechab were to accompany Fakredeen and Tancred,
Hassan and his Jellaheens, in a contrary direction of the
Desert, until they arrived at Gaza, where they were to await
further orders from the young Emir.

No sooner was this intelligence circulated, than the
silence which had pervaded the Desert ruins at once ceased.
Men came out of every tent and tomb. All was bustle and
noise. They chattered, they sang, they talked to their
horses, they apprised their camels of the intended expedition. They declared that the camels had consented to
go; they anticipated a prosperous journey; they speculated
on what tribes they might encounter.

It required all the consciousness of great duties, all the
inspiration of a great purpose, to sustain Tancred under
this sudden separation from Eva. Much he regretted that
it was not also his lot to traverse the Syrian wilderness,

but it was not for him to interfere with arrangements which he could neither control nor comprehend. All that passed amid the ruins of this Desert city was as incoherent and restless as the incidents of a dream; yet not without the bright passages of strange fascination, which form part of the mosaic of our slumbering reveries. At dawn a prisoner, at noon a free man, yet still, from his position, unable to move without succour, and without guides; why he was captured, how he was enfranchised, alike mysteries; Tancred yielded without a struggle to the management of that individual who was clearly master of the situation. Fakredeen decided upon everything, and no one was inclined to impugn the decrees of him whose rule commenced by conferring freedom.

It was only half an hour to sunset. The advanced guard of the children of Rechab, mounted on their dromedaries, and armed with lances, had some hours ago quitted the ruins. The camels, laden with the tents and baggage, attended by a large body of footmen with matchlocks, and who, on occasion, could add their own weight to the burden of their charge, were filing through the mountains; some horsemen were galloping about the plain and throwing the jereed; a considerable body, most of them dismounted, but prepared for the seat, were collected by the river side; about a dozen steeds of the purest race, one or two of them caparisoned, and a couple of dromedaries, were picketed before the pavilion of the great Sheikh, which was not yet struck, and about which some grooms were squatted, drinking coffee, and every now and then turning to the horses, and addressing them in tones of the greatest affection and respect.

Suddenly one of the grooms jumped up and said, 'He comes;' and then going up to a bright bay mare, whose dark prominent eye equalled in brilliancy, and far exceeded in intelligence, the splendid orbs of the antelope, he addressed her, and said, ' O Diamond of Derayeh, the Princess of the Desert can alone ride on thee!'

There came forth from his pavilion the great Amalek, accompanied by some of his Sheikhs; there came forth from the pavilion Eva, attended by her gigantic Nubian and her maidens; there came forth from the pavilion the Emir Fakredeen and Lord Montacute.

'There is but one God,' said the great Sheikh as he pressed his hand to his heart, and bade farewell to the Emir and his late prisoner. 'May he guard over us all!'

'Truly, there is but one God,' echoed the attendant Sheikhs. 'May you find many springs!'

The maidens were placed on their dromedaries; the grooms, as if by magic, had already struck the pavilion of their Sheikh, and were stowing it away on the back of a camel; Eva, first imprinting on the neck of the mare a gentle embrace, vaulted into the seat of the Diamond of Derayeh, which she rode in the fashion of Zenobia. To Tancred, with her inspired brow, her cheek slightly flushed, her undulating figure, her eye proud of its dominion over the beautiful animal which moved its head with haughty satisfaction at its destiny, Eva seemed the impersonation of some young classic here going forth to conquer a world.

Striving to throw into her countenance and the tones of her voice a cheerfulness which was really at this moment strange to them, she said, 'Farewell, Fakredeen!' and then, after a moment's hesitation, and looking at Tancred with a faltering glance which yet made his heart tremble, she added, 'Farewell, Pilgrim of Sinai.'

CHAPTER XI.

THE Emir of the Lebanon and his English friend did not depart from the Desert city until the morrow, Fakredeen being so wearied by his journey that he required repose. Unsustained by his lively conversation, Tancred felt all the depression natural to his position; and, restless and dis-

quieted, wandered about the valley in the moonlight, recalling the vanished images of the past. After some time,
unable himself to sleep, and finding Baroni disinclined to
slumber, he reminded his attendant of the promise he had
once given at Jerusalem, to tell something of his history.
Baroni was a lively narrator, and, accompanied by his
gestures, his speaking glance, and all the pantomime of his
energetic and yet controlled demeanour, the narrative, as
he delivered it, would have been doubtless much more
amusing than the calmer form in which, upon reflection,
we have thought fit to record some incidents, which the
reader must not in any degree suppose to form merely an
episode in this history. With this observation we solicit
attention to

The History of the Baroni Family.

BEING A CHAPTER IN THE LIFE OF SIDONIA.

1.

' I HAD no idea that you had a garrison here,' said Sidonia,
as the distant sounds of martial music were wafted down
a long, ancient street, that seemed narrower than it was
from the great elevation of its fantastically-shaped houses,
into the principal square in which was situate his hotel.
The town was one of the least frequented of Flanders; and
Sidonia, who was then a youth, scarcely of twenty summers, was on his rambling way to Frankfort, where he
then resided.

' It is not the soldiers,' said the Flemish maiden in
attendance, and who was dressed in one of those pretty
black silk jackets that seem to blend so well with the
sombre yet picturesque dwellings of the Spanish Nether-
lands. ' It is not the soldiers, sir; it is only the Baroni
family.'

' And who are the Baroni family?'

' They are Italians, sir, and have been here this week
past, giving some representations.'

' Of what kind ? '

' I hardly know, sir, only I have heard that they are very beautiful. There is tumbling, I know for certain; and there was the Plagues of Egypt; but I believe it changes every night.'

' And you have not yet seen them ? '

' Oh no, sir, it is not for such as me; the second places are half a franc ! '

' And what is your name ? ' said Sidonia.

' Therese; at your service, sir.'

' You shall go and see the Baroni family to-night, Therese, if your mistress will let you.'

' I am sure she would if you would ask her, sir,' said Therese, looking down and colouring with delight. The little jacket seemed very agitated.

' Here they come ! ' said Sidonia, looking out of the window on the great square.

A man, extremely good-looking and well made, in the uniform of a marshal of France, his cocked hat fringed and plumed, and the colour of his coat almost concealed by its embroidery, played a clarionet like a master; four youths of a tender age, remarkable both for their beauty and their grace, dressed in very handsome scarlet uniforms, with white scarfs, performed upon French horns and similar instruments with great energy and apparent delight; behind them an honest Blouse, hired for the occasion, beat the double drum.

' Two of them are girls,' said Therese; 'and they are all the same family, except the drummer, who belongs, I hear, to Ypres. Sometimes there are six of them, two little ones, who, I suppose, are left at home to-day; they look quite like little angels; the boy plays the triangle and his sister beats a tambourine.'

' They are great artistes,' murmured Sidonia to himself, as he listened to their performance of one of Donizetti's finest compositions. The father stood in the centre of the great square, the other musicians formed a circle round him; they continued their performance for about ten minutes to a considerable audience, many of whom had followed them, while the rest had collected at their appearance. There was an inclination in the curious multitude to press around the young performers, who would have been in a great degree hidden from general view by this discourteous movement, and even the sound of their instruments in some measure suppressed. Sidonia marked with interest the calm and commanding manner with which, under these circumstances, the father controlled the people. They yielded in an instant to his will: one tall blacksmith seemed scarcely to relish his somewhat imperious demeanour, and stood rooted to the ground; but Baroni, placing only one hand on the curmudgeon's brawny shoulder, while he still continued playing on his instrument with the other, whirled him away like a puppet. The multitude laughed, and the disconcerted blacksmith slunk away.

When the air was finished, Baroni took off his grand hat, and in a loud voice addressed the assembled people, informing them that this evening, in the largest room of the Auberge of St. Nicholas, there would be a variety of entertainments, consisting of masterpieces of strength and agility, dramatic recitations, dancing and singing, to conclude with the mystery of the Crucifixion of our blessed Lord and Saviour; in which all the actors in that memorable event, among others the blessed Virgin, the blessed St. Mary Magdalene, the Apostles, Pontius Pilate, the High Priest of the Jews, and many others, would appear, all to be represented by one family.

The speaker having covered himself, the band again formed and passed the window of Sidonia's hotel, followed by a stream of idle amateurs, animated by the martial strain, and attracted by the pleasure of hearing another fine performance at the next quarter of the town, where the Baroni family might halt to announce the impending amusements of the evening.

The moon was beginning to glitter, when Sidonia threw his cloak around him, and asked the way to the Auberge of St. Nicholas. It was a large, ungainly, whitewashed house, at the extremity of a suburb where the straggling street nearly ceased, and emptied itself into what in England would have been called a green. The many windows flared with lights, the doorway was filled with men smoking, and looking full of importance, as if, instead of being the usual loungers of the tavern, they were about to perform a principal part in the exhibition; they made way with respectful and encouraging ceremony to any one who entered to form part of the audience, and rated with sharp words, and sometimes a ready cuff, a mob of little boys who besieged the door, and implored every one who entered to give them tickets to see the Crucifixion. ' It's the last piece,' they perpetually exclaimed, ' and we may come in for five sous a head.'

Sidonia mounted the staircase, and, being a suitor for a ticket for the principal seats, was received with a most gracious smile by a pretty woman, fair-faced and arch, with a piquant nose and a laughing blue eye, who sat at the door of the room. It was a long and rather narrow apartment; at the end, a stage of rough planks, before a kind of curtain, the whole rudely but not niggardly lighted. Unfortunately for the Baroni family, Sidonia found himself the only first-class spectator. There was a tolerable sprinkling of those who paid half a franc for their amusement. These were separated from the first row, which Sidonia alone was to occupy; in the extreme distance was a large space not fitted up with benches, where the miscellaneous multitude, who could summon up five sous apiece later in the evening, to see the Crucifixion, were to be stowed.

' It hardly pays the lights,' said the pretty woman at the door. ' We have not had good fortune in this town. It seems hard, when there is so much for the money, and the children take such pains in going the rounds in the morning.'

'And you are Madame Baroni?' said Sidonia.

'Yes; I am the mother,' she replied.

'I should have thought you had been their sister,' said Sidonia.

'My eldest son is fifteen! I often wish that he was anything else but what he is, but we do not like to separate. We are all one family, sir, and that makes us bear many things.'

'Well, I think I know a way to increase your audience,' said Sidonia.

'Indeed! I am sure it is very kind of you to say so much; we have not met with a gentleman like you the whole time we have been here.'

Sidonia descended the stairs; the smoking amateurs made way for him with great parade, and pushed back with equal unkindness the young and wistful throng who still hovered round the portal.

'Don't you see the gentleman wants to go by? Get back, you boys!'

Sidonia halted on the doorway, and, taking advantage of a momentary pause, said, 'All the little boys are to come in free.'

What a rush!

The performances commenced by the whole of the Baroni family appearing in a row, and bowing to the audience. The father was now dressed in a Greek costume, which exhibited to perfection his compact frame : he looked like the captain of a band of Palikari; on his left appeared the mother, who, having thrown off her cloak, seemed a sylph or a sultana, for her bonnet had been succeeded by a turban. The three girls were on her left hand, and on the right of her husband were their three brothers. The eldest son, Francis, resembled his father, or rather was what his father must have been in all the freshness of boyhood; the same form of blended strength and symmetry; the same dark eye, the same determined air and regular features which in time would become strongly marked. The second boy,

Alfred, about eleven, was delicate, fair, and fragile, like his mother; his sweet countenance full of tenderness, changed before the audience with a rapid emotion. The youngest son, Michel, was an infant of four years, and with his large blue eyes and long golden hair, might have figured as one of the seraphs of Murillo.

There was analogy in the respective physical appearances of the brothers and the sisters. The eldest girl, Josephine, though she had only counted twelve summers, was in stature, and almost in form, a woman. She was strikingly handsome, very slender, and dark as night. Adelaide, in colour, in look, in the grace of every gesture, and in the gushing tenderness of her wild, yet shrinking glance, seemed the twin of Alfred. The little Carlotta, more than two years older than Michel, was the miniature of her mother, and had a piquant coquettish air, mixed with an expression of repose in one so young quite droll, like a little opera dancer. The father clapped his hands, and all, except himself, turned round, bowed to the audience, and retired, leaving Baroni and his two elder children. Then commenced a variety of feats of strength. Baroni stretched forth his right arm, and Josephine, with a bound, instantly sprang upon his shoulder; while she thus remained, balancing herself only on her left leg, and looking like a flying Victory, her father stretched forth his left arm, and Francis sprang upon the shoulder opposite to his sister, and formed with her a group which might have crowned a vase. Infinite were the postures into which, for more than half an hour, the brother and sister threw their flexible forms, and all alike distinguished for their agility, their grace, and their precision. At length, all the children, with the exception of Carlotta, glided from behind the curtain, and clustered around their father with a quickness which baffled observation. Alfred and Adelaide suddenly appeared, mounted upon Josephine and Francis, who had already resumed their former positions on the shoulders of their father, and stood immovable with outstretched arms, while their brother and sister balanced themselves above. This being arranged, Baroni caught up the young Michel, and, as it were, flung him up on high; Josephine received the urchin, and tossed him up to Adelaide, and in a moment the beautiful child was crowning the living pyramid, his smiling face nearly touching the rough ceiling of the chamber, and clapping his little hands with practised triumph, as Baroni walked about the stage with the breathing burden.

He stopped, and the children disappeared from his shoulders, like birds from a tree when they hear a sound. He clapped his hands, they turned round, bowed, and vanished.

'As this feat pleases you,' said the father, 'and as we have a gentleman here to-night who has proved himself a liberal patron of artists, I will show you something that I rarely exhibit; I will hold the whole of the Baroni family with my two hands;' and hereupon addressing some stout-looking fellows among his audience, he begged them to come forward and hold each end of a plank that was leaning against the wall, one which had not been required for the quickly-constructed stage. This they did with some diffidence, and with that air of constraint characteristic of those who have been summoned from a crowd to perform something which they do not exactly comprehend.

'Be not afraid, my good friends,' said Baroni to them, as Francis lightly sprang on one end of the plank, and Josephine on the other; then Alfred and Adelaide skipped up together at equal distances; so that the four children were now standing in attitude upon the same basis, which four stout men endeavoured, with difficulty, to keep firm. At that moment Madame Baroni, with the two young children, came from behind the curtain, and vaulted exactly on the middle of the board, so that the bold Michel on the one side, and the demure Carlotta on the other, completed the group. 'Thank you, my friends,' said Baroni, slipping under the plank, which was raised to a height which just admitted him to pass under it, 'I will release you,' and with his outstretched hands he sustained the whole burthen, the whole of the Baroni family supported by the father.

After this there was a pause of a few minutes, the stage was cleared, and Baroni, in a loose great-coat, appeared at its side with a violin. He played a few bars, then turning to the audience, said with the same contemptuous expression, which always distinguished him when he addressed them, 'Now you are going to hear a scene from a tragedy of the great Racine, one of the greatest tragedy writers that ever existed, if you may never have heard of him; but if you were at Paris, and went to the great theatre, you would find that what I am telling you is true.' And Josephine advanced, warmly cheered by the spectators, who thought that they were going to have some more tumbling. She advanced, however, as Andromache. It seemed to Sidonia that he had never listened to a voice more rich and passionate, to an elocution more complete; he gazed with admiration on her lightning glance and all the tumult of her noble brow. As she finished, he applauded her with vehemence. He was standing near to her father leaning against the wall.

'Your daughter is a great actress,' he said to Baroni.

'I sometimes think so,' said the father, turning round with some courtesy to Sidonia, whom he recognised as the liberal stranger who had so kindly increased his meagre audience; 'I let her do this to please herself. She is a good girl, but very few of the respectable savages here speak French. However, she likes it. Adelaide is now going to sing; that will suit them better.'

Then there were a few more bars scraped on the violin, and Adelaide, glowing rather than blushing, with her eyes first on the ground and then on the ceiling, but in all her movements ineffable grace, came forward and courtesied. She sang an air of Auber and of Bellini: a voice of the rarest quality, and, it seemed to Sidonia, promising almost illimitable power.

'Your family is gifted,' he said to Baroni, as he applauded his second daughter as warmly as the first; and the audience applauded her too.

'I sometimes think so. They are all very good. I am afraid, however, that this gift will not serve her much. The good-natured savages seem pleased. Carlotta now is going to dance; that will suit them better. She has had good instruction. Her mother was a dancer.'

And immediately, with her lip a little curling, a look of complete self-possession, willing to be admired, yet not caring to conceal her disgust, the little Carlotta advanced, and, after pointing her toe, threw a glance at her father to announce that he might begin. He played with more care and energy than for the other sisters, for Carlotta was exceedingly wilful and imperious, and, if the music jarred, would often stop, shrug her shoulders, and refuse to proceed. Her mother doted on her; even the austere Baroni, who ruled his children like a Pacha, though he loved them, was a little afraid of Carlotta.

The boards were coarse and rough, some even not sufficiently tightened, but it seemed to Sidonia, experienced as he was in the schools of Paris, London, and Milan, that he had never witnessed a more brilliant facility than that now displayed by this little girl. Her soul, too, was entirely in her art; her countenance generally serious and full of thought, yet occasionally, when a fine passage had been successfully achieved, radiant with triumph and delight. She was cheered, and cheered, and cheered; but treated the applause, when she retired, with great indifference. Fortunately, Sidonia had a rose in his button-hole, and he stepped forward and presented it to her. This gratified Carlotta, who bestowed on him a glance full of coquetry.

'And now,' said Baroni to the people, 'you are going to see the crucifixion of Jesus Christ: all the tableaux are taken from pictures by the most famous artists that ever

lived, Raphael, Rubens, and others. Probably you never
heard of them. I can't help that; it is not my fault; all I
can say is, that if you go to the Vatican and other galleries,
you may see them. There will be a pause of ten minutes,
for the children want rest.'

Now there was a stir and a devouring of fruit; Baroni,
who was on the point of going behind the curtain, came
forward, and there was silence again to listen to him.

'I understand,' he said, roughly, 'there is a collection
going to be made for the children; mind, I ask no one to
subscribe to it; no one obliges me by giving anything to
it; it is for the children and the children alone, they
have it to spend, that is all.'

The collectors were Michel and Adelaide. Michel was
always successful at a collection. He was a great favourite,
and wonderfully bold; he would push about in the throng
like a Hercules, whenever anyone called out to him to
fetch a liard. Adelaide, who carried the box, was much too
retiring, and did not like the business at all; but it was her
turn, and she could not avoid it. No one gave them more
than a sou. It is due, however, to the little boys who
were admitted free, to state that they contributed hand-
somely; indeed, they expended all the money they had in
the exhibition room, either in purchasing fruit, or in bestowing backsheesh on the performers.

'Encore un liard pour Michel,' was called out by several
of them, in order to make Michel rush back, which he did
instantly at the exciting sound, ready to overwhelm the
hugest men in his resistless course.

At last, Adelaide, holding the box in one hand and her
brother by the other, came up to Sidonia, and cast her eyes
upon the ground.

'For Michel,' said Sidonia, dropping a five-franc piece
into the box.

'A piece of a hundred sous!' said Michel.

'And a piece of a hundred sous for yourself and each of

your brothers and sisters, Adelaide,' said Sidonia, giving her a purse.

Michel gave a shout, but Adelaide blushed very much, kissed his hand, and skipped away. When she had got behind the curtain, she jumped on her father's neck, and burst into tears. Madame Baroni, not knowing what had occurred, and observing that Sidonia could command from his position a view of what was going on in their sanctuary, pulled the curtain, and deprived Sidonia of a scene which interested him.

About ten minutes after this, Baroni again appeared in his rough great-coat, and with his violin. He gave a scrape or two, and the audience became orderly. He played an air, and then turning to Sidonia, looking at him with great scrutiny, he said, ' Sir, you are a prince.'

' On the contrary,' said Sidonia, ' I am nothing; I am only an artist like yourself.'

' Ah ! ' said Baroni, ' an artist like myself ! I thought so. You have taste. And what is your line ? Some great theatre, I suppose, where even if one is ruined, one at least has the command of capital. 'Tis a position. I have none. But I have no rebels in my company, no traitors. With one mind and heart we get on, and yet sometimes ——' and here a signal near him reminded him that he must be playing another air, and in a moment the curtain separated in the middle, and exhibited a circular stage on which there were various statues representing the sacred story.

There were none of the usual means and materials of illusion at hand ; neither space, nor distance, nor cunning lights; it was a confined tavern room with some glaring tapers, and Sidonia himself was almost within arm's reach of the performers. Yet a representation more complete, more finely conceived, and more perfectly executed, he had never witnessed. It was impossible to credit that these marble forms, impressed with ideal grace, so still, so sad, so sacred, could be the little tumblers, who, but half-an-hour before, were disporting on the coarse boards at his side.

The father always described, before the curtain was withdrawn, with a sort of savage terseness, the subject of the impending scene. The groups did not continue long; a pause of half a minute, and the circular stage revolved, and the curtain again closed. This rapidity of representation was necessary, lest delay should compromise the indispensable immovableness of the performers.

'Now,' said Baroni, turning his head to the audience, and slightly touching his violin, 'Christ falls under the weight of the cross.' And immediately the curtain parted, and Sidonia beheld a group in the highest style of art, and which, though deprived of all the magic of colour, almost expressed the passion of Correggio.

'It is Alfred,' said Baroni, as Sidonia evinced his admiration. 'He chiefly arranges all this, under my instructions. In drapery his talent is remarkable.'

At length, after a series of representations, which were all worthy of being exhibited in the pavilions of princes, Baroni announced the last scene.

'What you are going to see now is the Descent from the Cross; it is after Rubens, one of the greatest masters that ever lived, if you ever heard of such a person,' he added, in a grumbling voice, and then turning to Sidonia, he said, 'This crucifixion is the only thing which these savages seem at all to understand; but I should like you, sir, as you are an artist, to see the children in some Greek or Roman story: Pygmalion, or the Death of Agrippina. I think you would be pleased.'

'I cannot be more pleased than I am now,' said Sidonia. 'I am also astonished.'

But here Baroni was obliged to scrape his fiddle, for the curtain moved.

'It is a triumph of art,' said Sidonia, as he beheld the immortal group of Rubens reproduced with a precision and an exquisite feeling which no language can sufficiently convey, or too much extol.

The performances were over, the little artists were summoned to the front scene to be applauded, the scanty audience were dispersing : Sidonia lingered.

'You are living in this house, I suppose?' he said to Baroni.

Baroni shook his head.   'I can afford no roof except my own.'

'And where is that?'

'On four wheels, on the green here. We are vagabonds, and, I suppose, must always be so ; but, being one family, we can bear it. I wish the children to have a good supper to-night, in honour of your kindness. I have a good deal to do. I must put these things in order,' as he spoke he was working ; 'there is the grandmother who lives with us ; all this time she is alone, guarded, however, by the dog. I should like them to have meat to-night, if I can get it. Their mother cooks the supper. Then I have got to hear them say their prayers. All this takes time, particularly as we have to rise early, and do many things before we make our first course through the city.'

'I will come and see you to-morrow,' said Sidonia, 'after your first progress.'

'An hour after noon, if you please,' said Baroni.   'It is pleasant for me to become acquainted with a fellow artist, and one so liberal as yourself'

'Your name is Baroni,' said Sidonia, looking at him earnestly.

'My name is Baroni.'

'An Italian name.'

'Yes, I come from Cento.'

'Well, we shall meet to-morrow.   Good night, Baroni. I am going to send you some wine for your supper, and take care the grandmamma drinks my health.'

II.

It was a sunny morn : upon the green contiguous to the Auberge of St. Nicholas was a house upon wheels, a sort of monster omnibus, its huge shafts idle on the ground, while three fat Flemish horses cropped the surrounding pasture. From the door of the house were some temporary steps, like an accommodation ladder, on which sat Baroni, dressed something like a Neapolitan fisherman, and mending his clarionet; the man in the blouse was eating his dinner, seated between the shafts, to which also was fastened the little dog, often the only garrison, except the grandmother, of this strange establishment.

The little dog began barking vociferously, and Baroni, looking up, instantly bade him be quiet. It was Sidonia, whose appearance in the distance had roused the precautionary voice.

' Well,' said Sidonia, 'I heard your trumpets this morning.'

' The grandmother sleeps,' said Baroni, taking off his cap, and slightly rising. 'The rest also are lying down after their dinner. Children will never repose unless there are rules, and this with them is invariable.'

'But your children surely cannot be averse to repose, for they require it.'

' Their blood is young,' continued Baroni, still mending his clarionet; 'they are naturally gay, except my eldest son. He is restless, but he is not gay.'

' He likes his art ? '

'Not too much; what he wants is to travel, and, after all, though we are always moving, the circle is limited.'

'Yes; you have many to move. And can this ark contain them all ? ' said Sidonia, seating himself on some timber that was at hand.

' With convenience even,' replied Baroni; 'but everything can be effected by order and discipline. I rule and regulate my house like a ship. In a vessel, there is not as much accommodation for the size as in a house of this kind; yet nowhere is there more decency and cleanliness than on board ship.'

'You have an obedient crew,' said Sidonia, 'and that is much.'

'Yes; when they wake, my children say their prayers,

and then they come to embrace me and their mother. This they have never omitted during their lives. I have taught them from their birth to obey God and to honour their parents. These two principles have made them a religious and a moral family. They have kept us united, and sustained us under severe trials.'

'Yet such talents as you all possess,' said Sidonia, 'should have exempted you from any very hard struggle, especially when united, as apparently in your case, with well-ordered conduct.'

'It would seem that they should,' said Baroni, 'but less talents than we possess would, probably, obtain as high a reward. The audiences that we address have little feeling for art, and all these performances, which you so much applauded last night, would not, perhaps, secure even the feeble patronage we experience, if they were not preceded by some feats of agility or strength.'

'You have never appealed to a higher class of audience?'

'No; my father was a posture-master, as his father was before him. These arts are traditionary in our family, and I care not to say for what length of time and from what distant countries we believe them to have been received by us. My father died by a fall from a tight rope in the midst of a grand illumination at Florence, and left me a youth. I count now only six-and-thirty summers. I married, as soon as I could, a dancer at Milan. We had no capital, but our united talents found success. We loved our children; it was necessary to act with decision, or we should have been separated and trampled into the mud. Then I devised this house and wandering life, and we exist in general as you see us. In the winter, if our funds permit it, we reside in some city, where we educate our children in the arts which they pursue. The mother can still dance, sings prettily, and has some knowledge of music. For myself, I can play in some fashion upon every instrument, and have almost taught them as much; I can paint, too, a scene, compose a group, and with the aid of my portfolio of prints, have picked up more knowledge of the costume of different centuries than you would imagine. If you see Josephine to-night in the Maid of Orleans you would perhaps be sur-prised. A great judge, like yourself a real artist, once told me at Bruxelles, that the grand opera could not pro-duce its equal.'

'I can credit it,' said Sidonia, 'for I perceive in Josephine, as well as indeed in all your children, a rare ability.'

'I will be frank,' said Baroni, looking at Sidonia very earnestly, and laying down his clarionet. 'I conclude from what you said last night, and the interest that you take in the children, that you are something in our way, though on a great scale. I apprehend you are looking out for novelties for the next season, and sometimes in the provinces things are to be found. If you will take us to London or Paris, I will consent to receive no remuneration if the venture fail ; all I shall then require will be a decent maintenance, which you can calculate beforehand : if the speculation answer, I will not demand more than a third of the profits, leaving it to your own liberality to make me any regalo in addition, that you think proper.'

'A very fair proposal,' said Sidonia.

'Is it a bargain ? '

'I must think over it,' said Sidonia.

'Well; God prosper your thoughts, for, from what I see of you, you are a man I should be proud to work with.'

'Well, we may yet be comrades.'

The children appeared at the door of the house, and, not to disturb their father, vaulted down. They saluted Sidonia with much respect, and then withdrew to some distance. The mother appeared at the door, and, leaning down, whis-pered something to Baroni, who, after a little hesitation, said to Sidonia, 'The grandmother is awake ; she has a wish to thank you for your kindness to the children. It will not trouble you; merely a word ; but women have their fancies, and we like always to gratify her, because she is much alone and never complains.'

' By all means,' said Sidonia.

Whereupon they ushered forward a venerable woman with
a true Italian face; hair white as snow, and eyes still glittering with fire, with features like a Roman bust, and an
olive complexion.   Sidonia addressed her in Italian, which
greatly pleased her.   She was profuse, even solemn, in her
thanks to him; she added, she was sure, from all that she
had heard of him, if he took the children with him, he would
be kind to them.

' She has overheard something I said to my wife,' said
Baroni, a little embarrassed.

' I am sure I should be kind to them,' said Sidonia, ' for
many reasons, and particularly for one;' and he whispered
something in Baroni's ear.

Baroni started from his seat with a glowing cheek, but
Sidonia, looking at his watch and promising to attend their
evening performance, bade them adieu.

III.

The performances were more meagrely attended this evening than even on the preceding one, but had they been conducted in the royal theatre of a capital, they could not have
been more elaborate, nor the troop have exerted themselves
with greater order and effect.   It mattered not a jot to
them whether their benches were thronged or vacant; the
only audience for whom the Baroni family cared was the
foreign manager, young, generous, and speculative, whom
they had evidently without intention already pleased, and
whose good opinion they resolved to-night entirely to secure.
And in this they perfectly succeeded.   Josephine was a
tragic muse; all of them, even to little Carlotta, performed
as if their destiny depended on the die.   Baroni would not
permit the children's box to be carried round to-night, as
he thought it an unfair tax on the generous stranger, whom
he did not the less please by this well-bred abstinence.   As
for the mediæval and historic groups, Sidonia could recall

nothing equal to them; and what surprised him most was the effect produced by such miserable materials. It seemed that the whole was effected with some stiffened linen and paper; but the divine touch of art turned everything to gold. One statue of Henri IV. with his flowing plume, and his rich romantic dress, was quite striking. It was the very plume that had won at Ivry, and yet was nothing more than a sheet of paper cut and twisted by the plastic finger of little Alfred.

There was to be no performance on the morrow; the niggard patronage of the town had been exhausted. Indeed, had it not been for Sidonia, the little domestic troop would, ere this, have quitted the sullen town, where they had laboured so finely, and achieved such an ungracious return. On the morrow, Baroni was to ride one of the fat horses over to Berg, a neighbouring town of some importance, where there was even a little theatre to be engaged, and if he obtained the permission of the mayor, and could make fair terms, he proposed to give there a series of representations. The mother was to stay at home and take care of the grandmother; but the children, all the children, were to have a holiday, and to dine with Sidonia at his hotel.

It would have been quite impossible for the most respectable burgher, even of the grand place of a Flemish city, to have sent his children on a visit in trim more neat, proper, and decorous, than that in which the Baroni family figured on the morrow, when they went to pay their respects to their patron. The girls were in clean white frocks with little black silk jackets, their hair beautifully tied and plaited, and their heads uncovered, according to the fashion of the country: not an ornament or symptom of tawdry taste was visible; not even a necklace, although they necessarily passed their lives in fanciful or grotesque attire; the boys, in foraging caps all of the same fashion, were dressed in blouses of holland, with bands and buckles, their broad shirt collars thrown over their shoulders. It is astonishing, as Baroni

said, what order and discipline will do ; but how that wonderful house upon wheels contrived to contain all these
articles of dress, from the uniform of the marshal of France
to the diminutive blouse of little Michel, and how their
wearers always managed to issue from it as if they came
forth from the most commodious and amply-furnished
mansion, was truly yet pleasingly perplexing. Sidonia took
them all in a large landau to see a famous château a few
miles off, full of pictures and rich old furniture, and built in
famous gardens. This excursion would have been delightful to them, if only from its novelty, but, as a substitute
for their daily progress through the town, it offered an additional gratification.

The behaviour of these children greatly interested and
pleased Sidonia. Their conduct to each other was invariably tender and affectionate : their carriage to him, though
full of respect, never constrained, and touched by an engaging simplicity. Above all, in whatever they did or said,
there was grace. They did nothing awkwardly ; their voices
were musical ; they were merry without noise, and their
hearts sparkled in their eyes.

‘ I begin to suspect that these youthful vagabonds, struggling for life, have received a perfect education,’ thought the
ever-musing Sidonia, as he leaned back in the landau, and
watched the group that he had made so happy. ‘ A sublime
religious principle sustains their souls ; a tender morality
regulates their lives ; and with the heart and the spirit thus
developed, they are brought up in the pursuit and pro-
duction of the beautiful. It is the complete culture of
philosophic dreams ! ’

IV.

The children had never sat down before to a regular
dinner, and they told Sidonia so. Their confession added
a zest to the repast. He gave them occasional instructions,
and they listened as if they were receiving directions for a
new performance. They were so quick and so tractable,

that their progress was rapid ; and at the second course Josephine was instructing Michel, and Alfred guiding the rather helpless but always self-composed Carlotta. After dinner, while Sidonia helped them to sugar-plums, he without effort extracted from each their master wish. Josephine desired to be an actress, while Adele confessed that, though she sighed for the boards, her secret aspirations were for the grand opera. Carlotta thought the world was made to dance.

'For my part,' said Francis, the eldest son, 'I have no wish to be idle; but there are two things which I have always desired : first, that I should travel ; and, secondly, that nobody should ever know me.'

' And what would Alfred wish to be ? ' said Sidonia.

'Indeed, sir, if it did not take me from my brothers and sisters, I should certainly wish to be a painter.'

'Michel has not yet found out what he wishes,' said Sidonia.

' I wish to play upon the horn,' said Michel, with great determination.

When Sidonia embraced them before their departure, he gave each of the girls a French shawl; to Francis he gave a pair of English pistols, to guard him when he travelled ; Alfred received a portfolio full of drawings of costume. It only arrived after dinner, for the town was too poor to supply anything good enough for the occasion, and Sidonia had sent a special messenger, the day before, for it to Lille. Michel was the guardian of a basket laden with good things, which he was to have the pleasure of dividing among the Baroni family. 'And if your papa come back to-night,' said Sidonia to Josephine, ' tell him I should like to have a word with him.'

v.

Sidonia had already commenced that habit which, during subsequent years, he has so constantly and successfully pursued, namely, of enlisting in his service all the rare talent

which he found lying common and unappropriated in the
great wilderness of the world, no matter if the object to
which it would apply might not immediately be in sight.
The conjuncture would arrive when it would be wanted.
Thus he generally had ready the right person for the occasion; and, whatever might be the transaction, the human
instrument was rarely wanting. Independent of the power
and advantage which this system gave him, his abstract
interest in intellect made the pursuit delightful to him. He
liked to give ability of all kinds its scope. Nothing was
more apt to make him melancholy, than to hear of persons
of talents dying without having their chance. A failure is
nothing; it may be deserved, or it may be remedied. In
the first instance, it brings self-knowledge; in the second,
it develops a new combination usually triumphant. But
incapacity, from not having a chance of being capable, is a
bitter lot, which Sidonia was ever ready to alleviate.

The elder Baroni possessed Herculean strength, activity
almost as remarkable, a practised courage, and a controlling
mind. He was in the prime of manhood, and spoke several
languages. He was a man, according to Sidonia's views,
of high moral principle, entirely trustworthy. He was too
valuable an instrument to allow to run to seed as the stroll-
ing manager of a caravan of tumblers; and it is not improbable that Sidonia would have secured his services, even
if he had not become acquainted with the Baroni family.
But they charmed him. In every member of it he recognised character, and a predisposition which might even be
genius. He resolved that every one of them should have a
chance.

When therefore Baroni, wearied and a little disgusted
with an unpromising journey, returned from Berg in the
evening, and, in consequence of the message of his children,
repaired instantly to the hotel of Sidonia, his astonishment
was great when he found the manager converted into a
millionaire, and that too the most celebrated in Europe.
But no language can convey his wonder when he learnt

the career that was proposed to him, and the fortunes that were carved out for his children. He himself was to repair, with all his family, except Josephine and her elder brother, at once to Vienna, where he was to be installed into a post of great responsibility and emolument. He was made superintendent of the couriers of the house of Sidonia in that capital, and especially of those that conveyed treasure. Though his duties would entail frequent absences on him, he was to be master of a constant and complete establishment. Alfred was immediately to become a pupil of the Academy of Painters, and Carlotta of that of dancing; the talents of Michel were to be watched, and to be reported to Sidonia at fitting periods. As for Adele, she was consigned to a lady who had once been a celebrated prima donna, with whom she was to pursue her studies, although still residing under the paternal roof.

'Josephine will repair to Paris at once with her brother,' said Sidonia. 'My family will guard over her. She will enjoy her brother's society until I commence my travels. He will then accompany me.'

It is nearly twenty years since these incidents occurred, and perhaps the reader may feel not altogether uninterested in the subsequent fate of the children of Baroni. Mademoiselle Josephine is at this moment the glory of the French stage; without any question the most admirable tragic actress since Clairon, and inferior not even to her. The spirit of French tragedy has risen from the imperial couch on which it had long slumbered since her appearance, at the same time classical and impassioned, at once charmed and commanded the most refined audience in Europe. Adele, under the name of Madame Baroni, is the acknowledged Queen of Song in London, Paris, Berlin, and St. Petersburgh; while her younger sister, Carlotta Baroni, shares the triumphs, and equals the renown, of a Taglioni and a Cerito. At this moment, Madame Baroni performs to enthusiastic audiences in the first opera of her brother Michel, who promises to be the rival of Meyerbeer and

Mendelssohn ; all delightful intelligence to meet the ear of
the soft-hearted Alfred, who is painting the new chambers
of the Papal palace, a Cavaliere, decorated with many orders,
and the restorer of the once famous Roman school.

'Thus,' continued Baroni to Tancred, 'we have all succeeded in life because we fell across a great philosopher,
who studied our predisposition. As for myself, I told M.
de Sidonia that I wished to travel and to be unknown, and
so he made of me, a secret agent.'

'There is something most interesting,' said Tancred, 'in
this idea of a single family issuing from obscurity, and disseminating their genius through the world, charming mankind with so many spells. How fortunate for you all that
Sidonia had so much feeling for genius!'

'And some feeling for his race,' said Baroni.

'How?' said Tancred, startled.

'You remember he whispered something in my father's
ear?'

'I remember.'

'He spoke it in Hebrew, and he was understood.'

'You do not mean that you, too, are Jews?'

'Pure Sephardim, in nature and in name.'

'But your name surely is Italian?'

'Good Arabic, my lord. Baroni; that is, the son of
Aaron; the name of old clothesmen in London, and of
caliphs at Bagdad.'

CHAPTER XII.

'How do you like my forest?' asked Fakredeen of Tancred,
as, while descending a range of the Lebanon, an extensive
valley opened before them, covered with oak trees, which
clothed also, with their stout trunks, their wide-spreading
branches, and their rich starry foliage, the opposite and undulating hills, one of which was crowned with a convent.

'It is the only oak forest in Syria. It will serve some day to build our fleet.'

At Gaza, which they had reached by easy journeys, for Fakredeen was very considerate of the health of Tancred, whose wound had scarcely healed, and over whom he watched with a delicate solicitude which would have almost become a woman, the companions met Scheriff Effendi. The magic signature of Lord Montacute settled the long-vexed question of the five thousand muskets, and secured also ten thousand piastres for the commander of the escort to deliver to his chief. The children of Rechab, in convoy of the precious charge, certain cases of which were to be delivered to the great Sheikh, and the rest to be deposited in indicated quarters of the Lebanon, here took leave of the Emir and his friend, and pursued their course to the north of Hebron and the Dead Sea, in the direction of the Hauraan, where they counted, if not on overtaking the great Sheikh, at least on the additional security which his neighbourhood would ensure them. Their late companions remained at Gaza, awaiting Tancred's yacht, which Baroni fetched from the neighbouring Jaffa. A favourite breeze soon carried them from Gaza to Beiroot, where they landed, and where Fakredeen had the political pleasure of exhibiting his new and powerful ally, a prince, an English prince, the brother perhaps of a queen, unquestionably the owner of a splendid yacht, to the admiring eye of all his, at the same time, credulous and rapacious creditors.

The air of the mountains invigorated Tancred. His eye had rested so long on the ocean and the Desert, that the effect produced on the nerves by the forms and colours of a more varied nature were alone reviving.

There are regions more lofty than the glaciered crests of Lebanon; mountain scenery more sublime, perhaps even more beautiful: its peaks are not lost in the clouds like the mysterious Ararat; its forests are not as vast and strange as the towering Himalaya; it has not the volcanic splendour of the glowing Andes; in lake and in cataract it

z

must yield to the European Alps; but for life, vigorous,
varied, and picturesque, there is no highland territory in
the globe that can for a moment compare with the great
chain of Syria.

Man has fled from the rich and servile plains, from the
tyranny of the Turk and from Arabian rapine, to clothe the
crag with vines, and rest under his fig tree on the mountain
top.   An ingenious spirit, unwearied industry, and a bland
atmosphere have made a perpetual garden of the Syrian
mountains.   Their acclivities sparkle with terraces of corn
and fruit.   Castle and convent crown their nobler heights,
and flat-roofed villages nestle amid groves of mulberry
trees.   Among these mountains we find several human
races, several forms of government, and several schemes of
religion, yet everywhere liberty: a proud, feudal aristocracy;
a conventual establishment, which in its ramifications
recalls the middle ages; a free and armed peasantry, whatever their creed, Emirs on Arabian steeds, bishops worthy
of the Apostles, the Maronite monk, the horned head-gear
of the Druses.

Some of those beautiful horses, for which Fakredeen was
celebrated, had awaited the travellers at Beiroot.   The
journey through the mountain was to last three days before
they reached Canobia.   They halted one night at a mountain village, where the young Emir was received with
enthusiastic devotion, and on the next at a small castle
belonging to Fakredeen, and where resided one of his kins-
men.   Two hours before sunset, on the third day, they
were entering the oak forest to which we referred, and
through whose glades they journeyed for about half an
hour.   On arriving at the convent-crowned height opposite,
they beheld an expanse of country; a small plain amid the
mountains; in many parts richly cultivated, studded by
several hamlets, and watered by a stream, winding amid
rich shrubberies of oleander.   Almost in the middle of this
plain, on a height superior to the immediate elevations
which bounded it, rose a mountain of gradual ascent,

covered with sycamores, and crowned by a superb Saracenic castle.

'Canobia!' said Fakredeen to Tancred, 'which I hope you never will quit.'

'It would be difficult,' rejoined Tancred, animated. 'I have seldom seen a sight more striking and more beautiful.'

In the meantime, Freeman and Trueman, who were far in the rear amid Fakredeen's attendants, exchanged congratulating glances of blended surprise and approbation.

'This is the first gentleman's seat I have seen since we left England,' said Freeman.

'There must have been a fine coming of age here,' rejoined Trueman.

'As for that,' replied Freeman, 'comings of age depend in a manner upon meat and drink. They ain't in noways to be carried out with coffee and pipes. Without oxen roasted whole, and broached hogsheads, they ain't in a manner legal.'

A horseman, who was ahead of the Emir and Tancred, now began beating with a stick on two small tabors, one on each side of his saddle, and thus announced to those who were already on the watch, the approach of their lord. It was some time, however, before the road, winding through the sycamore trees and gradually ascending, brought them to the outworks of the castle, of which, during their progress, they enjoyed a variety of views. It was a very extensive pile, in excellent condition, and apparently strongly fortified. A number of men in showy dresses and with ornamented arms, were clustered round the embattled gateway, which introduced the travellers into a quadrangle of considerable size, and of which the light and airy style pleasingly and suitably contrasted with the sterner and more massive character of the exterior walls. A fountain rose in the centre of the quadrangle which was surrounded by arcades. Ranged round this fountain, in a circle, were twenty saddled steeds of the highest race, each held by a groom, and each attended by a man-at-arms. All

pressed their hands to their hearts as the Emir entered, but
with a gravity of countenance which was never for a
moment disturbed. Whether their presence were habitual,
or only for the occasion, it was unquestionably impressive.
Here the travellers dismounted, and Fakredeen ushered
Tancred through a variety of saloons, of which the furniture, though simple, as becomes the East, was luxurious,
and, of its kind, superb; floors of mosaic marbles, bright
carpets, arabesque ceilings, walls of carved cedar, and broad
divans of the richest stuffs of Damascus.

'And this divan is for you,' said Fakredeen, showing
Tancred into a chamber, which opened upon a flower-
garden shaded by lemon trees. 'I am proud of my mirror,'
he added, with some exultation, as he called Tancred's
attention to a large French looking-glass, the only one in
Lebanon. 'And this,' added Fakredeen, leading Tancred
through a suite of marble chambers, 'this is your bath.'

In the centre of one chamber, fed by a perpetual fountain,
was a large alabaster basin, the edges of which were strewn
with flowers just culled. The chamber was entirely of
porcelain; a golden flower on a ground of delicate green.

'I will send your people to you,' said Fakredeen; 'but, in
the meantime, there are attendants here who are, perhaps,
more used to the duty;' and, so saying, he clapped his
hands, and several servants appeared, bearing baskets of
curious linen, whiter than the snow of Lebanon, and a
variety of robes.

END OF BOOK IV.

BOOK V.

CHAPTER I.

It has been long decreed that no poet may introduce the Phœnix. Scylla and Charybdis are both successfully avoided even by provincial rhetoric. The performance of Hamlet with the part of Hamlet omitted, and Mahomet's unhappy coffin, these are illustrations that have long been the prerogative of dolts and dullards. It is not for a moment to be tolerated that an oasis should be met with anywhere except in the Desert.

We sadly lack a new stock of public images. The current similes, if not absolutely counterfeit, are quite worn out. They have no intrinsic value, and serve only as counters to represent the absence of ideas. The critics should really call them in. In the good old days, when the superscription was fresh, and the mint mark bright upon the metal, we should have compared the friendship of two young men to that of Damon and Pythias. These were individuals then still well known in polite society. If their examples have ceased to influence, it cannot be pretended that the extinction of their authority has been the consequence of competition. Our enlightened age has not produced them any rivals.

Of all the differences between the ancients and ourselves, none more striking than our respective ideas of friendship. Grecian friendship was indeed so ethereal, that it is difficult to define its essential qualities. They must be sought rather in the pages of Plato, or the moral essays of Plutarch perhaps, and in some other books not quite as well known, but not less interesting and curious. As for modern friendship, it will be found in clubs. It is violent at a house dinner, fervent in a cigar shop, full of devotion at a cricket or a pigeon match, or in the gathering of a steeple chase. The nineteenth century is not entirely sceptical on the head of friendship, but fears 'tis rare. A man may have friends, but then, are they sincere ones ? Do not they abuse you behind your back, and blackball you at societies where they have had the honour to propose you ? It might philosophically be suggested, that it is more agreeable to be abused behind one's back than to one's face; and, as for the second catastrophe, it should not be forgotten that, if the sincere friend may occasionally put a successful veto on your election, he is always ready to propose you again. Generally speaking, among sensible persons, it would seem that a rich man deems that friend a sincere one who does not want to borrow his money ; while, among the less favoured with fortune's gifts, the sincere friend is generally esteemed to be the individual who is ready to lend it.

As we must not compare Tancred and Fakredeen to Damon and Pythias, and as we cannot easily find in Pall Mall or Park Lane a parallel more modish, we must be content to say, that youth, sympathy, and occasion combined to create between them that intimacy which each was prompt to recognise as one of the principal sources of his happiness, and which the young Emir, at any rate, was persuaded must be as lasting as it was fervent and profound.

Fakredeen was seen to great advantage among his mountains. He was an object of universal regard, and, anxious to maintain the repute of which he was proud, and which was to be the basis of his future power, it seemed that he was always in a gracious and engaging position. Brilliant, sumptuous, and hospitable, always doing something kind, or saying something that pleased, the Emirs and Sheikhs, both Maronite and Druse, were proud of the princely scion of their greatest house, and hastened to repair to Canobia, where they were welcome to ride any of his two hundred steeds, feast on his flocks, quaff his golden wine of Lebanon, or smoke the delicate tobaccos of his celebrated slopes.

As for Tancred, his life was novel, interesting, and exciting. The mountain breezes soon restored his habitual health; his wound entirely healed; each day brought new scenes, new objects, new characters; and there was ever at his side a captivating companion, who lent additional interest to all he saw and heard by perpetually dwelling on the great drama which they were preparing, and in which all these personages and circumstances were to perform their part and advance their purpose.

At this moment Fakredeen proposed to himself two objects: the first was, to bring together the principal chiefs of the mountain, both Maronite and Druse, and virtually to carry into effect at Canobia, that reconciliation between the two races which had been formally effected at Beiroot, in the preceding month of June, by the diplomatic interference of the Great Powers, and through the signature of certain articles of peace to which we have alluded. His second object was to increase his already considerable influence with these personages, by exhibiting to them, as his guest and familiar friend, an English prince, whose presence could only be accounted for by duties too grave for ordinary envoys, and who was understood to represent, in their fullest sense, the wealth and authority of the richest and most potent of nations.

The credulous air of Syria was favourable to the great mystification in which Lord Montacute was an unconscious agent. It was as fully believed in the mountain, by all the Habeishes and the Eldadahs, the Kazins and the Elvasuds, the Elheires and the Haidars, great Maronite families, as well as by the Druse Djinblats and their rivals the House of Yezbeck, or the House of Talhook, or the House of Abuneked, that the brother of the Queen of England was a guest at Canobia as it was in the stony wilderness of Petræa. Ahmet Raslan the Druse and Butros Kerauney the Maronite, who agreed upon no other point, were resolved on this. And was it wonderful, for Butros had already received privately two hundred muskets since the arrival of Tancred, and Raslan had been promised in confidence a slice of the impending English loan by Fakredeen ?

The extraordinary attention, almost homage, which the Emir paid his guest, entirely authorised these convictions, although they could justify no suspicion on the part of Tancred. The natural simplicity of his manners, indeed, and his constitutional reserve, recoiled from the state and ceremony with which he found himself frequently surrounded and too often treated ; but Fakredeen peremptorily stopped his remonstrances by assuring him that it was the custom of the country, and that every one present would be offended if a guest of distinction were not entertained with this extreme respect. It is impossible to argue against the customs of a country with which you are not acquainted, but coming home one day from a hawking party, a large assembly of the most influential chieftains, Fakredeen himself bounding on a Kochlani steed, and arrayed in a dress that would have become Solyman the Magnificent, Tancred about to dismount, the Lord of Canobia pushed forward, and, springing from his saddle, insisted on holding the stirrup of Lord Montacute.

'I cannot permit this,' said Tancred, reddening, and keeping his seat.

'If you do not, there is not a man here who will not take it as a personal insult,' said the Emir, speaking rapidly between his teeth, yet affecting to smile. 'It has been the custom of the mountain for more than seven hundred years.'

'Very strange,' thought Tancred, as he complied and dismounted.

All Syria, from Gaza to the Euphrates, is feudal. The system, generally prevalent, flourishes in the mountain region even with intenseness. An attempt to destroy feudalism occasioned the revolt against the Egyptians in 1840, and drove Mehemet Ali from the country which had cost him so much blood and treasure. Every disorder that has subsequently occurred in Syria since the Turkish restoration may be traced to some officious interposition or hostile encroachment in this respect. The lands of Lebanon are divided into fifteen Mookatas, or feudal provinces, and the rights of the mookatadgis, or landlords, in these provinces, are power of punishment not extending to death, service in war, and labour in peace, and the collection of the imperial revenue from the population, who are in fact their vassals, on which they receive a percentage from the Porte. The administration of police, of the revenue, and indeed the whole internal government of Lebanon, are in the hands of the mookatadgis, or rather of the most powerful individuals of this class, who bear the titles of Emirs and Sheikhs, some of whom are proprietors to a very great extent, and many of whom, in point of race and antiquity of established family, are superior to the aristocracy of Europe.

There is no doubt that the founders of this privileged and territorial class, whatever may be the present creeds of its members, Moslemin, Maronite, or Druse, were the old Arabian conquerors of Syria. The Turks, conquerors in their turn, have succeeded in some degree in the plain to the estates and immunities of the followers of the first caliphs; but the Ottomans never substantially prevailed in the Highlands, and their authority has been recognised mainly by management, and as a convenient compromise amid the rivalries of so many local ambitions.

Always conspicuous among the great families of the Lebanon, during the last century and a half pre-eminent, has been the house of Shehaab, possessing entirely one of the provinces, and widely disseminated and powerfully endowed in several of the others. Since the commencement of the eighteenth century, the virtual sovereignty of the country has been exercised by a prince of this family, under the title of Chief Emir. The chiefs of all the different races have kissed the hand of a Shehaab; he had the power of life and death, could proclaim war and confer honours. Of all this family, none were so supreme as the Emir Bescheer, who governed Lebanon during the Egyptian invasion, and to whose subdolous career and its consequences we have already referred. When the Turks triumphed in 1840, the Emir Bescheer was deposed, and with his sons sent prisoner to Constantinople. The Porte, warned at that time by the too easy invasion of Syria and the imminent peril which it had escaped, wished itself to assume the government of Lebanon, and to garrison the passes with its troops; but the Christian Powers would not consent to this proposition, and therefore Kassim Shehaab was called to the Chief Emirate. Acted upon by the patriarch of the Maronites, Kassim, who was a Christian Shehaab, countenanced the attempts of his holiness to destroy the feudal privileges of the Druse mookatadgis, while those of the Maronites were to be retained. This produced the civil war of 1841 in Lebanon, which so perplexed and scandalised England, and which was triumphantly appealed to by France as indubitable evidence of the weakness and unpopularity of the Turks, and the fruitlessness of our previous interference. The Turks had as little to do with it as M. Guizot or Lord Palmerston; but so limited is our knowledge upon these subjects, that the cry was successful, and many who had warmly supported the English minister during the previous year, and probably in equal ignorance of the real merits of the question, began now to shake their heads and fear that we had perhaps been too precipitate.

The Porte adroitly took advantage of the general anarchy to enforce the expediency of its original proposition, to which the Great Powers, however, would not assent. Kassim was deposed, after a reign of a few months, amid burning villages and their slaughtered inhabitants; and, as the Porte was resolved not to try another Shehaab, and the Great Powers were resolved not to trust the Porte, diplomacy was obliged again to interfere, and undertake to provide Lebanon with a government.

It was the interest of two parties, whose co-operation was highly essential to the settlement of this question, to prevent the desired adjustment, and these were the Turkish government and the family of Shehaab and their numerous adherents. Anarchy was an argument in the mouth of each, that the Lebanon must be governed by the Porte, or that there never could be tranquillity without a Shehaab prince. The Porte in general contented itself with being passive and watching the fray, while the agents of the Great Powers planned and promulgated their scheme of polity. The Shehaabs were more active, and their efforts were greatly assisted by the European project which was announced.

The principal feature of this administrative design was the institution of two governors of Lebanon, called Caimacams, one of whom was to be a Maronite and govern the Maronites, and the other a Druse and govern his fellow-countrymen. Superficially, this seemed fair enough, but reduced into practice the machinery would not work. For instance, the populations in many places were blended. Was a Druse Caimacam to govern the Christians in his district? Was the government of the two Caimacams to be sectarian or geographical? Should the Christian Caimacam govern all the Christians, and the Druse Caimacam govern all the Druses of the Lebanon? Or should the Christian Caimacam govern the Christian Mookatas, as well as such Druses as lived mixed with the Christians in the Christian Mookatas, and the Druse Camaicam in the Druse country exercise the same rights?

Hence arose the terms of mixed Druses and mixed Christians; mixed Druses meaning Druses living in the Christian country, and mixed Christians those living in the Druse country. Such was the origin of the mixed population question, which entirely upset the project of Downing Street; happy spot, where they draw up constitutions for Syria and treaties for China with the same self-complacency and the same success!

Downing Street (1842) decided upon the sectarian government of the Lebanon. It was simple, and probably
satisfactory, to Exeter Hall; but Downing Street was quite
unaware, or had quite forgotten, that the feudal system
prevailed throughout Lebanon. The Christians in the
Druse districts were vassals of Druse lords. The direct
rule of a Christian Caimacam was an infringement on all
the feudal rights of the Djinblats and Yezbecks, of the Talhooks and the Abdel-Maleks. It would be equally fatal
to the feudal rights of the Christian chiefs, the Kazins and
the Eldadahs, the Elheires and the El Dahers, as regarded
their Druse tenantry, unless the impossible plan of the
patriarch of the Maronites, which had already produced a
civil war, had been adopted. Diplomacy, therefore, seemed
on the point of at length succeeding in uniting the whole
population of Lebanon in one harmonious action, but unfortunately against its own project.

The Shehaab party availed themselves of these circumstances with great dexterity and vigour. The party was
powerful. The whole of the Maronites, a population of
more than 150,000, were enrolled in their ranks. The Emir
Bescheer was of their faith; so was the unfortunate Kassim.
True, there were several Shehaab princes who were Moslemin, but they might become Christians, and they were not
Druses, at least only two or three of them. The Maronite
clergy exercised an unquestioned influence over their flocks.
It was powerfully organised: a patriarch, numerous monas-
teries, nine prelates, and an active country priesthood.

Previously to the civil war of 1841, the feeling of the
Druses had been universally in favour of the Shehaabs.
The peril in which feudalism was placed revived their ancient sentiments. A Shehaab committee was appointed,
with perpetual sittings at Deir El Kamar, the most considerable place in the Lebanon; and, although it was chiefly
composed of Christians, there were several Druses at least
in correspondence with it. But the most remarkable institution which occurred about this time (1844) was that of

'Young Syria.' It flourishes: in every town and village of Lebanon, there is a band of youth who acknowledge the title, and who profess nationality as their object, though, behind that plea, the restoration of the house of Shehaab generally peeps out.

Downing Street, frightened, gave up sectarian diplomacy, and announced the adoption of the geographical principle of government. The Druses, now that their feudal privileges were secured, cooled in their ardour for nationality. The Shehaabs, on the other hand, finding that the Druses were not to be depended on, changed their note. 'Is it to be tolerated for a moment, that a Christian should be governed by a Druse? Were it a Moslem, one might bear it; these things will happen; but a Druse, who adores a golden calf, worshippers of Eblis! One might as well be governed by a Jew.'

The Maronite patriarch sent 200,000 piastres to his children to buy arms; the superior of the convent of Maashmooshi forwarded little less, saying it was much better to spend their treasure in helping the Christians than in keeping it to be plundered by the Druses. Bishop Tubia gave his bond for a round sum, but afterwards recalled it; Bishop Joseph Djezini came into Sidon with his pockets full, and told the people that a prince of the house of Shehaab would soon be at their head, but explained on a subsequent occasion that he went thither merely to distribute charity.

In this state of affairs, in May 1845 the civil war broke out. The Christians attacked the Druses in several districts on the same day. The attack was unprovoked, and eventually unsuccessful. Twenty villages were seen burning at the same time from Beiroot. The Druses repulsed the Christians and punished them sharply; the Turkish troops, at the instigation of the European authorities, marched into the mountain and vigorously interfered. The Maronites did not show as much courage in the field as in the standing committee at Deir ^J Kamar but several of the Shehaab princes who headed them, especially the Emir Kais, maintained the reputation of their house and displayed a brilliant courage. The Emir Fakredeen was at Canobia at the time of the outbreak, which, as it often happens, though not unpremeditated, was unexpected. He marched to the scene of action at the head of his troops, and, when he found that Kais had been outflanked and repulsed, that the Maronites were disheartened in proportion to their previous vanity and insolence, and that the Turkish forces had interfered, he assumed the character of mediator. Taking advantage of the circumstances and the alarm of all parties at the conjuncture and its yet unascertained consequences, he obtained for the Maronites a long-promised indemnity from the Porte for the ravages of the Druses in the civil war of 1841, which the Druses had been unable to pay, on condition that they should accept the geographical scheme of government; and, having signed, with other Emirs and Sheikhs, the ten articles of peace, he departed, as we have seen, on that visit to Jerusalem, which exercised such control over the career of Lord Montacute, and led to such strange results and such singular adventures.

CHAPTER II.

GALLOPED up the winding steep of Canobia the Sheikh Said Djinblat, one of the most popular chieftains of the Druses; amiable and brave, trustworthy and soft-mannered. Four of his cousins rode after him: he came from his castle of Mooktara, which was not distant. He was in the prime of manhood, tall and lithe; enveloped in a bornous which shrouded his dark eye, his white turban, and his gold-embroidered vests; his long lance was couched in its rest, as he galloped up the winding steep of Canobia.

Came slowly, on steeds dark as night, up the winding steep of Canobia, with a company of twenty men on foot armed with muskets and handjars, the two ferocious brothers Abuneked, Nasif and Hamood. Pale is the cheek of the daughters of Maron at the fell name of Abuneked. The Abunekeds were the Druse lords of the town of Deir el Kamar, where the majority of the inhabitants were Christian. When the patriarch tried to deprive the Druses of their feudal rights, the Abunekeds attacked and sacked their own town of Deir el Kamar. The civil war being terminated, and it being agreed, in the settlement of the indemnities from the Druses to the Maronites, that all plunder still in possession of the plunderers should be restored, Nasif Abuneked said, ' I have five hundred silver horns, and each of them I took from the head of a Christian woman. Come and fetch them.'

But all this is forgotten now; and least of all should it be remembered by the meek-looking individual who is at this moment about to ascend the winding steep of Canobia. Riding on a mule, clad in a coarse brown woollen dress, in Italy or Spain we should esteem him a simple Capuchin, but in truth he is a prelate, and a prelate of great power; Bishop Nicodemus, to wit, prime councillor of the patriarch, and chief prompter of those measures that occasioned the civil war of 1841. A single sacristan walks behind him, his only retinue, and befitting his limited resources; but the Maronite prelate is recompensed by universal respect; his vanity is perpetually gratified, and, when he appears, Sheikh and peasant are alike proud to kiss the hand which his reverence is ever prompt to extend.

Placed on a more eminent stage, and called upon to control larger circumstances, Bishop Nicodemus might have rivalled the Bishop of Autun; so fertile was he in resource, and so intuitive was his knowledge of men. As it was, he wasted his genius in mountain squabbles, and in regulating the discipline of his little church; suspending priests, interdicting monks, and inflicting public penance on the laity. He rather resembled De Retz than Talleyrand, for he was naturally turbulent and intriguing. He could under no circumstances let well alone. He was a thorough Syrian, at once subtile and imaginative. Attached to the house of Shehaab by policy, he was devoted to Fakredeen as much by sympathy as interest, and had contrived the secret mission of Archbishop Murad to Europe, which had so much perplexed M. Guizot, Lord Cowley, and Lord Aberdeen ; and which finally, by the intervention of the same Bishop Nicodemus, Fakredeen had disowned.

Came caracolling up the winding steep of Canobia a troop of horsemen, showily attired, and riding steeds that danced in the sunny air. These were the princes Kais and Abdullah Shehaab, and Francis El Kazin, whom the Levantines called Caseno, and the principal members of the Young Syria party ; some of them beardless Sheikhs, but all choicely mounted, and each holding on his wrist a falcon ; for this was the first day of the year that they might fly. But those who cared not to seek a quarry in the partridge or the gazelle, might find the wild boar or track the panther in the spacious woods of Canobia.

And the Druse chief of the house of Djezbek, who for five hundred years had never yielded precedence to the house of Djinblat, and Sheikh Fahour Kangé, who since the civil war had never smoked a pipe with a Maronite, but who now gave the salaam of peace to the crowds of Habeishs and Dahdahes who passed by ; and Butros Keramy, the nephew of the patriarch, himself a great Sheikh, who inhaled his nargilly as he rode, and who looked to the skies and puffed forth his smoke whenever he met a son of Eblis ; and the house of Talhook, and the house of Abdel-Malek, and a swarm of Elvasuds, and Elheires, and El Dahers, Emirs and Sheikhs on their bounding steeds, and musketeers on foot, with their light jackets and bare legs and wooden sandals, and black slaves, carrying vases and tubes ; everywhere a brilliant and animated multitude, and all mounting the winding steep of Canobia.

The great court of the castle was crowded with men and horses, and fifty mouths at once were drinking at the central basin; the arcades were full of Sheikhs, smoking and squatted on their carpets, which in general they had spread in this locality in preference to the more formal saloons, whose splendid divans rather embarrassed them; though even these chambers were well attended, the guests principally seated on the marble floors covered with their small bright carpets. The domain immediately around the castle was also crowded with human beings. The moment anyone arrived, his steed was stabled or picketed; his attendants spread his carpet, sought food for him, which was promptly furnished, with coffee and sherbets, and occasionally wine; and when he had sufficiently refreshed himself, he lighted his nargilly. Everywhere there was a murmur, but no uproar; a stir, but no tumult. And what was most remarkable amid these spears and sabres, these muskets, handjars, and poniards, was the sweet and perpetually recurring Syrian salutation of ' Peace.'

Fakredeen, moving about in an immense turban, of the most national and unreformed style, and covered with costly shawls and arms flaming with jewels, recognised and welcomed everyone. He accosted Druse and Maronite with equal cordiality, talked much with Said Djinblat, whom he specially wished to gain, and lent one of his choicest steeds to the Djezbek, that he might not be offended. The Talhook and the Abdel-Malek could not be jealous of the Habeish and the Eldadah. He kissed the hand of Bishop Nicodemus, but then he sent his own nargilly to the Emir Ahmet Raslan, who was Caimacam of the Druses.

In this strange and splendid scene, Tancred, dressed in a velvet shooting-jacket built in St. James' Street and a wide-awake which had been purchased at Bellamont market, and leaning on a rifle which was the masterpiece of Purday, was not perhaps the least-interesting personage. The Emirs and Sheikhs, notwithstanding the powers of dissimulation for which the Orientals are renowned, their habits of self-restraint, and their rooted principle never to seem surprised about anything, have a weakness in respect to

arms.   After eyeing Tancred for a considerable time with
imperturbable countenances, Francis El Kazin sent to Fakredeen to know whether the English prince would favour
them by shooting an eagle.   This broke the ice, and
Fakredeen came, and soon the rifle was in the hands of
Francis El Kazin.   Sheikh Said Djinblat, who would have
died rather than have noticed the rifle in the hands of
Tancred, could not resist examining it when in the possession of a brother Sheikh.   Kais Shehaab, several Habeishes
and Eldadahs gathered round ; exclamations of wonder and
admiration arose ; sundry asseverations that God was great
followed.

Freeman and Trueman, who were at hand, were summoned to show their lord's double-barrelled gun, and his
pistols with hair-triggers.   This they did, with that stupid
composure and dogged conceit which distinguish English
servants in situations which must elicit from all other
persons some ebullition of feeling.   Exchanging between
themselves glances of contempt at the lords of Lebanon,
who were ignorant of what everybody knows, they exhibited the arms without the slightest interest or anxiety to
make the Sheikhs comprehend them ; till Tancred, mortified
at their brutality, himself interfered, and, having already
no inconsiderable knowledge of the language of the country,
though, from his reserve, Fakredeen little suspected the extent of his acquirements, explained felicitously to his companions the process of the arms ; and then taking his rifle,
and stepping out upon the terrace, he levelled his piece at
a heron which was soaring at a distance of upwards of
one hundred yards, and brought the bird down amid the
applause both of Maronite and Druse.

'He is sent here, I understand,' said Butros Keramy, 'to
ascertain for the Queen of the English whether the country
is in favour of the Shehaabs.   Could you believe it, but
I was told yesterday at Deir el Kamar, that the English
consul has persuaded the Queen that even the patriarch was
against the Shehaabs?'

'Is it possible?' said Rafael Farah, a Maronite of the house of Eldadah. "It must be the Druses who circulate these enormous falsehoods.'

'Hush!' said Young Syria, in the shape of Francis El Kazin, 'there is no longer Maronite or Druse: we are all Syrians, we are brothers.'

'Then a good many of my brothers are sons of Eblis,' said Butros Keramy. 'I hope he is not my father.'

'Truly, I should like to see the mountain without the Maronite nation,' said Rafael Farah. 'That would be a year without rain.'

'And mighty things your Maronite nation has done!' rejoined Francis El Kazin. 'If there had been the Syrian nation instead of the Maronite nation, and the Druse nation, and half a dozen other nations besides, instead of being conquered by Egypt in 1832, we should have conquered Egypt ourselves long ago, and have held it for our farm. We have done mighty things truly with our Maronite nation!'

'To hear an El Kazin speak against the Maronite nation!' exclaimed Rafael Farah, with a look of horror; 'a nation that has two hundred convents!'

'And a patriarch,' said Butros Keramy, 'very much re-spected even by the Pope of Rome.'

'And who were disarmed like sheep,' said Francis.

'Not because we were beaten,' said Butros, who was brave enough.

'We were persuaded to that,' said Rafael.

'By our monks,' said Francis; 'the convents you are so proud of.'

'They were deceived by sons of Eblis,' said Butros. 'I never gave up my arms. I have some pieces now, that, although they are not as fine as those of the English prince, could pick a son of Eblis off behind a rock, whether he be Egyptian or Druse.'

'Hush!' said Francis El Kazin. 'You love our host, Butros; these are not words that will please him——'

'Or me, my children,' said Bishop Nicodemus. 'This is
a great day for Syria! to find the chiefs of both nations
assembled at the castle of a Shehaab. Why am I here but
to preach peace and love? And Butros Keramy, my friend,
my dearly beloved brother Butros, if you wish to please
the patriarch, your uncle, who loves you so well, you will
no longer call Druses sons of Eblis.'

'What are we to call them?' asked Rafael Farah, pettishly.

'Brothers,' replied Bishop Nicodemus; 'misguided, but
still brothers. This is not a moment for brawls, when the
great Queen of the English has sent hither her own brother
to witness the concord of the mountain.'

Now arose the sound of tabors, beaten without any attempt
at a tune, but with unremitting monotony, then the baying
of many hounds more distant. There was a bustle. Many
Sheikhs slowly rose; their followers rushed about; some
looked at their musket locks, some poised their pikes and
spears, some unsheathed their handjars, examined their
edge, and then returned them to their sheath. Those who
were in the interior of the castle came crowding into the
great court, which, in turn, poured forth its current of
population into the table-land about the castle. Here, held
by grooms, or picketed, were many steeds. The mares of
the Emir Fakredeen were led about by his black slaves.
Many of the Sheikhs, mounted, prepared for the pastime
that awaited them.

There was to be a grand chase in the oak forest, through
part of which Tancred had already travelled, and which
spread over a portion of the plain and the low hilly country
that encompassed it. Three parties, respectively led by the
Emir Fakredeen, and the Caimacams of the two nations,
were to penetrate into this forest at different and distant
points, so that the sport was spread over a surface of many
miles. The heads of the great houses of both nations accompanied the Emir of Canobia; their relatives and followers,
by the exertions of Francis El Kazin and Young Syria,

were in general so distributed, that the Maronites were
under the command of the Emir Raslan, the Druse Caimacam, while the Druses followed the Emir Haidar. This
great hunting party consisted of more than eight hundred
persons, about half of whom were mounted, but all were
armed; even those who held the dogs in leash were entitled to join in the sport with the same freedom as the
proudest Sheikh. The three leaders having mounted and
bowed gracefully to each other, the cavalcades separated
and descended into the plain. The moment they reached
the level country, the horsemen shouted and dispersed,
galloping in all directions, and many of them throwing
their spears; but, in a short time, they had collected again
under their respective leaders, and the three distinct bodies,
each a moving and many-coloured mass, might be observed
from the castled heights, each instant diminishing in size
and lustre, until they vanished at different points in the
distance, and were lost amid the shades of the forest.

For many hours throughout this region nothing was
heard but the firing of guns, the baying of hounds, the
shouting of men; not a human being was visible, except
some groups of women in the villages, with veils suspended
on immense silver horns, like our female headgear of the
middle ages. By-and-by, figures were seen stealing forth
from the forest, men on foot, one or two, then larger parties;
some reposed on the plain, some returned to the villages,
some re-ascended the winding steeps of Canobia. The
firing, the shouting, the baying had become more occasional.
Now a wearied horseman picked his slow way over the
plain; then came forth a brighter company, still bounding
along. And now they issued, but slowly and in small
parties, from various and opposite quarters of the woodland.
A great detachment, in a certain order, were then observed
to cross the plain and approach the castle. They advanced
very gradually, for most of them were on foot, and, joining
together, evidently carried burdens; they were preceded
and followed by a guard of cavalry. Soon it might be per-

ceived that the produce of the chase was arriving : twenty-five wild boars carried on litters of green branches; innumerable gazelles borne by their victors; transfixed by four spears, and carried by four men, a hyena.

Not very long after this caravan had reached the castle, the firing, which had died away, recommenced ; the sounds were near at hand ; there was a volley, and almost simultaneously there issued from various parts of the forest the great body of the hunt. They maintained no order on their return, but dispersed over the plain, blending together, galloping their steeds, throwing their lances, and occasionally firing a shot. Fakredeen and his immediate friends rode up to the Caimacam of the Druses, and they offered each other mutual congratulations on the sport of the morning. They waited for the Caimacam of the Maronites, who, however, did not long detain them ; and, when he appeared, their suites joined, and, cantering off at a brisk pace, they soon mounted in company the winding steeps of Canobia.

The kitchen of Canobia was on a great scale, though simple as it was vast. It was formed for the occasion. About fifty square pits, some four feet in length, and about half as deep, had been dug on the table-land in the vicinity of the castle. At each corner of each pit was a stake, and the four supported a rustic gridiron of green wood, suspended over each pit, which was filled with charcoal, and which yielded an equal and continuous heat to the animal reposing on the gridiron : in some instances a wild boar, in others a sheep—occasionally a couple of gazelles. The sheep had been skinned, for there had been time for the operation ; but the game had only been split open, cleared out, and laid on its back, with its feet tied to each of the stakes, so as to retain its position. While this roasting was going on, they filled the stomachs of the animals with lemons gashed with their daggers, and bruised pomegranates, whose fragrant juice, uniting with the bubbling fat, produced an aromatic and rosy gravy. The huntsmen were the cooks, but the greatest order was preserved ;

and though the Emirs and the great Sheikhs, heads of houses, retiring again to their divans, occupied themselves with their nargillies, many a mookatadgi mixed with the servants and the slaves, and delighted in preparing this patriarchal banquet, which indeed befitted a castle and a forest. Within the walls they prepared rice, which they piled on brazen and pewter dishes, boiled gallons of coffee, and stewed the liver of the wild boars and the gazelles in thè golden wine of Lebanon.

The way they dined was this. Fakredeen had his carpet spread on the marble floor of his principal saloon, and the two Caimacams, Tancred and Bishop Nicodemus, Said Djinblat, the heads of the houses of Djezbek, Talhook, and Abdel-Malek, Hamood Abuneked, and five Maronite chieftains of equal consideration, the Emirs of the house of Shehaab, the Habeish, and the Eldadah, were invited to sit with him. Round the chamber which opened to the air, other chieftains were invited to spread their carpets also ; the centre was left clear. The rest of the Sheikhs and mookatadgis established themselves in small parties, grouped in the same fashion, in the great court and under the arcades, taking care to leave free egress and regress to the fountain. The retainers feasted, when all was over, in the open air.

Every man found his knife in his girdle, forks were unknown. Fakredeen prided himself on his French porcelain, which the Djinblats, the Talhooks, and the Abunekeds glanced at very queerly. This European luxury was confined to his own carpet. There was, however, a considerable supply of Egyptian earthenware, and dishes of pewter and brass. The retainers, if they required a plate, found one in the large flat barley cake with which each was supplied. For the principal guests there was no want of coarse goblets of Bohemian glass ; delicious water abounded in vases of porous pottery, which might be blended, if necessary, with the red or white wine of the mountain. The rice, which had been dressed with a savoury sauce, was eaten with wooden spoons by those who were supplied with these instruments; but in general the guests served themselves by handfuls.

Ten men brought in a framework of oaken branches placed transversely, then covered with twigs, and over these, and concealing everything, a bed, fully an inch thick, of mulberry leaves. Upon this fragrant bier reposed a wild boar; and on each side of him reclined a gazelle. Their bodies had closed the moment their feet had been loosened from the stakes, so that the gravy was contained within them. It required a most skilful carver not to waste this precious liquid. The chamber was filled with an invigorating odour as the practised hand of Habas of Deir el Kamar proceeded to the great performance. His instruments were a silver cup, a poniard, and a handjar. Making a small aperture in the side of the animal, he adroitly introduced the cup, and proportionately baled out the gravy to a group of plates that were extended to him; then, plunging in the long poniard on which he rested, he made an incision with the keen edge and broad blade of the handjar, and sent forth slice after slice of white fat and ruby flesh.

The same ceremony was performing in the other parts of the castle. Ten of the pits had been cleared of their burden to appease the first cravings of the appetite of the hunters. The fires had been replenished, the gridirons again covered, and such a supply kept up as should not only satisfy the chieftains, but content their followers. Tancred could not refrain from contrasting the silent, business-like way in which the Shehaabs, the Talhooks, the Djinblats, and the Habeish performed the great operation that was going on, with the conversation which is considered an indispensable accompaniment of a dinner in Franguestan; for we must no longer presume to call Europe by its beautiful oriental name of Christendom. The Shehaabs, the Talhooks, the Djinblats, and the Habeish were sensible men, who were of opinion, that if you want to talk you should not by any means eat, since from such an attempt at a united performance it generally results, that you neither converse nor refresh yourself in a satisfactory manner.

There can be no question that, next to the corroding cares of Europeans, principally occasioned by their love of accumulating money which they never enjoy, the principal cause of the modern disorder of dyspepsia prevalent among them, is their irrational habit of interfering with the process of digestion by torturing attempts at repartee, and racking their brain, at a moment when it should be calm, to remind themselves of some anecdote so appropriate that they have forgotten it. It has been supposed that the presence of women at our banquets has occasioned this fatal and inopportune desire to shine; and an argument has been founded on this circumstance in favour of their exclusion, from an incident which, on the whole, has a tendency to impair that ideal which they should always study and cherish. It may be urged that if a woman eats she may destroy her spell; and that, if she will not eat, she destroys our dinner.

Notwithstanding all this, and without giving any opinion on this latter point, it should be remembered, that at dinners strictly male, where there is really no excuse for anything of the kind, where, if you are a person of ascertained position, you are invited for that position and for nothing else, and where, if you are not a person of ascertained position, the more agreeable you make yourself the more you will be hated, and the less chance you will have of being asked there again, or anywhere else, still this fatal frenzy prevails; and individuals are found who, from soup to coffee, from egg to apple, will tell anecdotes, indulge in jests, or, in a tone of levity approaching to jesting, pour forth garrulous secret history with which everyone is acquainted, and never say a single thing which is new that is not coolly invented for the occasion.

The princes of the house of Shehaab, Kais, and Assaad, and Abdullah, the Habeish and the Eldadah, the great houses of the Druses, the Djinblat and the Yezbek, the Abuneked, the Talhook, and the Abdel-Malek, were not of this school. Silently, determinedly, unceasing, unsatiated, they proceeded with the great enterprise on which they had embarked. If the two nations were indeed to be united, and form a great whole under the sceptre of a Shehaab, let not this banquet pass like the hypocritical hospitality of ordinary life, where men offer what they desire not to be accepted by those who have no wish to receive. This, on the contrary, was a real repast, a thing to be remembered. Practice made the guests accustomed to the porcelain of Paris and the goblets of Prague. Many was the goodly slice of wild boar, succeeded by the rich flesh of the gazelle, of which they disposed. There were also wood-pigeons, partridges, which the falconers had brought down, and quails from the wilderness. At length they called again for rice, a custom which intimated that their appetite for meat was satisfied, and immediately Nubian slaves covered them with towels of fine linen fringed with gold, and, while they held their hands over the basin, poured sweet waters from the ewer.

In the meantime, Butros Keramy opened his heart to Rafael Farah.

' I begin,' said Butros, quaffing a cup of the Vino d'Oro, ' to believe in nationality.'

' It cannot be denied,' said Rafael Farah, judiciously shaking his head, ' that the two nations were once under the same prince. If the great powers would agree to a Shehaab, and we could sometimes meet together in the present fashion, there is no saying, prejudices might wear off.'

' Shall it ever be said that I am of the same nation as Hamood Abuneked ? ' said Butros.

' Ah ! it is very dreadful,' said Rafael ; ' a man who has burned convents ! '

' And who has five hundred Maronite horns in his castle,' said Butros.

' But suppose he restores them ? ' said Francis El Kazin.

' That would make a difference,' said Rafael Farah.

' There can be no difference while he lives,' said Butros.

' I fear 'tis an affair of blood,' said Rafael Farah.

' Taking horns was never an affair of blood,' said Francis El Kazin.

' What should be an affair of blood,' said Butros, ' if——'

' But nothing else but taking horns can be proved,' said Francis El Kazin.

' There is a good deal in that ! ' said Rafael Farah.

After confectionary which had been prepared by nuns, and strong waters which had been distilled by the hands of priors, the chieftains praised God, and rose, and took their seats on the divan, when immediately advanced a crowd of slaves, each bearing a nargilly, which they presented to the guests. Then gradually the conversation commenced. It was entirely confined to the exploits of the day, which had been rich in the heroic feats of forest huntsmen. There had been wild boars, too, as brave as their destroyers ; some slight wounds, some narrow escapes. Sheikh Said Djinblat inquired of Lord Montacute whether there were hyenas in England, but was immediately answered by the lively and well-informed Kais Shehaab, who apprised him that there were only lions and unicorns. Bishop Nicodemus, who watched the current of observations, began telling hunting stories of the time of the Emir Bescheer, when that prince resided at his splendid castle of Bteddeen, near Deir El Kamar. This was to recall the days when the mountain had only one ruler, and that ruler a Shehaab, and when the Druse lords were proud to be classed among his most faithful subjects.

In the meantime smoking had commenced throughout the castle, but this did not prevent the smokers from drinking raki as well as the sober juice of Mocha. Four hundred men, armed with nargilly or chibouque, inhaling and puffing with that ardour and enjoyment which men, after a hard day's hunting, and a repast of unusual solidity, can alone experience ! Without the walls, almost as many individuals were feasting in the open air ; brandishing their handjars as they cut up the huge masses of meat before them, plunging their eager hands into the enormous dishes of rice, and slaking their thirst by emptying at a draught a vase of water, which they poured aloft as the Italians would a flask of wine or oil.

'And the most curious thing,' said Freeman to Trueman, as they established themselves under a pine tree, with an ample portion of roast meat, and armed with their travelling knives and forks, 'and the most curious thing is, that they say these people are Christians! Who ever heard of Christians wearing turbans?'

'Or eating without knives and forks?' added Trueman.

'It would astonish their weak minds in the steward's room at Bellamont, if they could see all this, John,' said Mr. Freeman, pensively. 'A man who travels has very great advantages.'

'And very great hardships too,' said Trueman. 'I don't care for work, but I do like to have my meals regular.'

'This is not bad picking, though,' said Mr. Freeman; 'they call it gazelle, which I suppose is the foreign for venison.'

'If you called this venison at Bellamont,' said Trueman, 'they would look very queer in the steward's room.'

'Bellamont is Bellamont, and this place is this place, John,' said Mr. Freeman. 'The Hameer is a noble gentleman, every inch of him, and I am very glad my lord has got a companion of his own kidney. It is much better than monks and hermits, and low people of that sort, who are not by no means fit company for somebody I could mention, and might turn him into a papist into the bargain.'

'That would be a bad business,' said Trueman; 'my lady could never abide that. It would be better that he should turn Turk.'

'I am not sure it wouldn't,' said Mr. Freeman. 'It would be in a manner more constitutional. The Sultan of Turkey may send an Ambassador to our Queen, but the Pope of Rome may not.'

'I should not like to turn Turk,' said Trueman, very thoughtfully.

'I know what you are thinking of, John,' said Mr. Freeman, in a serious tone. 'You are thinking, if anything were to happen to either of us in this heathen land, where we should get Christian burial.'

'Lord love you, Mr. Freeman, no I wasn't. I was thinking of a glass of ale.'

'Ah!' sighed Freeman, 'it softens the heart to think of such things away from home, as we are. Do you know, John, there are times when I feel very queer, there are indeed. I catched myself a singing "Sweet Home" one night, among those savages in the wilderness. One wants consolation, John, sometimes, one does, indeed; and, for my part, I do miss the family prayers and the home-brewed.'

As the twilight died away, they lighted immense bonfires, as well to cheer them during their bivouac, as to deter any adventurous panther, stimulated by the savoury odours, or hyena, breathing fraternal revenge, from reconnoitring their encampment. By degrees, however, the noise of the revellers without subsided, and at length died away. Having satisfied their hunger, and smoked their chibouques, often made from the branch which they had cut since their return from hunting, with the bud still alive upon the fresh green tube, they wrapped themselves in their cloaks and sheepskins, and sunk into a deep and well-earned repose.

Within, the Sheikhs and mookatadgis gradually, by no means simultaneously, followed their example. Some, taking off their turbans and loosening their girdles, ensconced themselves under the arcades, lying on their carpets, and covered with their pelisses and cloaks; some strolled into the divaned chambers, which were open to all, and more comfortably stowed themselves upon the well-stuffed cushions; others, overcome with fatigue and their revel, were lying in deep sleep, outstretched in the open court, and picturesque in the blazing moonlight.

The hunting party was to last three days, and few intended to leave Canobia on the morrow; but it must not be supposed that the guests experienced any very unusual hardships in what the reader may consider a far from satisfactory mode of passing their night. To say nothing of the warm and benignant climate, the Easterns have not the custom of retiring or rising with the formality of the Occidental nations. They take their sleep when they require it, and meet its embrace without preparation. One cause of this difference undoubtedly is, that the Orientals do not connect the business of the toilet with that of rest. The daily bath, with its elaborate processes, is the spot where the mind ponders on the colour of a robe or the fashion of a turban; the daily bath, which is the principal incident of Oriental habits, and which can scarcely be said to exist among our own.

Fakredeen had yielded even his own chambers to his friends. Every divan in Canobia was open, excepting the rooms of Tancred. These were sacred, and the Emir had requested his friend to receive him as a guest during the festival, and apportion him one of his chambers. The head of the house of Talhook was asleep with the tube of his nargilly in his mouth; the Yezbek had unwound his turban, cast off his sandals, wrapped himself in his pelisses, and fairly turned in; Bishop Nicodemus was kneeling in a corner, and kissing a silver cross; and Hamood Abuneked had rolled himself up in a carpet, and was snoring as if he were blowing through one of the horns of the Maronites. Fakredeen shot a glance at Tancred, instantly recognised. Then, rising and giving the salaam of peace to his guests, the Emir and his English friend made their escape down a corridor, at the bottom of which was one of the few doors that could be found in the castle of Canobia. Baroni received them, on the watch lest some cruising Sheikh should appropriate their resting-place. The young moon, almost as young and bright as it was two months before at Gaza, suffused with lustre the beautiful garden of fruit and flowers without. Under the balcony, Baroni had placed a divan with many cushions, a lamp with burning coffee, and some fresh nargillies.

'Thank God, we are alone!' exclaimed Fakredeen. 'Tell me, my Tancred, what do you think of it all?'

CHAPTER III.

'It has been a great day,' said Tancred, 'not to be forgotten.'

'Yes; but what do you think of them? Are they the fellows I described; the men that might conquer the world?'

'To conquer the world depends on men not only being good soldiers, but being animated by some sovereign principle that nothing can resist,' replied Tancred.

'But that we have got,' rejoined Fakredeen.

'But have they got it?'

'We can give it to them.'

'I am not so sure of that. It seems to me that we are going to establish a theocratic equality by the aid of the feudal system.'

'That is to say, their present system,' replied Fakredeen. 'Islamism was propagated by men who were previously idolaters, and our principle may be established by those whose practice at the present time is directly opposed to it.'

'I still cling to my first idea of making the movement from the Desert,' said Tancred: 'the Arabians are entirely unsophisticated; they are now as they were in the time of Mahomet, of Moses, of Abraham: a sublime devotion is natural to them, and equality, properly developed, is in fact the patriarchal principle.'

'But these are Arabians,' said Fakredeen; 'I am an

Arabian; there is not a mookatadgi, whatever his present creed, who does not come from Yemen, or the Hedjaz, or the Nejid.'

'That is a great qualification,' said Tancred, musingly.

'And, see what men these are!' continued Fakredeen, with great animation. 'Lebanon can send forth more than fifty thousand well-armed, and yet let enough stay at home to guard the mulberry trees and the women. Then you can keep them for nothing; a Bedoueen is not more temperate than a Druse, if he pleases: he will get through a campaign on olives and cheese; they do not require even tents; they bivouac in a sheepskin.'

'And yet,' said Tancred, 'though they have maintained themselves, they have done nothing; now the Arabs have always succeeded.'

'I will tell you how that is,' said Fakredeen. 'It is very true that we have not done much, and that, when we descended into the plain, as we did in '63, under the Emir Yousef, we were beat, beaten back even by the Mutualis; it is that we have no cavalry. They have always contrived to enlist the great tribes of the Syrian Desert against us, as, for instance, under Daher, of whom you must have heard: it was that which has prevented our development; but we have always maintained ourselves. Lebanon is the key of Syria, and the country was never unlocked, unless we pleased. But this difficulty is now removed. Through Amalek we shall have the Desert on our side; he is omnipotent in the Syrian wilderness; and if he sends messengers through Petræa to Derayeh, the Nejid, and through the Hedjaz, to Yemen and Oman, we could easily get a cavalry as efficient and not less numerous than our foot.'

'The instruments will be found,' said Tancred, 'for it is decreed that the deed should be done. But the favour of Providence does not exempt man from the exercise of human prudence. On the contrary, it is an agent, on whose co-operation they are bound to count. I should like to see something of the great Syrian cities. I should like also to see Bagdad. It appears to me, at the first glance, that the whole country to the Euphrates might be conquered in a campaign; but then I want to know how far artillery is necessary, whether it be indispensable. Then again, the Lesser Asia; we should never lose sight of the Lesser Asia as the principal scene of our movements; the richest regions in the world, almost depopulated, and a position from which we might magnetise Europe. But suppose the Turks, through Lesser Asia, conquer Lebanon, while we are overrunning the Babylonian and Assyrian monarchies? That will never do. I see your strength here with your own people and the Druses, and I do not underrate their qualities: but who is to garrison the north of Syria? Who is to keep the passes of the North? What population have you to depend on between Tripoli and Antioch, or between Aleppo and Adanah? Of all this I know nothing.'

Fakredeen had entirely imbibed the views of Tancred; he was sincere in his professions, fervent in his faith. A great feudal proprietor, he was prepared to forsake his beautiful castle, his farms and villages, his vineyards, and mulberry orchards, and forests of oaks, to assist in establishing, by his voice and his sabre, a new social system, which was to substitute the principle of association for that of dependence as the foundation of the Commonwealth, under the sanction and superintendence of the God of Sinai and of Calvary. True it was that the young Syrian Emir intended, that among the consequences of the impending movement should be his enthronement on one of the royal seats of Asia. But we should do him injustice, were we to convey the impression that his ardent co-operation with Tancred at this moment was impelled merely, or even principally, by these coarsely selfish considerations. Men certainly must be governed, whatever the principle of the social system, and Fakredeen felt born with a predisposition to rule.

But greater even than his desire for empire was his

thirst for action. He was wearied with the glittering cage in which he had been born. He panted for a wider field and a nobler theatre, interests more vast and incidents more dazzling and comprehensive; he wished to astonish Europe instead of Lebanon, and to use his genius in baffling and controlling the thrones and dominations of the world, instead of managing the simple Sheikhs and Emirs of his mountains. His castle and fine estates were no sources of satisfaction to him. On the contrary, he viewed Canobia with disgust. It entailed duties, and brought no excitement. He was seldom at home and only for a few passing days: continued residence was intolerable to his restless spirit. He passed his life in perpetual movement, scudding about on the fleetest dromedaries, and galloping over the Deserts on steeds of the highest race.

Though proud of his ancient house, and not unequal, when necessary, to the due representation of his position, unlike the Orientals in general, he disliked pomp, and shrank from the ceremony which awaited him. His restless. intriguing, and imaginative spirit revelled in the incognito. He was perpetually in masquerade; a merchant, a Mamlouk, a soldier of fortune, a Tartar messenger, sometimes a pilgrim, sometimes a dervish, always in pursuit of some improbable but ingenious object, or lost in the mazes of some fantastic plot. He enjoyed moving alone, without a single attendant; and seldom in his mountains, he was perpetually in Egypt, Bagdad, Cyprus, Smyrna, and the Syrian cities. He sauntered away a good deal of his time indeed in the ports and towns of the coast, looking after his creditors; but this was not the annoyance to him which it would be to most men.

Fakredeen was fond of his debts; they were the source indeed of his only real excitement, and he was grateful to them for their stirring powers. The usurers of Syria are as adroit and callous as those of all other countries, and possess no doubt all those repulsive qualities which are the consequence of an habitual control over every generous emotion. But, instead of viewing them with feelings of vengeance or abhorrence, Fakredeen studied them unceasingly with a fine and profound investigation, and found in their society a deep psychological interest. His own rapacious soul delighted to struggle with their rapine, and it charmed him to baffle with his artifice their fraudulent dexterity. He loved to enter their houses with his glittering eye and face radiant with innocence, and, when things were at the very worst and they remorseless, to succeed in circumventing them. In a certain sense, and to a certain degree, they were all his victims. True, they had gorged upon his rents and menaced his domains; but they had also advanced large sums, and he had so involved one with another in their eager appetite to prey upon his youth, and had so complicated the financial relations of the Syrian coast in his own respect, that sometimes they tremblingly calculated that the crash of Fakredeen must inevitably be the signal of a general catastrophe.

Even usurers have their weak side; some are vain, some envious; Fakredeen knew how to titillate their self-love, or when to give them the opportunity of immolating a rival. Then it was, when he had baffled and deluded them, or with that fatal frankness, of which he sometimes blushingly boasted, had betrayed some sacred confidence that shook the credit of the whole coast from Scanderoon to Gaza, and embroiled individuals whose existence depended on their mutual goodwill, that, laughing like one of the blue-eyed hyenas of his forests, he galloped away to Canobia, and, calling for his nargilly, mused in chuckling calculation over the prodigious sums he owed to them, formed whimsical and airy projects for his quittance, or delighted himself by brooding over the memory of some happy expedient or some daring feat of finance.

'What should I be without my debts?' he would sometimes exclaim; 'dear companions of my life that never desert me! All my knowledge of human nature is owing to them: it is in managing my affairs that I have sounded

the depths of the human heart, recognised all the combinations of human character, developed my own powers,
and mastered the resources of others. What expedient in
negotiation is unknown to me? What degree of endurance
have I not calculated? What play of the countenance
have I not observed? Yes, among my creditors, I have
disciplined that diplomatic ability, that shall some day con-
found and control cabinets. Oh, my debts, I feel your presence like that of guardian angels! If I be lazy, you prick
me to action; if elate, you subdue me to reflection : and
thus it is that you alone can secure that continuous yet
controlled energy which conquers mankind.'

Notwithstanding all this, Fakredeen had grown sometimes a little wearied even of the choice excitement of
pecuniary embarrassment. It was too often the same
story, the adventures monotonous, the characters identical.
He had been plundered by every usurer in the Levant, and
in turn had taken them in. He sometimes delighted his
imagination by the idea of making them disgorge ; that is
to say, when he had established that supremacy which
he had resolved sooner or later to attain. Although he
never kept an account, his memory was so faithful that he
knew exactly the amount of which he had been defrauded
by every individual with whom he had had transactions.
He longed to mulct them, to the service of the State, in
the exact amount of their unhallowed appropriations. He
was too good a statesman ever to confiscate; he confined
himself to taxation. Confiscation is a blunder that destroys
public credit; taxation, on the contrary, improves it; and
both come to the same thing.

That the proud soul of Tancred of Montacute, with its
sublime aspirations, its inexorable purpose, its empyrean
ambition, should find a votary in one apparently so whimsical, so worldly, and so worthless, may at the first glance
seem improbable; yet a nearer and finer examination may
induce us to recognise its likelihood. Fakredeen had a
brilliant imagination and a passionate sensibility; his heart

was controlled by his taste, and, when that was pleased and satisfied, he was capable of profound feeling and of earnest conduct. Moral worth had no abstract charms for him, and he could sympathise with a dazzling reprobate; but virtue in an heroic form, lofty principle, and sovereign duty invested with all the attributes calculated to captivate his rapid and refined perception, exercised over him a resistless and transcendent spell. The deep and disciplined intelligence of Tancred, trained in all the philosophy and cultured with all the knowledge of the West, acted with magnetic power upon a consciousness, the bright vivacity of which was only equalled by its virgin ignorance of all that books can teach, and of those great conclusions which the studious hour can alone elaborate. Fakredeen hung upon his accents like a bee, while Tancred poured forth, without an effort, the treasures of his stored memory and long musing mind. He went on, quite unconscious that his companion was devoid of that previous knowledge, which, with all other persons, would have been a preliminary qualification for a profitable comprehension of what he said. Fakredeen gave him no hint of this: the young Emir trusted to his quick perception to sustain him, although his literary training was confined to an Arabic grammar, some sentences of wise men, some volumes of poetry, and mainly and most profitably to the clever Courier de Smyrne, and occasionally a packet of French journals which he obtained from a Levantine consul.

It was therefore with a feeling not less than enthusiastic that Fakredeen responded to the suggestive influence of Tancred. The want that he had long suffered from was supplied, and the character he had long mused over had appeared. Here was a vast theory to be reduced to practice, and a commanding mind to give the leading impulse. However imperfect may have been his general conception of the ideas of Tancred, he clearly comprehended that their fulfilment involved his two great objects, change and action. Compared with these attainments on a great scale, his present acquisition and position sank into nothingness. A futurity consisting of a Syrian Emirate and a mountain castle figured as intolerable, and Fakredeen, hoping all things and prepared for anything, flung to the winds all consideration for his existing ties, whether in the shape of domains or of debts.

The imperturbable repose, the grave and thoughtful daring, with which Tancred developed his revolutionary projects, completed the power with which he could now dispose of the fate of the young Emir. Sometimes, in fluttering moments of disordered reverie, Fakredeen had indulged in dreams of what, with his present companion, it appeared was to be the ordinary business of their lives, and which he discussed with a calm precision which alone half convinced Fakredeen of their feasibility. It was not for an impassioned votary to intimate a difficulty; but if Fakredeen, to elicit an opinion, sometimes hinted an adverse suggestion, the objection was swept away in an instant by an individual whose inflexible will was sustained by the conviction of divine favour.

CHAPTER IV.

'Do you know anything of a people in the north of this country, called the Ansarey?' inquired Tancred of Baroni.

'No, my lord; and no one else. They hold the mountainous country about Antioch, and will let no one enter it; a very warlike race; they beat back the Egyptians; but Ibrahim Pacha loaded his artillery with piastres the second time he attacked them, and they worked very well with the Pacha after that.'

'Are they Moslemin?'

'It is very easy to say what they are not, and that is about the extent of any knowledge that we have of them; they are not Moslemin, they are not Christians, they are not Druses, and they are not Jews, and certainly they are not Guebres, for I have spoken of them to the Indians at Djedda, who are fire-worshippers, and they do not in any degree acknowledge them.'

'And what is their race? Are they Arabs?'

'I should say not, my lord; for the only one I ever saw was more like a Greek or an Armenian than a son of the Desert.'

'You have seen one of them?'

'It was at Damascus: there was a city brawl, and M. de Sidonia saved the life of a man, who turned out to be an Ansarey, though disguised. They have secret agents at most of the Syrian cities. They speak Arabic; but I have heard M. de Sidonia say they have also a language of their own.'

'I wonder he did not visit them.'

'The plague raged at Aleppo when we were there, and the Ansarey were doubly rigid in their exclusion of all strangers from their country.'

'And this Ansarey at Damascus, have you ever seen anything of him since?'

'Yes; I have been at Damascus several times since I travelled with M. de Sidonia, and I have sometimes smoked a nargilly with this man: his name is Darkush, and he deals in drugs.'

Now this was the reason that induced Tancred to inquire of Baroni respecting the Ansarey. The day before, which was the third day of the great hunting party at Canobia, Fakredeen and Tancred had found themselves alone with Hamood Abuneked, and the lord of Canobia had thought it a good occasion to sound this powerful Sheikh of the Druses. Hamood was rough, but frank and sincere. He was no enemy of the house of Shehaab; but the Abunekeds had suffered during the wars and civil conflicts which had of late years prevailed in Lebanon, and he was evidently disinclined to mix in any movement which was not well matured and highly promising of success. Fakredeen, of course, concealed his ulterior purpose from the Druse, who associated with the idea of union between the two nations merely the institution of a sole government under one head, and that head a Shehaab, probably dwelling at Canobia.

'I have fought by the side of the Emir Bescheer,' said Hamood, 'and would he were in his palace of Bteddeen at this moment! And the Abunekeds rode with the Emir Yousef against Djezzar. It is not the house of Abuneked that would say there should be two weak nations when there might be one strong one. But what I say is sealed with the signet of truth; it is known to the old, and it is remembered by the wise; the Emir Bescheer has said it to me as many times as there are oranges on that tree, and the Emir Yousef has said it to my father. The northern passes are not guarded by Maronite or by Druse.'

'And as long as they are not guarded by us?' said Fakredeen, inquiringly.

'We may have a sole prince and a single government,' continued Hamood, 'and the houses of the two nations may be brothers, but every now and then the Osmanli will enter the mountain, and we shall eat sand.'

'And who holds the northern passes, noble Sheikh?' inquired Tancred.

'Truly, I believe,' replied Hamood, 'very sons of Eblis, for the whole of that country is in the hands of the Ansarey, and there never has been evil in the mountain that they have not been against us.'

'They never would draw with the Shehaabs,' said Fakredeen; 'and I have heard the Emir Bescheer say that, if the Ansarey had acted with him, he would have baffled, in '40, both the Porte and the Pacha.'

'It was the same in the time of the Emir Yousef,' said Sheikh Hamood. 'They can bring twenty-five thousand picked men into the plain.'

'And, I suppose, if it were necessary, would not be afraid to meet the Osmanli in Anatoly?' said Fakredeen.

'If the Turkmans or the Kurds would join them,' said Sheikh Hamood, 'there is nothing to prevent their washing their horses' feet in the Bosphorus.'

'It is strange,' said Fakredeen, 'but frequently as I have been at Aleppo and Antioch, I have never been in their country. I have always been warned against it, always kept from it, which indeed ought to have prompted my earliest efforts, when I was my own master, to make them a visit. But, I know not how it is, there are some prejudices that do stick to one. I have a prejudice against the Ansarey, a sort of fear, a kind of horror. 'Tis vastly absurd. I suppose my nurse instilled it into me, and frightened me with them when I would not sleep. Besides, I had an idea that they particularly hated the Shehaabs. I recollect so well the Emir Bescheer, at Bteddeen, bestowing endless imprecations on them.'

'He made many efforts to win them, though,' said Sheikh Hamood, 'and so did the Emir Yousef.'

'And you think without them, noble Sheikh,' said Tancred, 'that Syria is not secure?'

'I think, with them and peace with the Desert, that Syria might defy Turk and Egyptian.'

'And carry the war into the enemy's quarters, if necessary?' said Fakredeen.

'If they would let us alone, I am content to leave them,' said Hamood.

'Hem!' said the Emir Fakredeen. 'Do you see that gazelle, noble Sheikh? How she bounds along! What if we follow her, and the pursuit should lead us into the lands of the Ansarey?'

'It would be a long ride,' said Sheikh Hamood. 'Nor should I care much to trust my head in a country governed by a woman.'

'A woman!' exclaimed Tancred and Fakredeen.

'They say as much,' said Sheikh Hamood; 'perhaps it is only a coffee-house tale.'

'I never heard it before,' said Fakredeen. 'In the time of my uncle, Elderidis was Sheikh. I have heard indeed that the Ansarey worship a woman.'

'Then they would be Christians,' said Sheikh Hamood, 'and I never heard that.'

CHAPTER V.

It was destined that Napoleon should never enter Rome, and Mahomet never enter Damascus. What was the reason of this? They were not uninterested in those cities that interest all. The Emperor selected from the capital of the Cæsars the title of his son; the Prophet, when he beheld the crown of Syria, exclaimed that it was too delightful, and that he must reserve his paradise for another world. Buonaparte was an Italian, and must have often yearned after the days of Rome triumphant. The son of Abdallah was descended from the patriarchs, whose progenitor had been moulded out of the red clay of the most ancient city in the world. Absorbed by the passionate pursuit of the hour, the two heroes postponed a gratification which they knew how to appreciate, but which, with all their success, all their power, and all their fame, they were never permitted to indulge. What moral is to be drawn from this circumstance? That we should never lose an occasion. Opportunity is more powerful even than conquerors and prophets.

The most ancient city of the world has no antiquity. This flourishing abode is older than many ruins, yet it does not possess one single memorial of the past. In vain has it conquered or been conquered. Not a trophy, a column, or an arch, records its warlike fortunes. Temples have been raised here to unknown gods and to revealed Divinity; all have been swept away. Not the trace of a palace or a prison, a public bath, a hall of justice, can be discovered in this wonderful city, where everything has been destroyed, and where nothing has decayed.

Men moralise among ruins, or, in the throng and tumult of successful cities, recall past visions of urban desolation for prophetic warning. London is a modern Babylon; Paris has aped imperial Rome, and may share its catastrophe. But what do the sages say to Damascus? It had municipal rights in the days when God conversed with

Abraham. Since then, the kings of the great monarchies have swept over it; and the Greek and the Roman, the Tartar, the Arab, and the Turk have passed through its walls; yet it still exists and still flourishes; is full of life, wealth, and enjoyment. Here is a city that has quaffed the magical elixir and secured the philosopher's stone, that is always young and always rich. As yet, the disciples of Progress have not been able exactly to match this instance of Damascus, but it is said that they have great faith in the future of Birkenhead.

We moralise among ruins: it is always when the game is played that we discover the cause of the result. It is a fashion intensely European, the habit of an organisation that, having little imagination, takes refuge in reason, and carefully locks the door when the steed is stolen. A community has crumbled to pieces, and it is always accounted for by its political forms, or its religious modes. There has been a deficiency in what is called checks in the machinery of government; the definition of the suffrage has not been correct; what is styled responsibility has, by some means or other, not answered; or, on the other hand, people have believed too much or too little in a future state, have been too much engrossed by the present, or too much absorbed in that which was to come. But there is not a form of government which Damascus has not experienced, excepting the representative, and not a creed which it has not acknowledged, excepting the Protestant. Yet, deprived of the only rule and the only religion that are right, it is still justly described by the Arabian poets as a pearl surrounded by emeralds.

Yes, the rivers of Damascus still run and revel within and without the walls, of which the steward of Sheikh Abraham was a citizen. They have encompassed them with gardens, and filled them with fountains. They gleam amid their groves of fruit, wind through their vivid meads, sparkle among perpetual flowers, gush from the walls, bubble in the courtyards, dance and carol in the streets:

everywhere their joyous voices, everywhere their glancing
forms, filling the whole world around with freshness, and
brilliancy, and fragrance, and life.   One might fancy, as
we track them in their dazzling course, or suddenly making
their appearance in every spot and in every scene, that they
were the guardian spirits of the city.   You have explained
then, says the utilitarian, the age and flourishing fortunes of
Damascus : they arise from its advantageous situation ; it is
well supplied with water. Is it better supplied than the ruins
of contiguous regions ?   Did the Nile save Thebes ?   Did the
Tigris preserve Nineveh ?   Did the Euphrates secure Babylon ?

Our scene lies in a chamber vast and gorgeous.   The
reader must imagine a hall, its form that of a rather long
square, but perfectly proportioned.   Its coved roof, glowing with golden and scarlet tints, is highly carved in the
manner of the Saracens, such as we may observe in the
palaces of Moorish Spain and in the Necropolis of the
Mamlouk Sultauns at Cairo, deep recesses of honeycomb
work, with every now and then pendants of daring grace
hanging like stalactites from some sparry cavern.   This
roof is supported by columns of white marble, fashioned in
the shape of palm trees, the work of Italian artists, and
which form arcades around the chamber.   Beneath these
arcades runs a noble divan of green and silver silk, and the
silken panels of the arabesque walls have been covered
with subjects of human interest by the finest artists of
Munich.   The marble floor, with its rich mosaics, was also
the contribution of Italian genius, though it was difficult at
the present moment to trace its varied, graceful, and
brilliant designs, so many were the sumptuous carpets, the
couches, sofas, and cushions that were spread about it.
There were indeed throughout the chamber many indications of furniture, which are far from usual even among
the wealthiest and most refined Orientals : Indian tables,
vases of china, and baskets of agate and porcelain filled
with flowers.   From one side, the large Saracenic windows
of this saloon, which were not glazed, but covered only

bringing sweetmeats from the Queen and goblets of iced water. They bowed; Keferinis indicated their purpose, and when they had fulfilled their office they disappeared; but the seasonable interruption had turned the conversation, and prevented Fakredeen making a sharp retort. Now they talked of the Queen, who, Keferinis said, would be graciously pleased not to see them to-day, and might not even see them for a week, which agreeable intelligence was communicated in the most affable manner, as if it were good news, or a compliment at least.

'The name of the Queen's father was Suedia,' said Fakredeen.

'The name of the Queen's father was Suedia,' replied Keferinis.

'And the name of the Queen's mother ——'

'Is of no consequence,' observed Keferinis, 'for she was a slave, and not one of us, and therefore may with singular exactitude be described as nothing.'

'Is she the first Queen who has reigned over the Ansarey?' inquired Tancred.

'The first since we have settled in these mountains,' replied Keferinis.

'And where were you settled before?' inquired Fakredeen.

'Truly,' replied Keferinis, 'in cities which never can be forgotten, and therefore need never be mentioned.'

Tancred and Fakredeen were very desirous of learning the name of the Queen, but were too well-bred directly to make the inquiry of Keferinis. They had endeavoured to obtain the information as they travelled along, but although every Ansarey most obligingly answered their inquiry, they invariably found, on comparing notes, that every time they were favoured with a different piece of information. At last, Baroni informed them that it was useless to pursue their researches, as he was, from various reasons, convinced that no Ansarey was permitted to give any information of his country, race, government, or creed, although he was far too civil ever to refuse an apparently satisfactory answer to every question. As for Keferinis, although he was very conversable, the companions observed that he always made it a rule to dilate upon subjects and countries with which he had no acquaintance, and he expressed himself in so affected a manner, and with such an amplification of useless phraseology, that, though he was always talking, they seemed at the end of the day to be little more acquainted with the Ansarey and their sovereign than when Baroni first opened the subject of their visit to Darkush at Damascus.

CHAPTER II.

'AWAY, away, Cypros! I can remain no more; my heart beats so.'

'Sweet lady,' replied Cypros, 'it is surprise that agitates you.'

'Is it surprise, Cypros? I did not know it was surprise. Then I never was surprised before.'

'I think they were surprised, sweet lady,' said Cypros, smiling.

'Hush, you are laughing very loud, my Cypros.'

'Is that laughter, sweet lady? I did not know it was laughter. Then I never laughed before.'

'I would they should know nothing either of our smiles or of our sighs, my Cypros.'

She who said this was a girl of eighteen summers; her features very Greek, her complexion radiant, hair dark as night, and eyes of the colour of the violet. Her beautiful countenance, however, was at this moment nearly shrouded by her veil, although no one could possibly behold it, excepting her attendant, younger even than herself, and fresh and fair as a flower.

They were hurrying along a wooden gallery, which led, behind the upper part of the divan occupied by the tra vellers, to the great square central tower of the quadrangle, which we have already noticed, and as the truth must always, or at least eventually, come out, it shall not be concealed that, availing themselves of a convenient, perhaps irresistible position, the fair fugitives had peeped into the chamber, and had made even minute observations on its inhabitants with impunity. Suddenly, Fakredeen rising from his seat, a panic had seized them and they hurried away.

The gallery led to a flight of steps, and the flight of steps into the first of several chambers without decoration, and with no other furniture than an eastern apartment always offers, the cushioned seat, which surrounds at least two-thirds of the room. At length they entered a small alcove, rudely painted in arabesque, but in a classic Ionic pattern; the alcove opened into a garden, or rather court of myrtles with a fountain. An antelope, an Angora cat, two Persian greyhounds, were basking on the sunny turf, and there were many birds about, in rude but capacious cages.

'We are safe,' said the lady, dropping on the divan; 'I think we must have been seen.'

'That was clearly impossible,' said Cypros.

'Well, we must be seen at last,' said the lady. 'Heigho! I never shall be able to receive them, if my heart beat so.'

'I would let them wait a few days, sweet lady,' said Cypros, 'and then you would get more used to them.'

'I shall never be more used to them. Besides, it is rude and inhospitable not to see them. Yesterday there was an excuse: they were wearied, or I had a right to suppose they were, with their travelling; and to-day, there ought to be an excuse for not receiving them to-day. What is it, Cypros?'

'I dare say they will be quite content, if to-day you fix the time when you will receive them, sweet lady.'

'But I shall not be content, Cypros. Having seen them once, I wish to see them again, and one cannot always be walking by accident in the gallery.'

'Then I would see them to-day, sweet lady. Shall I send for the noble Keferinis ? '

'I wish I were Cypros, and you were —— Hark ! what is that ? '

''Tis only the antelope, sweet lady.'

'I thought it was —— Now tell me, my Cypros, which of these two princes do you think is he who is one of us ? '

'Oh, really, sweet lady, I think they are both so handsome !'

'Yet so unlike,' said the lady.

'Well, they are unlike,' said Cypros, 'and yet ——'

'And what ? '

'The fair one has a complexion almost as radiant as your own, sweet lady.'

'And eyes as blue : no, they are too light. And so, as there is a likeness, you think he is the one ? '

'I am sure I wish they were both belonging to us,' said Cypros.

'Ah, me!' said the lady, ''tis not the bright-faced prince whom I hold to be one of us. No, no, my Cypros. Think awhile, sweet girl. The visage, the head of the other, have you not seen them before ? Have you not seen something like them ? That head so proudly placed upon the shoulders; that hair, that hyacinthine hair, that lofty forehead, that proud lip, that face so refined and yet so haughty, does it not recall anything ? Think, Cypros; think !'

'It does, sweet lady.'

'Tell me; whisper it to me; it is a name not to be lightly mentioned.'

Cypros advanced, and bending her head, breathed a word in the ear of the lady, who instantly, blushing deeply murmured with a faint smile, 'Yes.'

'It is he then,' said Cypros, 'who is one of us.'

CHAPTER III.

Our travellers were speculating, not very sanguinely, on the possible resources which Gindarics might supply for the amusement of a week, when, to their great relief, they were informed by Keferinis, that the Queen had fixed noon, on this the day after their arrival, to receive them. And accordingly at that time some attendants, not accompanying, however, the chief minister, waited on Tancred and Fakredeen, and announced that they were commanded to usher them to the royal presence. Quitting their apartments, they mounted a flight of steps, which led to the wooden gallery, along which they pursued their course. At its termination were two sentries with their lances. Then they descended a corresponding flight of stairs and entered a chamber where they were received by pages; the next room, of larger size, was crowded, and here they remained for a few minutes. Then they were ushered into the presence.

The young Queen of the Ansarey could not have received them with an air more impassive had she been holding a levée at St. James'. Seated on her divan, she was clothed in a purple robe; her long dark hair descended over her shoulders, and was drawn off her white forehead, which was bound with a broad circlet of pure gold, and of great antiquity. On her right hand stood Keferinis, the captain of her guard, and a priestly-looking person with a long white beard, and then at some distance from these three personages, a considerable number of individuals, between whose appearance and that of her ordinary subjects there was little difference. On her left hand were immediately three female attendants, young and pretty; at some distance from them, a troop of female slaves; and again, at a still further distance, another body of her subjects in their white turbans and their black dresses. The chamber was spacious, and rudely painted in the Ionic style.

' It is most undoubtedly requested, and in a vein of the

most condescending friendship, by the perfectly irresistible
Queen, that the princes should be seated,' said Keferinis,
and accordingly Tancred occupied his allotted seat on the
right of the Queen, though at some distance, and the
young Emir filled his on the left. Fakredeen was dressed
in Syrian splendour, a blaze of shawls and jewelled arms;
but Tancred retained on this, as he had done on every
other occasion, the European dress, though in the present
instance it assumed a somewhat more brilliant shape than
ordinary, in the dark green regimentals, the rich embroidery,
and the flowing plume of the Bellamont yeomanry cavalry.

'You are a prince of the English,' said the Queen to
Tancred.

'I am an Englishman,' he replied, 'and a subject of our
Queen, for we also have the good fortune to be ruled over
by the young and the fair.'

'My fathers and the house of Shehaab have been ever
friends,' she continued, turning to Fakredeen.

'May they ever continue so!' he replied. 'For if the
Shehaabs and the Ansarey are of one mind, Syria is no
longer earth, but indeed paradise.'

'You live much in ships?' said the Queen, turning to
Tancred.

'We are an insular people,' he answered, somewhat con-
fusedly, but the perfectly-informed Keferinis came to the
succour both of Tancred and of his sovereign.

'The English live in ships only during six months of the
year, principally when they go to India, the rest entirely
at their country houses.'

'Ships are required to take you to India?' said her
majesty.

Tancred bowed assent.

'Is your Queen about my age?'

'She was as young as your majesty when she began to
reign.'

'And how long has she reigned?'

'Some seven years or so.'

' Has she a castle ? '

' Her majesty generally resides in a very famous castle.'

' Very strong, I suppose ? '

' Strong enough.'

' The Emir Bescheer remains at Stambool ? '

' He is now, I believe, at Brusa,' replied Fakredeen.

' Does he like Brusa ? '

' Not as much as Stambool.'

' Is Stambool the largest city in the world ? '

' I apprehend by no means,' said Fakredeen.

' What is larger ? '

' London is larger, the great city of the English, from which the prince comes; Paris is also larger, but not so large as London.'

' How many persons are there in Stambool ? '

' More than half a million.'

'Have you seen Antakia (Antioch) ? ' the Queen inquired of Tancred.

' Not yet.'

' You have seen Beiroot ? '

' I have.'

' Antakia is not nearly so great a place as Beiroot,' said the Queen; ' yet once Antakia was much larger than Stambool; as large, perhaps, as your great city.'

' And far more beautiful than either,' said Tancred.

' Ah! you have heard of these things ! ' exclaimed the Queen, with much animation. ' Now tell me, why is Antakia no longer a great city, as great as Stambool and the city of the English, and far more beautiful ? '

'It is a question that might perplex the wise,' said Tancred.

' I am not wise,' said the Queen, looking earnestly at Tancred, ' yet I could solve it.'

' Would that your majesty would deign to do so.'

' There are things to be said, and there are things not to be said,' was the reply, and the Queen looked at Keferinis.

' Her majesty has expressed herself with infinite exactitude and with condescending propriety,' said the chief minister.

The Queen was silent for a moment, thoughtful, and then waved gracefully her hands; whereupon the chamber was immediately cleared. The princes, instructed by Keferinis, alone remained, with the exception of the minister, who, at the desire of his sovereign, now seated himself, but not on the divan. He sat opposite to the Queen on the floor.

' Princes,' said the Queen, 'you are welcome to Gindarics, where nobody ever comes. For we are people who wish neither to see nor to be seen. We are not like other people, nor do we envy other people. I wish not for the ships of the Queen of the English, and my subjects are content to live as their fathers lived before them. Our mountains are wild and barren; our vales require for their cultivation unceasing toil. We have no gold or silver, no jewels; neither have we silk. But we have some beautiful and consoling thoughts, and more than thoughts, which are shared by all of us and open to all of us, and which only we can value or comprehend. When Darkush, who dwells at Damascus, and was the servant of my father, sent to us the ever-faithful messenger, and said that there were princes who wished to confer with us, he knew well it was vain to send here men who would talk of the English and the Egyptians, of the Porte and of the nations of Franguestan. These things to us are like the rind of fruit. Neither do we care for cottons, nor for things which are sought for in the cities of the plains, and it may be, noble Emir, cherished also in the mountains of Lebanon. This is not Lebanon, but the mountains of the Ansarey, who are as they have ever been, before the name of Turk or English was known in Syria, and who will remain as they are, unless that happens which may never happen, but which is too beautiful not to believe may arrive. Therefore I speak to you with frankness, princes of strange countries: Darkush, the servant of my father, and also mine, told me, by the ever-faithful messenger, that it was not of these things,

which are to us like water spilt on sand, that you wished
to confer, but that there were things to be said which
ought to be uttered. Therefore it is I sent back the faithful messenger, saying, Send then these princes to Gindarics, since their talk is not of things which come and go,
making a noise on the coast and in the cities of the plains,
and then passing away. These we infinitely despise ; but
the words of truth uttered in the spirit of friendship
will last, if they be grave, and on matters which authorise
journeys made by princes to visit queens.'

Her Majesty ceased, and looked at Keferinis, who bowed
profound approbation. Tancred and Fakredeen also exchanged glances, but the Emir waved his hand, signifying
his wish that Tancred should reply, who, after a moment's
hesitation, with an air of great deference, thus ventured to
express himself:

'It seems to me and to my friend, the Prince of the
Lebanon, that we have listened to the words of wisdom.
They are in every respect just. We know not, ourselves,
Darkush, but he was rightly informed when he apprised
your majesty that it was not upon ordinary topics, either
political or commercial, that we desired to visit Gindarics.
Nor was it out of such curiosity as animates travellers.
For we are not travellers, but men who have a purpose
which we wish to execute. The world, that, since its
creation, has owned the spiritual supremacy of Asia, which
is but natural, since Asia is the only portion of the world
which the Creator of that world has deigned to visit, and
in which he has ever conferred with man, is unhappily
losing its faith in those ideas and convictions that hitherto
have governed the human race. We think, therefore, the
time has arrived when Asia should make one of its periodi-
cal and appointed efforts to reassert that supremacy. But
though we are acting, as we believe, under a divine impulse,
it is our duty to select the most fitting human agents to
accomplish a celestial mission. We have thought, therefore, that it should devolve on Syria and Arabia, countries

in which our God has even dwelt, and with which he has been from the earliest days in direct and regular communication, to undertake the solemn task. Two races of men alike free, one inhabiting the Desert, the other the mountains, untainted by any of the vices of the plains, and the virgin vigour of their intelligence not dwarfed by the conventional superstitions of towns and cities, one prepared at once to supply an unrivalled cavalry, the other an army ready equipped of intrepid foot-soldiers, appear to us to be indicated as the natural and united conquerors of the world. We wish to conquer that world, with angels at our head, in order that we may establish the happiness of man by a divine dominion, and, crushing the political atheism that is now desolating existence, utterly extinguish the grovelling tyranny of self-government.'

The Queen of the Ansarey listened with deep and agitated attention to Tancred. When he had concluded, she said, after a moment's pause, 'I believe also in the necessity of the spiritual supremacy of our Asia. And since it has ceased, it seems not to me that man and man's life have been either as great or as beautiful as heretofore. What you have said assures me, that it is well that you have come hither. But when you speak of Arabia, of what God is it you speak?'

'I speak of the only God, the Creator of all things, the God who spoke on the Arabian Mount Sinai, and expiated our sins upon the Syrian Mount Calvary.'

'There is also Mount Olympus,' said the Queen, 'which is in Anatolia. Once the gods dwelt there.'

'The gods of poets,' said Tancred.

'No; the gods of the people; who loved the people, and whom the people loved.'

There was a pause, broken by the Queen, who, looking at her minister, said, 'Noble Keferinis, the thoughts of these princes are divine, and in every respect becoming celestial things. Is it not well that the gates of the beautiful and the sacred should not be closed?'

'In every sense, irresistible Queen, it is well that the gates of the beautiful and the sacred should not be closed.'

'Then let them bring garlands. Princes,' the Queen continued, 'what the eye of no stranger has looked upon, you shall now behold. This also is Asian and divine.'

Immediately the chamber again filled. The Queen, looking at the two princes and bowing, rose from her seat. They instantly followed her example. One came forward, offering to the Queen, and then to each of them, a garland. Garlands were also taken by Keferinis and a few others. Cypros and her companions walked first, then Keferinis and one who had stood near the royal divan; the Queen, between her two guests, followed, and after her a small and ordered band.

They stopped before a lofty portal of bronze, evidently of ancient art. This opened into a covered and excavated way, in some respects similar to that which had led them directly to the castle of Gindarics; but, although obscure, not requiring artificial light, yet it was of no inconsiderable length. It emerged upon a platform cut out of the natural rock; on all sides were steep cliffs, above them the bright blue sky. The ravine appeared to be closed on every side.

The opposite cliff, at the distance of several hundred yards, reached by a winding path, presented, at first, the appearance of the front of an ancient temple; and Tancred, as he approached it, perceived that the hand of art had assisted the development of an intimation of nature: a pediment, a deep portico, supported by Ionic columns, and a flight of steps, were carved out of the cliff, and led into vast caverns, which art also had converted into lofty and magnificent chambers. When they had mounted the steps, the Queen and her companions lifted their garlands to the skies, and joined in a chorus, solemn and melodious, but which did not sound as the language of Syria. Passing through the portico, Tancred found himself apparently in a vast apartment, where he beheld a strange spectacle.

At the first glance it seemed that, ranged on blocks of the surrounding mountains, were a variety of sculptured figures of costly materials and exquisite beauty; forms of heroic majesty and ideal grace; and, themselves serene and unimpassioned, filling the minds of the beholders with awe and veneration. It was not until his eye was accustomed to the atmosphere, and his mind had in some degree recovered from the first strange surprise, that Tancred gradually recognised the fair and famous images over which his youth had so long and so early pondered. Stole over his spirit the countenance august, with the flowing beard and the lordly locks, sublime on his ivory throne, in one hand the ready thunderbolt, in the other the cypress sceptre; at his feet the watchful eagle with expanded wings: stole over the spirit of the gazing pilgrim, each shape of that refined and elegant hierarchy made for the worship of clear skies and sunny lands; goddess and god, genius, and nymph, and faun, all that the wit and heart of man can devise and create, to represent his genius and his passion, all that the myriad developments of a beautiful nature can require for their personification. A beautiful and sometimes flickering light played over the sacred groups and figures, softening the ravages of time, and occasionally investing them with, as it were, a celestial movement.

'The gods of the Greeks!' exclaimed Tancred.

'The gods of the Ansarey,' said the Queen; 'the gods of my fathers!'

'I am filled with a sweet amazement,' murmured Tancred. 'Life is stranger than I deemed. My soul is, as it were, unsphered.'

'Yet you know them to be gods,' said the Queen; 'and the Emir of the Lebanon does not know them to be gods?'

'I feel that they are such,' said Fakredeen.

'How is this, then?' said the Queen, 'How is it that you, the child of a northern isle ——'

'Should recognise the Olympian Jove,' said Tancred.

' It seems strange; but from my earliest youth I learnt these things.'

' Ah, then,' murmured the Queen to herself, and with an expression of the greatest satisfaction, ' Darkush was rightly informed; he is one of us.'

' I behold then, at last, the gods of the Ansarey,' said Fakredeen.

' All that remains of Antioch, noble Emir; of Antioch the superb, with its hundred towers, and its sacred groves and fanes of flashing beauty.'

' Unhappy Asia!' exclaimed the Emir; 'thou hast indeed fallen!'

' When all was over,' said the Queen; ' when the people refused to sacrifice, and the gods, indignant, quitted earth, I hope not for ever, the faithful few fled to these mountains with the sacred images, and we have cherished them. I told you we had beautiful and consoling thoughts, and more than thoughts. All else is lost, our wealth, our arts, our luxury, our invention, all have vanished. The niggard earth scarcely yields us a subsistence; we dress like Kurds, feed hardly as well; but if we were to quit these mountains, and wander like them on the plains with our ample flocks, we should lose our sacred images, all the traditions that we yet cherish in our souls, that in spite of our hard lives preserve us from being barbarians; a sense of the beautiful and the lofty, and the divine hope that, when the rapidly consummating degradation of Asia has been fulfilled, mankind will return again to those gods who made the earth beautiful and happy; and that they, in their celestial mercy, may revisit that world which, without them, has become a howling wilderness.'

' Lady,' said Tancred, with much emotion, 'we must, with your permission, speak of these things.. My heart is at present too full.'

' Come hither,' said the Queen, in a voice of great softness; and she led Tancred away.

They entered a chamber of much smaller dimensions.

which might be looked upon as a chapel annexed to the cathedral or Pantheon which they had quitted. At each end of it was a statue. They paused before one. It was not larger than life, of ivory and gold; the colour purer than could possibly have been imagined, highly polished, and so little injured, that at a distance the general effect was not in the least impaired.

'Do you know that?' asked the Queen, as she looked at the statue, and then she looked at Tancred.

'I recognise the god of poetry and light,' said Tancred; 'Phœbus Apollo.'

'Our god: the god of Antioch, the god of the sacred grove! Who could look upon him, and doubt his deity!'

'Is this indeed the figure,' murmured Tancred, 'before which a hundred steers have bled? before which libations of honeyed wine were poured from golden goblets? that lived in a heaven of incense?'

'Ah! you know all.'

'Angels watch over us!' said Tancred, 'or my brain will turn. And who is this?'

'One before whom the pilgrims of the world once kneeled. This is the Syrian goddess; the Venus of our land, but called among us by a name which, by her favour, I also bear, ASTARTE.'

CHAPTER IV.

'AND when did men cease from worshipping them?' asked Fakredeen of Tancred; 'before the Prophet?'

'When truth descended from Heaven in the person of Christ Jesus.'

'But truth had descended from Heaven before Jesus,' replied Fakredeen; 'since, as you tell me, God spoke to Moses on Mount Sinai, and since then to many of the prophets and the princes of Israel.'

'Of whom Jesus was one,' said Tancred; 'the descendant

of King David as well as the Son of God. But through this last and greatest of their princes it was ordained that the inspired Hebrew mind should mould and govern the world. Through Jesus God spoke to the Gentiles, and not to the tribes of Israel only. That is the great worldly difference between Jesus and his inspired predecessors. Christianity is Judaism for the multitude, but still it is Judaism, and its development was the death-blow of the Pagan idolatry.'

'Gentiles,' murmured Fakredeen ; 'Gentiles! you are a Gentile, Tancred ? '

'Alas! I am,' he answered, 'sprung from a horde of Baltic pirates, who never were heard of during the greater annals of the world, a descent which I have been educated to believe was the greatest of honours. What we should have become, had not the Syro-Arabian creeds formed our minds, I dare not contemplate. Probably we should have perished in mutual destruction. However, though rude and modern Gentiles, unknown to the Apostles, we also were in time touched with the sacred symbol, and originally endowed with an organisation of a high class, for our ancestors wandered from Caucasus; we have become kings and princes.'

'What a droll thing is history,' said Fakredeen. 'Ah! if I were only acquainted with it, my education would be complete. Should you call me a Gentile ? '

'I have great doubts whether such an appellation could be extended to the descendants of Ishmael. I always look upon you as a member of the sacred race. It is a great thing for any man ; for you it may tend to empire.'

'Was Julius Cæsar a Gentile ? '

'Unquestionably.'

'And Iskander ? ' (Alexander of Macedon.)

'No doubt ; the two most illustrious Gentiles that ever existed, and representing the two great races on the shores of the Mediterranean, to which the apostolic views were first directed.'

'Well, their blood, though Gentile, led to empire,' said Fakredeen.

'But what are their conquests to those of Jesus Christ?' said Tancred, with great animation. 'Where are their dynasties? where their subjects? They were both deified: who burns incense to them now? Their descendants, both Greek and Roman, bow before the altars of the house of David. The house of David is worshipped at Rome itself, at every seat of great and growing empire in the world, at London, at St. Petersburg, at New York. Asia alone is faithless to the Asian; but Asia has been overrun by Turks and Tatars. For nearly five hundred years the true Oriental mind has been enthralled. Arabia alone has remained free and faithful to the divine tradition. From its bosom we shall go forth and sweep away the mouldering remnants of the Tataric system; and then, when the East has resumed its indigenous intelligence, when angels and prophets again mingle with humanity, the sacred quarter of the globe will recover its primeval and divine supremacy; it will act upon the modern empires, and the faint-hearted faith of Europe, which is but the shadow of a shade, will become as vigorous as befits men who are in sustained communication with the Creator.'

'But suppose,' said Fakredeen, in a captious tone that was unusual with him, 'suppose, when the Tataric system is swept away, Asia reverts to those beautiful divinities that we beheld this morning?'

More than once, since they quitted the presence of Astarte, had Fakredeen harped upon this idea. From that interview the companions had returned moody and unusually silent. Strange to say, there seemed a tacit understanding between them to converse little on that subject which mainly engrossed their minds. Their mutual remarks on Astarte were few and constrained; a little more diffused upon the visit to the temple; but they chiefly kept up the conventional chat of companionship by rather common-place observations on Keferinis and other incidents when required by curtains of green and silver silk, now drawn aside, looked on a garden; vistas of quivering trees, broad parterres of flowers, and everywhere the gleam of glittering fountains, which owned, however, fealty to the superior stream, that bubbled in the centre of the saloon, where four negroes, carved in black marble, poured forth its refreshing waters from huge shells of pearl, into the vast circle of a jasper basin.

At this moment the chamber was enlivened by the presence of many individuals. Most of these were guests; one was the master of the columns and the fountains; a man much above the middle height, though as well proportioned as his sumptuous hall; admirably handsome, for beauty and benevolence blended in the majestic countenance of Adam Besso. To-day his Syrian robes were not unworthy of his palace; the cream-white shawl that encircled his brow with its ample folds was so fine that the merchant who brought it to him carried it over the ocean and the Desert in the hollow shell of a pomegranate. In his girdle rested a handjar, the sheath of which was of a rare and vivid enamel, and the hilt entirely of brilliants.

A slender man of middle size, who, as he stood by Besso, had a diminutive appearance, was in earnest conversation with his host. This personage was adorned with more than one order, and dressed in the Frank uniform of one of the Great Powers, though his head was shaven, for he wore a tarboush or red cap, although no turban. This gentleman was Signor Elias de Laurella, a wealthy Hebrew merchant at Damascus, and Austrian consul-general *ad honorem*; a great man, almost as celebrated for his diplomatic as for his mercantile abilities; a gentleman who understood the Eastern question; looked up to for that, but still more, in that he was the father of the two prettiest girls in the Levant.

The Mesdemoiselles de Laurella, Thérèse and Sophonisbe, had just completed their education, partly at Smyrna, the last year at Marseilles. This had quite turned their heads;

they had come back with a contempt for Syria, the bitter‑
ness of which was only veiled by the high style of Euro‑
pean nonchalance, of which they had a supreme command,
and which is, perhaps, our only match for Eastern repose.
The Mesdemoiselles de Laurella were highly accomplished,
could sing quite ravishingly, paint fruits and flowers, and
drop to each other, before surrounding savages, mysterious
allusions to feats in ball-rooms, which, alas! no longer
could be achieved. They signified, and in some degree
solaced, their intense disgust at their present position by
a haughty and amusingly impassable demeanour, which
meant to convey their superiority to all surrounding cir‑
cumstances. One of their favourite modes of asserting
this pre-eminence was wearing the Frank dress, which
their father only did officially, and which no female mem‑
ber of their family had ever assumed, though Damascus
swarmed with Laurellas. Nothing in the dreams of
Madame Carson, or Madame Camille, or Madame Devey,
nothing in the blazoned pages of the Almanachs des Dames
and Belle Assemblée, ever approached the Mdlles. Laurella,
on a day of festival. It was the acme. Nothing could be
conceived beyond it; nobody could equal it. It was taste
exaggerated, if that be possible; fashion baffling pursuit, if
that be permitted. It was a union of the highest moral
and material qualities; the most sublime contempt and the
stiffest cambric. Figure to yourself, in such habiliments,
two girls, of the same features, the same form, the same
size, but of different colour: a nose turned up, but choicely
moulded, large eyes, and richly fringed, fine hair, beautiful
lips and teeth, but the upper lip and the cheek bones
rather too long and high, and the general expression of
the countenance, when not affected, more sprightly than
intelligent. Therèse was a brunette, but her eye wanted
softness as much as the blue orb of the brilliant Sophonisbe.
Nature and Art had combined to produce their figures,
and it was only the united effort of two such firstrate
powers that could have created anything so admirable.

This was the first visit of the Mesdemoiselles Laurella to the family of Besso, for they had only returned from Marseilles at the beginning of the year, and their host had not resided at Damascus until the summer was much advanced. Of course they were well acquainted by reputation with the great Hebrew house of which the lord of the mansion was the chief. They had been brought up to esteem it the main strength and ornament of their race and religion. But the Mesdemoiselles Laurella were ashamed of their race, and not fanatically devoted to their religion, which might be true, but certainly was not fashionable. Thérèse, who was of a less sanguineous temperament than her sister, affected despair and unutterable humiliation, which permitted her to say before her own people a thousand disagreeable things with an air of artless frankness. The animated Sophonisbe, on the contrary, was always combating prejudice, felt persuaded that the Jews would not be so much disliked if they were better known; that all they had to do was to imitate as closely as possible the habits and customs of the nation among whom they chanced to live; and she really did believe that eventually, such was the progressive spirit of the age, a difference in religion would cease to be regarded, and that a respectable Hebrew, particularly if well dressed and well mannered, might be able to pass through society without being discovered, or at least noticed. Consummation of the destiny of the favourite people of the Creator of the universe!

Notwithstanding their practised nonchalance, the Mesdemoiselles Laurella were a little subdued when they entered the palace of Besso, still more so when they were presented to its master, whose manner, void of all art, yet invested with a natural dignity, asserted in an instant its superiority. Eva, whom they saw for the first time, received them like a queen, and in a dress which offered as complete a contrast to their modish attire as the beauty of her sublime countenance presented to their pretty and sparkling visages.

Madame Laurella, the mother of these young ladies,
would in Europe have been still styled young. She was a
Smyrniote, and had been a celebrated beauty. The rose
had since then too richly expanded, but even now, with
her dark eyelash charged with yamusk, her cheek touched
with rouge, and her fingers tipped with henna, her still
fine hair exaggerated by art or screened by her jewelled
turban, she would have been a striking personage, even if
it had not been for the blaze of jewels with which she was
suffused and environed. The existence of this lady was
concentred in her precious gems. An extreme susceptibility on this head is very prevalent among the ladies of
the Levant, and the quantity of jewels that they accumu-
late far exceeds the general belief. Madame Laurella was
without a rival in this respect, and resolved to maintain
her throne; diamonds alone did not satisfy her; immense
emeralds, rubies as big as pigeons' eggs, prodigious ropes
of pearls, were studded and wound about every part of her
rich robes. Every finger glittered, and bracelets flashed
beneath her hanging sleeves. She sat in silent splendour
on a divan, now and then proudly moving a fan of feathers,
lost in criticism of the jewels of her friends, and in contemplation of her own.

A young man, tall and well-looking, dressed as an
Oriental, but with an affected, jerking air, more French
than Syrian, moved jauntily about the room, speaking to
several persons for a short time, shrugging his shoulders
and uttering commonplaces as if they were poignant origi-
nalities. This was Hillel Besso, the eldest son of the Besso
of Aleppo, and the intended husband of Eva. Hillel, too,
had seen the world, passed a season at Pera, where he had
worn the Frank dress, and, introduced into the circles by
the lady of the Austrian Internuncio, had found success
and enjoyed himself. He had not, however, returned to
Syria with any of the disgust shared by the Mesdemoiselles
Laurella. Hillel was neither ashamed of his race nor his
religion: on the contrary, he was perfectly satisfied with

this life, with the family of Besso in general, and with himself particularly. Hillel was a little philosophical, had read Voltaire, and, free from prejudices, conceived himself capable of forming correct opinions. He listened smiling and in silence to Eva asserting the splendour and superiority of their race, and sighing for the restoration of their national glory, and then would say, in a whisper to a friend, and with a glance of epigrammatic airiness, ' For my part, I am not so sure that we were ever better off than we are.'

He stopped and conversed with Therèse Laurella, who at first was unbending, but when she found that he was a Besso, and had listened to one or two anecdotes, which indicated personal acquaintance not only with ambassadors but with ambassadors' ladies, she began to relax. In general, however, the rest of the ladies did not speak, or made only observations to each other in a hushed voice. Conversation is not the accomplishment of these climes and circles. They seemed content to show their jewels to their neighbours. There was a very fat lady, of prodigious size, the wife of Signor Yacoub Picholoroni, who was also a consul, but not a consul-general *in honorem.* She looked like a huge Chinese idol; a perpetual smile played upon her immense good-natured cheeks, and her little black eyes twinkled with continuous satisfaction. There were the Mourad Farhis and the Nassim Farhis. There were Moses Laurella and his wife, who shone with the reflected splendour of the great Laurellas, but who were really very nice people; sensible and most obliging, as all travellers must have found them. Moses Laurella was vice-consul to his brother. The Farhis had no diplomatic lustre, but they were great merchants, and worked with the house of Besso in all their enterprises. They had married two sisters, who were also their cousins. Madame Mourad Farhi was in the zenith of her renowned beauty; in the gorgeous Smyrniote style, brilliant yet languid, like a panther basking in the sunshine. Her sister also had a rich countenance, and a figure like a palm tree, while her fine brow beamed alike with intelligence and beauty. Madame Nassim was highly cultured, enthusiastic for her race, and proud of the friendship of Eva, of which she was worthy.

There were also playing about the room three or four children of such dazzling beauty and such ineffable grace, that no pen can picture their seraphic glances or gestures of airy frolic. Sometimes serious, from exhaustion not from thought; sometimes wild with the witchery of infant riot; a laughing girl with hair almost touching the ground, and large grey eyes bedewed with lustrous mischief, tumbles over an urchin who rises doubtful whether to scream or shout; sometimes they pull the robe of Besso while he talks, who goes on, as if unconscious of the interruption; sometimes they rush up to their mother or Eva for an embrace; sometimes they run up to the fat lady, look with wondering gravity in her face, and then, bursting into laughter, scud away. These are the children of a sister of Hillel Besso's, brought to Damascus for change of air. Their mother is also here, sitting at the side of Eva: a soft and pensive countenance, watching the children with her intelligent blue eyes, or beckoning to them with a beautiful hand.

The men in general remained on their legs apart, conversing as if they were on the Bourse.

Now entered, from halls beyond of less dimensions, but all decorated with similar splendour, a train of servants, two of whom carried between them a large broad basket of silver filagree, filled with branches of the palm tree entwined with myrtle, while another bore a golden basket of a different shape, and which was filled with citrons just gathered. These they handed to the guests, and each guest took a branch with the right hand and a citron with the left. The conversation of Besso with Elias Laurella had been broken by their entrance, and a few minutes afterwards, the master of the house, looking about, held up his branch, shook it with a rustling sound, and immediately Eva was at his side.

The daughter of Besso wore a vest of white silk, fitting close to her shape and descending to her knees ; it was buttoned with large diamonds and restrained by a girdle of pearls; anklets of brilliants peeped also, every now and then, from beneath her large Mamlouk trowsers of rose-coloured silk that fell over her slippers, powdered with diamonds. Over her vest she wore the Syrian jacket, made of cherry-coloured velvet, its open arms and back richly embroidered, though these were now much concealed by her outer pelisse, a brocade of India, massy with gold, and yet relieved from heaviness by the brilliancy of its light blue tint and the dazzling fantasy of its pattern. This was loosely bound round her waist by a Moorish scarf of the colour of a blood-red orange, and bordered with a broad fringe of precious stones. Her head-dress was of the same fashion as when we first met her in the kiosk of Bethany, except that, on this occasion, her Syrian cap on the back of her head was covered only with diamonds, and only with diamonds was braided her long dark hair.

' They will never come,' said Besso to his daughter. ' It was one of his freaks. We will not wait.'

'I am sure, my father, they will come,' said Eva, earnestly. And indeed, at this very moment, as she stood at his side, holding in one hand her palm branch, which was reposing on her bosom, and in the other her fresh citron, the servants appeared again, ushering in two guests who had just arrived. One was quite a stranger, a young man dressed in the European fashion ; the other was recognised at once by all present as the Emir of Canobia.

CHAPTER VI.

Eva had withdrawn from her father to her former remote position, the moment that she had recognised the two friends, and was, therefore, not in hearing when her father received them, and said, ' Welcome, noble stranger ! the noble Emir here, to whom a thousand welcomes, told me that you would not be averse from joining a festival of my people.'

'I would seize any opportunity to pay my respects to you,' replied Tancred; 'but this occasion is most agreeable to me.'

'And when, noble traveller, did you arrive at Esh Sham?'

'But this morning; we were last from Hasbeya.'

Tancred then inquired after Eva, and Besso led him to his daughter.

In the meantime the arrival of the new guests made a considerable sensation in the chamber, especially with the Mesdemoiselles Laurella. A young prince of the Lebanon, whatever his religion, was a distinguished and agreeable accession to their circle, but in Tancred they recognised a being at once civilised and fashionable, a Christian who could dance the Polka. Refreshing as springs in the desert to their long languishing eyes were the sight of his white cravat and his boots of Parisian polish.

'It is one of our great national festivals,' said Eva, slightly waving her palm branch; 'the celebration of the Hebrew vintage, the Feast of Tabernacles.'

The vineyards of Israel have ceased to exist, but the eternal law enjoins the children of Israel still to celebrate the vintage. A race that persist in celebrating their vintage, although they have no fruits to gather, will regain their vineyards. What sublime inexorability in the law! But what indomitable spirit in the people!

It is easy for the happier Sephardim, the Hebrews who have never quitted the sunny regions that are laved by the Midland Ocean; it is easy for them, though they have lost their heritage, to sympathise, in their beautiful Asian cities or in their Moorish and Arabian gardens, with the graceful rites that are, at least, an homage to a benignant nature. But picture to yourself the child of Israel in the dingy suburb or the squalid quarter of some bleak northern town, where there is never a sun that can at any rate ripen grapes

Yet he must celebrate the vintage of purple Palestine! The law has told him, though a denizen in an icy clime, that he must dwell for seven days in a bower, and that he must build it of the boughs of thick trees; and the Rabbins have told him that these thick trees are the palm, the myrtle, and the weeping willow. Even Sarmatia may furnish a weeping willow. The law has told him that he must pluck the fruit of goodly trees, and the Rabbins have explained that goodly fruit on this occasion is confined to the citron. Perhaps, in his despair, he is obliged to fly to the candied delicacies of the grocer. His mercantile connections will enable him, often at considerable cost, to procure some palm leaves from Canaan, which he may wave in his synagogue while he exclaims, as the crowd did when the Divine descendant of David entered Jerusalem, ' Hosannah in the highest!'

There is something profoundly interesting in this devoted observance of Oriental customs in the heart of our Saxon and Sclavonian cities; in these descendants of the Bedoueens, who conquered Canaan more than three thousand years ago, still celebrating that success which secured their forefathers, for the first time, grapes and wine.

Conceive a being born and bred in the Judenstrasse of Hamburg or Frankfort, or rather in the purlieus of our Houndsditch or Minories, born to hereditary insult, without any education, apparently without a circumstance that can develop the slightest taste, or cherish the least sentiment for the beautiful, living amid fogs and filth, never treated with kindness, seldom with justice, occupied with the meanest, if not the vilest, toil, bargaining for frippery, speculating in usury, existing for ever under the concurrent influence of degrading causes which would have worn out, long ago, any race that was not of the unmixed blood of Caucasus, and did not adhere to the laws of Moses; conceive such a being, an object to you of prejudice, dislike, disgust, perhaps hatred. The season arrives, and the mind and heart of that being are filled with images and passions

that have been ranked in all ages among the most beautiful
and the most genial of human experience; filled with a
subject the most vivid, the most graceful, the most joyous,
and the most exuberant; a subject which has inspired poets,
and which has made gods; the harvest of the grape in the
native regions of the Vine.

He rises in the morning, goes early to some Whitechapel
market, purchases some willow boughs for which he has
previously given a commission, and which are brought,
probably, from one of the neighbouring rivers of Essex,
hastens home, cleans out the yard of his miserable tene-
ment, builds his bower, decks it, even profusely, with the
finest flowers and fruits that he can procure, the myrtle and
the citron never forgotten, and hangs its roof with varie-
gated lamps. After the service of his synagogue, he sups
late with his wife and his children in the open air, as if he
were in the pleasant villages of Galilee, beneath its sweet
and starry sky.

Perhaps, as he is giving the Keedush, the Hebrew blessing
to the Hebrew meal, breaking and distributing the bread,
and sanctifying, with a preliminary prayer, the goblet of
wine he holds, the very ceremony which the Divine Prince
of Israel, nearly two thousand years ago, adopted at the
most memorable of all repasts, and eternally invested with
eucharistic grace; or, perhaps, as he is offering up the peculiar thanksgiving of the Feast of Tabernacles, praising
Jehovah for the vintage which his children may no longer
cull, but also for his promise that they may some day again
enjoy it, and his wife and his children are joining in a pious
Hosanna, that is, Save us! a party of Anglo-Saxons, very
respectable men, ten-pounders, a little elevated it may be,
though certainly not in honour of the vintage, pass the
house, and words like these are heard:

'I say, Buggins, what's that row?'

'Oh! it's those cursed Jews! we've a lot of 'em here. It
is one of their horrible feasts. The Lord Mayor ought to
interfere. However, things are not as bad as they used to

be: they used always to crucify little boys at these hulla-baloos, but now they only eat sausages made of stinking pork.'

'To be sure,' replies his companion, 'we all make progress.'

In the meantime, a burst of music sounds from the gardens of Besso of Damascus. He advances, and invites Tancred and the Emir to follow him, and, without any order or courtesy to the softer sex, who, on the contrary, follow in the rear, the whole company step out of the Saracenic windows into the gardens. The mansion of Besso, which was of great extent, appeared to be built in their midst. No other roof or building was in any direction visible, yet the house was truly in the middle of the city, and the umbrageous plane trees alone produced that illimitable air which is always so pleasing and effective. The house, though lofty for an eastern mansion, was only one story in height, yet its front was covered with an external and double staircase. This, after a promenade in the garden, the guests approached and mounted. It led to the roof or terrace of the house, which was of great size, an oblong square, and which again was a garden. Myrtle trees of a considerable height, and fragrant with many flowers, were arranged in close order along the four sides of this roof forming a barrier which no eye from the city beneath or any neighbouring terrace could penetrate. This verdant bulwark, however, opened at each corner of the roof, which was occupied by a projecting pavilion of white marble, a light cupola of chequered carving supported by wreathed columns. From these pavilions the most charming views might be obtained of the city and the surrounding country : Damascus, itself a varied mass of dark green groves, white minarets, bright gardens, and hooded domes; to the south and east, at the extremity of its rich plain, the glare of the Desert; to the west the ranges of the Lebanon; while the city was backed on the north by other mountain regions which Tancred had not yet penetrated.

In the centre of the terrace was a temporary structure of a peculiar character. It was nearly forty feet long, half as many broad, and proportionately lofty. Twelve palm trees clustering with ripe fruit, and each of which seemed to spring from a flowering hedge of myrtles, supported a roof, formed with much artifice of the braided boughs of trees. These, however, only furnished an invisible framework, from which were suspended the most beautiful and delicious fruits, citron and pomegranate, orange, and fig, and banana, and melon, in such thickness and profusion that they formed, as it were, a carved ceiling of rich shades and glowing colours, like the Saracenic ceiling of the mansion, while enormous bunches of grapes every now and then descended like pendants from the main body of the roof. The spaces between the palm trees were filled with a natural trellis-work of orange trees in fruit and blossom, leaving at intervals arches of entrance, whose form was indicated by bunches of the sweetest and rarest flowers.

Within was a banqueting-table covered with thick white damask silk, with a border of gold about a foot in breadth, and before each guest was placed a napkin of the same fashion. The table, however, lacked none of the conveniences and luxuries and even ornaments of Europe. What can withstand the united influence of taste, wealth, and commerce? The choicest porcelain of France, golden goblets chiselled in Bond Street, and the prototypes of which had perhaps been won at Goodwood or Ascot, mingled with the rarest specimens of the glass of Bohemia, while the triumphant blades of Sheffield flashed in that very Syrian city whose skill in cutlery had once been a proverb. Around the table was a divan of amber-coloured satin with many cushions, so arranged that the guests might follow either the Oriental or the European mode of seating themselves. Such was the bower or tabernacle of Besso of Damascus, prepared to celebrate the seventh day of his vintage feast.

CHAPTER VII.

'WE ought to have met at Jerusalem,' said Tancred to Besso, on whose right hand he was seated, 'but I am happy to thank you for all your kindness, even at Damascus.'

'My daughter tells me you are not uninterested in our people, which is the reason I ventured to ask you here.'

'I cannot comprehend how a Christian can be uninterested in a people who have handed down to him immortal truths.'

'All the world is not as sensible of the obligation as your-self, noble traveller.'

'But who are the world? Do you mean the inhabitants of Europe, which is a forest not yet cleared; or the inhabit-ants of Asia, which is a ruin about to tumble?'

'The railroads will clear the forest,' said Besso.

'And what is to become of the ruin?' asked Tancred.

'God will not forget his land.'

'That is the truth; the government of this globe must be divine, and the impulse can only come from Asia.'

'If your government only understood the Eastern ques-tion!' said Mr. Consul-General Laurella, pricking up his ears at some half phrase that he had caught, and addressing Tancred across the table. 'It is more simple than you ima-gine, and before you return to England to take your seat in your parliament, I should be very happy to have some conversation with you. I think I could tell you some things ——' and he gave a glance of diplomatic mystery. Tancred bowed.

'For my part,' said Hillel Besso, shrugging his shoulders, and speaking in an airy tone, 'it seems to me that your Eastern question is a great imbroglio that only exists in the cabinets of diplomatists. Why should there be any Eastern question? All is very well as it is. At least we might be worse: I think we might be worse.'

'I am so happy to find myself once more among you,'

whispered Fakredeen to his neighbour, Madame Mourad Farhi. ' This is my real home.'

'All here must be happy and honoured to see you, too, noble Emir.'

'And the good Signor Mourad: I am afraid I am not a favourite of his?' pursued Fakredeen, meditating a loan.

' I never heard my husband speak of you, noble Emir, but with the greatest consideration.'

'There is no man I respect so much,' said Fakredeen; 'no one in whom I have such a thorough confidence. Excepting our dear host, who is really my father, there is no one on whose judgment I would so implicitly rely. Tell him all that, my dear Madame Mourad, for I wish him to respect me.'

' I admire his hair so much,' whispered Therèse Laurella, in an audible voice to her sister, across the broad form of the ever-smiling Madame Picholoroni. ' 'Tis such a relief after our dreadful turbans.'

'And his costume, so becoming! I wonder how any civilised being can wear the sort of things we see about us. 'Tis really altogether like a wardrobe of the Comedie.'

' Well, Sophonisbe,' said the sensible Moses Laurella, 'I admire the Franks very much; they have many qualities which I could wish our Levantines shared; but I confess that I do not think that their strong point is their costume.'

' Oh, my dear uncle!' said Therèse; 'look at that beautiful white cravat. What have we like it? So simple, so distinguished! Such good taste! And then the boots. Think of our dreadful slippers! powdered with pearls and all sorts of trash of that kind, by the side of that lovely French polish.'

'He must be terribly ennuyé here,' said Therèse to Sophonisbe, with a look of the initiated.

' Indeed, I should think so: no balls, not an opera; I quite pity him. What could have induced him to come here?'

' I should think he must be attached to some one,' said Therèse; ' he looks unhappy.'

'There is not a person near him with whom he can have an idea in common.'

'Except Mr. Hillel Besso,' said Thérèse. 'He appears to be quite enlightened. I spoke to him a little before dinner. He has been a winter at Pera, and went to all the balls.'

'Lord Palmerston understood the Eastern question to a certain degree,' said Mr. Consul-General Laurella; 'but, had I been in the service of the Queen of England, I could have told him some things;' and he mysteriously paused.

'I cannot endure this eternal chatter about Palmerston,' said the Emir, rather pettishly. 'Are there no other statesmen in the world besides Palmerston? And what should he know about the Eastern question, who never was in the East?'

'Ah, noble Emir, these are questions of the high diplomacy. They cannot be treated unless by the cabinets which have traditions.'

'I could settle the Eastern question in a month, if I were disposed,' said Fakredeen.

Mr. Consul-General Laurella smiled superciliously, and then said, 'But the question is, what is the Eastern question?'

'For my part,' said Hillel Besso, in a most epigrammatic manner, 'I do not see the use of settling anything.'

'The Eastern question is, who shall govern the Mediterranean?' said the Emir. 'There are only two powers who can do it: Egypt and Syria. As for the English, the Russians, the Franks, your friends the Austrians, they are strangers. They come, and they will go; but Syria and Egypt will always remain.'

'Egypt has tried, and failed.'

'Then let Syria try, and succeed.'

'Do you visit Egypt before you return from the East, noble sir?' asked Besso, of Tancred.

'I have not thought of my return; but I should not be sorry to visit Egypt. It is a country that rather perplexes us in Europe. It has undergone great changes.'

Besso shook his head, and slightly smiled.

'Egypt,' said he, 'never changes. 'Tis the same land as in the days of the Pharaohs: governed on their principles of political economy, with a Hebrew for prime minister.'

'A Hebrew for prime minister!'

'Even so: Artim Bey, the present prime minister of Egypt, formerly the Pacha's envoy at Paris, and by far the best political head in the Levant, is not only the successor but the descendant of Joseph.'

'He must be added then to your friend M. de Sidonia's list of living Hebrew statesmen,' said Tancred.

'We have our share of the government of the world,' said Besso.

'It seems to me that you govern every land except your own.'

'That might have been done in '39,' said Besso musingly; 'but why speak of a subject which can little interest you?'

'Can little interest me!' exclaimed Tancred. 'What other subject should interest me? More than six centuries ago, the government of that land interested my ancestor, and he came here to achieve it.'

The stars were shining before they quitted the Arabian tabernacle of Besso. The air was just as soft as a sweet summer English noon, and quite as still. The pavilions of the terrace and the surrounding bowers were illuminated by the varying tints of a thousand lamps. Bright carpets and rich cushions were thrown about for those who cared to recline; the brothers Farhi, for example, and indeed most of the men, smoking inestimable nargillies. The Consul-General Laurella begged permission to present Lord Monta-cute to his daughters Thérèse and Sophonisbe, who, resolved to show to him that Damascus was not altogether so barbarous as he deemed it, began talking of new dances and the last opera. Tancred would have found great difficulty in sustaining his part in the conversation, had not the young ladies fortunately been requested to favour those present with a specimen of the art in which they excelled, which they did after much solicitation, vowing that they had no voice to-night, and that it was impossible at all times to sing, except in a chamber.

'For my part,' said Hillel Besso, with an extremely piquant air, 'music in a chamber is very charming, but I think also in the open air it is not so bad.'

Tancred took advantage of this movement to approach Eva, who was conversing, as they took their evening walk, with the soft-eyed sister of Hillel and Madame Nassim Farhi; a group of women, that the drawing-rooms of Europe and the hareems of Asia could perhaps not have rivalled.

'The Mesdemoiselles Laurella are very accomplished,' said Tancred, 'but at Damascus I am not content to hear anything but sackbuts and psalteries.'

'But in Europe your finest music is on the subjects of our history,' said Eva.

'Naturally,' said Tancred, 'music alone can do justice to such themes. They baffle the uninspired pen.'

'There is a prayer which the Mesdemoiselles Laurella once sang, a prayer of Moses in Egypt,' said Madame Nassim, somewhat timidly. 'It is very fine.'

'I wish they would favour us with it,' said Eva; 'I will ask Hillel to request that kindness;' and she beckoned to Hillel, who sauntered toward her, and listened to her whispered wish with a smile of supercilious complacency.

'At present they are going to favour us with Don Pasquale,' he said, shrugging his shoulders. 'A prayer is a very fine thing, but for my part, at this hour, I think a serenade is not so bad.'

'And how do you like my father?' said Eva to Tancred, in a hesitating tone, and yet with a glance of blended curiosity and pride.

'He is exactly what Sidonia prepared me for; worthy not only of being your father, but the father of mankind.'

'The Moslemin say that we are near paradise at Damascus,' said Madame Nassim, 'and that Adam was fashioned out of our red earth.'

'He much wished to see you,' said Eva, 'and your meeting is as unexpected as to him it is agreeable.'

'We ought to have met long before,' said Tancred. 'When I first arrived at Jerusalem, I ought to have hastened to his threshold. The fault and the misfortune were mine. I scarcely deserved the happiness of knowing you.'

'I am happy we have all met, and that you now understand us a little. When you go back to England, you will defend us when we are defamed? You will not let them persecute us, as they did a few years back, because they said we crucified their children at the feast of our passover?'

'I shall not go back to England,' said Tancred, colouring; 'and if you are persecuted, I hope I shall be able to defend you here.'

The glowing sky, the soft mellow atmosphere, the brilliant circumstances around, flowers and flashing gems, rich dresses and ravishing music, and every form of splendour and luxury, combined to create a scene, that to Tancred was startling, as well from its beauty as its novel character. A rich note of Thérèse Laurella for an instant arrested their conversation. They were silent while it lingered on their ear. Then Tancred said to the soft-eyed sister of Hillel, 'All that we require here to complete the spell are your beautiful children.'

'They sleep,' said the lady, 'and lose little by not being present, for, like the Queen of Sheba, I doubt not they are dreaming of music and flowers.'

'They say that the children of our race are the most beautiful in the world,' said Eva, ' but that when they grow up, they do not fulfil the promise of their infancy.'

'That were scarcely possible,' said the soft-eyed mother.

'It is the sense of shame that comes on them and dims their lustre,' said Eva. 'Instead of joyousness and frank hilarity, anxiety and a shrinking reserve are soon impressed upon the youthful Hebrew visage. It is the seal of ignominy. The dreadful secret that they are an expatriated and persecuted race is soon revealed to them, at least among the humbler classes. The children of our house are bred in noble thoughts, and taught self-respect. Their countenances will not change.'

And the countenance, from whose beautiful mouth issued those gallant words, what of that ? It was one that might wilder the wisest. Tancred gazed upon it with serious yet fond abstraction. All heavenly and heroic thoughts gathered around the image of this woman. From the first moment of their meeting at Bethany to this hour of sacred festival, all the passages of his life in which she had been present flashed through his mind. For a moment he was in the ruins of the Arabian Desert, and recalled her glance of sweet solicitude, when, recovered by her skill and her devotion, he recognised the fair stranger whose words had, ere that, touched the recesses of his spirit, and attuned his mind to high and holiest mysteries. Now again their eyes met ; an ineffable expression suffused the countenance of Lord Montacute. He sighed.

At this moment Hillel and Fakredeen advanced with a hurried air of gaiety. Hillel offered his hand to Eva with jaunty grace, exclaiming at the same time, ' Ladies, if you like to follow us, you shall see a casket just arrived from Marseilles, and which Eva will favour me by carrying to Aleppo. It was chosen for me by the Lady of the Austrian Internuncio, who is now at Paris. For my part, I do not see much advantage in the diplomatic corps, if occasionally they do not execute a commission for one.'

Hillel hurried Eva away, accompanied by his sister and Madame Nassim. Tancred and Fakredeen remained behind.

' Who is this man ? ' said Tancred.

' 'Tis her affianced,' said the Emir ; ' the man who has robbed me of my natural bride. It is to be hoped, however, that, when she is married, Besso will adopt me as his son, which in a certain sense I am, having been fostered by his wife. If he do not leave me his fortune, he ought at least to take up all my bills in Syria. Don't you think so, my Tancred ? '

' What ? ' said Tancred, with a dreamy look.

There was a burst of laughter in the distance.

' Come, come,' said Fakredeen, ' see how they are all gathering round the marriage casket. Even Nassim Farhi has risen. I must go and talk to him : he has impulses, that man, at least compared with his brother ; Mourad is a stone, a precious stone though, and you cannot magnetise him through his wife, for she has not an idea ; but Madame Nassim is immensely mesmeric. Come, come, Tancred.'

' I follow.'

But instead of following his friend, Tancred entered one of the marble pavilions that jutted out from each corner of the terraced roof, and commanded splendid views of the glittering and gardened city. The moon had risen over that unrivalled landscape ; the white minarets sparkled in its beam, and the vast hoods of the cupolaed mosques were suffused with its radiancy or reposed in dark shadow, almost as black as the cypress groves out of which they rose. In the extreme distance, beyond the fertile plain, was the Desert, bright as the line of the sea, while otherwise around him extended the chains of Lebanon and of the North.

The countenance of Tancred was more than serious, it was sad, as, leaning against one of the wreathed marble pillars, he sighed and murmured : ' If I were thou, most beautiful Damascus, Aleppo should not rob me of such a gem ! But I must tear up these thoughts from my heart by their roots, and remember that I am ordained for other deeds.'

CHAPTER VIII.

AFTER taking the bath on his arrival at Damascus, having his beard arranged by a barber of distinction, and dressing himself in a fresh white suit, as was his custom when in residence, with his turban of the same colour arranged a little aside, for Baroni was scrupulous as to his appearance, he hired a donkey and made his way to the great bazaar.

The part of the city through which he proceeded was very crowded and bustling: narrow streets, with mats slung across, to shield from the sun the swarming population beneath. His accustomed step was familiar with every winding of the emporium of the city; he threaded without hesitation the complicated mazes of those interminable arcades. Now he was in the street of the armourers, now among the sellers of shawls; the prints of Manchester were here unfolded, there the silks of India; sometimes he sauntered by a range of shops gay with yellow papooshes and scarlet slippers, and then hurried by the stalls and shelves stored with the fatal frippery of the East, in which it is said the plague in some shape or other always lurks and lingers. This locality, however, indicated that Baroni was already approaching the purlieus of the chief places; the great population had already much diminished, the brilliancy of the scene much dimmed; there was no longer the swarm of itinerant traders who live by promptly satisfying the wants of the visitors to the bazaar in the shape of a pipe or an ice, a cup of sherbet or of coffee, or a basket of delicious fruit. The passengers were few, and all seemed busy: some Armenians, a Hebrew physician and his page, the gliding phantoms of some winding-sheets, which were in fact women.

Baroni turned into an arcade, well built, spacious, airy, and very neatly fitted up. This was the bazaar of the dealers in drugs. Here, too, spices are sold, all sorts of dye-woods, and especially the choice gums for which Arabia is still celebrated, and which Syria would fain rival by the aromatic juices of her pistachio and her apricot trees.

Seated on what may be called his counter, smoking a nargilly, in a mulberry-coloured robe bordered with fur, and a dark turban, was a middle-aged man of sinister countenance and air, a long hook nose and a light blue eye.

'Welcome, Effendi,' he said, when he observed Baroni; 'many welcomes! And how long have you been at Esk Sham?'

'Not too long,' said Baroni; 'and have you been here since my last visit?'

'Here and there,' said the man, offering him his pipe.

'And how are our friends in the mountains?' said Baroni, touching the tube with his lips and returning it.

'They live,' said the man.

'That's something,' said Baroni.

'Have you been in the land of the Franks?' said the man.

'I am always in the land of the Franks,' said Baroni, 'and about.'

'You don't know any one who wants a parcel of scammony?' said the man.

'I don't know that I don't,' said Baroni, mysteriously.

'I have a very fine parcel,' said the man; 'it is very scarce.'

'No starch or myrrh in it?' asked Baroni.

'Do you think I am a Jew?' said the man.

'I never could make out what you were, friend Darkush; but as for scammony, I could throw a good deal of business in your way at this moment, to say nothing of galls and tragacanth.'

'As for tragacanth,' said Darkush, 'it is known that no one in Esh Sham has pure tragacanth except me; as for galls, every foundling in Syria thinks he can deal in afis, but is it afis of Moussoul, Effendi?'

'What you say are the words of truth, good Darkush; I could recommend you with a safe conscience. I dreamt last night that there would many piastres pass between us this visit.'

'What is the use of friends unless they help you in the hour of adversity?' exclaimed Darkush.

'You speak ever the words of truth. I am myself in a valley of dark shadows. I am travelling with a young English capitani, a prince of many tails, and he has declared that he will entirely extinguish my existence unless he pays a visit to the Queen of the Ansarey.'

Let him first pay a visit to King Soliman in the cities of the Gin,' said Darkush, doggedly.

'I am not sure that he will not, some time or other,' replied Baroni, 'for he is a man who will not take nay. But now let us talk of scammony,' he added, vaulting on the counter, and seating himself by the side of Darkush; 'one might get more by arranging this visit to your mountains than by enjoying an appalto of all its gums, friend Darkush; but if it cannot be, it cannot be.'

'It cannot be.'

'Let us talk then of scammony. You remember my old master, Darkush?'

'There are many things that are forgotten, but he is not one.'

'This capitani with whom I travel, this prince of many tails, is his friend. If you serve me now, you serve also him who served you.'

'There are things that can be done, and there are things that cannot be done.'

'Let us talk then of scammony. But fifteen years ago, when we first met, friend Darkush, you did not say nay to M. de Sidonia. It was the plague alone that stopped us.'

'The snow on the mountain is not the same snow as fifteen years ago, Effendi. All things change!'

'Let us talk then of scammony. The Ansarey have friends in other lands, but if they will not listen to them, many kind words will be lost. Things also might happen which would make everybody's shadow longer, but if there be no sun, their shadows cannot be seen.'

Darkush shrugged his shoulders.

'If the sun of friendship does not illumine me,' resumed Baroni, 'I am entirely lost in the bottomless vale. Truly, I would give a thousand piastres if I could save my head by taking the capitani to your mountains.'

'The princes of Franguestan cannot take off heads,' observed Darkush. 'All they can do is to banish you to islands inhabited by demons.'

'But the capitani of whom I speak is prince of many tails, is the brother of queens. Even the great Queen of the English, they say, is his sister.'

'He who serves queens may expect backsheesh.'

'And you serve a queen, Darkush?'

'Which is the reason I cannot give you a pass for the mountains, as I would have done, fifteen years ago, in the time of her father.'

'Are her commands, then, so strict?'

'That she should see neither Moslem nor Christian. She is at war with both, and will be for ever, for the quarrel between them is beyond the power of man to remove.'

'And what may it be?'

'That you can learn only in the mountains of the Ansarey,' said Darkush, with a malignant smile.

Baroni fell into a musing mood. After a few moments' thought, he looked up, and said : 'What you have told me, friend Darkush, is very interesting, and throws light on many things. This young prince, whom I serve, is a friend to your race, and knows well why you are at war both with Moslem and Christian, for he is so himself. But he is a man sparing of words, dark in thought, and terrible to deal with. Why he wishes to visit your people I dared not inquire, but now I guess, from what you have let fall, that he is an Ansarey himself. He has come from a far land merely to visit his race, a man who is a prince among the people, to whom piastres are as water. I doubt not he has much to say to your Queen : things might have happened that would have lengthened all our shadows ; but never mind, what cannot be, cannot be : let us talk then of scammony.'

'You think he is one?' said Darkush, in a lower tone, and looking very inquiringly.

'I do,' said Baroni.

'And what do you mean by one?' said Darkush.

'That is exactly the secret which I never could penetrate.'

'I cannot give a pass to the mountains,' said Darkush,

but the sympathy of friends is a river flowing in a fair garden. If this prince, whose words and thoughts are dark, should indeed be one —— Could I see him, Effendi ? '

' It is a subject on which I dare not speak to him,' said Baroni. ' I hinted at his coming here : his brow was the brow of Eblis, his eye flashed like the red lightning of the Kamsin : it is impossible ! What cannot be done, cannot be done. He must return to the land of his fathers, unseen by your Queen, of whom he is perhaps a brother ; he will live, hating alike Moslem and Christian, but he will banish me for ever to islands of many demons.'

' The Queen shall know of these strange things,' said Darkush, ' and we will wait for her words.'

' Wait for the Mecca caravan !' exclaimed Baroni. ' You know not the child of storms, who is my master, and that is ever a reason why I think he must be one of you. For had he been softened by Christianity or civilised by the Koran —— '

' Unripe figs for your Christianity and your Koran !' exclaimed Darkush. ' Do you know what we think of your Christianity and your Koran ? '

' No,' said Baroni, quietly. ' Tell me.'

' You will learn in our mountains,' said Darkush.

' Then you mean to let me go there ? '

' If the Queen permit you.' said Darkush.

' It is three hundred miles to your country, if it be an hour's journey,' said Baroni. ' What with sending the message and receiving the answer, to say nothing of the delays which must occur with a woman and a queen in the case, the fountains of Esh Sham will have run dry before we hear that our advance is forbidden.'

Darkush shook his head, and yet smiled.

' By the sunset of to-morrow, Effendi, I could say, ay or nay. Tell me what scammony you want, and it shall be done.'

' Write down in your tablets how much you can let me have,' said Baroni, ' and I will pay you for it to-morrow.

As for the goods themselves, you may keep them for me, until I ask you for them; perhaps the next time I travel with a capitani who is one of yourselves.'

Darkush threw aside the tube of his nargilly, and, putting his hand very gently into the breast of his robe, he drew out a pigeon, dove-coloured, but with large bright black eyes. The pigeon seemed very knowing and very proud, as he rested on his master's two fingers.

' Hah, hah ! my Karaguus, my black eyes,' exclaimed Darkush. ' What, is he going on a little journey to some-body ! Yes, we can trust Karaguus, for he is one of us. Effendi, to-morrow at sunset, at your khan, for the bazaar will be closed, you shall hear from me.'

END OF BOOK V.

BOOK VI.

CHAPTER I.

At the black gorge of a mountain pass sat, like sentries, two horsemen. Their dress was that of the Kurds: white turbans, a black shirt girt with cords, on their back a long lance, by their side a crooked sword, and in their girdle a brace of pistols.

Before them extended a wide, but mountainous landscape: after the small and very rugged plain on the brink of which they were posted, many hilly ridges, finally a lofty range. The general character of the scene was severe and savage; the contiguous rocks were black and riven, the hills barren and stony, the granite peaks of the more eminent heights uncovered, except occasionally by the snow. Yet, notwithstanding the general aridity of its appearance, the country itself was not unfruitful. The concealed vegetation of the valleys was not inconsiderable, and was highly cherished; the less precipitous cliffs, too, were cut into terraces, and covered with artificial soil. The numerous villages intimated that the country was well populated. The inhabitants produced sufficient wine and corn for their own use, were clothed in garments woven by themselves, and possessed some command over the products of other countries by the gums, the bees-wax, and the goats' wool which they could offer in exchange.

'I have seen two eagles over Gibel Kiflis twice this morning,' said one of the horsemen to his companion. 'What does that portend?'

'A good backsheesh for our Queen, comrade. If these children of Franguestan can pay a princess's dower to visit some columns in the Desert, like Tadmor, they may well give us the golden keys of their treasury when they enter where none should go but those who are ——'

'But they say that this Frank is one.'

'It has never been known that there were any among the Franks,' replied his comrade, shaking his head. 'The Franks are all Nazareny, and, before they were Nazareny, they were savages, and lived in caves.'

'But Keferinia has given the word, that all are to guard over the strangers as over the Queen herself, and that one is a prince, who is unquestionably one of us.'

'My father had counted a hundred and ten years when he left us, Azaz, and he had twenty-four children, and when he was at the point of death he told us two things : one was, never to forget what we were ; and the other, that never in his time had one like us ever visited our country.'

'Eagles again fly over Gibel Kiflis : methinks the strangers must be at hand.'

'May their visit lead to no evil to them or to us !'

'Have you misgivings ?'

'We are alone among men : let us remain so.'

'You are right. I was once at Haleb (Aleppo) ; I will never willingly find myself there again.'

'Give me the mountains, the mountains of our fathers, and the beautiful things that can be seen only by one of us !'

'They are not to be found in the bazaars of Haleb ; in the gardens of Damascus they are not to be sought.'

'Oh ! who is like the Queen who reigns over us ? I know to whom she is to be compared, but I will not say ; yet you too know, my brother in arms.'

'Yes ; there are things which are not known in the bazaars of Haleb ; in the gardens of Damascus they are not to be sought.'

Karaguus, the black-eyed pigeon, brought tidings to the Queen of the Ansarey, from her agent Darkush, that two young princes, one a Syrian the other a Frank, wished to enter her territories to confer with her on grave matters, and that he had reason to believe that one of the princes, the Frank, strange, incredible as it might sound, was one of themselves. On the evening of the next day, very weary, came Rubylips, the brother of Blackeyes, with the reply of her majesty, ordering Darkush to grant the solicited pass, but limiting the permission of entrance into her dominions to the two princes and two attendants. As one of these, Baroni figured. They did not travel very rapidly. Tancred was glad to seize the occasion to visit Hameh and Aleppo on his journey.

It was after quitting the latter city, and crossing the river Koweik, that they approached the region which was the object of their expedition. What certainly did not contribute to render their progress less difficult and dangerous, was the circumstance that war at this moment was waged between the Queen of the Ansarey and the Pacha of Aleppo. The Turkish potentate had levied tribute on some villages which owned her sway, and which, as he maintained, were not included in the ancient composition paid by the Ansarey to the Porte in full of all demands. The consequence was, that parties of the Ansarey occasionally issued from their passes and scoured the plain of Aleppo. There was also an understanding between the Ansarey and the Kurds, that, whenever any quarrel occurred between the mountaineers and the Turks, the Kurds, who resembled the inhabitants of the mountain in their general appearance, should, under the title of Ansarey, take this opportunity of ravage. Darkush, however, had given Baroni credentials to the secret agent of the Ansarey at Aleppo; and, with his instructions and assistance, the difficulties, which otherwise might have been insuperable, were overcome; and thus it was that the sentries stationed at the mouth of the black ravine, which led to the fortress palace of the Queen, were now hourly expecting the appearance of the princes.

A horseman at full gallop issued from the hills, and came bounding over the stony plain; he shouted to the sentries as he passed them, announcing the arrival of the strangers,

and continued his pace through the defile. Soon afterwards appeared the cavalcade of the princes; themselves,
their two attendants, and a party of horsemen with white
turbans and long lances.

Tancred and Fakredeen rode horses of a high race. But
great as is the pleasure of being well mounted, it was not
that circumstance alone which lit up their eyes with even
unwonted fire, and tinged their cheeks with a triumphant
glow. Their expedition had been delightful; full of adventure, novelty, and suspense. They had encountered
difficulties and they had overcome them. They had a great
purpose, they were on the eve of a stirring incident. They
were young, daring, and brilliant.

'A strong position,' said Tancred, as they entered the defile.

'O! my Tancred, what things we have seen together!'
exclaimed Fakredeen. 'And what is to follow!'

The defile was not long, and it was almost unbending.
It terminated in a table-land of very limited extent, bounded
by a rocky chain, on one of the front and more moderate
elevations of which was the appearance of an extensive
fortification; though, as the travellers approached it, they
perceived that, in many instances, art had only availed itself
of the natural advantages of the position, and that the
towers and turrets were carved out of the living rock
which formed the impregnable bulwarks and escarpments.

The cavalcade, at a quick pace, soon gained the ascending and winding road that conducted them to a tall and
massy gateway, the top of which was formed of one prodigious stone. The iron portal opening displayed a covered
way cut out of the rock, and broad enough to permit the
entrance of two horsemen abreast. This way was of considerable length, and so dark that they were obliged to be
preceded by torch-bearers. Thence they issued into a
large courtyard, the sunshine of which was startling and
almost painful, after their late passage. The court was
surrounded by buildings of different styles and proportions;
the further end, and, as it were, centre of the whole, being

a broad, square, and stunted brick tower, immediately behind which rose the granite peaks of the mountains.

There were some horsemen in the court, and many
attendants on foot, who came forward and assisted the
guests to alight. Tancred and Fakredeen did not speak, but
exchanged glances which expressed their secret thoughts.
Perhaps they were of the same opinion as Baroni, that,
difficult as it was to arrive there, it might not be more easy
to return. However, God is great! a consolatory truth
that had sustained Baroni under many trials.

They were ushered into a pavilion at the side of the
court, and thence into a commodious divan, which opened
upon another and smaller court, in which were some acacia
trees. As usual, pipes and coffee were brought. Baroni
was outside, with the other attendant, stowing away the
luggage. A man plainly but neatly dressed, slender and
wrinkled, with a stooping gait but a glittering eye, came
into the chamber, and, in a hushed voice, with many smiles,
much humility, but the lurking air of a master, welcomed
them to Gindarics. Then, seating himself on the divan, he
clapped his hands, and an attendant brought him his nargilly.

' I presume,' said Tancred, ' that the Emir and myself
have the honour of conversing with the Lord Keferinis.'
Thus he addressed this celebrated eunuch, who is prime
minister of the Queen of the Ansarey.

' The Prince of England,' replied Keferinis, bowing, and
speaking in a very affected voice and in a very affected
manner, ' must not expect the luxuries of the world amid
these mountains. Born in London, which is surrounded
by the sea, and with an immense slave population at your
command, you have advantages with which the Ansarey
cannot compete, unjustly deprived, as they have been, of
their port; and unable, in the present diminished supply of
the markets, to purchase slaves as heretofore from the
Turkomans and the Kurds.'

' I suppose the Russians interfere with your markets ? '
said Fakredeen.

'The noble Emir of the Lebanon has expressed himself with infinite exactitude,' said Keferinis. 'The Russians now entirely stock their hareems from the north of Asia.'

'The Lord Keferinis has been a great traveller, I apprehend?' said Tancred

'The Prince of England has expressed himself with extreme exactitude, and with flattering grace,' replied Keferinis. 'I have indeed visited all the Syrian cities, except Jerusalem, which no one wishes to see, and which,' he added, in a sweet calm tone, 'is unquestionably a place fit only for hogs.'

Tancred started, but repressed himself.

'Have you been in Lebanon?' asked Fakredeen.

'Noble Emir, I have been the guest of princes of your illustrious house. Conversations have passed between me and the Emir Bescheer,' he added, with a significant look. 'Perhaps, had events happened which did not occur, the great Emir Bescheer might not at this moment have been a prisoner at Stambool, among those who, with infinite exactitude, may be described as the most obscene sons of very intolerable barbarians.'

'And why did not you and the Emir Bescheer agree?' inquired Fakredeen, eagerly. 'Why has there never been a right understanding between your people and the house of Shehaab? United, we should not only command Syria, but we might do more: we might control Asia itself!'

'The noble Emir has expressed himself with inexpressible grace. The power of the Ansarey cannot be too highly estimated!'

'Is it true that your sovereign can bring five and twenty thousand men into the field?' asked Tancred.

'Five and twenty thousand men,' replied Keferinis, with insinuating courtesy, 'each of whom could beat nine Maronites, and consequently three Druses.'

'Five and twenty thousand figs for your five and twenty thousand men!' exclaimed Fakredeen, laughing.

At this moment entered four pages and four maidens

and persons comparatively of little interest and importance.

After their audience, they lined with the minister, not
exactly in the manner of Downing Street, nor even with
the comparative luxury of Canobia; but the meal was an
incident, and therefore agreeable. A good pilaff was more
acceptable than some partridges dressed with oil and honey :
but all Easterns are temperate, and travel teaches abstinence
to the Franks. Neither Fakredeen nor Tancred were men
who criticised a meal : bread, rice, and coffee, a bird or a
fish, easily satisfied them. The Emir affected the Moslem
when the minister offered him the wine of the mountains,
which was harsh and rough after the delicious Vino d'Oro
of Lebanon ; but Tancred contrived to drink the health
of Queen Astarte without any wry expression of countenance.

'I believe,' said Keferinis, 'that the English, in their
island of London, drink only to women ; the other natives
of Franguestan chiefly pledge men ; we look upon both as
barbarous.'

'At any rate, you worship the god of wine,' remarked
Tancred, who never attempted to correct the self-complacent minister. 'I observed to-day the statue of Bacchus.'

'Bacchus !' said Keferinis, with a smile, half of inquiry,
half of commiseration. 'Bacchus : an English name, I
apprehend ! All our gods came from the ancient Antakia
before either the Turks or the English were heard of.
Their real names are in every respect sacred ; nor will they
be uttered, even to the Ansarey, until after the divine
initiation has been performed in the perfectly admirable
and inexpressibly delightful mysteries,' which meant, in
simpler tongue, that Keferinis was entirely ignorant of the
subject on which he was talking.

After their meal, Keferinis, proposing that in the course
of the day they should fly one of the Queen's hawks, left
them, when the conversation, of which we have given a
snatch, occurred. Yet, as we have observed, they were

on the whole moody and unusually silent.   Fakredeen in particular was wrapt in reverie, and when he spoke, it was always in reference to the singular spectacle of the morning.   His musing forced him to inquiry, having never before heard of the Olympian hierarchy, nor of the woods of Daphne, nor of the bright lord of the silver bow.

Why were they moody and silent ?

With regard to Lord Montacute, the events of the morning might sufficiently account for the gravity of his demeanour, for he was naturally of a thoughtful and brooding temperament.   This unexpected introduction to Olympus was suggestive of many reflections to one so habituated to muse over divine influences.   Nor need it be denied that the character of the Queen greatly interested him.   Her mind was already attuned to heavenly thoughts.   She already believed that she was fulfilling a sacred mission. Tancred could not be blind to the importance of such a personage as Astarte in the great drama of divine regeneration, which was constantly present to his consideration. Her conversion might be as weighty as ten victories.   He was not insensible to the efficacy of feminine influence in the dissemination of religious truth, nor unaware how much the greatest development of the Arabian creeds, in which the Almighty himself deigned to become a personal actor, was assisted by the sacred spell of woman.   It is not the Empress Helene alone who has rivalled, or rather surpassed, the exploits of the most illustrious apostles.   The three great empires of the age, France, England, and Russia, are indebted for their Christianity to female lips. We all remember the salutary influence of Clotilde and Bertha which bore the traditions of the Jordan to the Seine and the Thames : it should not be forgotten that to the fortunate alliance of Waldimir, the Duke of Moscovy, with the sister of the Greek Emperor Basil, is to be ascribed the remarkable circumstance, that the intellectual development of all the Russias has been conducted on Arabian principles.   It was the fair Giselle, worthy successor of the soft-hearted women of Galilee, herself the sister of the Emperor Henry the Second, who opened the mind of her husband, the King of Hungary, to the deep wisdom of the Hebrews, to the laws of Moses and the precepts of Jesus. Poland also found an apostle and a queen in the sister of the Duke of Bohemia, and who revealed to the Sarmatian Micislas the ennobling mysteries of Sinai and of Calvary.

Sons of Israel, when you recollect that you created Christendom, you may pardon the Christians even their Autos da Fè !

Fakredeen Shehaab, Emir of Canobia, and lineal descendant of the standard-bearer of the Prophet, had not such faith in Arabian principles as to dream of converting the Queen of the Ansarey. Quite the reverse; the Queen of the Ansarey had converted him. From the first moment he beheld Astarte, she had exercised over him that magnetic influence of which he was peculiarly susceptible, and by which Tancred at once attracted and controlled him. But Astarte added to this influence a power to which the Easterns in general do not very easily bow, the influence of sex. With the exception of Eva, woman had never guided the spirit or moulded the career of Fakredeen; and, in her instance, the sovereignty had been somewhat impaired by that acquaintance of the cradle, which has a tendency to enfeeble the ideal, though it may strengthen the affections. But Astarte rose upon him commanding and complete, a star whose gradual formation he had not watched, and whose unexpected brilliancy might therefore be more striking even than the superior splendour which he had habitually contemplated. Young, beautiful, queenly, impassioned, and eloquent, surrounded by the accessories that influence the imagination, and invested with fascinating mystery, Fakredeen, silent and enchanted, had yielded his spirit to Astarte, even before she revealed to his unaccustomed and astonished mind the godlike forms of her antique theogony.

Eva and Tancred had talked to him of gods; Astarte
had shown them to him. All visible images of their
boasted divinities of Sinai and of Calvary with which he
was acquainted were enshrined over the altars of the convents of Lebanon. He contrasted those representations
without beauty or grace, so mean, and mournful, and
spiritless, or if endued with attributes of power, more
menacing than majestic, and morose rather than sublime,
with those shapes of symmetry, those visages of immortal
beauty, serene yet full of sentiment, on which he had
gazed that morning with a holy rapture. The Queen had
said that, besides Mount Sinai and Mount Calvary, there
was also Mount Olympus. It was true; even Tancred had
not challenged her assertion. And the legends of Olympus
were as old as, nay, older than, those of the convent or the
mosques.

This was no mythic fantasy of the beautiful Astarte; the
fond tradition of a family, a race, even a nation. These
were not the gods merely of the mountains: they had
been, as they deserved to be, the gods of a great world, of
great nations, and of great men. They were the gods of
Alexander and of Caius Julius; they were the gods under
whose divine administration Asia had been powerful, rich,
luxurious and happy. They were the gods who had
covered the coasts and plains with magnificent cities,
crowded the midland ocean with golden galleys, and filled
the provinces that were now a chain of wilderness and
desert with teeming and thriving millions. No wonder
the Ansarey were faithful to such deities. The marvel was
why men should ever have deserted them. But man had
deserted them, and man was unhappy. All; Eva, Tancred,
his own consciousness, the surrounding spectacles of his
life, assured him that man was unhappy; degraded, or discontented; at all events, miserable. He was not surprised
that a Syrian should be unhappy, even a Syrian prince, for
he had no career; he was not surprised that the Jews were
unhappy, because they were the most persecuted of the

human race, and, in all probability, very justly so, for such an exception as Eva proved nothing; but here was an Englishman, young, noble, very rich, with every advantage of nature and fortune, and he had come out to Syria to tell them that all Europe was as miserable as themselves. What if their misery had been caused by their deserting those divinities who had once made them so happy.

A great question; Fakredeen indulged in endless combinations while he smoked countless nargillies. If religion were to cure the world, suppose they tried this ancient and once popular faith, so very popular in Syria. The Queen of the Ansarey could command five and twenty thousand approved warriors, and the Emir of the Lebanon could summon a host, if not as disciplined, far more numerous. Fakredeen, in a frenzy of reverie, became each moment more practical. Asian supremacy, cosmopolitan regeneration, and theocratic equality, all gradually disappeared. An independent Syrian kingdom, framed and guarded by a hundred thousand sabres, rose up before him; an established Olympian religion, which the Druses, at his instigation, would embrace, and toleration for the Maronites till he could bribe Bishop Nicodemus to arrange a general conformity, and convert his great principal from the Patriarch into the Pontiff of Antioch. The Jews might remain, provided they negotiated a loan which should consolidate the Olympian institutions and establish the Gentile dynasty of Fakredeen and Astarte.

CHAPTER V.

WHEN Fakredeen bade Tancred as usual good night, his voice was different from its accustomed tones; he had replied to Tancred with asperity several times during the evening; and when he was separated from his companion, he felt relieved. All unconscious of these changes and symptoms was the heir of Bellamont. Though grave, one indeed who never laughed and seldom smiled, Tancred was blessed with the rarest of all virtues, a singularly sweet temper. He was grave, because he was always thinking, and thinking of great deeds. But his heart was soft, and his nature most kind, and remarkably regardful of the feelings of others. To wound them, however unintentionally, would occasion him painful disturbance. Though naturally rapid in the perception of character, his inexperience of life, and the self-examination in which he was so frequently absorbed, tended to blunt a little his observation of others. With a generous failing, which is not uncommon, he was prepared to give those whom he loved credit for the virtues which he himself possessed, and the sentiments which he himself extended to them. Being profound, stedfast, and most loyal in his feelings, he was incapable of suspecting that his elected friend could entertain sentiments towards him less deep, less earnest, and less faithful. The change in the demeanour of the Emir was, therefore, unnoticed by him. And what might be called the sullen irritability of Fakredeen was encountered with the usual gentleness and total disregard of self which always distinguished the behaviour of Lord Montacute.

The next morning they were invited by Astarte to a hawking party, and, leaving the rugged ravines, they descended into a softer and more cultivated country, where they found good sport. Fakredeen was an accomplished falconer, and loved to display his skill before the Queen. Tancred was quite unpractised, but Astarte seemed resolved that he should become experienced in the craft among her mountains, which did not please the Emir, as he caracoled in sumptuous dress on a splendid steed, with the superb falcon resting on his wrist.

The princes dined again with Keferinis; that, indeed, was to be their custom during their stay; afterwards, accompanied by the minister, they repaired to the royal divan, where they had received a general invitation. Here they found Astarte alone, with the exception of Cypros and her companions, who worked with their spindles apart and here, on the pretext of discussing the high topics on which they had repaired to Gindarics, there was much conversation on many subjects. Thus passed one, two, and even three days; thus, in general, would their hours be occupied at Gindarics. In the morning the hawks, or a visit to some green valley, which was blessed with a stream and beds of oleander, and groves of acacia or sycamore. Fakredeen had no cause to complain of the demeanour of Astarte towards him, for it was most gracious and encouraging. Indeed, he pleased her; and she was taken, as many had been, by the ingenuous modesty, the unaffected humility, the tender and touching deference of his manner; he seemed to watch her every glance, and hang upon her every accent: his sympathy with her was perfect; he agreed with every sentiment and observation that escaped her. Blushing, boyish, unsophisticated, yet full of native grace, and evidently gifted with the most amiable disposition, it was impossible not to view with interest, and even regard, one so young and so innocent.

But while the Emir had no cause to be dissatisfied with the demeanour of Astarte to himself, he could not be unaware that her carriage to Tancred was different, and he doubted whether the difference was in his favour. He hung on the accents of Astarte, but he remarked that the Queen hung upon the accents of Tancred, who, engrossed with great ideas, and full of a great purpose, was unconscious of what did not escape the lynx-like glance of his companion. However, Fakredeen was not, under any circumstances, easily disheartened; in the present case, there were many circumstances to encourage him. This was a great situation; there was room for combinations. He felt that he was not unfavoured by Astarte; he had confidence, and a just confidence, in his power of fascination. He had to combat a rival, who was, perhaps, not thinking of conquest; at any rate, who was unconscious of success. Even had he the advantage, which Fakredeen was not now disposed to admit, he might surely be baffled by a competitor with a purpose, devoting his whole intelligence to his object, and hesitating at no means to accomplish it.

Fakredeen became great friends with Keferinis. He gave up his time and attentions much to that great personage; anointed him with the most delicious flattery, most dexterously applied; consulted him on great affairs which had no existence; took his advice on conjunctures which never could occur; assured Keferinis that, in his youth, the Emir Bescheer had impressed on him the importance of cultivating the friendly feelings, and obtaining the support of the distinguished minister of the Ansarey; gave him some jewels, and made him enormous promises.

On the fourth day of the visit, Fakredeen found himself alone with Astarte, at least, without the presence of Tancred, whom Keferinis had detained in his progress to the royal apartment. The young Emir had pushed on, and gained an opportunity which he had long desired.

They were speaking of the Lebanon; Fakredeen had been giving Astarte, at her request, a sketch of Canobia, and intimating his inexpressible gratification were she to honour his castle with a visit; when, somewhat abruptly, in a suppressed voice, and in a manner not wholly free from embarrassment, Astarte said, 'What ever surprises me is, that Darkush, who is my servant at Damascus, should have communicated, by the faithful messenger, that one of the princes seeking to visit Gindarics was of our beautiful and ancient faith; for the Prince of England has assured me, that nothing was more unfounded or indeed impossible; that the faith, ancient and beautiful, never prevailed in the land of his fathers; and that the reason why he was acquainted with the god-like forms is, that in his country it is the custom (custom to me most singular, and indeed incomprehensible) to educate the youth by teaching them the ancient poems of the Greeks, poems quite lost to us, but in which are embalmed the sacred legends.'

'We ought never to be surprised at anything that is done by the English,' observed Fakredeen; 'who are, after all, in a

certain sense, savages. Their country produces nothing;
it is an island, a mere rock, larger than Malta, but not so
well fortified. Everything they require is imported from
other countries; they get their corn from Odessa, and their
wine from the ports of Spain. I have been assured at
Beiroot that they do not grow even their own cotton, but that
I can hardly believe. Even their religion is an exotic; and as
they are indebted for that to Syria, it is not surprising that
they should import their education from Greece.'

'Poor people!' exclaimed the Queen; 'and yet they travel;
they wish to improve themselves?'

'Darkush, however,' continued Fakredeen, without noticing the last observation of Astarte, 'was not wrongly
informed.'

'Not wrongly informed?'

'No: one of the princes who wished to visit Gindarics
was, in a certain sense, of the ancient and beautiful faith,
but it was not the Prince of the English.'

'What are these pigeons that you are flying without
letters!' exclaimed Astarte, looking very perplexed.

'Ah! beautiful Astarte,' said Fakredeen, with a sigh;
'you did not know my mother.'

'How should I know your mother, Emir of the castles of
Lebanon? Have I ever left these mountains, which are
dearer to me than the pyramids of Egypt to the great Pacha?
Have I ever looked upon your women, Maronite or Druse,
walking in white sheets, as if they were the children of ten
thousand Ghouls; with horns on their heads, as if they were
the wild horses of the Desert?'

'Ask Keferinis,' said Fakredeen, still sighing; 'he has
been at Bteddeen, the court of the Emir Bescheer. He
knew my mother, at least by memory. My mother, beautiful
Astarte, was an Ansarey.'

'Your mother was an Ansarey!' repeated Astarte, in a
tone of infinite surprise; 'your mother an Ansarey? Of
what family was she a child?'

'Ah!' replied Fakredeen, 'there it is; that is the secret

sorrow of my life. A mystery hangs over my mother, for I lost both my parents in extreme childhood; I was at her heart,' he added, in a broken voice, 'and amid outrage, tumult, and war. Of whom was my mother the child? I am here to discover that, if possible. Her race and her beautiful religion have been the dream of my life. All I have prayed for has been to recognise her kindred and to behold her gods.'

'It is very interesting,' murmured the Queen.

'It is more than interesting,' sighed Fakredeen. Ah! beautiful Astarte! if you knew all, if you could form even the most remote idea of what I have suffered for this unknown faith;' and a passionate tear quivered on the radiant cheek of the young prince.

'And yet you came here to preach the doctrines of another,' said Astarte.

'I came here to preach the doctrines of another!' replied Fakredeen, with an expression of contempt; his nostril dilated, his lip curled with scorn. 'This mad Englishman came here to preach the doctrines of another creed, and one with which, it seems to me, he has as little connection as his frigid soil has with palm trees. They produce them, I am told, in houses of glass, and they force their foreign faith in the same manner; but, though they have temples, and churches, and mosques, they confess they have no miracles; they admit that they never produced a prophet; they own that no God ever spoke to their people, or visited their land; and yet this race, so peculiarly favoured by celestial communication, aspire to be missionaries!'

'I have much misapprehended you,' said Astarte; 'I thought you were both embarked in a great cause.'

'Ah, you learnt that from Darkush!' quickly replied Fakredeen. 'You see, beautiful Astarte, that I have no personal acquaintance with Darkush. It was the intendant of my companion who was his friend; and it is through him that Darkush has learnt anything that he has communicated. The mission, the project, was not mine; but when I found my comrade had the means, which had hitherto evaded me, of reaching Gindarics, I threw no obstacles in his crotchetty course. On the contrary, I embraced the opportunity even with fervour, and, far from discouraging my friend from views to which I know he is fatally, even ridiculously, wedded, I looked forward to this expedition as the possible means of diverting his mind from some opinions, and, I might add, some influences, which I am persuaded can eventually entail upon him nothing but disappointment and disgrace.' And here Fakredeen shook his head, with that air of confidential mystery which so cleverly piques curiosity.

'Whatever may be his fate,' said Astarte, in a tone of seriousness, 'the English prince does not seem to me to be a person who could ever experience disgrace.'

'No, no,' quickly replied his faithful friend; 'of course I did not speak of personal dishonour. He is extremely proud and rash, and not in any way a practical man; but he is not a person who ever would do anything to be sent to the bagnio or the galleys. What I mean by disgrace is, that he is mixed up with transactions, and connected with persons who will damage, cheapen, in a worldly sense dishonour him, destroy all his sources of power and influence. For instance, now, in his country, in England, a Jew is never permitted to enter England; they may settle in Gibraltar, but in England, no. Well, it is perfectly well known among all those who care about these affairs, that this enterprise of his, this religious-politico-military adventure, is merely undertaken because he happens to be desperately enamoured of a Jewess at Damascus, whom he cannot carry home as his bride.'

'Enamoured of a Jewess at Damascus!' said Astarte, turning pale.

'To folly, to frenzy; she is at the bottom of the whole of this affair; she talks Cabala to him, and he Nazareny to her; and so, between them, they have invented this grand scheme, the conquest of Asia, perhaps the world, with our Syrian sabres, and we are to be rewarded for our pains by eating passover cakes.'

'What are they?'

'Festival bread of the Hebrews, made in the new moon, with the milk of he-goats.'

'What horrors!'

'What a reward for conquest!'

'Will the Queen of the English let one of her princes marry a Jewess?'

'Never; he will be beheaded, and she will be burnt alive, eventually; but, in the meantime, a great deal of mischief may occur, unless we stop it.'

'It certainly should be stopped.'

'What amuses me most in this affair,' continued Fakredeen, 'is the cool way in which this Englishman comes to us for our assistance. First, he is at Canobia, then at Gindarics; we are to do the business, and Syria is spoken of as if it were nothing. Now the fact is, Syria is the only practical feature of the case. There is no doubt that, if we were all agreed, if Lebanon and the Ansarey were to unite, we could clear Syria of the Turks, conquer the plain, and carry the whole coast in a campaign, and no one would ever interfere to disturb us. Why should they? The Turks could not, and the natives of Franguestan would not. Leave me to manage them. There is nothing in the world I so revel in as hocussing Guizot and Aberdeen. You never heard of Guizot and Aberdeen? They are the two Reis Effendis of the King of the French and the Queen of the English. I sent them an archbishop last year, one of my fellows, Archbishop Murad, who led them a pretty dance. They nearly made me King of the Lebanon, to put an end to disturbances which never existed except in the venerable Murad's representations.'

'These are strange things! Has she charms, this Jewess? Very beautiful, I suppose?'

'The Englishman vows so; he is always raving of her; talks of her in his sleep.'

'As you say, it would indeed be strange to draw our sabres for a Jewess. Is she dark or fair?'

' I think, when he writes verses to her, he always calls her a moon or a star ; that smacks nocturnal and somewhat sombre.'

' I detest the Jews ; but I have heard their women are beautiful.'

' We will banish them all from our kingdom of Syria,' said Fakredeen, looking at Astarte earnestly.

' Why, if we are to make a struggle, it should be for something.   There have been Syrian kingdoms.'

' And shall be, beauteous Queen, and you shall rule them. I believe now the dream of my life will be realised.'

' Why, what's that?'

' My mother's last aspiration, the dying legacy of her passionate soul, known only to me, and never breathed to human being until this moment.'

' Then you recollect your mother ? '

' It was my nurse, long since dead, who was the depositary of the injunction, and in due time conveyed it to me.'

' And what was it?'

' To raise, at Deir el Kamar, the capital of our district, a marble temple to the Syrian goddess.'

' Beautiful idea!'

' It would have drawn back the mountain to the ancient faith; the Druses are half-prepared, and wait only my word.'

' But the Nazareny bishops,' said the Queen, ' whom you find so useful, what will they say ? '

' What did the priests and priestesses of the Syrian goddess say, when Syria became Christian ?   They turned into bishops and nuns.   Let them turn back again.'

CHAPTER VI.

TANCRED and Fakredeen had been absent from Gindarics for two or three days, making an excursion in the neighbouring districts, and visiting several of those chieftains whose future aid might be of much importance to them.   Away from the unconscious centre of many passions and intrigues, excited by the novelty of their life, sanguine of the ultimate triumph of his manœuvres, and at times still influenced by his companion, the demeanour of the young Emir of Lebanon to his friend resumed something of its wonted softness, confidence, and complaisance. They were once more in sight of the wild palace-fort of Astarte; spurring their horses, they dashed before their attendants over the plain, and halted at the huge portal of iron, while the torches were lit, and preparations were made for the passage of the covered way.

When they entered the principal court, there were unusual appearances of some recent and considerable occurrence : groups of Turkish soldiers, disarmed, reclining camels, baggage and steeds, and many of the armed tribes of the mountain.

'What is all this?' inquired Fakredeen.

''Tis the hareem of the Pacha of Aleppo,' replied a warrior, 'captured on the plain, and carried up into the mountains to our Queen of queens.'

'The war begins,' said Fakredeen, looking round at Tancred with a glittering eye.

'Women make war on women,' he replied.

''Tis the first step,' said the Emir, dismounting; 'I care not how it comes. Women are at the bottom of everything. If it had not been for the Sultana Mother, I should have now been Prince of the Mountain.'

When they had regained their apartments the lordly Keferinis soon appeared, to offer them his congratulations on their return. The minister was peculiarly refined and mysterious this morning, especially with respect to the great event, which he involved in so much of obscurity, that, after much conversation, the travellers were as little acquainted with the occurrence as when they entered the courtyard of Gindarics.

'The capture of a pacha's hareem is not water spilt on sand, lordly Keferinis,' said the Emir. 'We shall hear more of this.'

' What we shall hear,' replied Keferinis, 'is entirely an affair of the future; nor is it in any way to be disputed, that there are few men who do not find it more difficult to foretell what is to happen than to remember what has taken place.'

' We sometimes find that memory is as rare a quality as prediction,' said Tancred.

' In England,' replied the lordly Keferinis; ' but it is never to be forgotten, and indeed, on the contrary, should be entirely recollected, that the English, being a new people, have nothing indeed which they can remember.'

Tancred bowed.

' And how is the most gracious lady, Queen of queens?' inquired Fakredeen.

' The most gracious lady, Queen of queens,' replied Keferinis, very mysteriously, ' has at this time many thoughts.'

' If she require any aid,' said Fakredeen, ' there is not a musket in Lebanon that is not at her service.'

Keferinis bent his head, and said, ' It is not in any way to be disputed that there are subjects which require for their management the application of a certain degree of force, and the noble Emir of the Lebanon has expressed himself in that sense with the most exact propriety; there are also subjects which are regulated by the application of a certain number of words, provided they are well chosen, and distinguished by an inestimable exactitude. It does not by any means follow that from what has occurred there will be sanguinary encounters between the people of the gracious lady, Queen of queens, and those that dwell in plains and cities; nor can it be denied that war is a means by which many things are brought to a final conjuncture. At the same time courtesy has many charms, even for the Turks, though it is not to be denied, or in any way concealed, that a Turk, especially if he be a pacha, is, of all obscene and utter children of the devil, the most entirely contemptible and thoroughly to be execrated.'

'If I were the Queen, I would not give up the hareem,' said Fakredeen ; 'and I would bring affairs to a crisis. The garrison at Aleppo is not strong ; they have been obliged to march six regiments to Deir el Kamar, and, though affairs are comparatively tranquil in Lebanon for the moment, let me send a pigeon to my cousin Francis El Kazin, and young Syria will get up such a stir that old Wageah Pacha will not spare a single man. I will have fifty bonfires on the mountain near Beiroot in one night, and Colonel Rose will send off a steamer to Sir Canning to tell him there is a revolt in the Lebanon, with a double despatch for Aberdeen, full of smoking villages and slaughtered women!' and the young Emir inhaled his nargilly with additional zest as he recollected the triumphs of his past mystifications.

At sunset it was announced to the travellers that the Queen would receive them. Astarte appeared much gratified by their return, was very gracious, although in a different way, to both of them, inquired much as to what they had seen and what they had done, with whom they had conversed, and what had been said. At length she observed, ' Something has also happened at Gindarics in your absence, noble princes. Last night, they brought part of the hareem of the Pacha of Aleppo captive hither. This may lead to events.'

' I have already ventured to observe to the lordly Keferinis,' said Fakredeen, ' that every lance in the Lebanon is at your command, gracious Queen.'

' We have lances,' said Astarte ; ' it is not of that I was thinking. Nor indeed do I care to prolong a quarrel for this capture. If the Pacha will renounce the tribute of the villages, I am for peace ; if he will not, we will speak of those things, of which there has been counsel between us. I do not wish this affair of the hareem to be mixed up with what has preceded it. My principal captive is a most beautiful woman, and one, too, that greatly interests and charms me. She is not a Turk, but, I apprehend, a Christian lady of the cities. She is plunged in grief, and weeps

sometimes with so much bitterness that I quite share her
sorrow; but it is not so much because she is a captive, but
because some one, who is most dear to her, has been slain
in this fray. I have visited her, and tried to console her;
and begged her to forget her grief and become my companion. But nothing soothes her, and tears flow for ever
from eyes which are the most beautiful I ever beheld.'

'This is the land of beautiful eyes,' said Tancred, and
Astarte almost unconsciously glanced at the speaker.

Cypros, who had quitted the attendant maidens immediately on the entrance of the two princes, after an interval,
returned. There was some excitement on her countenance
as she approached her mistress, and addressed Astarte in a
hushed but hurried tone. It seemed that the fair captive of
the Queen of the Ansarey had most unexpectedly expressed
to Cypros her wish to repair to the divan of the Queen,
although, the whole day, she had frequently refused to
descend. Cypros feared that the presence of the two guests
of her mistress might prove an obstacle to the fulfilment of
this wish, as the freedom of social intercourse that prevailed among the Ansarey was unknown even among the
ever-veiled women of the Maronites and Druses. But the
fair captive had no prejudices on this head, and Cypros had
accordingly descended to request the royal permission, or
consult the royal will. Astarte spoke to Keferinis, who
listened with an air of great profundity, and finally bowed
assent, and Cypros retired.

Astarte had signified to Tancred her wish that he should
approach her, while Keferinis at some distance was engaged
in earnest conversation with Fakredeen, with whom he had
not had previously the opportunity of being alone. His report of all that had transpired in his absence was highly
favourable. The minister had taken the opportunity of the
absence of the Emir and his friend to converse often and
amply about them with the Queen. The idea of an united
Syria was pleasing to the imagination of the young sovereign. The suggestion was eminently practicable. It re-

quired no extravagant combinations, no hazardous chances
of fortune, nor fine expedients of political skill. A union
between Fakredeen and Astarte at once connected the most
important interests of the mountains without exciting the
alarm or displeasure of other powers. The union was
as legitimate as it would ultimately prove irresistible. It
ensured a respectable revenue and a considerable force;
and, with prudence and vigilance, the occasion would soon
offer to achieve all the rest. On the next paroxysm in the
dissolving empire of the Ottomans, the plain would be occupied by a warlike population descending from the mountains that commanded on one side the whole Syrian coast,
and on the other all the inland cities from Aleppo to
Damascus

The eye of the young Emir glittered with triumph as he
listened to the oily sentences of the eunuch. 'Lebanon,'
he whispered, 'is the key of Syria, my Keferinis, never
forget that; and we will lock up the land. Let us never
sleep till this affair is achieved. You think she does not
dream of a certain person, eh? I tell you, he must go, or
we must get rid of him: I fear him not, but he is in the
way; and the way should be smooth as the waters of El
Arish. Remember the temple to the Syrian goddess at
Deir el Kamar, my Keferinis! The religion is half the
battle. How I shall delight to get rid of my bishops and
those accursed monks: drones, drivellers, bigots, drinking
my golden wine of Canobia, and smoking my delicate
Latakia. You know Canobia, my Keferinis; but you have
heard of it. You have been at Bteddeen? Well, Bteddeen
to Canobia is an Arab moon to a Syrian sun. The marble
alone at Canobia cost a million of piastres. The stables are
worthy of the steeds of Solomon. You may kill anything
you like in the forest, from panthers to antelopes. Listen,
my Keferinis, let this be done, and done quickly, and
Canobia is yours.'

'Do you ever dream?' said Astarte to Tancred.

'They say that life is a dream.'

'I sometimes wish it were. Its pangs are too acute for a shadow.'

'But you have no pangs.'

'I had a dream when you were away, in which I was much alarmed,' said Astarte.

'Indeed!'

'I thought that Gindarics was taken by the Jews. I suppose you have talked of them to me so much that my slumbering memory wandered.'

'It is a resistless and exhaustless theme,' said Tancred; 'for the greatness and happiness of everything, Gindarics included, are comprised in the principles of which they were the first propagators.'

'Nevertheless, I should be sorry if my dream came to be true,' said Astarte.

'May your dreams be as bright and happy as your lot, royal lady!' said Tancred.

'My lot is not bright and happy,' said the Queen; 'once I thought it was, but I think so no longer.'

'But why?'

'I wish you could have a dream and find out,' said the Queen. 'Disquietude is sometimes as perplexing as pleasure. Both come and go like birds.'

'Like the pigeon you sent to Damascus,' said Tancred.

'Ah! why did I send it?'

'Because you were most gracious, lady.'

'Because I was very rash, noble prince.'

'When the great deeds are done to which this visit will lead, you will not think so.'

'I am not born for great deeds; I am a woman, and I am content with beautiful ones.'

'You still dream of the Syrian goddess,' said Tancred.

'No; not of the Syrian goddess. Tell me: they say the Hebrew women are very lovely, is it so?'

'They have that reputation.'

'But do you think so!'

'I have known some distinguished for their beauty'

'Do they resemble the statue in our temple?'

'Their style is different,' said Tancred; 'the Greek and the Hebrew are both among the highest types of the human form.'

'But you prefer the Hebrew?'

'I am not so discriminating a critic,' said Tancred; 'I admire the beautiful.'

'Well, here comes my captive,' said the Queen; 'if you like, you shall free her, for she wonderfully takes me. She is a Georgian, I suppose, and bears the palm from all of us. I will not presume to contend with her: she would vanquish, perhaps, even that fair Jewess of whom, I hear, you are so enamoured.'

Tancred started, and would have replied, but Cypros advanced at this moment with her charge, who withdrew her veil as she seated herself, as commanded, before the Queen. She withdrew her veil, and Fakredeen and Tancred beheld EVA!

CHAPTER VII.

IN one of a series of chambers excavated in the mountains, yet connected with the more artificial portion of the palace, chambers and galleries which in the course of ages had served for many purposes, sometimes of security, sometimes of punishment; treasuries not unfrequently, and occasionally prisons; in one of these vast cells, feebly illumined from apertures above, lying on a rude couch with her countenance hidden, motionless and miserable, was the beautiful daughter of Besso, one who had been bred in all the delights of the most refined luxury, and in the enjoyment of a freedom not common in any land, and most rare among the Easterns.

The events of her life had been so strange and rapid during the last few days that, even amid her woe, she revolved in her mind their startling import. It was little more than ten days since, under the guardianship of her father, she had commenced her journey from Damascus to Aleppo. When they had proceeded about half way, they were met at the city of Homs by a detachment of Turkish soldiers, sent by the Pacha of Aleppo, at the request of Hillel Besso, to escort them, the country being much troubled in consequence of the feud with the Ansarey. Notwithstanding these precautions, and although, from the advices they received, they took a circuitous and unexpected course, they were attacked by the mountaineers within half a day's journey of Aleppo; and with so much strength and spirit, that their guards, after some resistance, fled and dispersed, while Eva and her attendants, after seeing her father cut down in her defence, was carried a prisoner to Gindarics.

Overwhelmed by the fate of her father, she was at first insensible to her own, and was indeed so distracted that she delivered herself up to despair. She was beginning in some degree to collect her senses, and to survey her position with some comparative calmness, when she learnt from the visit of Cypros that Fakredeen and Tancred were, by a strange coincidence, under the same roof as herself. Then she recalled the kind sympathy and offers of consolation that had been evinced and proffered to her by the mistress of the castle, to whose expressions at the time she had paid but an imperfect attention. Under these circumstances she earnestly requested permission to avail herself of a privilege, which had been previously offered and refused, to become the companion, rather than the captive of the Queen of the Ansarey; so that she might find some opportunity of communicating with her two friends, of inquiring about her father, and of consulting with them as to the best steps to be adopted in her present exigency.

The interview, from which so much was anticipated, had turned out as strange and as distressful as any of the recent incidents to which it was to have brought balm and solace. Recognised instantly by Tancred and the young Emir, and greeted with a tender respect, almost equal to the surprise and sorrow which they felt at beholding her, Astarte, hitherto so unexpectedly gracious to her captive, appeared suddenly agitated, excited, haughty, even hostile. The Queen had immediately summoned Fakredeen to her side, and there passed between them some hurried and perturbed explanations; subsequently she addressed some inquiries to Tancred, to which he replied without reserve. Soon afterwards, Astarte, remaining intent and moody, the court was suddenly broken up; Keferinis signifying to the young men that they should retire, while Astarte, without bestowing on them her usual farewell, rose, and, followed by her maidens, quitted the chamber. As for Eva, instead of returning to one of the royal apartments which had been previously allotted to her, she was conducted to what was in fact a prison.

There she had passed the night and a portion of the ensuing day, visited only by Cypros, who, when Eva would have inquired the cause of all this mysterious cruelty and startling contrast to the dispositions which had preceded it, only shook her head and pressed her finger to her lip, to signify the impossibility of her conversing with her captive.

It was one of those situations where the most gifted are deserted by their intelligence; where there is as little to guide as to console; where the mystery is as vast as the misfortune; and the tortured apprehension finds it impossible to grapple with irresistible circumstances.

In this state, the daughter of Besso, plunged in a dark reverie, in which the only object visible to her mind's eye was the last glance of her dying father, was roused from her approaching stupor by a sound, distinct yet muffled, as if some one wished to attract her attention, without startling her by too sudden an interruption. She looked up; again she heard the sound, and then, in a whispered tone, her name ——

'Eva!'

'I am here.'

'Hush!' said a figure, stealing into the caverned chambɔr, and then throwing off his Syrian cloak, revealing to her one whom she recognised.

'Fakredeen,' she said, starting from her couch, ' what is all this ?'

The countenance of Fakredeen was distressed and agitated ; there was an expression of alarm, almost of terror, stamped upon his features.

'You must follow me,' he said ; 'there is not a moment to lose ; you must fly !'

'Why and whither ?' said Eva. 'This capture is one of plunder not of malice, or was so a few hours back. It is not sorrow for myself that overwhelmed me. But yesterday, the sovereign of these mountains treated me with a generous sympathy, and, if it brought me no solace, it was only because events have borne, I fear, irremediable woe. And now, I suddenly find myself among my friends; friends, who, of all others, I should most have wished to encounter at this moment, and all is changed. I am a prisoner, under every circumstance of harshness, even of cruelty, and you speak to me as if my life, my immediate existence, was in peril.'

'It is.'

'But why ?'

Fakredeen wrung his hands, and murmured, 'Let us go.'

'I scarcely care to live,' said Eva ; 'and I will not move until you give me some clue to all this mystery.'

'Well, then, she is jealous of you ; the queen, Astarte ; she is jealous of you with the English prince, that man that has brought us all so many vexations.'

'Is it he that has brought us so many vexations ?' replied Eva. 'Tho Queen jealous of me, and with the English prince ! 'Tis very strange. We scarcely exchanged a dozen sentences together, when all was disturbed and broken up. Jealous of me ! Why then was she anxious that I should descend to her divan ? This is not the truth, Fakredeen.'

'Not all; but it is the truth ; it is, indeed. The Queen is jealous of you : she is in love with Tancred ; a curse be on

him and her both ! and somebody has told her that Tancred
is in love with you.'

'Somebody ! When did they tell her ? '

'Long ago ; long ago. She knew, that is, she had been
told, that Tancred was affianced to the daughter of Besso of
Damascus ; and so this sudden meeting brought about a
crisis. I did what I could to prevent it ; vowed that you
were only the cousin of the Besso that she meant ; did everything, in short, I could to serve and save you ; but it was of
no use. She was wild, is wild, and your life is in peril.'

Eva mused a moment. Then, looking up, she said, ' Fakredeen, it is you who told the Queen this story. You are
the somebody who has invented this fatal falsehood. What
was your object I care not to inquire, knowing full well,
that, if you had an object, you never would spare friend or
foe. Leave me. I have little wish to live ; but I believe in
the power of truth. I will confront the Queen and tell her
all. She will credit what I say ; if she do not, I can meet
my fate ; but I will not, now or ever, entrust it to you.'

Thereupon Fakredeen burst into a flood of passionate
tears, and, throwing himself on the ground, kissed Eva's
feet, and clung to her garments which he embraced, sob-
bing, and moaning, and bestowing on her endless phrases
of affection, mixed with imprecations on his own head and
conduct.

'O Eva ! my beloved Eva, sister of my soul, it is of no
use telling you any lies ! Yes, I am that villain and that
idiot, who has brought about all this misery, misery enough
to turn me mad, and which, by a just retribution, has destroyed all the brilliant fortunes which were at last opening
on me. This Frank stranger was the only bar to my union
with the sovereign of these mountains, whose beauty you
have witnessed, whose power, combined with my own,
would found a kingdom. I wished to marry her. You cannot be angry with me, Eva, for that. You know very well
that, if you had married me yourself, we should neither of
us have been in the horrible situation in which we now find
ourselves. Ah ! that would have been a happy union !

But let that pass. I have always been the most unfortunate of men; I have never had justice done me. Well, she loved this prince of Franguestan. I saw it; nothing escapes me. I let her know that he was devoted to another. Why I mentioned your name I cannot well say; perhaps because it was the first that occurred to me; perhaps because I have a lurking suspicion that he really does love you. The information worked. My own suit prospered. I bribed her minister. He is devoted to me. All was smiling. How could I possibly have anticipated that you would ever arrive here! When I saw you, I felt that all was lost. I endeavoured to rally affairs, but it was useless. Tancred has no finesse; his replies neutralised, nay, destroyed, all my counter representations. The Queen is a whirlwind. She is young; she has never been crossed in her life. You cannot argue with her when her heart is touched. In short, all is ruined;' and Fakredeen hid his weeping face in the robes of Eva.

'What misery you prepare for yourself, and for all who know you!' exclaimed Eva. 'But that has happened which makes me insensible to further grief.'

'Yes; but listen to what I say, and all will go right. I do not care in the least for my own disappointment. That now is nothing. It is you, it is of you only that I think, whom I wish to save. Do not chide me : pardon me, pardon me, as you have done a thousand times; pardon and pity me. I am so young and really so inexperienced; after all, I am only a child; besides, I have not a friend in the world except you. I am a villain, a fool; all villains are. I know it. But I cannot help it. I did not make myself. The question now is, How are we to get out of this scrape? How are we to save your life?'

'Do you really mean, Fakredeen, that my life is in peril?'

'Yes, I do,' said the Emir, crying like a child.

'You do not know the power of truth, Fakredeen. You have no confidence in it. Let me see the Queen.'

'Impossible!' he said, starting up, and looking very much alarmed.

'Why ?'

'Because, in the first place, she is mad. Keferinis, that is, her minister, one of my creatures, and the only person who can manage her, told me this moment that it was a perfect kamsin, and that, if he approached her again, it would be at his own risk; and, in the second place, bad as things are, they would necessarily be much worse if she saw you, because (and it is of no use concealing it any longer) she thinks you already, dead.'

'Dead! Already dead!'

'Yes.'

'And where is your friend and companion?' said Eva. 'Does he know of these horrors?'

'No one knows of them except myself. The Queen sent for me last night to speak to me of the subject generally. It was utterly vain to attempt to disabuse her; it would only have compromised all of us. She would only have supposed the truth to be an invention for the moment. I found your fate sealed. In my desperation, the only thing that occurred to me was to sympathise with her indignation and approve of all her projects. She apprised me that you should not live four-and-twenty hours. I rather stimulated her vengeance, told her in secresy that your house had nearly effected my ruin, and that there was no sacrifice I would not make, and no danger that I would not encounter, to wreak on your race my long-cherished revenge. I assured her that I had been watching my opportunity for years. Well, you see how it is, Eva; she consigned to me the commission which she would have whispered to one of her slaves. I am here with her cognisance; indeed, by this time she thinks 'tis all over. You comprehend?'

'You are to be my executioner?'

'Yes; I have undertaken that office, in order to save your life.'

'I care not to save my life. What is life to me, since he perhaps is gone who gave me that life, and for whom alone I lived!'

'O Eva! Eva! don't distract me; don't drive me abso-lutely mad! When a man is doing what I am for your sake, giving up a kingdom, and more than a kingdom, to treat him thus! But you never did me justice.' And Fa-kredeen poured forth renewed tears. 'Keferinis is in my pay; I have got the signet of the covered way. Here are two Mamlouk dresses; one you must put on. Without the gates are two good steeds, and in eight-and-forty hours we shall be safe, and smiling again.'

'I shall never smile again,' said Eva. 'No, Fakredeen,' she added, after a moment's pause, 'I will not fly, and you cannot fly. Can you leave alone in this wild place that friend, too faithful, I believe, whom you have been the means of leading hither?'

'Never mind him,' said the Emir. 'I wish we had never seen him. He is quite safe. She may keep him a prisoner perhaps. What then? He makes so discreet a use of his liberty that a little durance will not be very injurious. His life will be safe enough. Cutting off his head is not the way to gain his heart. But time presses. Come, my sister, my beloved Eva! In a few hours it may not be in my power to effect all this. Come, think of your father, of his anxiety, his grief. One glimpse of you will do him more service than the most cunning leech.'

Eva burst into passionate tears. 'He will never see us again. I saw him fall; never shall I forget that moment!' and she hid her face in her hands.

'But he lives,' said Fakredeen. 'I have been speaking to some of the Turkish prisoners. They also saw him fall; but he was borne off the field, and, though insensible, it was believed that the wound was not fatal. Trust me, he is at Aleppo.'

'They saw him borne off the field?'

'Safe, and, if not well, far from desperate.'

'O God of my fathers!' said Eva, falling on her knees; 'thine is indeed a mercy-seat!'

'Yes, yes; there is nothing like the God of your fathers,

Eva. If you knew the things that are going on in this place, even in these vaults and caverns, you would not tarry here an instant. They worship nothing but graven images, and the Queen has fallen in love with Tancred, because he resembles a marble statue older than the times of the pre-Adamite Sultauns. Come, come!'

'But how could they know that he was far from desperate?'

'I will show you the man who spoke to him,' said Fakredeen; 'he is only with our horses. You can ask him any questions you like. Come, put on your Mamlouk dress, every minute is golden.'

'There seems to me something base in leaving him here alone,' said Eva. 'He has eaten our salt, he is the child of our tents, his blood will be upon our heads.'

'Well, then, fly for his sake,' said Fakredeen; 'here you cannot aid him; but when you are once in safety, a thousand things may be done for his assistance. I could return, for example.'

'Now, Fakredeen,' said Eva, stopping him, and speaking in a solemn tone, 'if I accompany you, as you now require, will you pledge me your word, that the moment we pass the frontier you will return to him.'

'I swear it, by our true religion, and by my hopes of an earthly crown.'

CHAPTER VIII.

THE sudden apparition of Eva at Gindarics, and the scene of painful mystery by which it was followed, had plunged Tancred into the greatest anxiety and affliction. It was in vain that, the moment they had quitted the presence of Astarte, he appealed to Fakredeen for some explanation of what had occurred, and for some counsel as to the course they should immediately pursue to assist one in whose fate they were both so deeply interested. The Emir, for the first time since their acquaintance, seemed entirely to have lost himself. He looked perplexed, almost stunned; his language was incoherent, his gestures those of despair. Tancred, while he at once ascribed all this confused demeanour to the shock which he had himself shared at finding the daughter of Besso a captive, and a captive under circumstances of doubt and difficulty, could not reconcile such distraction, such an absence of all resources and presence of mind, with the exuberant means and the prompt expedients which in general were the characteristics of his companion, under circumstances the most difficult and unforeseen.

When they had reached their apartments, Fakredeen threw himself upon the divan and moaned, and, suddenly starting from the couch, paced the chamber with agitated step wringing his hands. All that Tancred could extract from him was an exclamation of despair, an imprecation on his own head, and an expression of fear and horror at Eva having fallen into the hands of pagans and idolaters.

It was in vain also that Tancred endeavoured to communicate with Keferinis. The minister was invisible, not to be found, and the night closed in, when Tancred, after fruitless counsels with Baroni, and many united but vain efforts to open some communication with Eva, delivered himself not to repose, but to a distracted reverie over the present harassing and critical affairs.

When the dawn broke, he rose and sought Fakredeen, but, to his surprise, he found that his companion had already quitted his apartment. An unusual stillness seemed to pervade Gindarics this day; not a person was visible. Usually at sunrise all were astir, and shortly afterwards Keferinis generally paid a visit to the guests of his sovereign; but this day Keferinis omitted the ceremony, and Tancred, never more anxious for companions and counsellors, found himself entirely alone; for Baroni was about making observations, and endeavouring to find some clue to the position of Eva.

Tancred had resolved, the moment that it was practicable, to solicit an audience of Astarte on the subject of Eva, and to enter into all the representations respecting her, which, in his opinion, were alone necessary to secure for her immediately the most considerate treatment, and ultimately a courteous release.   The very circumstance that she was united to the Emir of Canobia by ties so dear and intimate, and was also an individual to whom he himself was indebted for such generous aid and such invaluable services, would, he of course assumed, independently of her own interesting personal qualities, enlist the kind feelings of Astarte in her favour.   The difficulty was to obtain this audience of Astarte, for neither Fakredeen nor Keferinis was to be found, and no other means of achieving the result were obvious.

About two hours before noon, Baroni brought word that he had contrived to see Cypros, from whom he gathered that Astarte had repaired to the great temple of the gods.   Instantly, Tancred resolved to enter the palace, and if possible to find his way to the mysterious sanctuary.   That was a course by no means easy; but the enterprising are often fortunate, and his project proved not to be impossible.   He passed through the chambers of the palace, which were entirely deserted, and with which he was familiar, and he reached without difficulty the portal of bronze, which led to the covered way that conducted to the temple, but it was closed. Baffled and almost in despair, a distant chorus reached his ear, then the tramp of feet, and then slowly the portal opened. He imagined that the Queen was returning; but, on the contrary, pages and women and priests swept by without observing him, for he was hidden by one of the opened valves, but Astarte was not there ; and, though the venture was rash, Tancred did not hesitate, as the last individual in the procession moved on, to pass the gate.   The portal shut instantly with a clang, and Tancred found himself alone and in comparative darkness. His previous experience, however, sustained him.   His eye, fresh from the sunlight, at first wandered in obscurity, but by degrees, habituated to the atmosphere, though dim, the way was sufficiently indicated, and he advanced, till the light became each step more powerful, and soon he emerged upon the platform, which faced the mountain temple at the end of the ravine: a still and wondrous scene, more striking now, if possible, when viewed alone, with his heart the prey of many emotions. How full of adventure is life! It is monotonous only to the monotonous. There may be no longer fiery dragons, magic rings, or fairy wands, to interfere in its course and to influence our career; but the relations of men are far more complicated and numerous than of yore; and in the play of the passions, and in the devices of creative spirits, that have thus a proportionately greater sphere for their action, there are spells of social sorcery more potent than all the necromancy of Merlin or Friar Bacon.

Tancred entered the temple, the last refuge of the Olympian mind. It was race that produced these inimitable forms, the idealised reflex of their own peculiar organisation. Their principles of art, practised by a different race, do not produce the same results. Yet we shut our eyes to the great truth into which all truths merge, and we call upon the Pict, or the Sarmatian, to produce the forms of Phidias and Praxiteles.

Not devoid of that awe which is caused by the presence of the solemn and the beautiful, Tancred slowly traced his steps through the cavern sanctuary. No human being was visible. Upon his right was the fane to which Astarte led him on his visit of initiation. He was about to enter it, when, kneeling before the form of the Apollo of Antioch, he beheld the fair Queen of the Ansarey, motionless and speechless, her arms crossed upon her breast, and her eyes fixed upon her divinity, in a dream of ecstatic devotion.

The splendour of the ascending sun fell full upon the statue, suffusing the ethereal form with radiancy, and spreading around it for some space a broad and golden halo. As Tancred, recognising the Queen, withdrew a few paces, his shadow, clearly defined, rested on the glowing wall of the

rook temple. Astarte uttered an exclamation, rose quickly
from her kneeling position, and, looking round, her eyes
met those of Lord Montacute. Instantly she withdrew her
gaze, blushing deeply.

'I was about to retire,' murmured Tancred.

'And why should you retire ?' said Astarte, in a soft voice,
looking up.

'There are moments when solitude is sacred.'

'I am too much alone : often, and of late especially, I feel
a painful isolation.'

She moved forward, and they re-entered together the chief
temple, and then emerged into the sunlight. They stood
beneath the broad Ionic portico, beholding the strange scene
around. Then it was that Tancred, observing that Astarte
cared not to advance, and deeming the occasion very favour
able to his wishes, proceeded to explain to her the cause of
his venturing to intrude on her this morning. He spoke
with that earnestness, and, if the phrase may be used, that
passionate repose, which distinguished him. He enlarged
on the character of Besso, his great virtues, his amiable
qualities, his benevolence and unbounded generosity; he
sought in every way to engage the kind feelings of Astarte
in favour of his family, and to interest her in the character
of Eva, on which he dilated with all the eloquence of his
heart. Truly, he almost did justice to her admirable qualities, her vivid mind, and lofty spirit, and heroic courage ;
the occasion was too delicate to treat of the personal charms
of another woman, but he did not conceal his own deep
sense of obligation to Eva for her romantic expedition to the
Desert on his behalf.

'You can understand then,' concluded Tancred, 'what
must have been my astonishment and grief when I found
her yesterday a captive. It was some consolation to me to
remember in whose power she had fallen, and I hasten to
throw myself at your feet to supplicate for her safety and
her freedom.'

'Yes, I can understand all this,' said Astarte, in a low tone.

Tancred looked at her. Her voice had struck him with pain; her countenance still more distressed him. Nothing could afford a more complete contrast to the soft and glowing visage that a few moments before he had beheld in the fane of Apollo. She was quite pale, almost livid; her features, of exquisite shape, had become hard and even distorted; all the bad passions of our nature seemed suddenly to have concentred in that face which usually combined perfect beauty of form with an expression the most gentle, and in truth most lovely.

'Yes, I can understand all this,' said Astarte, 'but I shall not exercise any power which I may possess to assist you in violating the laws of your country, and outraging the wishes of your sovereign.'

'Violating the laws of my country!' exclaimed Tancred, with a perplexed look.

'Yes, I know all. Your schemes truly are very heroic and very flattering to our self-love. We are to lend our lances to place on the throne of Syria one who would not be permitted to reside in your own country, much less to rule in it?'

'Of whom, of what, do you speak?'

'I speak of the Jewess whom you would marry,' said Astarte, in a hushed yet distinct voice, and with a fell glance, 'against all laws, divine and human.'

'Of your prisoner?'

'Well you may call her my prisoner; she is secure.'

'Is it possible you can believe that I even am a suitor of the daughter of Besso?' said Tancred, earnestly. 'I wear the Cross, which is graven on my heart, and have a heavenly mission to fulfil, from which no earthly thought shall ever distract me. But even were I more than sensible to her charms and virtues, she is affianced, or the same as affianced; nor have I the least reason to suppose that he who will possess her hand does not command her heart.'

'Affianced?'

'Not only affianced, but, until this sad adventure, on the

very point of being wedded. She was on her way from Damascus to Aleppo, to be united to her cousin, when she was brought hither, where she will, I trust, not long remain your prisoner.'

The countenance of Astarte changed , but, though it lost its painful and vindictive expression, it did not assume one of less distress. After a moment's pause, she murmured, ' Can this be true ? '

' Who could have told you otherwise ? '

' An enemy of hers, of her family,' continued Astarte, in a low voice, and speaking as if absorbed in thought; ' one who admitted to me his long-hoarded vengeance against her house.'

Then turning abruptly, she looked Tancred full in the face, with a glance of almost fierce scrutiny. His clear brow and unfaltering eye, with an expression of sympathy and even kindness on his countenance, met her searching look.

' No,' she said ; ' it is impossible that you can be false.'

' Why should I be false ? or what is it that mixes up my name and life with these thoughts and circumstances ? '

' Why should you be false ! Ah ! there it is,' said Astarte, in a sweet and mournful voice. ' What are any of us to you ! ' And she wept.

' It grieves me to see you in sorrow,' said Tancred, approaching her, and speaking in a tone of kindness.

' I am more than sorrowful : this unhappy lady ——' and the voice of Astarte was overpowered by her emotion.

' You will send her back in safety and with honour to her family,' said Tancred, soothingly. ' I would fain believe her father has not fallen. My intendant assures me that there are Turkish soldiers here who saw him borne from the field. A little time, and their griefs will vanish. You will have the satisfaction of having acted with generosity, with that good heart which characterises you ; and as for the daughter of Besso, all will be forgotten as she gives one hand to her father and the other to her husband.'

' It is too late,' said Astarte in an almost sepulchral voice.

' What is that ? '

' It is too late!   The daughter of Besso is no more.'

' Jesu preserve us!' exclaimed Tancred, starting. ' Speak it again : what is it that you say ? '

Astarte shook her head.

'Woman!' said Tancred, and he seized her hand, but his thoughts were too wild for utterance, and he remained pallid and panting.

' The daughter of Besso is no more ; and I do not lament it, for you loved her.'

' Oh, grief ineffable ! ' said Tancred, with a groan, looking up to heaven, and covering his face with his hands : ' I loved her, as I loved the stars and sunshine.' Then, after a pause, he turned to Astarte, and said, in a rapid voice, ' This dreadful deed ; when, how, did it happen ? '

' Is it so dreadful ? '

' Almost as dreadful as such words from woman's lips. A curse be on the hour that I entered these walls ! '

'No, no, no! ' said Astarte, and she seized his arm distractedly. ' No, no !   No curse ! '

' It is not true ! ' said Tancred. ' It cannot be true ! She is not dead.'

' Would she were not, if her death is to bring me curses.'

' Tell me when was this ? '

' An hour ago, at least.'

' I do not believe it.   There is not an arm that would have dared to touch her.   Let us hasten to her.   It is not too late.'

' Alas! it is too late,' said Astarte. ' It was an enemy's arm that undertook the deed.'

' An enemy !   What enemy among your people could the daughter of Besso have found ? '

' A deadly one, who seized the occasion offered to a long cherished vengeance ; one who for years has been alike the foe and the victim of her race and house.   There is no hope!'

' I am indeed amazed.   Who could this be ? '

'Your friend; at least, your supposed friend, the Emir of the Lebanon.'

'Fakredeen?'

'You have said it.'

'The assassin and the foe of Eva!' exclaimed Tancred, with a countenance relieved yet infinitely perplexed. 'There must be some great misconception in all this. Let us hasten to the castle.'

'He solicited the office,' said Astarte; 'he wreaked his vengeance, while he vindicated my outraged feelings.'

'By murdering his dearest friend, the only being to whom he is really devoted, his more than friend, his foster-sister, nursed by the same heart; the ally and inspiration of his life, to whom he himself was a suitor, and might have been a successful one, had it not been for the custom of her religion and her race, which shrink from any connection with strangers and with Nazarenes.'

'His foster-sister!' exclaimed Astarte.

At this moment Cypros appeared in the distance, hastening to Astarte with an agitated air. Her looks were disturbed; she was almost breathless when she reached them; she wrung her hands before she spoke.

'Royal lady!' at length she said, 'I hastened, as you instructed me, at the appointed hour, to the Emir Fakredeen, but I learnt that he had quitted the castle. Then I repaired to the prisoner; but, woe is me! she is not to be found.'

'Not to be found!'

'The raiment that she wore is lying on the floor of her prison. Methinks she has fled.'

'She has fled with him who was false to us all,' said Astarte, 'for it was the Emir of the Lebanon who long ago told me that you were affianced to the daughter of Besso, and who warned me against joining in any enterprise which was only to place upon the throne of Syria one whom the laws of your own country would never recognise as your wife.'

'Intriguer!' said Tancred. 'Vile and inveterate intriguer!'

'It is well,' said Astarte. 'My spirit is more serene.'

'Would that Eva were with any one else!' said Tancred, thoughtfully, and speaking, as it were, to himself.

'Your thoughts are with the daughter of Besso,' said Astarte. 'You wish to follow her, to guard her, to restore her to her family.'

Tancred looked round and caught the glance of the Queen of the Ansarey, mortified, yet full of affection.

'It seems to me,' he said, 'that it is time for me to terminate a visit that has already occasioned you, royal lady, too much vexation.'

Astarte burst into tears.

'Let me go,' she said, 'you want a throne; this is a rude one, yet accept it. You require warriors, the Ansarey are invincible. My castle is not like those palaces of Antioch, of which we have often talked, and which were worthy of you, but Gindarics is impregnable, and will serve you for your head-quarters until you conquer that world which you are born to command.'

'I have been the unconscious agent in petty machinations,' said Tancred. 'I must return to the Desert to recover the purity of my mind. It is Arabia alone that can regenerate the world.'

At this moment Cypros, who was standing apart, waved her scarf, and exclaimed, 'Royal lady, I perceive in the distance the ever-faithful messenger;' whereupon Astarte looked up, and, as yet invisible to the inexperienced glance of Tancred, recognised what was an infinitely small dusky speck, each moment becoming more apparent, until at length a bird was observed by all of them winging its way towards the Queen.

'Is it the ever-faithful Karaguus,' said Astarte; 'or is it Rubylips that ever brings good news?'

'It is Karaguus,' said Cypros, as the bird drew nearer and nearer; 'but it is not Karaguus of Damascus. By the ring on its neck, it is Karaguus of Aleppo.'

The pigeon now was only a few yards above the head of

the Queen.   Fatigued, but with an eye full of resolution, it
fluttered for a moment, and then fell upon her bosom.
Cvpros advanced and lifted its weary wing, and untied the
cartel which it bore, brief words, but full of meaning, and a
terrible interest.

' *The Pacha, at the head of five thousand regular troops,
leaves Haleb to-morrow to invade our land.*'

' Go,' said Astarte to Tancred ; 'to remain here is now
dangerous.   Thanks to the faithful messenger, you have
time to escape with ease from that land which you scorned
to rule, and which loved you too well.'

' I cannot leave it in the hour of peril,' said Tancred.
' This invasion of the Ottomans may lead to results of
which none dream.   I will meet them at the head of your
warriors ! '

CHAPTER IX.

' Is there any news ? ' asked Adam Besso of Issachar, the
son of Selim, the most cunning leech at Aleppo, and who
by day and by night watched the couch which bore the
suffering form of the pride and mainstay of the Syrian
Hebrews.

' There is news, but it has not yet arrived,' replied
Issachar, the son of Selim, a man advanced in life, but
hale, with a white beard, a bright eye, and a benignant
visage.

' There are pearls in the sea, but what are they worth ? '
murmured Besso.

' I have taken a Cabala,' said Issachar, the son of Selim,
' and three times that I opened the sacred book, there were
three words, and the initial letter of each word is the name
of a person who will enter this room this day, and every
person will bring news.'

' But what news ? ' sighed Besso.   ' The news of Tophet
and of ten thousand demons ? '

'I have taken a Cabala,' said Issachar, the son of Selim, 'and the news will be good.'

'To whom and from whom ? Good to the Pacha, but not to me! good to the people of Haleb, but not, perhaps, to the family of Besso.'

' God will guard over his own. In the meanwhile, I must replace this bandage, noble Besso. Let me rest your arm upon this cushion and you will endure less pain.'

'Alas ! worthy Issachar, I have wounds deeper than any you can probe.'

The resignation peculiar to the Orientals had sustained Besso under his overwhelming calamity. He neither wailed nor moaned. Absorbed in a brooding silence, he awaited the result of the measures which had been taken for the release of Eva, sustained by the chance of success, and caring not to survive if encountering failure. The Pacha of Aleppo, long irritated by the Ansarey, and meditating for some time an invasion of their country, had been fired by the all-influential representations of the family of Besso instantly to undertake a step which, although it had been for some time contemplated, might yet, according to Turkish custom, have been indefinitely postponed. Three regiments of the line, disciplined in the manner of Europe, some artillery, and a strong detachment of cavalry, had been ordered at once to invade the contiguous territory of the Ansarey. Hillel Besso had accompanied the troops, leaving his uncle under his paternal roof, disabled by his late conflict, but suffering from wounds which in themselves were serious rather than perilous.

Four days had elapsed since the troops had quitted Aleppo. It was the part of Hillel, before they had recourse to hostile movements, to obtain, if possible, the restoration of the prisoners by fair means ; nor were any resources wanting to effect this purpose. A courier had arrived at Aleppo from Hillel, apprising Adam Besso that the Queen of the Ansarey had not only refused to give up the prisoners, but even declared that Eva had been already released ; but

Hillel concluded that this was merely trifling. This parleying had taken place on the border ; the troops were about to force the passes on the following day.

About an hour before sunset, on the very same day that Issachar, the son of Selim, had taken more than one Cabala, some horsemen, in disorder, were observed from the walls by the inhabitants of Aleppo, galloping over the plain. They were soon recognised as the cavalry of the Pacha, the irregular heralds, it was presumed, of a triumph achieved. Hillel Besso, covered with sweat and dust, was among those who thus early arrived. He hastened at a rapid pace through the suburb of the city, scattering random phrases to those who inquired after intelligence as he passed, until he reached the courtyard of his own house.

' 'Tis well,' he observed, as he closed the gate. ' A battle is a fine thing, but, for my part, I am not sorry to find myself at home.'

' What is that ? ' inquired Adam Besso, as a noise reached his ear.

' 'Tis the letter of the first Cabala,' replied Issachar, the son of Selim.

' Uncle, it is I,' said Hillel, advancing.

' Speak,' said Adam Besso, in an agitated voice ; ' my sight is dark.'

' Alas, I am alone ! ' said Hillel.

' Bury me in Jehoshaphat,' murmured Besso, as he sank back.

' But, my uncle, there is hope.'

' Speak then of hope,' replied Besso, with sudden vehemence, and starting from his pillow.

' Truly I have seen a child of the mountains, who persists in the tale that our Eva has escaped.'

' An enemy's device ! Are the mountains ours ? Where are the troops ? '

' Were the mountains ours, I should not be here, my uncle. Look from the ramparts, and you will soon see the plain covered with the troops, at least with all of them who have escaped the matchlocks and the lances of the Ansarey.'

'Are they such sons of fire?'

'When the Queen of the Ansarey refused to deliver up the prisoners, and declared that Eva was not in her power, the Pacha resolved to penetrate the passes, in two detachments, on the following morning. The enemy was drawn up in array to meet us, but fled after a feeble struggle. Our artillery seemed to carry all before it. But,' continued Hillel, shrugging his shoulders, 'war is not by any means a commercial transaction. It seemed that, when we were on the point of victory, we were in fact entirely defeated. The enemy had truly made a feigned defence, and had only allured us into the passes, where they fired on us from the heights, and rolled down upon our confused masses huge fragments of rock. Our strength, our numbers, and our cannon, only embarrassed us; there arose a confusion; the troops turned and retreated. And, when everything was in the greatest perplexity, and we were regaining the plain, our rear was pursued by crowds of cavalry, Kurds, and other Giaours, who destroyed our men with their long lances, uttering horrible shouts. For my own part, I thought all was over, but a good horse is not a bad thing, and I am here, my uncle, having ridden for twenty hours, nearly, without a pause.'

'And when did you see this child of the mountains who spoke of the lost one?' asked Besso, in a low and broken voice.

'On the eve of the engagement,' said Hillel. 'He had been sent to me with a letter, but, alas! had been plundered on his way by our troops, and the letter had been destroyed or lost. Nevertheless, he induced them to permit him to reach my tent, and brought these words, that the ever adorable had truly quitted the mountains, and that the lost letter had been written to that effect by the chieftain of the Ansarey.'

'Is there yet hope! What sound is that?'

' 'Tis the letter of the second Cabala,' said Issachar, the son of Selim.

And at this moment entered the chamber a faithful slave, who made signs to the physician, upon which Issachar rose, and was soon engaged in earnest conversation with him who had entered, Hillel tending the side of Besso. After a few minutes, Issachar approached the couch of his patient, and said, ' Here is one, my lord and friend, who brings good tidings of your daughter.'

' God of my fathers !' exclaimed Besso, passionately, and springing up.

' Still we must be calm,' said Issachar; ' still we must be calm.'

' Let me see him,' said Besso.

' It is one you know, and know well,' said Issachar. ' It is the Emir Fakredeen.'

' The son of my heart,' said Besso, ' who brings me news that is honey in my mouth.'

' I am here, my father of fathers,' said Fakredeen, gliding to the side of the couch.

Besso grasped his hand, and looked at him earnestly in the face. ' Speak of Eva,' he at length said, in a voice of chok-ing agitation.

' She is well, she is safe. Yes, I have saved her,' said Fakredeen, burying his face in the pillow, exhausted by emotion. ' Yes, I have not lived in vain.'

' Your flag shall wave on a thousand castles,' said Besso. ' My child is saved, and she is saved by the brother of her heart. Entirely has the God of our fathers guarded over us. Henceforth, my Fakredeen, you have only to wish : we are the same.' And Besso sank down almost insensible ; then he made a vain effort to rise again, murmuring ' Eva ! '

' She will soon be here,' said Fakredeen ; ' she only rests awhile after many hardships.'

' Will the noble Emir refresh himself after his long journey ?' said Hillel.

' My heart is too elate for the body to need relief,' said the Emir.

' That may be very true,' said Hillel. 'At the same time, for my part, I have always thought that the body should be maintained as well as the spirit.'

' Withdraw from the side of the couch,' said Issachar, the son of Selim, to his companions. ' My lord and friend has swooned.'

Gradually the tide of life returned to Besso, gradually the heart beat, the hand grew warm. At length he slowly opened his eyes, and said, ' I have been dreaming of my child, even now I see her.'

Yes, so vivid had been the vision, that even now, restored entirely to himself, perfectly conscious of the locality and the circumstances that surrounded him, knowing full well that he was in his brother's house at Aleppo, suffering and disabled, keenly recalling his recent interview with Fakredeen, notwithstanding all these tests of inward and outward perception, still before his entranced and agitated vision hovered the lovely visage of his daughter, a little paler than usual, and an uncommon anxiety blended with its soft expression, but the same rich eyes, and fine contour of countenance that her father had so often gazed on with pride, and recalled in her absence with brooding fondness. ' Even now I see her,' said Besso.

He could say no more, for the sweetest form in the world had locked him in her arms.

' 'Tis the letter of the third Cabala,' said Issachar, the son of Selim.

CHAPTER X.

Tancred had profited by his surprise by the children of Rechab in the passes of the Stony Arabia, and had employed the same tactics against the Turkish force. By a simulated defence on the borders, and by the careful dissemination of false intelligence, he had allowed the Pacha and his troops to penetrate the mountains, and principally by a pass which the Turks were assured by their spies that the Ansarey had altogether neglected. The success of these manœuvres had been as complete as the discomfiture and rout of the Turks. Tancred, at the head of the cavalry, had pursued them into the plain, though he had halted, for an instant, before he quitted the mountains, to send a courier to Astarte from himself with the assurance of victory, and the horsetails of the Pacha for a trophy.

It so happened, however, that, while Tancred, with very few attendants, was scouring the plain, and driving before him a panic-struck multitude, who, if they could only have paused and rallied, might in a moment have overwhelmed him, a strong body of Turkish cavalry, who had entered the mountains by a different pass from that in which the principal engagement had taken place, but who, learning the surprise and defeat of the main body, had thought it wise to retreat in order and watch events, debouched at this moment from the high country into the plain and in the rear of Tancred. Had they been immediately recognised by the fugitives, it would have been impossible for Tancred to escape; but the only impression of the routed Turks was, that a reinforcement had joined their foe, and their disorder was even increased by the appearance in the distance of their own friends. This misapprehension must, however, in time, have been at least partially removed; but Baroni, whose quick glance had instantly detected the perilous incident, warned Tancred immediately.

' We are surrounded, my lord ; there is only one course to pursue. To regain the mountains is impossible; if we advance, we enter only a hostile country, and must be soon overpowered. We must make for the Eastern Desert.'

Tancred halted and surveyed the scene : he had with him not twenty men. The Turkish cavalry, several hundreds strong, had discovered their quarry, and were evidently resolved to cut off their retreat.

' Very well,' said Tancred, ' we are well mounted, we

must try the mettle of our steeds. Farewell, Gindarics! Farewell, gods of Olympus! To the Desert, which I ought never to have quitted!' and, so speaking, he and his band dashed towards the East.

Their start was so considerable that they baffled their pursuers, who, however, did not easily relinquish their intended prey. Some shots in the distance, towards nightfall, announced that the enemy had given up the chase. After three hours of the moon, Tancred and his companions rested at a well not far from a village, where they obtained some supplies. An hour before dawn, they again pursued their way over a rich flat country, uninclosed, yet partially cultivated, with, every now and then, a village nestling in a jungle of Indian fig.

It was the commencement of December, and the country was very parched ; but the short though violent season of rain was at hand : this renovates in the course of a week the whole face of Nature, and pours into little more than that brief space the supplies which in other regions are distributed throughout the year. On the third day, before sunset, the country having gradually become desolate and deserted, consisting of vast plains covered with herds, with occasionally some wandering Turkomans or Kurds, Tancred and his companions came within sight of a broad and palmy river, a branch of the Euphrates.

The country round, far as the eye could range, was a kind of downs covered with a scanty herbage, now brown with heat and age. When Tancred had gained an undulating height, and was capable of taking a more extensive survey of the land, it presented, especially towards the south, the same features through an illimitable space.

' The Syrian Desert!' said Baroni ; ' a fortnight later, and we shall see this land covered with flowers and fragrant with aromatic herbs.'

' My heart responds to it,' said Tancred. ' What is Damascus, with all its sumptuousness, to this sweet liberty!'

Quitting the banks of the river, they directed their course to the south, and struck as it were into the heart of the Desert; yet, on the morrow, the winding waters again met them. And now there opened on their sight a wondrous scene: as far as the eye could reach innumerable tents; strings of many hundred camels going to, or returning from, the waters; groups of horses picketed about; processions of women with vases on their heads visiting the palmy banks; swarms of children and dogs; spreading flocks; and occasionally an armed horseman bounding about the environs of the vast encampment.

Although scarcely a man was visible when Tancred first caught a glimpse of this Arabian settlement, a band of horsemen suddenly sprang from behind a rising ground and came galloping up to them to reconnoitre and to inquire.

'We are brothers,' said Baroni, 'for who should be the master of so many camels but the lord of the Syrian pastures?'

'There is but one God,' said the Bedoueen, 'and none are lords of the Syrian pastures but the children of Rechab.'

'Truly, there is only one God,' said Baroni; 'go tell the great Sheikh that his friend the English prince has come here to give him a salaam of peace.'

Away bounded back the Bedoueens, and were soon lost in the crowded distance.

'All is right,' said Baroni; 'we shall sup to-night under the pavilion of Amalek.'

'I visit him then, at length, in his beautiful pastures,' said Tancred; 'but, alas! I visit him alone.'

They had pulled up their horses, and were proceeding leisurely towards the encampment, when they observed a cavalcade emerging from the outer boundary of the settlement. This was Amalek himself, on one of his steeds of race, accompanied by several of his leading Sheikhs, coming to welcome Tancred to his pavilion in the Syrian pastures. A joyful satisfaction sparkled in the bright eyes of the old chieftain, as, at a little distance, he waved his hand with graceful dignity, and pressed his hand to his heart.

'A thousand salaams,' he exclaimed, when he had reached Tancred; 'there is but one God. I press you to my heart of hearts. There are also other friends, but they are not here.'

'Salaam, great Sheikh! I feel indeed we are brothers. There are friends of whom we must speak, and indeed of many things.'

Thus conversing, and riding side by side, Amalek and Tancred entered the camp. Nearly five thousand persons were collected together in this wilderness, and two thousand warriors were prepared at a moment's notice to raise their lances in the air. There were nearly as many horses, and ten times as many camels. This wilderness was the principal and favourite resting-place of the great Sheikh of the children of Rechab, and the abundant waters and comparatively rich pasturage permitted him to gather around him a great portion of his tribe.

The lamps soon gleamed, and the fires soon blazed; sheep were killed, bread baked, coffee pounded, and the pipe of honour was placed in the hands of Tancred. For an Arabian revel, the banquet was long and rather elaborate. By degrees, however, the guests stole away; the women ceased to peep through the curtains; and the children left off asking Baroni to give them backsheesh. At length, Amalek and Tancred being left alone, the great Sheikh, who had hitherto evinced no curiosity as to the cause of the presence of his guest, said, 'There is a time for all things, for eating and for drinking, also for prayers. There is, also, a season to ask questions. Why is the brother of the Queen of the English in the Syrian Desert?'

'There is much to tell, and much to inquire,' said Tancred; 'but before I speak of myself, let me know whether you can get me tidings of Eva, the daughter of Besso.'

'Is she not living in rooms with many divans?' said Amalek.

'Alas!' said Tancred, 'she was a prisoner, and is now a fugitive.'

'What children of Gin have done this deed? Are there strange camels drinking at my wells? Is it some accursed Kurd that has stolen her sheep; or some Turkoman, blacker than night, that has hankered after her bracelets?'

'Nothing of all this, yet more than all this. All shall be told to you, great Sheikh, yet before I speak, tell me again, can you get me tidings of Eva, the daughter of Besso?'

'Can I fire an arrow that will hit its mark?' said Amalek; 'tell me the city of Syria, where Eva the daughter of Besso may be found, and I will send her a messenger that would reach her even in the bath, were she there.'

Tancred then gave the great Sheikh a rapid sketch of what had occurred to Eva, and expressed his fear that she might have been intercepted by the Turkish troops. Amalek decided that she must be at Aleppo, and, instantly summoning one of his principal men, he gave instructions for the departure of a trusty scout in that direction.

'Ere the tenth day shall have elapsed,' said the great Sheikh, 'we shall have sure tidings. And now let me know, prince of England, by what strange cause you could have found yourself in the regions of those children of hell, the Ansarey, who, it is well known, worship Eblis in every obscene form.'

'It is a long tale,' said Tancred, 'but I suppose it must be told; but now that you have relieved my mind by sending to Aleppo, I can hardly forget that I have ridden for more than three days, and with little pause. I am not, alas! a true Arab, though I love Arabia and Arabian thoughts; and, indeed, my dear friend, had we not met again, it is impossible to say what might have been my lot, for I now feel that I could not have much longer undergone the sleepless toil I have of late encountered. If Eva be safe, I am content, or would wish to feel so; but what is content, and what is life, and what is man? Indeed, great Sheikh, the longer I live and the more I think ——' and here the chibouque dropped gently from Tancred's mouth, and he himself sunk upon the carpet.

CHAPTER XI.

'BESSO is better,' said the Consul Pasqualigo to Barizy of the Tower, as he met him on a December morning in the Via Dolorosa.

'Yes, but he is by no means well,' quickly rejoined Barizy. 'The physician of the English prince told me ——'

'He has not seen the physician of the English prince!' screamed Pasqualigo, triumphantly.

'I know that,' said Barizy, rallying; 'but the physician of the English prince says for flesh-wounds ——'

'There are no flesh-wounds,' said the Consul Pasqualigo. 'They have all healed; 'tis an internal shock.'

'For internal shocks,' said Barizy of the Tower, 'there is nothing like rosemary stewed with salt, and so kept on till it simmers.'

'That is very well for a bruise,' said the Consul Pasqualigo.

'A bruise is a shock,' said Barizy of the Tower.

'Besso should have remained at Aleppo,' said the Consul.

'Besso always comes to Jerusalem when he is indisposed,' said Barizy; 'as he well says, 'tis the only air that can cure him; and, if he cannot be cured, why, at least, he can be buried in the Valley of Jehoshaphat.'

'He is not at Jerusalem,' said the Consul Pasqualigo, maliciously.

'How do you mean,' said Barizy, somewhat confused. 'I am now going to inquire after him, and smoke some of his Latakia.'

'He is at Bethany,' said the Consul.

'Hem!' said Barizy, mysteriously. 'Bethany! Will that marriage come off now, think you? I always fancy, when, eh? ——'

'She will not marry till her father has recovered,' said the Consul.

'This is a curious story,' said Barizy. 'The regular troops beaten by the Kurds.'

'They were not Kurds,' said the Consul Pasqualigo. 'They were Russians in disguise. Some cannon have been taken, which were cast at St. Petersburgh; and, besides, there is a portfolio of state papers found on a Cossack, habited as a Turkoman, which betrays all. The documents are to be published in numbers, with explanatory commentaries. Consul-General Laurella writes from Damascus that the Eastern question is more alive than ever. We are on the eve of great events.'

'You don't say so?' said Barizy of the Tower, losing his presence of mind from this overwhelming superiority of information. 'I always thought so. Palmerston will never rest till he gets Jerusalem.'

'The English must have markets,' said the Consul Pasqualigo.

'Very just,' said Barizy of the Tower. 'There will be a great opening here. I think of doing a little myself in cottons; but the house of Besso will monopolise everything.'

'I don't think the English can do much here,' said the Consul, shaking his head. 'What have we to give them in exchange? The people here had better look to Austria, if they wish to thrive. The Austrians also have cottons, and they are Christians. They will give you their cottons, and take your crucifixes.'

'I don't think I can deal in crucifixes,' said Barizy of the Tower.

'I tell you what, if you won't, your cousin Barizy of the Gate will. I know he has given a great order to Bethlehem.'

'The traitor!' exclaimed Barizy of the Tower. 'Well,

if people will purchase crucifixes and nothing else, they must be supplied. Commerce civilises man.'

'Who is this?' exclaimed the Consul Pasqualigo.

A couple of horsemen, well mounted, but travel-worn, and followed by a guard of Bedoueens, were coming up the Via Dolorosa, and stopped at the house of Hassan Nejid.

''Tis the English prince,' said Barizy of the Tower. 'He has been absent six months; he has been in Egypt.'

'To see the temples of the fire-worshippers, and to shoot crocodiles. They all do that,' said the Consul Pasqualigo.

'How glad he must be to get back to Jerusalem,' said Barizy of the Tower. 'There may be larger cities, but there are certainly none so beautiful.'

'The most beautiful city in the world is the city of Venice,' said Pasqualigo.

'You have never been there,' said Barizy.

'But it was built principally by my ancestors,' said the Consul, 'and I have a print of it in my hall.'

'I never heard that Venice was comparable to Jerusalem,' said Barizy.

'Jerusalem is, in every respect, an abode fit for swine, compared with Venice,' said Pasqualigo.

'I would have you to know, Monsieur Pasqualigo, who call yourself consul, that the city of Jerusalem is not only the city of God, but has ever been the delight and pride of man.'

'Pish!' said Pasqualigo.

'Poh!' said Barizy.

'I am not at all surprised that Besso got out of it as soon as he possibly could.'

'You would not dare to say these things in his presence,' said Barizy.

'Who says " dare " to the representative of a European Power!'

'I say " dare " to the son of the janissary of the Austrian Vice-Consul at Sidon.'

'You will hear more of this,' said Pasqualigo, fiercely.

' I shall make a representation to the Internonce at Stambool.'

'You had better go there yourself, as you are tired of El Khuds.'

Pasqualigo, not having a repartee ready, shot at his habitual comrade a glance of withering contempt, and stalked away.

In the meantime, Tancred dismounted and entered for the first time his house at Jerusalem, of which he had been the nominal tenant for half a year. Baroni was quite at home, as he knew the house in old days, and had also several times visited, on this latter occasion, the suite of Tancred. Freeman and Trueman, who had been forwarded on by the British Consul at Beiroot, like bales of goods, were at their post, bowing as if their master had just returned from a club. But none of the important members of the body were at this moment at hand. Colonel Brace was dining with the English Consul on an experimental plum-pudding, preliminary to the authentic compound, which was to appear in a few days. It was supposed to be the first time that a Christmas pudding had been concocted at Jerusalem, and the excitement in the circle was considerable. The Colonel had undertaken to supervise the preparation, and had been for several days instilling the due instructions into a Syrian cook, who had hitherto only succeeded in producing a result which combined the specific gravity of lead with the general flavour and appearance of a mass of kneaded dates, in a state of fermentation after a long voyage. The Reverend Mr. Bernard was at Bethlehem, assisting the Bishop in catechising some converts who had passed themselves off as true children of Israel, but who were in fact, older Christians than either of their examinants; being descendants of some Nestorian families, who had settled in the south of Palestine in the earlier ages of Christianity. As for Dr. Roby, he was culling simples in the valley of the Jordan; and thus it happened that, when Tancred at length did evince some disposition to settle down quietly under his own roof, and avail himself of the services and society of his friends, not one of them was present to receive and greet him.

Tancred roamed about the house, surveyed his court and garden, sighed, while Baroni rewarded and dismissed their escort. ' I know not how it is,' he at length said to his intendant, ' but I never could have supposed that I could have felt so sad and spiritless at Jerusalem.'

' It is the reaction, my lord, after a month's wandering in the Desert. It is always so : the world seems tame.'

' I am disappointed that Besso is not here. I am most anxious to see him.'

' Shall I send for the Colonel, my lord ? ' said Baroni, shaking Tancred's Arabian cloak.

' Well, I think I should let him return naturally,' said Tancred ; ' sending for him is a scene ; and I do not know why, Baroni, but I feel, I feel unstrung. I am surprised that there are no letters from England ; and yet I am rather glad too, for a letter ——'

' Received some months after its date,' said Baroni, ' is like the visit of a spectre. I shudder at the sight of it.'

' Heigho ! ' said Tancred, stretching his arm, and half-speaking to himself, ' I wish the battle of Gindarics had never ceased, but that, like some hero of enchantment, I had gone on for ever fighting.'

' Ah ! there is nothing like action,' said Baroni, unscrewing his pistols.

' But what action is there in this world ? ' said Tancred. ' The most energetic men in Europe are mere busybodies. Empires are now governed like parishes, and a great statesman is only a select vestryman. And they are right : unless we bring man nearer to heaven, unless government become again divine, the insignificance of the human scheme must paralyse all effort.'

' Hem ! ' said Baroni, kneeling down and opening Tancred's rifle-case. The subject was getting a little too deep for him. ' I perceive,' he said to himself, ' that my lord is very restless. There is something at the bottom of his mind which, perhaps, he does not quite comprehend himself; but it will come out.'

Tancred passed the day alone in reading, or walking about his room with an agitated and moody step. Often, when his eye rested on the page, his mind wandered from the subject, and he was frequently lost in profound and protracted reverie. The evening drew on ; he retired early to his room, and gave orders that he was not to be disturbed. At a later hour, Colonel Brace returned, having succeeded in his principal enterprise, and having also sung the national anthem. He was greatly surprised to hear that Lord Montacute had returned ; but Baroni succeeded in postponing the interview until the morrow. An hour after the Colonel, the Rev. Mr. Bernard returned from Bethlehem. He was in great tribulation, as he had been pursued by some of the vagabonds of that ruffianly district ; a shot had even been fired after him ; but this was only to frighten him. The fact is, the leader of the band was his principal catechumen, who was extremely desirous of appropriating a very splendid copy of the Holy Writings, richly bound, and adorned with massy golden clasps, which the Duchess of Bellamont had presented to the Rev. Mr. Bernard before his departure, and which he always, as a sort of homage to one whom he sincerely respected, displayed on any eminent instance of conversion.

The gates of the city were shut when Doctor Roby returned, laden with many rare balsams. The consequence was, he was obliged to find quarters in a tomb in the valley of Jehoshaphat. As his attendant was without food, when his employer had sunk into philosophic repose, he supped off the precious herbs and roots, and slaked his thirst with a draught from the fountain of Siloah.

Tancred passed a night of agitating dreams. Sometimes he was in the starry Desert, sometimes in the caverned dungeons of Gindarics. Then, again, the scene changed to Bellamont Castle, but it would seem that Fakredeen was its lord; and when Tancred rushed forward to embrace his mother, she assumed the form of the Syrian goddess, and yet the face was the face of Eva. Though disturbed, he slept, and when he woke, he was for a moment quite unconscious of being at Jerusalem. Although within a week of Christmas, no sensible difference had yet occurred in the climate. The golden sun succeeded the silver moon, and both reigned in a clear blue sky. You may dine at night on the terrace of your house at Jerusalem in January, and find a serene and benignant atmosphere.

Tancred rose early; no one was stirring in the house except the native servants, and Mr. Freeman, who was making a great disturbance about hot water. Tancred left a message with this gentleman for the Colonel and his companions, begging that they might all meet at breakfast, and adding that he was about to stroll for half an hour. Saying this, he quitted the house, and took his way by the gate of Stephen to the Mount of Olives.

It was a delicious morn, wonderfully clear, and soft, and fresh. It seemed a happy and a thriving city, that forlorn Jerusalem, as Tancred, from the heights of Olivet, gazed upon its noble buildings, and its cupolaed houses of freestone, and its battlemented walls and lofty gates. Nature was fair, and the sense of existence was delightful. It seemed to Tancred that a spicy gale came up the ravines of the wilderness, from the farthest Arabia.

Lost in prolonged reverie, the hours flew on. The sun was mounting in the heavens when Tancred turned his step, but, instead of approaching the city, he pursued a winding path in an opposite direction. That path led to Bethany.

CHAPTER XII.

The crest of the palm-tree in the garden of Eva glittered in the declining sun; and the lady of Bethany sat in her kiosk on the margin of the fountain, unconsciously playing with a flower, and gazing in abstraction on the waters. She had left Tancred with her father, now convalescent. They had passed the morning together, talking over the strange events that had occurred since they first became acquainted on this very spot; and now the lady of Bethany had retired to her own thoughts.

A sound disturbed her: she looked up and recognised Tancred.

'I could not refrain from seeing the sun set on Arabia,' he said; 'I had almost induced the noble Besso to be my companion.'

'The year is too old,' said Eva, not very composed.

'They should be Midsummer nights,' said Tancred, 'as on my first visit here; that hour thrice blessed!'

'We know not what is blessed in this world,' said Eva, mournfully.

'I feel I do,' murmured Tancred; and he also seated himself on the margin of the fountain.

'Of all the strange incidents and feelings that we have been talking over this day,' said Eva, 'there seems to me but one result; and that is, sadness.'

'It is certainly not joy,' said Tancred.

'There comes over me a great despondency,' said Eva, 'I know not why, my convictions are as profound as they were, my hopes should not be less high, and yet ——'

'And what?' said Tancred, in a low, sweet voice, for she hesitated.

'I have a vague impression,' said Eva, sorrowfully, 'that there have been heroic aspirations wasted, and noble energies thrown away; and yet, perhaps,' she added, in a faltering tone, 'there is no one to blame. Perhaps, all this time, we have been dreaming over an unattainable end, and the only source of deception is our own imagination.'

' My faith is firm,' said Tancred; ' but if anything could make it falter, it would be to find you wavering.'

' Perhaps it is the twilight hour,' said Eva, with a faint smile. ' It sometimes makes one sad.'

' There is no sadness where there is sympathy,' said Tancred, in a low voice. ' I have been, I am sad, when I am alone; but when I am with you, my spirit is sustained, and would be, come what might.

' And yet——' said Eva ; and she paused.

' And what ?'

' Your feelings cannot be what they were before all this happened; when you thought only of a divine cause, of stars, of angels, and of our peculiar and gifted land. No, no ; now it is all mixed up with intrigue, and politics, and management, and baffled schemes, and cunning arts of men. You may be, you are, free from all this, but your faith is not the same. You no longer believe in Arabia.'

' Why, thou to me art Arabia,' said Tancred, advancing and kneeling at her side. ' The angel of Arabia, and of my life and spirit! Talk not to me of faltering faith : mine is intense. Talk not to me of leaving a divine cause : why, thou art my cause, and thou art most divine! O Eva! deign to accept the tribute of my long agitated heart! Yes, I too, like thee, am sometimes full of despair; but it is only when I remember that I love, and love, perhaps, in vain !'

He had clasped her hand ; his passionate glance met her eye, as he looked up with adoration to a face infinitely distressed. Yet she withdrew not her hand, as she murmured, with averted head, ' We must not talk of these things; we must not think of them. You know all.'

' I know of nothing, I will know of nothing, but of my love.'

' There are those to whom I belong ; and to whom you

belong. 'Yes,' she said, trying to withdraw her hand.
'Fly, fly from me, son of Europe and of Christ!'

'I am a Christian in the land of Christ,' said Tancred,
'and I kneel to a daughter of my Redeemer's race. Why
should I fly?'

'Oh! this is madness!'

'Say, rather, inspiration,' said Tancred, 'for I will not
quit this fountain by which we first met until I am told, as
you now will tell me,' he added, in a tone of gushing tenderness, 'that our united destinies shall advance the sovereign purpose of our lives. Talk not to me of others, of
those who have claims on you or on myself. I have no
kindred, no country, and, as for the ties that would bind
you, shall such world-worn bonds restrain our consecrated
aim? Say but you love me, and I will trample them to
the dust.'

The head of Eva fell upon his shoulder. He impressed
an embrace upon her cheek. It was cold, insensible. Her
hand, which he still held, seemed to have lost all vitality.
Overcome by contending emotions, the principle of life
seemed to have deserted her. Tancred laid her reclining
figure with gentleness on the mats of the kiosk; he sprinkled
her pale face with some drops from the fountain; he chafed
her delicate hand. Her eyes at length opened, and she
sighed. He placed beneath her head some of the cushions
that were at hand. Recovering, she slightly raised herself,
leant upon the marble margin of the fountain, and looked
about her with a wildered air.

At this moment a shout was heard, repeated and increased; soon the sound of many voices and the tramp of
persons approaching. The vivid but brief twilight had
died away. Almost suddenly it had become night. The
voices became more audible, the steps were at hand. Tancred recognised his name, frequently repeated. Behold a
crowd of many persons, several of them bearing torches.
There was Colonel Brace in the van: on his right was the
Rev. Mr. Bernard; on his left, Doctor Roby. Freeman and

Trueman and several guides and native servants were in the rear, most of them proclaiming the name of Lord Montacute.

'I am here,' said Tancred, advancing from the kiosk, pale and agitated. 'Why am I wanted?'

Colonel Brace began to explain, but all seemed to speak at the same time.

The Duke and Duchess of Bellamont had arrived at Jerusalem.